LORI FOSTER

A PERFECT STORM

HQN™

Recycling programs
for this product may
not exist in your area.

ISBN-13: 978-0-373-77656-6

A PERFECT STORM

Copyright © 2012 by Lori Foster

All rights reserved. Except for use in any review, the reproduction or
utilization of this work in whole or in part in any form by any electronic,
mechanical or other means, now known or hereafter invented, including
xerography, photocopying and recording, or in any information storage
or retrieval system, is forbidden without the written permission of the
publisher, Harlequin Enterprises Limited, 225 Duncan Mill Road,
Don Mills, Ontario M3B 3K9, Canada.

This is a work of fiction. Names, characters, places and incidents are
either the product of the author's imagination or are used fictitiously,
and any resemblance to actual persons, living or dead, business
establishments, events or locales is entirely coincidental.

This edition published by arrangement with Harlequin Books S.A.

For questions and comments about the quality of this book
please contact us at Customer_eCare@Harlequin.ca.

® and TM are trademarks of the publisher. Trademarks indicated with
® are registered in the United States Patent and Trademark Office, the
Canadian Trade Marks Office and in other countries.

www.Harlequin.com

Printed in U.S.A.

Dear Reader,

From the moment Arizona Storm appeared on the page in *Savor the Danger*, I loved her. She's so vulnerable while still being kick-butt bold and, to me, adorably outrageous. And Spencer Lark...I think he might be my new favorite hero. Big, capable and oh-so-intuitive when it comes to Arizona. She really, really needed Spencer in her life. Eventually he realizes that he needs her as well. Lots of sparks, lots of sensuality, and—I hope—lots of fun!

A Perfect Storm is book four in my series of über-alpha private mercenaries who walk the edge of honor. You already met Dare Macintosh, Trace Rivers and Jackson Savor. Well, Arizona fits right in with the guys. But as Spencer can tell you, she's a woman through and through.

To see more about the books, including how they're related and more on the characters, visit my website, www.LoriFoster.com, and check out the "Related Books & Series" page under the "Booklists" link.

Feel free to chat with me on my Facebook fan page or visit me on Twitter or Goodreads.

I hope you enjoy the story!

Lori Foster

Also available from
LORI FOSTER
and HQN Books

Men Who Walk the Edge of Honor

The Guy Next Door
"Ready, Set, Jett"
When You Dare
Trace of Fever
Savor the Danger

Other must-reads

Forever Buckhorn
Buckhorn Beginnings
Bewitched
Unbelievable
Tempted
Bodyguard
Caught!
Heartbreakers
Fallen Angels
Enticing

Don't miss Lori Foster's
newest sizzling tale,
coming soon from HQN Books:

Run the Risk

And look for another classic
Buckhorn Brothers adventure,
also coming soon:

The Buckhorn Legacy

A PERFECT
STORM

CHAPTER ONE

ARIZONA STORM SAT QUIETLY on the overstuffed chair, her chin resting on her drawn-up knees, her fingers laced together around her shins.

Waiting.

In the quiet, shadowed room, she breathed in the unique aroma of aftershave and gun oil, and the headier scent of warm male. On the back of the chair behind her he'd tossed his jeans and a rumpled T-shirt. Close at hand on the nightstand, he'd placed his freshly cleaned gun and his deadly switchblade.

His discarded boxers lay on the floor.

He fascinated her.

After breaking into his house, she'd removed her sneakers and put them next to his boots by the front door. The air-conditioning, set on high, left her toes cold, but he'd covered himself with no more than a thin sheet.

Again and again, her gaze tracked over him, from one big foot sticking out over the side of the bed, up and over his flat, solid abs covered by the snowy-white sheet, to his chest—not covered by anything except enticing body hair.

With one arm behind his head, his underarm and the dark tuft of hair there were visible. Seeing that almost made him look vulnerable—except that, despite his relaxed pose, the positioning of his long arm made a thick biceps bulge.

At nearly six and a half feet tall, solidly built and finely sculpted, Spencer Lark was one of the biggest, strongest, most impressive men she'd ever met.

And she knew some really prime specimens.

His long lashes shadowed his high cheekbones, but that didn't detract from the bruising beneath one eye. A recent fight? She smiled while picturing it, sure that Spencer had come out ahead. His skill at fighting intrigued her even more than his big bod.

Amazing, but even his slightly crooked nose held her rapt. When and how had he broken it?

She inhaled a deep breath and let it out in a quiet sigh that, given the silence in his home and Spencer's acute instincts, disturbed his slumber.

Arizona admitted to herself that maybe she'd wanted to wake him. After all, she'd been watching him—and waiting—for a while now.

His head turned on the pillow, his legs shifted.

Holding herself perfectly still, she waited to see if he'd awaken, what he'd do, what he'd say. She didn't know him all that well, and yet...she did.

Sort of.

They'd met nearly a month ago while they were both on a sting. Immediately, they'd butted heads, and he'd infuriated her by interfering with her life.

But worse, he'd robbed her of the revenge she desperately craved.

Sure, he had his own need for revenge, so she understood his motives. She didn't forgive him. Not yet, anyway.

But she did understand.

At least, she thought she did. Once they talked it over, then she'd decide for sure.

He made a soft, gravelly sound as he stretched that long, strong body. His chin tucked in. Muscles flexed.

The sheet tented.

Eyes widening, Arizona stared, not really alarmed, but no longer so at ease, either. She had a very dark history with aroused men, so she doubted she'd ever be unaffected by them. But she didn't let it get in her way, not when she wanted something, not when she had a goal in mind.

She knew she should have taken Spencer's gun, at the very least moved it out of his reach. But instead she'd found him in the bed, and before she'd even thought it through, she'd taken the empty seat and settled in to study him while he slept.

Since that fateful day when her destiny had been stolen from her, she'd seen him only a handful of times. She'd tried to stay away. She'd tried to forget about him.

She hadn't been successful.

Stretching, he brought his hand out from behind his head, around to rub over his hair, across his face, down his chest.

As he gave a sleepy, growling groan, that hand disappeared under the sheet.

Arizona's lips parted, and her heartbeat tripped up. She cleared her throat. "Spence?"

Freezing, without moving any other body part, he opened his eyes and met her gaze.

She frowned at him.

He didn't look super-startled, and he said nothing. He just stared at her.

With his hand still under there.

"Yeah…" Semi-satisfied with his frozen reaction, she nodded at his lap. "You weren't going for a little tug, were you? Because as your spectator, I'd just as soon not see it."

He brought his hand out and put it back behind his head, still silent, still watching her. Almost...relaxed.

His gaze was so dark, so compelling, she felt like squirming, damn it. "I mean, I guess I could wait in the other room if it's really necessary. That is, if you don't take too long."

He disappointed her by not reacting. As if he often woke to an uninvited woman playing voyeur in his bedroom, he looked her over, from her bare toes up to her long, wind-tangled hair.

"Been here long?"

"Maybe half an hour or so." Curiosity prompted her to ask, "Were you going to...you know?" She nodded at his lap.

"Most men say hi to the boys first thing."

"Say hi?"

With no sign of discomfort, he shrugged one shoulder. "You broke in."

A statement, not a question. She gave her own casual shrug. "Since you're not dumb enough to leave the place unlocked, yeah, I had to."

He turned his head, but not to check on the time. He saw the gun still on the nightstand where he'd left it and brought his gaze back to hers again. "You know how to make coffee?"

One eyebrow lifted high. "Trying to get me out of the room so you can leave the bed? I'm not squeamish, you know. I mean, with my background, I've seen plenty of—"

He threw off the sheet and sat up, effectively shutting down her snide retort.

Ho boy.

"If you don't know how to make coffee, just say so." Spencer stretched again, harder, longer this time. Sitting on the side of the bed, he snagged up his boxers and stepped into them. As he stood, he pulled them up.

They fit like a glove.

He still had a tent going.

And she still stared.

He picked up the gun and, betraying some trust issues, checked to make sure she hadn't unloaded it. Discovering she hadn't touched it at all, he nodded in satisfaction.

As he passed her, he chucked her under the chin. "It's called morning wood, little girl. No reason for alarm." Gun in hand, he went on past her into the bathroom. The door closed quietly behind him.

Belatedly, Arizona shut her mouth. Oh, how she hated when he called her "little girl." As of today, she wasn't quite as young as he thought, and given her experiences, well, she hadn't felt like a kid in a very long time.

Her brows snapped down, and her spine stiffened. She would not let him get to her. Huh-uh. No way.

This was *her* game. She would call the shots, and if anyone had to be tongue-tied, it'd be him.

She shoved to her feet, but didn't stomp. Excesses of emotion gave away too much. She didn't want him to know how he affected her.

At the bathroom door, voice cold and collected, she stated, "I'll be the kitchen."

Minutes later, just to prove a point, she went about making coffee.

SPENCER STOOD WITH HIS HANDS braced on the porcelain sink, his head hanging, his muscles twitchy.

What the hell?

Sure, he knew Arizona Storm was a reckless, impetuous, headstrong girl. He'd figured that out in the first few seconds of making her acquaintance.

But breaking and entering?

Why the hell had she sat there watching him sleep?

He felt…violated. Angry.

He felt extreme pity. For her.

Damn, but he didn't want her, not in his house, not in his head. He could control the first.

Hadn't had much luck controlling the second.

Not trusting her to respect his privacy, knowing damn good and well she would snoop without remorse, he gave up the idea of a shower and shave and instead rushed through brushing his teeth, splashing his face and finger-combing his hair.

Since she wasn't in his bedroom anymore, he took the time to pull on his jeans, but rather than mess with the holster, he just stuck the gun in his waistband. He grabbed up his knife, opened it, closed it again and slid it into his pocket.

Barefoot and shirtless, he went in search of Arizona—and he had to admit, anticipation chased away the cobwebs of old memories and lack of sleep.

Seeing her slumped in a kitchen chair, arms crossed, one foot hooked behind a chair leg, jolted his senses even more.

God Almighty, she was a beauty.

Slim, long-legged and generously stacked, with a face like a wet dream, Arizona would turn heads wherever she went. Dark, wavy hair hung down her back, usually in disarray. Honey-colored skin seemed in direct contrast with light blue, heavily lashed eyes. A full mouth, a strong chin, high cheekbones…

He wondered at the mixed heritage that had produced such a dream.

As he stood unnoticed in the doorway, she chewed at a thumbnail. Arizona didn't wear makeup, or polish her nails, or do much of anything to enhance her looks—and she didn't need to. She could wear burlap and men would burn for her.

"Nervous?"

She went still before affecting a bored expression and swiveling her head to face him. "Do you always sleep 'til noon?"

"When I've been up all night, yes." He made a beeline for the coffeepot but didn't thank her for making it. After all, she'd come in uninvited. "You want a cup?"

"If you have sugar and milk."

"Creamer." He poured two cups and set them on the table, then got the creamer from the fridge. The sugar bowl sat in the middle of the table, framed by salt and pepper shakers.

Like many of the things in his kitchen, they resembled cows in one way or another.

His wife had bought the novelty items years ago.

While blowing on the hot coffee, Spencer ruthlessly quashed bad memories. Arizona loaded her coffee with two heaping spoonfuls of sugar and a liberal splash of the cream.

He watched her lush mouth as she sipped, sipped again.

Shaking himself, he took a drink, and nearly choked. Strong enough to peel the lining from his throat, it was the worst coffee he'd ever tasted. Arizona didn't seem to notice, though, so he manned up and drank without complaint.

The overdose of caffeine would do him good.

Silence dragged out while they each gave attention to their coffee. He wouldn't be the first to break.

Finally she eyed him. "How come you were out late? Carousing?"

Actually, he'd needed to expend some energy for reasons he wouldn't yet examine too closely. Shrugging, he said, "I hit up a bar, found a little trouble." He looked at her. "You know how it is, right?"

To his disgruntlement, she nodded. "Yeah, I did the same. But I fared better than you." Her mouth quirked in a small grin, and she winked. "No black eye."

Had she really been in a bar? Looking for trouble? *Again?*

He didn't need to defend himself, not to her, but still he said, "You should see the other three guys."

"Yeah? Only three?" Tsking, she let her gaze drift over him. "Any other bruises?"

"No."

She propped her chin on a fist. "One lucky punch, huh?"

Did she have to appear so amused by idiotic drinking and brawling? "Something like that." Actually it was a thrown chair that had caught him, but whatever. He wouldn't encourage her with details. "So tell me, little girl. What were you doing in a bar?"

She looked away. With one finger, she traced the rim of her coffee cup. "Sometimes," she said low, her voice almost whimsical, "I just need a distraction."

His chest tightened. He waited to see if she'd elaborate, if she'd share details of her tragic background with human traffickers. She had a need to even the score with people already dead, the monsters who'd hurt her badly.

Suddenly she leaned forward. "Can you keep a secret?"

Damn, he didn't want to play these games. "Depends."

She scowled. "On what?"

"On whether or not keeping it is in your best interest."

Sitting back in irritation, she demanded, "Why does that concern you?"

He countered with, "Why do you want to tell me?"

For long moments they stared at each other, and then she broke. "Fuck it. I don't. Not anymore." After downing the rest of her coffee, she scraped back her chair. "I'm outta here."

Spencer caught her wrist. And of course, that got her going.

Quick temper and a boulder-size chip on her shoulder had her swinging a fist. He dodged it, but she kicked and caught him in the shin. Luckily she didn't wear shoes, so it didn't hurt.

Much.

In the ensuing scuffle, his coffee cup hit the floor and broke.

Given they were both barefoot, he did the expedient thing and tossed her over his shoulder. Clamping a hand over her thighs, he warned, "Bite me, and I swear to God, you won't like the consequences."

Rather than struggle, she braced her elbows on his back. "You've threatened me before."

"Because you've attacked me before." Stepping over and around the mess on his floor, he went into the hallway, then figured, what the hell, and went on into the living room.

He dumped her on the couch.

She bounded right back off again.

Another scuffle, and damn it, it was too early and he was too tired to put up with it.

"Arizona!" He locked her in close in a now familiar hold—at least with her—keeping her back to his chest, her arms pinned down. He squeezed her tight enough to steal her breath. "Knock it off already, will you?"

Her head dropped back against his chest so she could glare at him. He waited, refusing to relent, driven by... God knew what.

She gave one sharp nod.

Spencer opened his arms but quickly stepped out of her reach. "Okay?"

"Screw you."

So much animosity, so much rage at the world. She'd never admit it, but Arizona needed a friend, a confidante, and if it put him through hell, well, so what? He'd been in hell for a while now. "You came to me, remember?"

"And now I'm trying to leave!"

His head pounded. If she walked out now, he'd spend the rest of the day worrying about her.

Or following her.

He worked his jaw, then said, "I'll keep your secret. What is it?"

"Oh, aren't you the generous one?"

He sighed. "The sneer is unappealing. Just tell me what it is."

The narrowing of her eyes emphasized their pale, bright blue color and the thickness of her long, inky lashes. She drew two deep breaths, making it tough for him to keep his attention off her chest.

"It's my birthday."

Huh. Of all the things he'd imagined, that wasn't one

of them. It wasn't even one of the top fifty. "Your birthday?" he said stupidly.

"Yeah, you know, the day I was born. Not under a rock, in case you're wondering." When he stayed mute, she added, "I'm twenty-one now. A legal adult. Not a little girl, like you keep saying."

Arizona didn't have family. She had a friend, Jackson, the man who had rescued her from death. She had Jackson's soon-to-be-wife, Alani. She had *their* family and friends.

But none of her own.

He shook his head. "That's it?" That's why she'd broken into his house? Why she'd sat on the chair and watched him sleep?

She rolled her eyes. "Yeah, what'd you expect? A confession of murder?"

"I don't know." With her, he could take nothing for granted. Why didn't she want anyone to know about her birthday? His rubbed his bristly jaw, studied her, but came up short of reason or even clear thought. He dropped his hand. "Happy birthday."

"Thanks."

They stood there staring at each other, and it would have been odd, but everything with Arizona was odd.

Especially the multitude of ways she affected him, the emotions she wrought and the needs she ignited.

As if her bizarre overreaction hadn't happened, she dropped back to sit on the couch. "I almost didn't remember. I mean, it's been a really long time since anyone made note of it. And even then, it was usually just my mom saying happy birthday to me. No biggie." She gave a crooked smile. "We weren't a cake and candles type of family."

So she'd never gotten a birthday gift? No one celebrated her life?

"It's not a big deal or anything. But I guess with you always accusing me of being young—"

"You are young. It's not an accusation, it's a fact." One he desperately needed to remember.

"But now I'm legal."

Meaning…what? At thirty-two, he was only eleven years older than her, but he felt twice her age. He massaged a kink in the back of his neck. Did she expect a gift? A night out? Jesus, he didn't know. "So…we could go get a cake." Or something.

Her small smile spread into a mocking grin. "Don't be an ass. I don't want or need anything like that. I'm just saying, no more calling me *little girl*."

At a loss, Spencer joined her on the couch. Instead of lounging back, he half turned toward her. "Why are you keeping it secret?"

She snorted. "You met Jackson. You know he'd make a big deal of it or something, and I don't want that." Half under her breath, she muttered, "I'm enough of a burden already."

"I don't think he'd agree with that." Jackson treated her like a kid sister, and he'd probably want to do whatever he could to commemorate the day, to somehow make it special for her—to make up for a past so dark, so depressing, that no young lady should have suffered through it.

"Yeah." She smoothed a hand over the corduroy of his couch. "Maybe not. But it's still true."

Since she didn't want him to, he wouldn't say anything, but he didn't like it. "You shouldn't keep stuff from him. He cares about you."

"I know." She crossed her arms over her middle. "But

he's got his hands full. Remember, he's planning a wedding."

Was she jealous of Alani? From what he'd seen, Arizona looked at Jackson with her heart in her eyes. He was the only person she had, so he meant a lot to her. "More like his fiancée is planning it."

"Alani is preggers, remember?"

"I had heard." He also knew the pregnancy was a happy surprise, and in no way had forced their decision to marry. "Does it bother you?"

"Of course not," she insisted. "But with all that going on, he doesn't need to be messing with me."

Dinner out, a small gift, cake and hugs…did she consider that too much fuss? "I think Jackson can handle it."

"Besides," she added, speaking over him, "I have a new identity, remember? No going back and especially no celebrating give-away dates like birthdays."

In an effort to help her, Jackson had covered her background, buried the past for her as much as he could, and for her safety, he'd given her a whole new identity, including a new name. It was a way to start over, to start fresh.

But none of that would help Arizona heal from the past.

Uncomfortable with the moment, Spencer floundered, trying to find something to say. He hadn't known her that long, and their acquaintance had been fraught with danger. As a bounty hunter, he'd been tracking criminal psychopaths—and the psychopaths had been tracking her.

Arizona, being outrageous in every way a person could imagine, had used herself as bait. Along the way,

Spencer had met Jackson and learned a little about their history.

They presented their relationship as that of friends, or maybe siblings. But the nuances of their connection made anything that simple impossible. Not with Arizona's looks and not when Jackson had saved her life.

Not when she'd once been held captive by human traffickers who, after using her, had tried to kill her as punishment for running away.

Her death would have been a lesson to remaining trapped victims. Instead, the bastards had died—and good riddance.

Luckily—at least for Spencer's peace of mind— Jackson was already in love with Alani, so his interest in Arizona wasn't romantic in any way. But for Arizona? He just didn't know.

Jackson was a good man. A protector.

And right now, Spencer felt like a destroyer of evil. Nothing protective in that.

"Oh, for crying out loud." Arizona slugged him in the shoulder. "What the hell is wrong with you? No one died. Lose the sad face, will you?"

He'd try. "So why are you here?" Remembering how she'd gotten in, he turned to look at the door. "You didn't damage my lock, did you?"

"Your lock is fine—shitty, but fine." She propped her feet on the table in front of the couch. "I'm good at picking locks."

"Why am I not surprised?"

She stared down the length of her legs and wiggled her toes. Nonchalantly, she said, "I need some help."

Apprehension shot through him. "With what?" Had she gotten herself into trouble somehow? Was someone after her again?

"Promise me that you won't tell Jackson about this, either, and then I'll tell you."

Fearful for her, he said, "Sure, whatever. I won't tell Jackson."

"Hmm." Her eyes narrowed. "That was a mighty quick agreement."

"But sincere." At the moment, his biggest concern was her safety. "Spill it."

"All right." She went back to rubbing the corduroy, and it was such a sensual thing, her hand moving slowly over the material, that Spencer felt mesmerized. "There's this restaurant. Well, it's actually a sleazy bar, but they do serve food during the day, too."

From any other woman, those words wouldn't cause much reaction. From Arizona, they boded a looming catastrophe. "What bar? Where?"

"Don't look like that," she complained. "Until I know you're on board, I'm not giving you details. Let's just say I suspect they're part of a large-scale trafficking ring and maybe using forced labor. I want to look into it. But I'm not dumb. I know I need some backup."

Dear God, *Jackson* looked into large-scale trafficking rings—not Arizona! And he didn't work alone—he worked with other men who were equally skilled.

They backed each other up—and they'd given Arizona computer duties in an effort to involve her, while keeping her away from the more dangerous action. She should have been doing no more than researching backgrounds on small-scale, local-level traffickers.

Research *only*.

"I was thinking I could be bait again. You know, put myself out there and see what happens. With you keeping watch, it'd be safe enough, right? If they try to grab me, then we—"

"No." His temper shot into overdrive, on a par with his alarm. He said again, with more force, *"No."*

Unmoved, Arizona met his angry gaze—and shrugged. "Fine. I thought you might want to team up, but I can figure it out on my own." She started to leave the couch.

He again caught her arm.

Slim, warm and so soft...

As she stared at him, her blue eyes lit from a very short fuse. "I'd suggest you stop trying to manhandle me."

Hearing the deadly tone in her voice, Spencer opened his fingers. "Give me a second to think, will you?"

"Huh." At her leisure, she dropped back again. "So 'no' with you isn't necessarily no? It might mean something else? It could mean that you just want time to think?"

She was making mincemeat out of him. He had to take control. "I don't want you anywhere near anything dangerous, especially by yourself."

"Yeah, but see, you aren't my daddy, aren't my boyfriend, and you sure as hell aren't anything in-between. So if you don't want to help, then it's none of your damn business."

What did she consider in-between? "I want to make a bet with you."

Her interest perked up. "You do? About what?"

Already knowing it wouldn't go over well, Spencer braced himself. "I bet you can't go a month without cursing."

Her chin tucked in, and her brows came down. "What does that have to do with anything?"

He had no idea, except that it annoyed him to hear her be so coarse. "Go a month without cursing." He hated himself, but he said, "Every time you slip, you owe me a kiss."

Icy stillness fell over her. Silence pulsed in the room. Tension gathered like storm clouds.

Pulling the tiger's tail, he asked, "Well?"

Eyes glittering, Arizona slowly pushed to her feet. "Fuck you," she whispered.

He could see a pulse tripping in her slim throat.

He could see the fear she tried so hard to hide.

"I suggested a kiss, Arizona. Nothing more. And despite what you said, 'no' does mean 'no' to me. You don't have to be afraid."

"I'm not!"

"You don't have to expect the worst, either." He didn't move from his position on the couch, but with their gazes locked, it felt as if he touched her all the same.

It disturbed him—so what would it do to her?

"I would never hurt you," he promised. "I'd do my best to protect you from anyone who would."

"I don't need you to protect me." Her eyes turned glassy, a little wet. "I can protect myself."

Not too long ago, she hadn't protected herself at all. And no one else had, either.

"You find kissing so repulsive?"

She shook her head but said, "I don't know." Then she added, "I haven't done much...kissing."

"No?"

Her teeth clenched; she spoke through stiff lips. "A guy who's paying for his time doesn't want to waste it on that." In defiance, she added, "Thank God."

Her words felt like a kick in the guts. "Arizona—"

"They saw me as unclean." Her chin jutted forward. "And I'm glad!"

Had she ever been given a sincere, caring, affectionate kiss? He just didn't know. But they had to start some-where, or she'd never be free of her past.

He sat forward. "Given your expression, the idea of kissing me would be insufferable, so I'm guessing it should be incentive enough to clean up your language. Right?"

She took a step back, then another. Arms loose, bare feet braced apart, she prepared to fight.

After everything that had happened to him in the past three years, his heart should have been encased in ice. Until Arizona, it had been.

Now, around her, everything felt as raw as a fresh, hot wound.

"You trust me," he pointed out.

She shook her head. "I don't trust anyone."

Slowly he stood and took a step toward her. "Yes, you do. You don't want to, and I understand that. I really do. But that's no way to live and you know it."

Shaking her head again, she whispered, "No." Then louder, "No!"

He stopped. "Why did you break into my house to tell me it's your birthday? If you don't trust me, why did you leave my gun and knife on the nightstand? If you're afraid of me, why are you here, asking me to partner up with you?"

She breathed harder.

As a warning, her small hand bunched into a fist. He didn't care. If she slugged him, maybe that'd finally make him see reason.

Maybe he'd finally be able to stop thinking about her.

"Damn you," she growled.

And his doorbell rang.

CHAPTER TWO

ARIZONA WATCHED AS CALM settled over Spencer's features. Oh, chaotic emotion had been there seconds before. She knew it. But now, he looked as collected as a college professor.

"Excuse me," he said with absurd formality, and turned to head for the front door.

The second his back was turned, she let out a pent-up breath and felt her knees weaken.

Why did he rattle her so much? Fear? Yeah, around him she felt it in spades. But it wasn't a normal kind of fear.

It wasn't anything familiar.

She'd lived with fear most of her life, first from her father and his cohorts, then from the awful traffickers and the swine who came to them for women. And then... from the idea of being alone, unable to help others.

Useless.

From where she stood, the open door blocked her view of his visitor, but she didn't need a visual, not with the husky female voice now crooning, "Spencer, I'm so glad you're home."

Arizona's spine went rigid.

Strength surged back into her legs.

So did petty animosity.

She strained her ears but heard nothing, and she suspected the woman was kissing Spencer.

"Sorry, doll," Spencer finally said low, "but it's not a good time."

Doll? Not a good time for *what?* Curiosity, and a few more unpleasant emotions, nudged Arizona closer.

"But it's been forever," purred the female, "and you promised me—"

"I don't make promises."

"I know." An exaggerated sigh. "That's not what I meant. But…" Silly female cajoling. "God, Spencer, I *need* you." Slim, pale hands came up and around Spencer's neck and drew him down.

This time she had no doubts at all about the silence. They were making out in his doorway, right there for God and the rest of the world to see.

Peeved, Arizona took a few quicker steps forward, and witnessed a pretty blonde delivering a scorching kiss. They both had their eyes closed. They fit together. And she saw a flash of tongue.

Fury narrowed her eyes.

Spencer *knew* she was waiting on him, but he didn't exactly fight off Blondie's attentions.

With one hand at her waist and the other keeping the door held open—probably to try to block Arizona from seeing—Spencer let the brazen broad kiss him.

Crossing her arms and propping her shoulder against the wall, Arizona asked, "Can I get an estimate on how long this is going to take?"

When they both looked at her, the blonde shocked, Spencer resigned, Arizona smiled.

"I mean, is this going somewhere? Should I skedaddle and leave you to it? Or should I just wait outside for a few?"

The blonde opened her mouth twice but said nothing. Her lips were now wet, her face flushed.

Spencer, appearing unaffected by it all, didn't say anything. He just watched Arizona.

When the blonde noticed that, she shoved out of Spencer's hold. "You bastard!" She turned and marched away.

"Hey, he doesn't make promises," Arizona called after her. "You should've remembered that!" Since Blondie didn't head for a car but instead crossed the lawn, Arizona assumed her to be a neighbor. How handy was that? He had "hanky-panky" living right next door.

Giving her a dirty look, Spencer pointed at her. *"Stay."* And with that, he went after the woman.

Like…maybe she mattered to him? *Who was she?*

Snuffing the hurt she felt, Arizona said, "Woof," so Spencer would know what she thought of his order, then she strode to the door to watch the theatrics.

Relationships confounded her; she'd never seen the appeal of having someone around, underfoot. The invasion to your privacy. The expectations. Obligations.

Sex.

No, she wanted no part of it.

And yet it infuriated her to see Spencer contain the woman by holding her oh-so-gently, and to see Blondie soften as he explained.

What did he tell her?

For certain, Spencer wouldn't admit that she'd watched him sleeping, that he'd gotten up and paraded around buck naked in front of her.

He wouldn't admit that they were both vigilantes, and that their only connection was a drive to bring the bad guys to justice.

But he talked about *something,* and when the woman looked toward Arizona with understanding and sympathy, her temper snapped.

What the hell?

Did that bimbo *pity* her?

Storming away, Arizona headed back to the kitchen. Along the way she threw a few shadow punches and kicks, then drew a slow deep breath. She'd already reconnoitered Spencer's house, so she knew she could slip out the back door and not have to see him again.

But she wouldn't. She'd be damned before she let him make her flee. She didn't run from anyone. Not anymore. Never again.

Hoping to hide her awful mix of emotions, she went about cleaning up the mess on the floor.

Making herself at home, she located Spencer's garbage can and unearthed a roll of paper towels. She was almost done when Spencer came in several minutes later.

The second she saw him, she tossed away the last paper towel and regained her feet. "You do her in the driveway?"

Appearing cautious, he said, "What?"

Holding one hand in a circle and extending the first finger of her other hand, Arizona created a crude simulation of sex.

His expression tightened. "That's enough."

"Is it?" She leaned on the counter. "You were gone long enough."

"Five minutes? I don't think so."

That stymied her for a moment, but what did she know of his sexual habits? Maybe he struggled. Maybe it took him longer. "Whatever you say."

He drew out a chair. "Jealous much?"

"No!"

"Then what do you care?"

Her molars clenched. "I don't." But her heart started thumping in a very strange way.

"You refused to kiss me," he reminded her.

Oh, surely he didn't think… "Damn right I refused!"

"Then it doesn't matter if I kiss her, does it?"

Her hand twitched with the need to zing the remaining coffee cup at his handsome face, but that would never do. It'd give away too much—and leave her with another mess to clean up.

Besides, he now blocked the exit from the kitchen to the front door, and she wasn't reckless enough to infuriate him when getting out the back would hinder her escape and make it possible for him to catch her—

"I will not hurt you, damn it!"

She almost jumped out of her skin with that deep, loud shout. But he looked more offended than threatening, alleviating her concern. "Sheesh. Stop my heart, why don't you?" At least his outburst had brought her back around, helping her to shake off those odd sensations of worry and…hurt.

He literally fumed. "You're standing there configuring escape routes."

"No way." How could he know that?

"I saw it in your eyes, Arizona. You have an expressive face."

"Seriously?" And here she'd thought just the opposite. Many, many times she'd hidden her emotions from others. Her sadness. Her fear. Her yearning. No one else had so easily picked up on her thoughts.

"Very expressive." He drew a deep breath, ran both hands through his hair. "But there's no need. Marla's a friend, that's all."

"A friend that you fuck?"

His teeth sawed together. "Occasionally. By mutual agreement."

Ah, God, why did that hurt so much? It shouldn't. It had nothing to do with her. "I interrupted a little nookie time for you, didn't I?" The sarcasm came through loud and clear. She shook her head in pity. "I am *soooo* sorry."

"No, you're not, so don't lie about it."

No, she wasn't sorry. Just the opposite, she was glad she'd kept him from boinking the blonde. "Marla, huh? She was sort of...full-figured, wasn't she?"

"She's got a lot of curves. So what?"

"You're a chubby chaser?"

He rubbed his face in exasperation. "Most men like a woman with some meat on her bones."

Unable to stop herself, Arizona glanced down at her trim limbs. No one would call her chubby. She had her own curves, but if he preferred—

"Stop it, Arizona."

"Stop what?"

"Comparing." His gaze went all over her, fast but thorough. He glanced away as he said, "You're incredibly sexy."

"Incredibly?" Okay, so she knew that men found her appealing. Usually it creeped her out.

Now...not so much.

"There are a lot of different body types, but most women are beautiful in their own way."

"Wow." Could he really believe that nonsense? "That sounded almost poetic."

"You know men find you attractive."

"I know they see...me." Her throat tightened, especially with the speculative way Spencer watched her. She flagged a hand and tried to sound negligent. "They look at me and they know things. That's all."

"What things?"

"Who I am, what I've done."

"No." His gaze darkened, softened. "They look at you

and see an extremely exotic, beautiful woman. That's all."

If he wanted to believe that, fine. She knew the truth: her ugly past clung to her like a wet shirt.

He dropped into the seat. "Let's get back to the bet, okay?"

She'd rather not. "What did you tell her about me?" It still rankled, seeing the way that woman had looked at her, all long-faced and sad-sacked.

Spencer sighed. "Does it really matter?"

"To me, yeah." She nudged her chin at him. "C'mon. Fess up. What'd you say?"

He worked his jaw. "I told her you were a one-night stand who didn't understand the concept."

Un-freaking-believable. "She bought that?"

"That you and I would have sex?" With a sardonic glare, he said, "Yeah, she bought it."

"No, I mean that I would track you down here and act all stalkerish and clingy and shit?"

His expression didn't change. "She bought it."

"Huh. That makes me sound really…dysfunctional. And maybe dangerous." She thought about it and grinned. "Not bad. I can live with that."

He rolled his eyes. "The bet?"

It wouldn't hurt to clean up her language. She'd always meant to anyway, but when she got annoyed, stuff just came out of her mouth. "I dunno. What do I get when I win?"

"What do you want?"

Perfect opening. Refusing to admit, even to herself, how much his answer mattered, she said, "Your help with checking out the bar and grill and, if necessary, righting things there."

His gaze searched hers for only a moment before he nodded agreement.

No way. That was too easy. "Seriously?"

He sat back in the seat and crossed his arms. "I'd have done that anyway. So yeah, why not?"

"You…" She closed her mouth and frowned. He'd planned to assist her all along? "You'll help me? For real?"

"I can't control you, so I know you're going to do it either way." Gently, he tacked on, "Did you really think I'd let you get involved on your own?"

Did he really think he'd have any say-so in that? Not likely.

Two emotions pulled at her: resentment that he wanted to control her, because no way in hell would she ever let that happen again, and a twinge of…maybe relief.

Because he seemed to care what happened to her.

Dumb, dumb, dumb. She worked best unhindered by emotion. It was tough enough worrying about Jackson, but she owed him big-time, so of course she wanted him safe. The last thing she needed was to start fretting about Spencer, too.

And thinking of Jackson…

While she had Spencer in an agreeable mood, why not press for more? Taking the seat opposite him at the table, she thought it through, then ventured cautiously, "Okay. Since that was already a given, maybe…" she drew a deep breath "…you could be my escort to Jackson's wedding?"

"Done." He thrust out his hand.

Whoa. His fast agreement left her feeling played. But damn it, she didn't want to go to a wedding. Since she had to go, she didn't want to go by herself.

He waited.

"If I can't swear," she warned, "you can't, either."

"No problem." He kept his hand extended, his expression expectant.

Uncertainty left her on edge. Oh, she trusted that she could win the stupid bet and all payments would be a moot point, but still… "What kind of kiss are we talking about?"

Suddenly his annoyance melted away. A small smile curled the corners of his mouth. "Nothing to distress you, I promise."

Yeah, well, the way he said that—with so much satisfaction—sort of distressed her more than anything. But Arizona shored up her pride and gripped his hand. "Get your suit ready, Spence, because I know I'll win the bet."

He let her slide on shortening his name—which was something she knew annoyed him. "If you say so." He retained his hold on her hand. "I would have gone with you to the wedding anyway, so it's no skin off my nose."

Touching him did funny things to her stomach, made her feel unsettled and jumpy and too warm. Pulling her hand free, she pushed from her seat and glared down at him. "If you would have already done both those things, then I'm not really getting anything in the bet!"

"But you already agreed." He smiled. "You even shook on it. And somehow, I just know you're true to your word."

Like he really knew jackola about her or her morals? Fat chance. She headed for the coffee carafe and a new mug. "Fine. Whatever. Now, about that bar…"

"Understand, Arizona. Even if you lose the bet—"

"I won't." She couldn't. Kisses? No, she couldn't, wouldn't let that happen.

"I'm still going with you to the wedding—"

"We'll see." But she was so relieved to hear it. Going with Spencer would make the formal affair a little more bearable.

"—and I'm still going to help you with the bar."

"Great. Glad to hear it."

"But I want you to listen to me, and listen good."

Here we go. She poured a fresh cup of coffee and came back to the table. "Let's hear it."

"Since you want my help, I have a few rules."

"Like?"

"Give me the name and address and I'll scope it out." He looked stern, even foreboding. "In the meantime, you will not do anything on your own. Don't go there, don't even go *near* there. I don't want them to know who you are."

Arizona laughed. "Sorry, Spence-my-buddy, but it's too late for that. I've been there twice already, and they've more than taken notice of me, so…" She shrugged. "I'm balls-deep in this thing, and we gotta go in tomorrow night, because they're expecting me. Be there or be square."

THE SECOND SPENCER STEPPED into the family-owned diner, he saw Trace sitting toward the back, drinking a Coke and eating a burger. Innocuous enough, or at least it should have been.

But no way in hell would anyone *not* notice Trace Miller. More than any other man he knew, this one exuded extreme capability. He was part of a trio that Spencer had met after tailing Arizona right into the middle of a setup. She'd been in danger, or so he'd thought. There was no way he could have known she had an elite ops group looking out for her. The trio had incredible contacts, far reaching influence and the ability to back up the badass swagger.

Not that any of them swaggered, really. Well, maybe Jackson, but that had more to do with Jackson as a man than with his expertise at utilizing deadly skill. If Spencer had to guess, he'd say Jackson was born cocky.

This one, Trace Miller—most likely an alias—was a cool cucumber. *GQ* looks didn't conceal his edge. As a bounty hunter, Spencer had learned to size up people quickly in order to gauge the danger in any situation. He'd pegged Trace as a take-charge, protect-the-innocent but get-it-done personality. Suave, wealthy, efficient… and deadly when necessary.

The trio seemed to trust him—to a degree. He had no illusions about their cautious natures. They'd already dug through his background, unearthed things he'd rather keep private, and probably knew him as well as he knew himself. Not that they said much about it. So far, there'd been no reason.

Spencer didn't take the association lightly, and beyond that, he hated to ask for favors. He especially hated to admit he might not be able to handle things on his own. If Arizona wasn't at risk, he'd do things his way and accept the consequences.

He wasn't without his own ability.

But she was involved. Hell, she was in it up to her pretty little nose, and that changed everything. He knew the trio cared about her, that they'd made her a priority. Having backup, just in case things went sideways, only made sense. *He wanted her safe, damn it.*

Feeling a little traitorous, Spencer crossed the restaurant floor. He'd only promised not to tell Jackson, he reminded himself.

He hadn't said a thing about Trace.

When he reached the table, Trace set aside his napkin and glanced up. "There a reason you stood there studying me before coming in?"

Since he hadn't been going for stealth, Spencer didn't mind the direct question. He shook his head and slid into the booth. "Not really. Just wondering about something. I know Jackson renamed Arizona. And I know that Alani's last name is different from yours, even though you're siblings. So was she renamed, too?"

"No."

Which meant Miller was an alias.

Figures. With a nod, because he really didn't care, Spencer said, "I have a problem."

With a half smile, Trace asked, "Is her name Arizona?"

Not funny. Or rather, it would be funny if it didn't involve him. "Bingo."

"What'd she do now?" Trace sat back in the booth. "And why aren't you going to Jackson? She's like a sister to him."

Was she? He knew Jackson felt that way—but Arizona? Sometimes he wondered. They had a very complicated relationship, but Spencer said only, "Arizona made me promise I wouldn't tell Jackson."

"Ah. Didn't mention keeping it from me or Dare, huh?"

"No. I guess she didn't think you two were an option." Dare was the third element in the team. The day Spencer had met them all, Dare had been on surveillance—meaning crouched on a hillside with high-powered rifles ready to pick off anyone planning an ambush. "I doubt Arizona even realizes we've stayed in touch since that cluster-fuck happened."

He shrugged. "It went as planned."

"She was in the middle of it all." It still made Spencer furious to think about it. Arizona had used herself to lure in the human traffickers. But she hadn't realized they were the same people she'd previously escaped—the same people who had once tossed her, bound and abused, over the side of a bridge and into a churning river to kill her.

If Jackson hadn't come upon them that night, if he hadn't been skilled enough and fast enough, Arizona would have drowned.

Sadly, few would have noticed her passing. Even fewer would have cared.

Spencer's guts cramped. So far in her young life, Arizona had been dealt a miserable hand. And still she was so...spirited.

"Since they wanted her dead, I'd say you were right." Trace studied him. "You seeing her much?"

"Not really." He didn't want to betray Arizona's trust, so he couldn't explain that he'd been trying to avoid her—and forget her—only to find her sitting in his bedroom, watching him sleep. "She stopped by."

Trace's expression didn't change. "To engage you in one of her stunts?"

Now he felt defensive on her behalf. "What she doesn't have in size and strength, she makes up for with brains and bravery."

"Bravery?" Eyebrow raised, Trace reached for his Coke. "I'd call it recklessness."

"Maybe." He didn't want to argue the point. "It bothers me that she doesn't show enough caution, and she puts no value on her own hide."

"I know." Almost as a warning, Trace said, "Whoever hooks up with the girl better have a lot of fortitude, because I don't see her easing off anytime soon."

Yeah…he didn't want to think about Arizona with anyone else. And the way she'd reacted to the idea of a kiss, he knew she still had a lot of hurt to overcome. People now cared for her, but she trusted only the ugly side of life.

Because that was all she knew.

With the Coke gone, Trace got serious. "I thought Jackson had her busy doing computer work."

Not busy enough, obviously. "She does that—and then some."

On a sigh, Trace asked, "So what's she into now?"

Spencer explained about the bar and grill, and Arizona's suspicions. "She told me she's been there a few times already and she's been noticed."

"That girl would get noticed anywhere."

An irrefutable fact. He'd never seen a woman as breathtakingly gorgeous as Arizona. "So at this point, for the sake of her safety, I have to assume there are some shady deals going on. Which means someone might have already followed her."

"They could know where she lives, the places she frequents. She could get grabbed right off the street." Trace gave him a long look. "Unfortunately, it happens all the time."

Which was why he wanted to protect her. "I have no choice but to get involved."

"No choice at all." Trace considered things. "Give me the name of the place and the location."

"The Green Goose, in downtown Middleville."

Expression arrested, Trace said, "Shit."

"What? You're aware of something going on in there?"

It took him a second, and then Trace laughed. "She's got great instincts, I'll give her that."

It hit Spencer like a ton of bricks. "She's right about the place, isn't she?"

"Afraid so. Luckily for your peace of mind, we were already on it. Early stages, though. Dare was running background checks on the owners, and I was planning a visit so I could scope out things from within."

"Arizona's already done that." He rubbed the bridge of his nose, but Trace had to know it all. "She says she sat at a table, and when a kid came to take her order, she noticed some bruises, what looked like a broken finger that hadn't been set right, and the boy wouldn't look her in the eyes. Probably not more than sixteen, though of course his age would be fudged."

Anger gathered in Trace's expression, but he sounded calm enough when he said, "I wish we'd moved on this sooner, damn it."

But they couldn't be everywhere at once, and cruelty existed far and wide, all the time. "When the boy brought her food, Arizona asked if it was a good place to work. She told him she was looking for a job."

"The boy's reaction?"

"He couldn't or wouldn't tell her what they made per hour."

Grim, Trace said, "Because he's not getting paid."

"That's Arizona's assumption. Around a lot of stammering and nervousness, the boy pointed out the man to talk to if she wanted to work there. Arizona said he's a tall, skinny guy, mid-forties, thinning brown hair, brown eyes, goatee, earring, some sort of colorful tribal tattoo on his left arm. From what she could find out, he's the owner of the place."

"Terry Janes." Trace crossed his arms. "Did some time when he was younger for peddling drugs, been in more trouble a handful of times for robbery, breaking and entering, suspected rape. He had a charge for beating a guy half to death, but that fell through the cracks. No way is he the owner."

God, it sounded worse than Spencer had suspected. "Later that night, Arizona kept watch on the place and only a few of the employees left. Janes, his bartender, his bouncer—just key people, I guess. He locked the door behind him. It's a shitty part of town, so bars on the windows make sense, but in this case—"

"They're there to keep the workers in." After a moment of thought, Trace leaned forward, arms resting on the table. "Please tell me that Arizona hasn't talked to him."

That was the only good news in the whole screwed scenario. "She says not, but she told the boy she'd be back tomorrow night—and she's pretty sure the guy overheard it all."

"Which was probably intentional on her part?"

"I assume so."

Trace shook his head. "So now they'll be watching for her."

"You met Arizona. That's her plan." Disgust rolled through him; he *hated* her plan. "She wants them to know, to make a move, so she can expose them."

"At least she had the good sense to come to you for backup." Trace pulled out his cell phone. "Where's Arizona now?"

"At this precise moment? No idea." And that was a problem, because it would take Arizona no more than a minute to get in over her head. When he couldn't see her, he worried about what she was doing, if she was safe.

He wondered if she thought about him even half as much as he thought about her.

It'd be nice to claim that altruistic motives drove him. But that wouldn't be the whole truth, and he knew it.

He glanced at his wristwatch. "She's coming by my place in a few hours so we can coordinate plans for tomorrow."

"Coordinating plans was the best you could come up with?"

Spencer shrugged. That had been the only excuse he could think of to gain himself time enough to talk to Trace—and to get a cake for her birthday.

Trace said, "Whatever you call it, get her to stay overnight with you, and keep her under wraps until she heads to the Green Goose."

No and no again. "How the hell am I supposed to do that?" *And not touch her?*

"I don't know. Find a way. Tell her you need to go over the rules with her."

Or just go over her. Spencer shook his head. "You think that'll take the whole night?"

"Guess that depends on how you drag it out, doesn't it?"

Spencer didn't miss the suggestion. But Trace had to be kidding. With a hand to the back of his neck, Spencer tried to rub away the growing tension. "The thing is, Arizona's…skittish."

What an understatement. Arizona was all brass and bravado, until someone showed intimate interest. Then her survival reaction of fight, flight or freeze kicked in.

So far, with him, she always chose to fight.

And every time it happened, the vise on his heart squeezed a little tighter. He had a plan to help her with that. A masochistic plan that was sure to make him nuts, but for Arizona…

"She knows you want her."

"No." Damn it, he'd said that too fast and sounded far too defensive.

Trace just looked at him.

"I'm too old for her." *God, just shut up, Spencer.*

"Given what she's been through and the way she lives, I'd say you're just what she needs."

Not a topic he'd discuss with Trace or anyone else.

As if he realized that himself, Trace didn't wait for confirmation. "Get her to your place, and I'll find a way to disable her car. It's as good an excuse as any for her to stay the night. Keeping her with you will give you more control until we shut down the joint."

The enormity of coercing Arizona to do anything was overshadowed by Spencer's surprise. "Shut it down?" Could it really be that easy to remove Arizona from danger—this time? "Just like that?"

"Yeah, just like that." Being enigmatic, Trace added, "We were on this anyway."

We, meaning Trace, Dare and Jackson? He didn't ask. He knew Trace wouldn't tell him. "Glad to hear it."

"Now, with Arizona ready to dive in… It could still take some time, but I'll do my best to accelerate things."

"I hope so, because if you know Arizona at all, you know I'm not going to be able to get her to pull back." Hell, he'd be lucky if he could get her to stop swinging for his head. "As for her staying with me…dicking with her car might work once, but after that? She won't like the idea of anyone protecting her."

Trace looked down at the table. "I understand her. After what she's been through, she hurts, physically and emotionally, thinking about anyone caught in that situation."

"She knows how it is," Spencer agreed softly. "She understands that unique misery only too well." And for

Arizona, the only escape from her memories would be to validate her current well-being by helping others. Otherwise, she'd feel like she had no justice at all.

They shared a somber moment, then Trace flipped open his phone and pressed a button. "Let me make this call, and then I'll tell you what we're going to do."

CHAPTER THREE

BRIGHT SUNSHINE SHONE in Arizona's eyes as she waited in her car for Spencer to return. Even adjusting the visor didn't help. Heat built—inside the car, inside her mind.

Growing bored, then quickly drowsy, she leaned her head back, closed her eyes against the glare…and drifted away to the day of that awful confrontation.

Spencer's voice sounded with conviction…and with caring. "Whatever Chandra did to you, she'll pay."

But Arizona knew that couldn't be true. Even thinking Chandra had died wasn't payment enough. And now, people she cared about, people she loved, were at risk.

Because of her.

Red-hot hatred, bone-deep fear, churned inside her.

It wasn't easy, but she pretended indifference to the situation. Not that she ever could be. Not faced with her tormentor—the one who'd orchestrated so much hurt and unthinkable disgrace, here in the flesh.

All this time, she'd thought Chandra dead, well out of reach of revenge.

And unable to cause more pain.

Yet there she stood. Smiling. Sick as always. Unfortunately, this time, Arizona wasn't her only target. Now Chandra planned to hurt others—Jackson, his girlfriend, Alani.

Spencer.

No, not Spencer. He'd skipped out seconds before the situation escalated. To where?

Who cared? She wouldn't. She couldn't.

Bravado would have to get her through. Summoning a snide smile to hide the hurt, Arizona sneered, "Usually dead women can't talk. And you are dead—whether you realize it yet or not."

A maniacal laugh. Chandra's awful, bone-chilling enjoyment of pain.

It left her pale, cold. Determined. Arizona didn't back down. "It's between us. Leave the others out of it." Let me have my revenge. Please.

Chandra disregarded the warning, saying, "If she speaks again, shoot her."

And they would. Chandra's bully boys would enjoy putting a bullet in her.

What to do? Stand back, as Jackson asked? She owed him so much, but...she couldn't. If she stayed safe, she couldn't strike out. And she wanted to. She desperately needed to.

So what if her hands were shaking?

So what if her heart thundered and her eyes burned and the urge to flee beat hard and fast in her chest? Never would she run away.

This was her hell.

She had the right to end it.

Determined, determined...but then everything happened at once. Multiple shots, chaos...

Spencer! He hadn't left. Not yet.

Expression fierce and jaw rock-hard, Spencer started toward her.

He'd stolen her revenge.

He hadn't left her.

Anger and relief built in combustible force, so confusing, so powerful—

"Yoo-hoo."

Jolted from the dark memory, Arizona bolted upright in her seat. Without thinking about it, she automatically reached for her knife and looked around at the same time.

Standing there by the passenger door, bending to look in the window, was Spencer's busty neighbor. She showed off a bright smile, a lot of cleavage and cunning resolve.

Perfect. Just what she deserved.

Still caught up in reliving the awful scenario that had stolen her purpose for being, Arizona breathed too hard, too fast. Sweat had gathered along her spine. Her palms felt damp.

Slowly, hoping the neighbor wouldn't notice, she drew her hand away from the knife hidden at the small of her back, then shoved her hair from her face.

Where the hell was Spencer? She'd pulled up twenty minutes ago but hadn't seen his truck. While trying to decide whether to hang around or to bolt, she'd taken an unplanned trip down memory lane.

So lame.

Surreptitiously she swiped a forearm over her brow and put up the car windows.

Never one to miss an opportunity, Arizona undid her seat belt and left her black Focus. "Yoo-hoo, yourself." Even saying it with sarcasm, she felt like an ass. But at least the intrusion had brought her back to the here and now. "You know where Spencer is?"

"He went out," Blondie said helpfully.

"No kidding?" Arizona circled the hood, leaned

against the fender and crossed her arms. "You don't miss much, do you?"

Blondie's smile slipped, making her almost feel mean.

"Sorry. I've had a rough day." She held out her hand. "Arizona."

"What?"

Well used to that reaction, she shrugged. "My name. It's Arizona."

"Oh." Wary, keeping the contact as brief as possible, the neighbor-lady shook her hand in a limp, barely there greeting. "Marla."

"Nice to meet you, Marla." Spencer had asked her to come back at six, and she was twenty minutes early, but so what? She couldn't break in again, not with the ever-alert Marla keeping tabs on things. Anything that happened now was Spencer's fault. "So, that stuff this morning... You and Spence got something going on, huh?"

Marla found her backbone. "Yes."

That was it? Arizona pursed her mouth and waited. Blondie would crack, no doubt about it.

Annnnnddd...she did.

"We've, ah, been seeing each other for a while now."

Seeing each other meant what? In the sack, or had Spencer taken her out on a date? Dancing, dinner, movies... Arizona really had no understanding of the concept. Never in her life had she been out on a legitimate "date."

This could be a great learning experience. She'd uncover details about Spencer that a cold file filled with facts couldn't give, and maybe get a better, more personal grasp of the whole relationship ritual.

"No kidding? How long is a while?"

Marla's bravery faltered. "Long enough."

Meaning...they were an item? "Well of course you have. Look at you." She gestured at Marla's boobs. "No guy would pass that up, right?"

That must've been the wrong thing to say, because Marla backed up two steps. "You looked lost in thought when I walked out."

Lost being the operative word. But not anymore. Never again. "Just waiting on Spence."

"Why?"

For some insane reason, maybe deeply rooted female vindictiveness, Arizona enjoyed telling her, "He wanted me to join him for dinner."

Putting her plump shoulders back, Marla tried for a level, nasty stare. "You're wasting your time."

A direct attack? Bravo, Marla. Grinning, Arizona said, "Well, look at you feeling all ballsy and possessive and stuff."

That got her a double take and more wariness. "I mean it." Marla visually worked up her courage. "Spencer and I might not be...committed—"

"Still up in the air, huh?"

"But we have an *understanding.*"

What did that mean? An understanding about what? "Enlighten me, why doncha?"

"You can't have him."

No misunderstanding that. "Didn't say I wanted him." Arizona pushed away from the car, and Blondie took another quick step back. "At least, not for what you're talking about."

"No?"

"Definitely no. You want to screw him?" Her throat tightened, but she got the words out. "Have at it. More power to you."

Marla soaked in the words, analyzed them, and gave a slow smile.

Arizona didn't trust that smile one bit. "What's funny?"

Overflowing with good humor, Marla said, "You haven't slept with him, have you?"

How would she know that? She couldn't. "I never kiss and tell."

Marla shook her head. "Spencer said you were a one-night stand, a mistake, but now I know that was a lie."

A mistake? That dick. She'd make him pay for that. "You calling Spence a liar?"

"I'm just saying that he made up a story for some reason. Maybe to protect you somehow. I know he's a bounty hunter. Could be you're undercover with him or something."

Huh. What exactly did she think bounty hunters did? Mocking her assumptions, Arizona said, "That's some imagination you've got."

Marla shrugged. "All I know is that you haven't slept with him."

"You're sure about that, are you?"

"Absolutely." Marla oozed satisfaction, even leaned in to taunt Arizona. "If you'd ever had him, you'd feel differently about having him again."

She sounded so convinced, she piqued Arizona's interest. "Yeah? Why's that?"

With significance, Marla purred, "For one thing, he's big *all over.*"

Arizona's heart almost stopped. In an appalled whisper, she asked, "You *like* that?"

Scowling, Marla pulled back. "Bigger is definitely better."

Visuals came to Arizona's mind, but she didn't have

quite the reaction Marla seemed to expect. She wrinkled her nose. "If you say so."

Marla shivered with pleasure. "He's delicious."

Yeaaaahhhh, she'd let that one go. "You're saying that even though he's big, you don't feel…" She couldn't think of an appropriate word and settled for, "maybe threatened?"

"With Spencer? Of course not."

Hmm. Okay, so Spencer was extra tall, extra muscular, solid, and loaded with ability. He had never hurt her.

Contained her, yes. Hurt her, no. "So you like it that he's big?"

"That, and the man knows things."

Fascinating. What things could he know that she didn't, that Marla found not only acceptable, but good enough to want again and again? "Give me an example."

"I'm not telling you!"

Provoking her—because she really did want details—Arizona said, "That's what I thought. You can't give an example because you don't know."

"He's *wonderful*."

Arizona snorted. "Wonderfully pushy."

"He's considerate and patient."

"So is my bookie," Arizona told her, "but I wouldn't want to screw him." She shuddered at just the thought.

Taking the bait, Marla leaned forward again. "He's the best, most generous lover I've ever had."

"How many have you had?"

"My God." Gasping, Marla drew back once more. "That is none of your business!"

"You brought it up." Still ripe with curiosity, Arizona asked, "So what does Spence do specifically that's so awesome you'd be willing to fight for him?"

Marla blanched. "Fight? But…but I never said anything about *fighting*."

"No? So then what's this?" Arizona waved a hand between them. "Some sort of warped social call?"

Her mouth worked, but it took her a few seconds to get anything out. "He said you're a stalker."

Considering she'd broken in and watched him sleep, she couldn't deny that. "Ehhhh…maybe."

Marla found her courage again. "Well, whatever reason you're here, you might as well give up on the idea of having him. He's mine, and he's staying mine."

Spencer drove up and, looking horrified to see the women together, pulled into his driveway and slammed the truck into Park.

Lifting a hand to shield her eyes from the sun, Arizona watched him cross the yard in a fast, long-legged stride. He wore a frown of concern. Sheesh. What did he think she'd do to his girlfriend?

"Last chance to tell me what's so special about him." In bed.

"That's personal, so forget it."

Knowing there'd be no more Q & A, Arizona said to Marla, "Spoilsport." And then she waited for Spencer to reach them.

WHILE ARIZONA ACTED as if nothing had happened, Spencer continued to stew. He didn't know if she truly lacked all social graces, or if she enjoyed pushing his buttons in any and every way possible.

There'd be hell to pay with Marla. She'd already started to get clingy, and now, seeing Arizona as a direct threat, she'd probably double her efforts.

Just what he didn't need.

Since losing his wife three years ago, he'd occasionally given in to his baser urges. He was a grown man, and between long bouts of celibacy, he needed relief.

He didn't fault himself for that.

But giving in to Marla had been a huge mistake. Their close proximity as neighbors was sticky enough; the fact that she had marriage in her eyes should have been the clincher.

Unfortunately, a few months after she'd moved in, she'd caught him at a weak moment, a moment he regretted, and after that...well, he'd slept with her a total of three times.

Idiotic. And regrettable.

But that was all before meeting Arizona, and since meeting her... No, he hadn't wanted Marla.

Straddling a chair, Arizona watched him intently as he went about cooking dinner. There was a new attentiveness to her gaze that hadn't been there before. He didn't understand it.

He didn't understand her.

They hadn't said much since he'd more or less dragged her inside—away from Marla—with rushed excuses. He felt her amusement, and it nettled him. He felt her curiosity, and that worried him more.

"Food smells good."

Standing at the stove turning chops, Spencer glanced back at her. An olive branch? From Arizona? He wasn't fool enough to reject it.

"Thanks. We would have had steaks on the grill, but—"

"You didn't want Marla to see us together." Arizona grinned. "I get it." She lifted her hand as if shooting a gun. "The lady's got you in her sights and she's taking aim."

The microwave dinged, so he took out the potatoes. "Marla misunderstands the situation."

"Nah, I don't think so. She knows you're not hooked yet, or she wouldn't be so insecure about things." Snorting, Arizona added, "I can't believe you told her we slept together."

His neck stiffened. "It was as good an excuse as any."

"Yeah, maybe. But now she knows better."

Going still, Spencer swallowed a groan. "You told her?" Marla would likely ramp up her efforts if she knew the truth.

"Not really on purpose." Arizona's gaze was so intent, it burned him.

He split the potatoes and dropped in butter. He almost hated to ask, but… "How does that conversation accidentally happen?"

"When she found out I wasn't going all she-devil over the idea of you boinking her, she said she knew." Nonchalantly, Arizona added, "Something about you being such a stud-muffin in the sack that if I'd ever had a taste of what you have to offer, I'd be fighting tooth and nail to keep it all to myself."

Heat crawled up his neck. "That's baloney."

"Hey, she said it, not me. I was notably skeptical."

Figured. "Questioned my prowess, huh?"

"She didn't really mention your, er, prowess. She just said you're well hung."

He damn near dropped the plate of potatoes. Slowly, he turned his head to stare at her.

Unfazed, Arizona asked, "Wouldn't that just make things more unpleasant?"

Oh, God. No way was he prepared for this conversation. Later, maybe. After he'd had time to formulate what to say, how to reassure her. How to approach the conversation in a detached, casual... Who was he kidding?

He couldn't discuss the size of his junk with her. Not ever.

He cleared his throat and turned back to his food prep. "Just like women, to stand around gossiping." He could only imagine Marla's reaction to Arizona and her uncensored ways.

"You know, I asked her for specifics, but she wouldn't share."

He jerked around to face her again. "You asked Marla for details about me in bed with her?"

Arizona shrugged. "She made me curious with all her moony-eyed, drooling enthusiasm."

Curious was...maybe good. Better than fear. He considered her candor, her ease in talking to him about such private things. That had to be a sign of trust, didn't it?

Brightening, Arizona said, "You're thinking of telling me?"

He shook his head. No, he wouldn't tell her a thing—not yet anyway. "Maybe later."

"Why wait?"

He turned off the stove. "Dinner is almost ready."

She frowned but said, "Good, because I'm starved."

Thank God for the safer subject. "When did you last eat?"

"I don't know."

Never the expected answer from Arizona. One day he'd get used to that. If he knew her long enough, which was doubtful. "What do you mean, you don't know?"

"I had a candy bar around lunchtime."

"Nothing since then?"

She shook her head.

"What'd you have for breakfast?"

"Coffee with you."

His head started to pound. "Dinner the night before?"

She thought about it, then shook her head again.

Frustration edged in. "Why would you not eat?"

"I just forget sometimes." She left her chair and approached the stove. "Can I do anything to help get the show on the road here? My stomach is growling."

While she sniffed the pork chops, Spencer looked at the top of her head, at the shiny dark hair, the crooked part. Everything about her seemed endearing.

If a hedgehog could be endearing. "You can set the table if you want."

"Sure thing." Bumping him with her hip, she grinned and said, "A proper place setting is one of the things I learned in the school that Jackson sent me to. But I'm guessing you're more into informality, right?"

"Casual works for me." After first meeting Arizona, he'd tried to look up her background but found very little. He assumed Jackson was responsible for keeping her off the grid; it was how that elite trio worked. The less info out there, the better they liked it.

It fascinated Spencer, watching Arizona move around his kitchen, seeing her go on tiptoe to reach into cabinets. She'd again left her sneakers by the front door, and her bare feet were narrow, cute. Slender hands, small wrists.

So fundamentally female—but such a live wire and always unpredictable.

Hoping to sound cavalier, he said, "Tell me about the school."

With no sign of offense, she said, "It was this exclusive all-girl finishing school. Real hoity-toity." She flashed him another grin. "Not exactly my speed, but

Jackson paid through the nose, so they were always nice."

Spencer stared at her. Good God, they still had those? "You're serious?"

"Sure." Carrying two plates to the table, Arizona said, "I mean, no one looking for me would have thought to find *me* there, right?"

"I can't imagine finding any young lady there." But Arizona? In a structured routine meant to stuff societal rules down her throat? "What was it like?"

"Just an education, and a few classes on things like—" She swept her hand over the table. "Etiquette. Not that this setting really counts, but you get my drift."

"You went along with that?"

"Why not? The idea was sort of twofold. I figured I could learn how to blend in, and though he didn't say it, Jackson figured he'd have me locked down and out of trouble." She shook her head with some fond memory. "Jackson can be a real card."

Jackson had his sympathy. Teasing, Spencer asked, "Were you getting into trouble even then?"

She paused, made a face. "I think mostly he wanted me out of his apartment because I came on to him."

Flattened, Spencer stood there, mute.

Arizona glanced at him. "Dumb, huh?"

"I never..." He shook himself. "You...?"

"Snap out of it, Spence. Sheesh, I didn't expect you to get all tongue-tied over sex."

"Sex?" Had she slept with Jackson then? A red haze gathered in his vision. That son of a—

"Keep up, will you?" She rolled her eyes. "I offered, Jackson refused, and then he was different. Maybe uncomfortable. How should I know?"

"He refused?"

Sighing, a little dreamy, Arizona said softly, "Yeah, he did."

Suddenly he understood. "You thought to repay him, didn't you?"

"No. Well…maybe." She made a face. "Something like that, I guess. But Jackson had this heart-to-heart with me, and he was…kind."

So kind that he'd packed her off to a stuffy school where she wouldn't fit in? "Yeah, he's a prince."

"I know." Still wearing that small smile, she said, "I suggested going to a school, but I didn't expect that school. I just wanted to not be dumb, you know? But we talked about it, and I liked the idea." She flashed him a look. "I had no idea it'd cost so much, though."

"Jackson paid for it all?"

"Yeah. Insane, huh?" Going back to the cabinets for tableware, she said, "The way that guy blows money—"

"Think of it as an investment in your future." If he hadn't met Jackson, if he didn't know him as an honorable man in love with a different woman, Spencer might have been a little jealous. Not that he had the right. Not that he even wanted to think along those lines.

But knowing that Arizona had once offered herself to the other man, he couldn't deny the twinge of resentment. Jackson had done the right thing in turning her down.

And when the time came, he would do the right thing, too. He would do what was best for her.

"That's almost exactly what Jackson said."

After stirring the steamed vegetables one more time, Spencer put them in a bowl and carried them to the table. He dropped a potato and one chop on Arizona's plate, then his own.

He had a lot more questions, but he also wanted to feed her. "What would you like to drink?"

"Milk would be good."

Why that surprised him, he couldn't say. "Milk it is." As he filled her glass, he asked, "So you liked the school?"

"It was okay." She wrinkled her nose. "Except that they tattled a lot. Their loyalty was to Jackson. I mean, he paid, so that makes sense. But still, I couldn't even dodge out for a day or two without them telling him."

Keeping himself in check, Spencer asked, "Why did you dodge out?"

"I get restless." She eyed her food with significance.

He joined her at the table with a glass of iced tea. "Go ahead. Dig in."

She surprised him again by showing impeccable manners. She put her napkin in her lap, cut a small piece of her pork chop, chewed quietly.

He took great pleasure in watching her. "Good?"

"Mmm. Delicious." Her bright gaze went over him. "Sex, cooking, kicking as—er, butt. Is there anything you aren't good at?"

"Good catch." She'd almost cursed—and then she would have owed him that kiss. Refusing to acknowledge his disappointment, Spencer forked up a big bite of buttered baked potato. "Don't take Marla's word on the sex. As for kicking butt, I can hold my own, but I've gotten my fair share of bruises."

"And modest, too." She finished another bite. "Why shouldn't I take Marla's word?"

"You said it yourself, she has me in her sights. Wouldn't do her much good to insult me, now, would it?"

"I guess not. But it was more than that. She made it

sound like you were something special. Something more than—"

"So…" Finding it prudent to interrupt, Spencer asked, "What did you mean by blending in?"

She stalled, then her slender shoulder rolled. "What did I know of polite society? Even before I got caught up with the traffickers, my family was not what you'd call normal."

"What would you call them?" he asked gently.

"Hmm. Well, my momma was mostly okay, I guess, except that she drank too often, and she put up with daddy and his cronies. And I can't tell you much about my dad since I can't curse." She grinned. "Let's just say he wouldn't win any awards for father of the year."

"That leaves open a whole lot of possibilities."

"Yeah, well, figure the worst, and that was my father." She lifted her glass of milk in salute.

The worst was…awful. But then, he'd already guessed as much.

She didn't give him time to sympathize. "After the traffickers had me, well, you know how it goes. You get the bare minimum of everything."

Minimum care, shelter…and food. His heart hurt. "No milk?"

"Not unless a customer gave it to me. And then I always figured it might be drugged or something. There was no real contact with the outside world except during a deal, so I had no way of staying up on current affairs. In other words, I was dumber than a rock, uneducated, uncouth… Even you noticed the way I talk, right?"

Guilt swamped him. The last thing she needed from him was criticism. "I know you choose to be coarse, honey. It's not that you don't know any other way."

"Because Jackson sent me to that school. End of story."

But it wasn't and he knew it. "You are far from dumb."

"I know."

"Do you?"

Because she had her last bite of food in her mouth, she just nodded.

He wanted to ask her if she'd finished the school, if she'd gotten a degree, but he feared the answer. When the opportunity presented itself, he'd ask Jackson. "All done?"

She sat back in her seat with a sigh. "That was great. Thanks. I can't remember the last time anyone cooked for me. Maybe Jackson, but that would have been before the school."

"Your mother cooked?"

She laughed but cut it off real quick. "Not really, no."

Pushing his plate aside and crossing his arms on the table, Spencer asked the question burning in his mind. "How did the traffickers get you?"

"You really want to hear this?"

More than anything, he wanted her to trust him. He had to think that confiding in someone else would help ease the pain she carried inside. "If you don't mind telling me."

"It's not like it's a secret. Well, I mean it is, to most people. But not to anyone who already knows me and what I do, and that I was..."

Spencer waited for her to wind down.

Bravado in place, she smirked at him. "My daddy traded me to them for drugs."

Leveled by a dozen different emotions, most prominently rage and pity, Spencer swallowed twice. "How old were you?"

"Seventeen." She chewed her bottom lip, lost in thought. "The older I got, the more his buddies noticed. I heard a few lewd suggestions, stuff said sort of as a joke—but not really, know what I mean?"

"Yes." Bastards.

"I sort of grew into my looks. Pretty soon, they weren't joking anymore."

Jesus. He knew how it worked; human trafficking wouldn't be profitable without buyers. But still, with it so personal, fury left him sick at heart. "Your father knew them?" *Knew what they'd do with her?* It couldn't get more personal than that.

"Yeah, he knew. I think he admired them for forcing girls into prostitution." Her lip curled. "The sick pricks."

"What about your mother?"

Arizona shrugged. "She let him get away with a lot, including using some of the other girls, even though she knew their situation. But I guess selling me off was too much for her." She looked down at her fork. "Unfortunately, when she tried to stop them, they killed her."

Jesus. And that meant her father would have been a loose end. Already knowing the answer, Spencer asked, "They killed your father, too?" Had she seen it all?

"They did, and I was glad."

So she'd had no one—not that her folks had been much to count on anyway. He had to focus on the fact that she'd eventually escaped. "How'd you get away?"

"After more than a month, I decided I couldn't take it anymore. I knew if I ran they'd try to kill me, but…" She shrugged as if it didn't matter. "I was pretty much dead anyway, you know?"

He had nothing to say to that.

"We were at a truck stop, about to make a transaction, but when I saw a female trucker in an idling semi, I figured that might be my only chance."

"You asked her for help?"

"Get real. I didn't have time for pleasantries." Her lips tilted in a half smile. "That poor woman. I ran over and jumped in her cab. My heart was pumping so fast and I was nearly hysterical. I locked the passenger door, and then I screamed right into her face—drive, drive, *drive*. Luckily for me…she did."

CHAPTER FOUR

No matter how she made light of it, the horror of the situation appalled Spencer. "I can imagine what she thought."

"Yeah." Arizona gave a soft laugh. "At first, she figured I was robbing her or something, and she looked ready to jump out of her skin. But then Jerry—"

"Jerry?"

"One of the goons hired as muscle to make sure no one got out of line." She waved that off as unimportant. "Anyway, he came toward us, all fuming with blood in his eyes. When he pulled out his gun, she put that big rig in gear and rolled right out of there. Of course she wanted an explanation, so as soon as we'd covered a little ground, I told her a guy was trying to rape me. Not really a lie, but not the whole truth, either. I just...I couldn't see going into all of it, you know?"

"I understand." And he did. Too many women felt shame at what had been forced on them. Relaying details to a stranger would be painful.

"She wanted to take me to the cops, but I just wanted to be free."

A small word—that meant so much.

"When she hit a quiet stretch of highway, I thanked her, and bailed."

On her own? The idea of a seventeen-year-old abused girl finding shelter and safety boggled his mind. It was a wonder she'd survived—but she had, with attitude galore.

"I know what you're thinking." She shook her head at him. "But it was okay. Luckily it wasn't a cold or rainy season. I boosted a car, but I still needed some paper, so I mugged a drug dealer."

Paper, meaning money. But…she'd tangled with a dealer? "I hope that's an exaggeration."

"Nah. He was a little creep, and I let him think I was interested." She snorted. "He rushed me to his room, and when he got all grabby, I snatched his gun from him."

Hiding his horror, Spencer asked, "You shot him?"

She looked at him like he was nuts. "A gunshot would've drawn attention."

And that had been her only reason for not murdering the guy? "I see."

"I went old-school and pistol-whipped the punk." She made a "clunk" motion with her hand. "Clubbed him right on his melon. I had to hit him twice to really put him out. The first one only dazed him. But when I left he was breathing."

"And then you took his cash?"

"Yeah. I was hoping for enough to get food, but the dude had five C-notes!"

"Five hundred dollars?" Spencer whistled. Losing that much would put any crook into a foul mood. Thank God she'd gotten away. "You left the area?"

"Scooted right out of there, with his money and his gun." Proud of herself, she grinned. "Within two days of running, I had a car, plenty of cash and a weapon. I headed to another town, found a place to stay. I figured what worked once would work again, so most of my spending money came from traveling to other areas and robbing drug dealers. Occasionally I cashed up by gambling."

The idea of her besting an armed thug should have been ludicrous, but he'd seen her in action. Given her size and how she looked, she probably took plenty of guys by surprise. "You learned to fight by fighting?"

"Survival is a good teacher." She smirked. "Back then, I preferred the gambling."

"And now you prefer fighting?"

She didn't answer that. "I win a lot because I'm a good cheat. I'm also a good thief, and I'm really good at picking locks."

Because she'd spent so much time locked in.

With an effort, Spencer kept his tone neutral. "If those skills are what helped you get by, then I'm glad you had them."

"Even though I broke into your house?"

Keeping his gaze on his tea glass, he offered, "You could have a key if you want."

"Seriously? You trust me?"

He didn't, not really. Not with everything. Definitely not with too much intimacy.

But with his belongings?

He met her mocking gaze. "Would you rob me?"

"No!"

"That's what I thought. So why not give you a key?"

Skepticism kept her quiet for a long study. Finally she smiled. "That's real big of you, Spence."

"Spencer," he corrected with strained patience. He knew she shortened his name whenever she got annoyed—or felt vulnerable.

"But I don't need a key." She turned away with feigned disinterest. "Not like I plan to come here that often."

Probably not, but he wouldn't mind if she did. Whether arguing with her, wrestling with her, or having dinner, he enjoyed her company. "Then feel free to break in whenever the mood strikes you."

"Pffft." She half laughed. "You just took all the fun out of it."

Spencer smiled in return, but he in no way felt amused. He couldn't imagine what kind of guts it took, or how it would shape a person, to live through what she'd described. He knew the basics from Jackson, but while she was in a talkative mood, he wanted to hear it—all of it—from her perspective.

"So how does Jackson factor in?"

"Yeah, that's the interesting part, huh?" A little livelier now, she leaned forward and smiled at him. "See, the bastards didn't take kindly to me getting away, but when they finally caught up to me, they didn't want me for the usual."

To sell, barter and abuse. Gently, he asked, "Why did they want you?"

"To teach the others a lesson—by killing me."

Under the circumstances, Spencer let the curse pass. They were bastards—and so much more. In contrast to the awful words, Arizona's cavalier mood made it all too clear how much it still hurt her.

"They…" She faltered, then rallied again. "They roughed me up. I tried to fight, but they tied my hands behind me, and then…" She hesitated, her brows pulling down in a small frown.

It gave him warning of the awfulness of the details she'd share. He braced himself, but not enough.

Voice quieter now, she whispered, "They tossed me over a bridge into a river."

Air left his lungs; his muscles bunched. He'd known,

but hearing it from her made it more—more vivid. "They wanted to drown you."

She shook off the melancholy. "It was such a miserable night, storming like crazy with lightning cracking everywhere and thunder so loud, you could feel it. I was so scared that when they threw me over, I barely had the sense to stop flailing and try to land feetfirst, to suck in air before that icy water closed in around me." Using both hands, she pushed her hair back from her face. "I pretty much figured I was dead."

"Jesus." His stomach bottomed out. He desperately wanted to hold her, to draw her into his lap and hug her tight and tell her…what? That nothing bad would ever happen to her again?

He knew she'd never allow that, so he settled on reaching for her hand. "I'm so sorry you went through that."

"Yeah, pretty sucky, right?" After one brief squeeze, she pulled away. "I managed to get my head above water, but it wasn't easy, and I knew I couldn't do that for long. And even if I found a way to make it to shore, they'd just throw me back in again. Or shoot me."

Imagining the panic she had to have suffered left Spencer hurting for her.

"For certain they weren't going anywhere until they knew I was gone for good. See, they'd already told me that they needed the police to find my body. That way, they could tell the other women about it and use it as discouragement—"

"I get the picture." And he wanted to kill them, all of them. But that satisfaction would be denied him; they were already dead.

"They weren't counting on Jackson, though." She propped her chin on a fist and smiled. "Poor guy just sort of stumbled onto the whole mess. I'll never understand why, but he jumped into the thick of things, annihilated the goons, and then…"

Spencer waited.

She sighed and met his gaze. "Jackson dove in after me."

Off a bridge during a storm into dark waters. Thank God Jackson had been there. "How many men were there?"

"Three." She grinned with delight at Jackson's ability. "But when I think of how he looked that night, I don't think it would've mattered if there was a dozen."

Spencer couldn't muster even the most meager smile. "Dead?"

"Eventually." She flapped a hand. "I don't know if he killed them or…"

"I know about the group, hon."

She went still, then tipped her head to study him. After a few seconds, she said, "I'm not your hon, but okay, if you know about them, then you already know none of those cretins survived that night."

Not touching her wasn't an option. He reached for her slender hand again and moved his thumb over her knuckles. "I'm glad."

"Yeah, me, too." Appearing disconcerted, she glanced down at their clasped hands, cleared her throat and eased away. "So that's it. You already know that Chandra, the head of the ring, got away that night. Because she hadn't been in the car or standing there on the bridge, the guys never knew she was there in the first place. I didn't know that they'd missed her presence, so I assumed she was part of the carnage."

"She can't ever again hurt you."

Arizona directed a frown at him. "Because *you* killed her, when it should have been my privilege."

He said, "I'm sorry," and he meant it.

"Well...now all of them are gone, and I'm left at loose ends."

Her mercurial mood swings kept him guessing. Yes, he'd shot Chandra, but he'd been tracking her for his own reasons, and it was debatable who had more right to vengeance.

That she felt robbed was a sad consequence of his actions. "Ready for dessert?"

Accepting the switch from morbid history to here and now, she said, "Dessert? Seriously? You do know how to treat a gal, don't you?"

ARIZONA WAS THINKING how nice it felt to share with Spencer. He didn't get all mushy on her, didn't try to console her or make a move. He listened.

And she knew he understood.

Sure, he'd done that odd hand-holding thing, but then, people did that. They touched. She'd seen it plenty of times with Jackson, Trace, Dare and their wives. She didn't hate it, but she wasn't crazy about it, either.

When it was Spencer doing the touching, for some reason, it affected her even more. It wasn't intolerable, really, but...she didn't know if she'd get used to it or not.

Then Spencer turned from the fridge—and she saw he held a small but fancy birthday cake.

Stunned, she slowly pushed back her chair and stood on suddenly wobbly legs. "What is *that?*"

Very matter-of-factly, he replied, "Vanilla cream cake with whipped frosting. I think it has raspberry filling between the layers." His gaze met hers. "But there are no hidden threats, Arizona. It's not poisoned, and I promise, it isn't something you need to freak over."

"I wasn't freaking!" But she was. The urge to escape left her heart hammering.

"Bull. You look ready to run away."

She tucked in her chin. How could he know that? And how dare he say it out loud? "I don't run from anyone."

He set the cake on the table in front of her and, with a smile, said, "Sometimes you should. But not now." Standing too close, all but towering over her, he whispered, "Not ever from me."

No way would she look at him, not while he sounded like that, all dominant, protective male. Instead she eyed the dessert. It had fancy sugared rosettes and the words "Happy Birthday!" written in pale blue frosting across the top.

A lump formed in her throat. "I told you not to do anything dumb."

In a touch so gentle it scared her half to death, he reached out and tucked her hair behind her ear. "I know. That's why I refrained from putting candles on it."

She snorted. "I'd have…"

"What? Socked me? Thrown the cake at my face?"

"Maybe." His close physical proximity made her jumpy. "Well, get back in your seat then if we're going to eat this thing."

Even though she didn't look at him, she *felt* his smile. "All right." He stepped away. "More milk? Or coffee?"

"Milk." Now that she had some breathing room, she filled her lungs. Grudgingly, she said, "It's a pretty cake. Thanks."

"My pleasure." He refilled her glass. "And for the record, in case you want to reciprocate, my birthday is right before Thanksgiving."

Even knowing he teased, Arizona imagined how it'd be. Buying a cake for someone, sharing that special day...like she was doing right now.

Such a normal thing to do. "Yeah, okay."

His smile widened. "I'll hold you to that." Using a cake server with a cow-shaped handle, he cut into the cake and put a big piece on a plate for her.

Maybe it was the "not knowing" that made her so anxious, but she couldn't refrain from trying to dissect his objective. "I told you how I made Jackson that offer."

Spencer looked up from cutting his own piece of the fancy cake. "The offer of...?"

"Sex." Giving Spencer a furtive glance, she added, "And he turned me down flat. You know why?"

Nodding, his tone solemn, he said, "You offered out of obligation."

She'd hoped to again take Spencer off guard with her candid speaking, but this time he rolled with the punches. "He'd done so much for me." And Spencer wanted to do things for her, too. But why? "Too much."

Seconds ticked by while he watched her. "I doubt Jackson saw it that way."

She knew exactly how Jackson saw it. "He felt...pity for me."

Spencer shook his head. "No."

"Well, it wasn't about the rescue." In a rush, she put voice to the turmoil of her thoughts. "He rescued Alani, too, but that didn't bother him. He chased her like crazy. That's because he didn't pity her."

Unconvinced, Spencer rubbed his upper lip as he measured his words and, after some hesitation, finally said, "I feel pity for what you suffered, Arizona, for all that was done to you. But I don't pity *you,* because I can see you're a survivor, not a victim."

Heart pumping hard, she locked gazes with him. "So...you want to have sex with me?"

More hesitation, and then with a shrug, "I'm breathing, aren't I?"

The words raked over her nerves like talons, stealing her breath and her nerve. "So—"

"Wanting you, and planning to do anything about it, are two very different things. There are a lot of things I want, but men, *good* men, control themselves. They don't abuse others, or—God forbid—take by force." He reached out a hand, palm up, and waited for her to accept him.

Though it felt cowardly, she...couldn't. She shook her head and crossed her arms tight around herself.

Letting his hand rest on the table, he accepted her decision without comment. "I can't deny that you're a beautiful girl—"

"Woman." Appalled at herself, Arizona bit her lip. Hard. *Idiot.* "I'm legit now," she stammered and felt even more foolish. "That's all I meant."

"You're a twenty-one-year-old woman," he agreed. "And you're stunning."

"Stunning." She made a mocking face. "Whatever." But she kind of liked that, after all the creeps who'd admired her, Spencer found her appealing, too.

"Most men who look at you are going to admire you, Arizona. And yes, they'll want you. They'll think about seeing you naked, about having sex with you. It's how men's minds work. We're visual, and we're sexual. But that's not a curse."

Good God. Talk about blunt. "Sure feels like a curse to me!"

"Even if you were willing, nothing like that will happen between us. *Not* because I pity you," he stressed, "but because you're too young for me, you've been through too much to totally understand what you want or need, and you don't entirely trust me."

And he was still in love with his wife.

But Arizona wasn't cruel enough to say that to him. Instead, she touched the cow-shaped handle on the serving knife. "I'm guessing your wife bought this?"

Drawing back, he stared at her—and shut down.

Undeterred, Arizona said, "It looks like the kind of stuff a wife would buy. A good wife, I mean."

Picking up his fork, he dug into his cake. "What would a bad wife buy?"

"Drugs. Alcohol. I don't know. That kind of stuff."

He paused. "Arizona…"

"Will you tell me about her?"

He took two slow breaths and shook his head. "Eat your cake."

"It's almost too pretty to eat." The sugar crystals on the flowers glittered. Between the layers, pinkish raspberry cream dripped out. She scooped up a big bite, ate it and groaned. "Oh, yeah. It tastes even better than it looks."

She was almost done with the piece of cake when he said, "I know you went through my background."

There'd be no point in denying it. "Yeah, well—"

"I don't mind. I attempted to go through yours, too."

He wouldn't have found much—but she had. She knew all about his wife, how she'd died, and how he'd avoided any commitments since then.

But she wanted to know more. She wanted to know the small things, the nuances that made a man and woman stay together. Stay in love. Enjoy intimacy. "So you'll tell me about her?"

Spencer took another drink of coffee and then set the cup down quietly. "No."

Arizona tried to quell her curiosity, but he'd been so nosy, why shouldn't she ask? It had been three years, after all. "Was she pretty?"

Slowly closing his eyes in a gesture of resignation, he put his forehead on a fist. He looked like he'd fallen asleep, but then he said, "She was pretty."

Feeling absurdly blessed that he'd take part in the conversation, Arizona warmed. "I saw a small picture," she volunteered. "But I couldn't tell much."

"Long brown hair." He straightened in his seat again. "Not as dark or wavy as yours. Brown eyes. Fair-skinned."

"Stacked?"

Shaking his head, he said, "Understated." Done with his cake, he left the table and carried his plate to the sink.

Arizona wolfed down the rest of hers and joined him. "I can do the dishes."

"I'll only rinse and put them in the dishwasher."

"Oh." He bumped into her, gave her a level look, and with an expression of apology, she moved to the side. But not too far away. "She was your first love?"

"She was…everything."

He made it sound as if he planned to be single the rest of his life, or as if he assumed he'd never fall in love again. "You married young?"

"Right after she finished college." He closed the dishwasher. Keeping his back to her, his hands braced on the sink, arms stiff, he said, "She was two years younger than me. A dental assistant with a quirky sense of style, as you can tell by all the cow decor everywhere."

"I like it." It made everything feel real homey. "It's a

nice house." Older, small but very neat, with hardwood floors, cove ceilings and tall baseboards.

Spencer nodded. "She loved this house. Loved being married, too, and she loved me. Eventually, she wanted kids. We were thinking another year or so, but then…"

Then her life had been cut short. Taking a cue from Spencer, Arizona tentatively touched his arm, and waited.

As if the gesture surprised him, Spencer stalled but only for a moment. "She stopped at a convenience store one night on her way home from work. Two men—"

"Part of a human trafficking ring," she supplied, knowing that from the background check she'd done on him.

"Yeah. They were trying to drag a woman out of there, my wife intervened…"

His hands fisted, and Arizona, feeling really, *really* awkward, moved her hand from his arm to his back. "I'm sorry."

"A store clerk died that day, too. Another customer was injured."

"Senseless. But that's how it always is. Senseless and cruel and—"

He stepped away from her. "Enough about that."

Her hand dropped. "You got the guys who shot her."

"I did. But they were only a small part of a bigger operation." He squared off with her. "I had as much right to go after Chandra as you did."

Chandra had been the brains behind that particular ring. Arizona knew, since it was Chandra who'd caught her, twice. Chandra who'd trafficked her. Chandra who'd arranged her street education.

Chandra who'd tried to kill her.

"That's sort of what I was thinking, actually." Arizona leaned back on the counter. "We have that in common, when usually I don't have anything in common with anyone. Since we both want the same things, I'd be willing to forgive how you robbed me of personal justice, if we work together."

On alert, Spencer took a stance and scowled at her. "We are working together. The Green Goose, right? That's what you're talking about?"

"Yeah, the bar and grill." She tried not to look unsure of herself. "But we could do more than that if you wanted. I could find trafficking rings, do some background on them, and you could be my muscle."

His eyes narrowed—not a promising sign.

"You're up for it, right?" Trying for a joke, Arizona reached out and squeezed his upper arm.

Solid with strength. And she knew firsthand about his fast reflexes.

No doubt about it: Spencer was a big bundle of raw power and astounding ability. She admired strength a lot. In his case…maybe too much.

Crossing her arms, she tried really hard to look and sound unaffected. "So, Spence. What do you say? You want to partner up with me on a more permanent basis?"

CHAPTER FIVE

"It's Spencer, and you know it." He took her arm and started her toward the living room. "Why do you insist on butchering my name?"

"Actually...I don't know." She put on her brakes. "Where are we going?"

"I figured we'd watch some television. Maybe a movie or something."

After a big yawn, she pulled free. "I need to get going. Burning the candle at both ends has me more tired than usual. I need some shut-eye."

Shit. He glanced at his watch. "It's only eight o'clock."

"Early to bed, early to rise and all that." She started for the front door and her shoes.

"You get up early?"

"I get up whenever I wake. And more often than not, I can't sleep. So—"

"Why can't you sleep?"

Impatient, she glanced back at him. "I'll tell you all about my sleeping habits—tomorrow." She bent and pulled on first one unlaced sneaker, then the other.

Arizona had "sloppy" down to a fine art. But it was a look that complemented her attitude. "We still need to talk about the Green Goose. How are we going in, what time, every little detail." Had Trace already disabled her car? She wanted to leave sooner than he'd anticipated—not that anyone could accurately anticipate anything with Arizona. "We have a lot of ground to cover."

"I've got some ideas for that. We can talk about it tomorrow morning." Her mouth curled in an acerbic smile. "Or do you have plans with Marla?"

Ignoring that, he said, "Why the big rush?"

She opened the door. "Told you. I'm tired."

Hot, humid air, thick with the threat of a storm, blasted him as he followed her out. He needed to think of a way to stall her.

Maybe if he hadn't been so touchy discussing his past... But no, he couldn't go there. As an alternative, he asked, "Where are you staying?"

Without looking at him, she said, "Just a motel."

Suspicions bloomed. "What motel?"

"A random dive." Halfway down the sidewalk, she glanced over at Marla's house. "Should you be dogging my heels like this? You know your girlfriend probably has her nose to the window, watching your every move."

"She's not my girlfriend." He glanced that way, too, and saw a shadow shift from the window. Damn. Catching Arizona before she reached her car, he said, "Forget Marla. Why are you dodging the question?"

"What question?"

He growled out an impatient breath. "The question about where you're staying."

"I wasn't." She opened her car door to let out the heat and then leaned on the fender. "Thing is, you haven't yet agreed to be my partner, so why should I tell you anything?"

"Blackmail?"

Her eyes, now bright with mischief, looked even bluer out in the natural light. "Coercion."

Tension mounted in the back of his neck. He rubbed

a knotted muscle, but it didn't help. "I'll think about the partnership thing." And he'd talk to Trace and Dare…

"Yeah." Her gaze went to his hand. "You do that."

With nothing else to say, Spencer stepped back, and she got into her car. "Whenever you wake up is a pretty loose time frame. Can't you narrow it down a little?"

She put the key in the ignition. "I don't know. Let's say between 5:00 a.m. and noon."

Would she sneak in again and watch him sleep? Not like he'd even be able to sleep with that possibility looming.

He gripped the frame of the open window. "I can track you down, you know. I can find out where you're staying."

"You think so?" She turned the key—and nothing happened. With a frown, she said, "We'll see."

And she tried the car again.

Dead. Completely.

Relieved, Spencer stepped back, wondering how she'd react.

It was something to see, the way her brows pulled down, her eyes glittered, and angry color flooded her face. She pumped the gas, tried again and, after visibly gathering steam, opened her car door and stepped out. She slammed her door. Hard.

It didn't take a genius to see she was pissed. *Really* pissed. The darkening sky had nothing on her.

Deadpan, he asked, "Car won't start?"

Her locked teeth sawed together. "Let's go."

Fascinating. He'd never seen a woman as visually expressive as Arizona. "Where to, exactly?"

"Back inside." She headed that way but said over her

shoulder, "Unless you want me to lose it out here, for all your nice, domestic neighbors to witness."

"Inside it is." A little amused, a lot pleased, he trailed behind her.

Unfortunately, Marla stepped out to her porch. Wearing a low-cut top and a look of censure, she opened her mouth, and Arizona swung around to her, snarling, *"Don't."* She sucked in a breath. "Just…don't." After that dire warning, she stormed on into his house.

Marla stood there looking hurt.

Double damn. Apologetic, Spencer said to her, "Sorry. She's having a bad day."

Marla's impressive chest heaved a little. "I suppose she'll have a better night?"

"Marla," he chided. "I told you it wasn't like that—for you or her."

She gathered herself. "I don't understand you."

"You do, you just don't want to."

"It was good between us."

"Yes." And maybe if he hadn't met Arizona…but he had. "I need to go."

"Wait!" She licked her lips. "Do you think it's going to storm?"

With a quick glance at the sky, he said, "Probably." He knew right where this was going. "Your roof's still leaking?"

"Yes." She leaned on the railing, deliberately giving him an eyeful of cleavage. "It's the ceiling in my bedroom. Any…suggestions?"

"Yeah. Put out a few buckets—and call a repairman as soon as you can. With these old roofs, they're as likely to cave in as leak." He'd have felt guilty for not offering any real help, except that her roof had been bad since winter, and she didn't repair it because she'd rather use it as a female ploy to get him back in bed.

Giving her a salute, Spencer went in. He'd barely gotten the door shut before Arizona was there, rising on tiptoe to blast him.

IN BATTLE MODE, Arizona jabbed him hard in the chest with one finger. "You told Jackson!"

"No." With his good mood quickly souring, he stepped around her.

She grabbed his arm. "You did! You said something to him, and that's why he disabled my car."

Infusing iron in his tone, Spencer said, "You realize you're calling me a liar, right?"

But she was too angry to relent. "I trusted you!"

"Baloney! You're about as trusting as a junkyard dog."

She gasped.

"But I did *not* tell Jackson, and I'd appreciate it if you'd quit yelling like a kid having a temper tantrum!"

Since he'd ended with his own yelling, the insult was ludicrous at best.

Fury colored her face and kept her eyes narrowed. "Okay, fine. Let's just see." And for an additional dig, she said, "Jackson will tell me the truth."

"You're going to call him?" That worked fine by him. She'd be the one to let her erstwhile protector know the score, and at the same time she'd learn the truth. Spencer gestured at her. "Feel free."

"I will!" She dug out her cell phone from her back pocket and hit a speed dial number.

Because he didn't want to miss a word, Spencer said, "Dare you to put it on speaker phone."

"Feeling nosy?" she sneered.

"I don't trust you to admit to my acquittal." He almost smiled, knowing she wouldn't be able to resist his taunt. "Or are you afraid of what I'll hear?"

"HA!" KEEPING HER ANGRY GAZE locked on his, Arizona hit the speaker button. Her car was dead, and she knew it wasn't by accident. She'd been around Jackson too long to miss the signs of interference.

Because she hadn't used the emergency number, Jackson answered with a greeting, instead of silence. "Hey, Arizona. What's up?"

At the sound of his voice, she brightened with triumph. "What did you do to my car?" Did they really think they could bully her? That she was too dumb to recognize how they worked? Fat chance. She wasn't an idiot.

"What's that?" A new alertness entered Jackson's tone. "Something's wrong with your car?"

Uh-oh. He sounded pretty sincere. "No use denying it," she pressed. "I know you disabled it somehow."

"Not me. Alani and I are at dinner with Dare and Molly." And then with suspicion, "Where did you say you are?"

Crap. Was it possible that the car's battery had died somehow? It didn't seem likely.

"Arizona?"

Deflated, she admitted, "I'm at Spencer's."

"Yeah?" A smile sounded through the call. "Doing what?"

"Never mind." Oh, this was awkward. And Spencer looked *so* smug. "My car won't start. It's totally dead. You sure you didn't tamper with it?"

"Why would I? What are you up to— Oh, wait."

She heard muted voices, a brief conversation, and

then Jackson came back on the line. "Reckon it was Trace." And before she could get riled about that, he said, "Why didn't you remind me that it was your birthday?"

No! No, no, no. How did he realize it *now?* She groaned, long and dramatic.

"Stop that," Jackson said. "You should have told me. More to the point, I should have remembered." His voice deepened. "I'm sorry that I've been distracted."

"Don't." Her throat closed up. She absolutely would not look at Spencer. "You're getting married, for crying out loud. You're going to be a dad. You have enough on your mind already."

"That's not a good excuse."

She needed to end this, and fast. "Honestly, it doesn't matter."

"The hell it doesn't."

Time to shoot off in a new direction. "What did Dare tell you? Why does he think it was Trace?"

"Spencer talked to Trace."

Aha! "That—"

"And Trace told Dare. But no one told me because *you* swore everyone to secrecy, and I have to tell you, that annoys the hell out of me."

"Oh. Umm…" She could practically feel Spencer gloating. "Yeah, about that. It's just that I…"

"You were supposed to be researching, hon. For *me*. You were not supposed to branch off on your own."

"Well, I…"

"Don't compound it now by fibbing to me." He laughed as he said that, removing any real insult. "I'm glad you're there with Spencer, and I'm doubly glad you had enough sense to get him involved rather than charging into a mess alone."

"I'm nothing if not cautious." Even she winced at the sarcasm.

"Yeah. Cautious. That's exactly how I'd describe you."

"Jackson—"

He cut her off to say, "Trace dicked with your car because he wants you to stay put, so that's what you'll do." He spoke over her again before she could get started. "Otherwise I'll have to uproot my tired butt from this nice dinner with my pregnant fiancée and friends, and you know you don't want me to do that."

No, she didn't. Turning her back on Spencer, she whispered, "I can't stay here."

Obtuse to the bitter end, Jackson asked, "Why not?"

Almost at the same time, Spencer said, "Why not?"

She groaned again. Men! "I don't want to, that's why."

Jackson discounted her reasoning. "C'mon, Arizona. You know that once you start snooping, you have to cover your ass. That means you have to alter your routine, avoid your normal stomping ground, and for certain you can't go back to whatever hole-in-the-wall you were using to bed down. That's not how it's done, honey."

Yeah, she knew that. She had planned to hop to another motel for the night. She even had her overnight bag in the car. "I'm not dumb, you know."

"Definitely not. But you are jumping the gun. Any operation requires planning." There was more muted conversation before Jackson laughed and came back to her. "Dare says that Trace has it under wraps, and before you feel guilty about that, he says it's a job they'd already started before you tripped in."

"Really?" That got her intrigued. "So I was right? It's a cover for a trafficking ring?"

"Most likely, but it's too soon to know for sure, and

it's definitely too soon to tip our hand. The sting is still in preliminary research." His voice lowered. "Put Spencer on the phone."

"No." *Hell,* no.

"Arizona…"

Her shoulders were so stiff, they ached. "I don't need anyone to babysit me. I'm fine."

"You'll stay put?"

"Mmm…maybe." It'd depend on what Spencer said and what he had planned. The men might be world-class protectors, but she knew she could look after herself.

Jackson sighed and then said, "Hang on, hon."

Seconds later, Spencer's cell phone rang. He grinned at her as he answered.

Un-freaking-believable.

And *his* phone wasn't on speaker, so she could only hear one side of the conversation.

Spencer said, "Yeah, hey. Sure. That's what I figured." He nodded. "Do my best, that's all I can promise. Yeah, okay. I would've done that anyway."

Arizona thought her hair might stand on end. When Jackson came back, she growled, "Satisfied?"

"Getting there." And in a lower voice, "Happy birthday, honey."

Oh. Heat rushed up her neck. "Yeah, uh, thanks."

"I promise I won't forget again."

She rolled her eyes. "Aren't men supposed to forget that stuff?"

"No."

Sheesh, did he have to sound so offended? "Look, don't sweat it, okay? Spencer got a cake and everything."

"Everything?" He didn't even try to hide his amusement. "Well, I owe you a gift, and no, don't argue. Alani will enjoy helping me pick it out. We'll hook up soon, okay?"

Feeling desperate, she was quick to say, "Not necessary, Jackson. I know you're busy with your wedding prep and—"

Again, he paid no attention to her protests. "We'll invite Spencer. Dare said this weekend would work at his house. What do you think?"

Oh, Gawd! He'd cornered her. "Look, I don't—"

"Great. Saturday at two. Bring a bathing suit and we'll hang at the lake. Do it up picnic style. Sound good?" Before she could answer, he said, "So we're all set. But now I need to go before my steak gets cold."

She wanted to deny him and his weekend plans, but she didn't want to keep him from his meal. "Okay, fine." She was such a dolt. Somehow she'd find a way around things—especially the bathing suit part of it all. "Sorry for interrupting."

"You didn't." There was a slight hesitation and then: "Love ya."

Happiness filled her heart. She swallowed back a swell of emotion. Keeping her back to Spencer, she said, "Love you, too."

After she pocketed the phone, she had no idea what to do. The moment was so awkward that she wanted to crawl off and hide.

Then Spencer said, "Told you so."

His self-righteous tone brought her snapping around. "You told Trace!"

He shrugged that off. "But only Trace…so you owe me an apology."

She opened her mouth to blast him…and then shut it again. Yeah, she did owe him. Grudgingly, she muttered, "Sorry."

His hand touched her chin, lifted her face. "I won't ever lie to you, Arizona."

Not for a second would she believe that. "Everyone lies. Big lies, little lies. No one is honest all the time."

"Including you?"

Especially her. She folded her arms under her breasts. "When necessary, I fudge things."

"I won't. Not with you."

Feeling herself waffle, Arizona looked around, wondering what to do now. Humiliation rolled over her. She'd disrupted everyone with her plans, when she'd really only wanted to disrupt Spencer.

That truth made her frown at herself.

He thought the frown was directed at him. "I had to tell Trace. You're smart, Arizona. You know that."

"And you knew that Trace would tell Jackson."

He crossed his arms, mimicking her stance. "You're distorting the facts. Trace said he wouldn't tell Jackson, and he didn't. He told Dare. And Dare didn't tell Jackson until *you* called up and spilled the beans. So exoncrate me. I held to my end of the bargain—so far as I could, anyway."

She shook her head in denial—but it was truc. Somehow, deep down, she'd known he would alert the others. "Why do you guys have this sick need to protect misfits?"

"Is that it?" He put his big hands on her shoulders. He didn't draw her closer, he just offered…support. "You're concerned about what Trace will think?"

"I know what he thinks. That I'm pathetic and I need a keeper."

He gave her a speculative look. "You've met Priss, Trace's wife."

"Yeah, so?" Priss was self-confident and funny, and Trace loved her a lot.

"Priss's life wasn't all roses, you know. Actually, no roses, just thorns."

The boys had been talking, it seemed. Had Jackson told Spencer about Priss? Had he told him about Dare's wife, Molly, too? "What's your point?"

"I told Trace because we need backup if we're going to do this—"

"We are." He couldn't change his mind on her now. She needed to stay busy, and she needed to feel as if she made a difference.

And…she kind of liked being around Spencer—but she wasn't about to admit it to him.

"Trace understands what you're going through." He gave her a gentle shake. "You and Priss have a lot in common. And if you think he pities his wife, you haven't seen the two of them together."

"I've seen them." While Jackson was easygoing—most of the time—Trace could be very heavy-handed. Yet Priss matched him in every way. Anyone could see that pity was the last thing Trace felt for Priss. "They make a nice couple."

"Yes, they do." His thumbs rubbed over her shoulders. "Fact is, you're looking at this all wrong. You're so busy defending your independence, and bearing that massive chip on your shoulder, that you've forgotten how it's done."

"It?"

"The whole undercover, covert, infiltration gig. You think Jackson ever approaches these situations alone? Or Trace or Dare? They always work as a team."

For him to know that, they had to have done a lot of

talking. Did Jackson really trust him so much? Apparently.

She raised her chin. "You don't."

"Until recently, I hadn't tampered in their league. The busts I made as a bounty hunter were small beans in comparison to what they do. But now, with human trafficking rings that have reach across the country, even out of the country, you can bet your sweet little butt that I wouldn't get in too deep without knowing someone else was on board, watching to make sure neither of us disappears."

Because that all made sense, Arizona paced away—and immediately felt the loss of Spencer's touch.

Standing where she'd left him in the middle of the floor, he waited.

She knew she'd relent. Heck, she didn't even want to go. Not really. But she wasn't quite ready to tell him that yet. "What did Jackson say to you?"

"He wanted me to follow you if you left, and to tail you all night if necessary." When her eyes widened, he added, "And I would have. *I will*—if you don't stay."

Going to the window, Arizona watched the rain start to fall. If she was going to get her bag, she should do it now.

From right behind her, his tone compelling, Spencer said, "Stay."

"You said you wouldn't lie."

"I won't."

"Okay, then…" Turning to face him, she asked in a rush, "If you're not trying to have sex with me, then why are you doing all this? Why are you being so…concerned and caring, and protective and understanding and stuff?"

"All that?" A smile flickered over his mouth. "Okay,

the truth. I want you to see a better way of things. I want you to be able to move on—"

Move on? "As in, be with some dude? Seriously?" The idea was so ludicrous, she laughed. "What, like in a marriage and all that? Not happening."

"Doesn't have to be marriage." His gaze moved over her face to her mouth and then back to her eyes. "Could just be a date."

"And you think dates are fun?"

He drew a short breath. "Most of the time, sure."

"You've had dates with Marla?"

"Ah…no."

"Just sex, huh?"

"Arizona…"

"And sex is fun?"

His gaze locked on hers. "Yes."

"Will you tell me about it?"

Face muscles tightened as he flexed his jaw. "What do you want to know?"

So many things, she hardly knew where to begin. "Is it the same with Marla as it was with your wife?"

His eyes darkened with disbelief and, maybe, sadness. "If you mean are women interchangeable, no. Not to good men. Not when a man cares about a woman."

That riled her. "So you care about Marla?"

"Not at all like I cared about my wife, no. But as a nice person, yes, of course I do." Putting his hands on his hips, he dropped his head forward, then gave in to a short laugh. "God, this is an awkward conversation."

She didn't care. He offered to explain, and she wanted to hear it, so she waited.

After releasing a long breath, he met her gaze again. "I was up front with Marla. I didn't lead her on. I haven't led on any woman."

Including her? His bet would curtail her language—but gain him a kiss if she slipped up. Was that really all he wanted? "So with Marla, it was sex, but only sex, huh?"

"It's not always about love."

"Boy, do I know that!"

"Sometimes," he continued as if she hadn't spoken, "the pleasure is enough."

"If you say so." She had her doubts about any real pleasure, though. She sure hadn't experienced it. "So how many women have there been?"

He made a sound of disgust. "They were few and far between. But I am a grown man, Arizona."

So defensive. Sharp with derision, she said, "And you have *needs?*"

"Everyone has those needs—including you." When she started to shake her head, he cut her off. "You *do*. And that brings us full circle. You know about abuse, but you don't know anything about the real give-and-take that's supposed to happen between the sheets."

"Not always between the sheets."

He paused. "No." He took a step closer, then stopped himself. "There are all kinds of sexual encounters, in lots of different places."

"And different positions?"

"Positions that you should enjoy." He reached out, but instead of touching her, he pulled back and ended up rubbing the back of his neck. "Only it doesn't start with sex."

"No?"

"It starts with an attraction. A *mutual* attraction."

"Can't prove it by me."

His gaze searched hers, his voice deepened. "I know. That's my point."

There was such gravity in his tone, she rolled her eyes. "Go on. Mutual attraction?" she prompted.

Slowly, he nodded. "Flirting, kissing, a touch or two. Foreplay for an hour, or a day. Wanted by both people, and shared by both people."

That did sound sort of...not awful. "I know that's how it's supposed to be." She wasn't a total social misfit. She'd seen romantic movies, and she'd seen real life. People walking together, talking together. In sync.

In love.

But he'd just negated the link between love and sex, and she wasn't sure she could ever trust in casual sex.

Almost as if he'd read her thoughts, he said softly, "It can be really good when both people are willing, eager participants."

"And you think I need to experience that, huh?"

"You're a healthy, energetic woman. I'd hate to see deliberate cruelty turn you off from knowing everything that nature intended."

For reasons she wouldn't analyze, his attitude irked her. "So let me get this straight. You want to do things to me, to get me all into the idea of screwing—and then you want me to go off to find some other guy to finalize the deal?" She smirked at him. "Know what, Spence? From my side of the table, that sort of makes you sound like a pimp. Only problem is, I can't figure out what you get from the deal."

CHAPTER SIX

WITH HER BREAKING DOWN his motives to the basest purpose, Spencer had to admit that it did sound bad. God knew he didn't *want* to send her off to anyone else. The thought of another man touching her left him raw with anger.

But he wasn't the man for her. Even if the age difference didn't exist, she deserved someone who'd be involved for the long haul. She deserved someone with a sunny outlook on life.

Not only was he opposed to settling down again, he was about as far from optimistic as a man could get.

"I wasn't trying to coerce you into having sex with anyone." What he wanted most was for her to not be… damaged. But he sure as hell couldn't say anything that stark to her. "What I'd really like is to break down those walls so you can let in people who care about you." He tried a smile that she didn't return. "All in all, you can be a pretty likable woman."

With one hand flattened to his chest, she pushed him back a step and moved out from between him and the window. "Whatever. If I'm staying over, I want Trace to fix my car."

The quick turnaround surprised him. "You'll stay put?" *With me.*

She made a gesture of indifference. "For now."

"Then I'll let Trace know." And they could all help keep an eye on her.

Her eyes narrowed. She hesitated, then she turned away. "I better go get my stuff."

It'd take time to convince her of his motives. Spencer accepted that, so he allowed the change of topic. "What stuff?"

"My duffel and laptop case. I'm not as dumb as you and the big macho boys want to believe." She opened the front door, and a heavy gust of wind carried a smattering of rain in around her. "Ho boy, look at those purple storm clouds blowing in."

Spencer closed the door. He could see why she'd keep the laptop close. But the other? "You brought an overnight bag with you?"

"Yeah, see, I had no intention of going back to my motel room tonight."

That surprised him, but he was pleased with her forethought, especially since she'd made the plans to protect herself, not someone else. He had a feeling that Arizona deliberately put herself at risk far too often.

Given the downpour, he caught her arm and moved her away. "I'll get your things for you."

"I don't melt."

Already rain dampened the front of her T-shirt and left her face dewy.

Physically, she was the most tempting woman he'd ever met. He didn't want to test his resolve by seeing her in soaked clothes that would cling to her shapely little body.

But beyond that, he worried. The sky had darkened, and he felt the turbulence in the air. Soon the rain would be a full-fledged storm—just like the night she'd been bound and thrown into a river, a night she would have died…and been forgotten.

Suffused with emotion, he eased a damp tendril of hair away from her cheek. "It looks like the rain will turn into a storm." No sooner had the words left his mouth than a flash of lightning cut across the darkening sky. Seconds later, thunder crashed down, rattling the windows.

Arizona smiled at his apprehension. "You think it'll bother me, don't you?"

He was afraid she'd be pulled into nightmarish memories. "Given what you went through, I'd understand if it did."

"Yeah." This time when she put her hand on his chest, Spencer suspected it was just to have contact. "You'd think it would spook me some, huh?"

Grateful that he had her with him, Spencer covered her hand with his own. Despite all her brass, she was small-boned and delicate. "Will it?"

She laughed. "You know what I always think of during stormy weather? How Jackson saved me that night. Up until then, life was something I had to bear. But after that, everything turned around for me." She stroked him once and dropped her hand. "Truthfully, I love storms."

Jackson had given her a new lease on life, and yet, she still wasn't comfortable with that life. Given half a chance she'd take on the world and to hell with the consequences. She recognized that Jackson put value on her life—but she didn't share that sentiment…yet.

One way or another, he planned to turn that around.

With more resolve than ever, Spencer moved her away from the door. "Sorry, honey, but I'm a gentleman. I'll get your things, end of conversation."

For several seconds, he watched as she considered fighting him over it. He knew the second she relented. "Fine, you want to get soaked? Suit yourself." She handed him her keys. "Everything is in the trunk. Blue duffel and a canvas laptop case. But don't you dare touch anything else." She turned and headed for the hall.

Now anxious to see what else she had in the trunk, Spencer dashed out the door. He was soaked within seconds of leaving the porch. Rather than cleansing the air, the rain thickened the existing hot September humidity. Steam rose from the blacktop roads, occasionally disrupted by battering winds.

Scanning the area but seeing no one and nothing amiss, Spencer unlocked the trunk.

Disbelief locked his knees; he became oblivious to the stinging rain. Among the array of survival items—water, blanket, first aid kit—neatly arranged in the trunk space, he noted a sniper rifle, night-vision binoculars, machete, bulletproof vest…shovel. In every nook and cranny she'd neatly stored weapons both common and unconventional.

Jesus. What the hell did she have planned? Or did she consider those things everyday necessities?

For fear that anyone else might see, he grabbed the duffel tucked in next to other overnight bags and the canvas case half hidden behind everything else, and slammed the trunk. Did Jackson know she carried around an arsenal? Did Trace and Dare know?

One of them could have clued him in!

Keeping both bags close to his body to protect them as much as he could from the storm, Spencer ran back up his walkway, up the porch steps and to the front door. The rain blew nearly horizontal, still hitting his back but not beating down on his head like needles.

He pried off his boots, stripped off his sodden shirt and stepped in on the foyer rug.

Arizona stood there. As she fixated on his chest, her cocky smiled faded away.

Ah, hell. He knew that look and what it meant.

Arizona might not realize it yet, but she was aware of him as a man. And damn if that didn't spark his own heated awareness.

Spencer set her things on the floor and dropped his shoes on the rug. When he straightened again, rain dripped over his temple, down his shoulder and into his chest hair.

She stared so hard, her expression almost tactile, that he felt himself stir. He forgot his disgruntlement over her store of weapons.

Palms itching with the need to touch her, Spencer shifted. "Do you realize how you're affecting me?"

Lashes lifting, Arizona met his gaze—and cracked a wry smile. "Sorry about that." Though dusky color tinted her cheeks, she thrust out a towel and spoke as naturally as ever. "Thought you might want to dry off."

"Thanks."

Her gaze flipped back to his chest.

"Arizona?"

"You're so darned big, and you have a really awesome bod."

With her staring like that, he was bound to get bigger by the second. Spencer touched her chin to raise her gaze. "I think your body is appealing, too."

Snorting, she said, "I'm not running around wet and topless."

Thank God. Fighting a smile at his own discomfort, Spencer said, "You could give it a try—"

"Ha!" She snatched up her duffel and turned away.

"Hope you don't mind, but I'm going to make use of your shower before the electricity goes out."

Arizona. In his shower. Naked and soap slick…

"Make it quick," he said to her retreating back. "It's not safe with all the lightning—"

His bathroom door closed while he was still midsentence.

Well, hell.

With no more reason for modesty, Spencer stripped off his jeans there in the foyer and carried everything into the laundry room, where he also peeled off his boxers and socks. Wrapped in the towel, he went to the more private bath in his bedroom. His shower would be cold, and then maybe, after he'd gotten his libido under control, he and Arizona could go over their plans for tomorrow.

And with any luck, she'd trust him enough to explain the weapons in her trunk and the forbidding inclusion of a shovel.

AFTER A DRAWN-OUT SHOWER that did nothing to ease her growing tension, Arizona brushed her teeth, blow-dried her hair and dressed in a big gray T-shirt with loose-legged, pull-on shorts. Normally she slept in just a T-shirt and panties, but since she'd be sharing this night with Spencer, she made a concession for modesty.

She tidied up the bathroom again, storing her discarded clothing back in her duffel and leaving no sign that she'd been in there. Spencer wasn't neat to the point of annoying, but he did keep things clean and uncluttered.

She loved his house, and the bathroom was especially cool with the vintage-looking black-and-white tiles. The towels matched the shower curtain matched the window covering matched the decorative pictures and knick-knacks.

His wife must've been a real homebody. Arizona imagined her in an apron, baking cookies with a sweet smile.

No wonder Spencer loved her. No wonder, even after three years, he couldn't get over losing her.

Knowing she'd taken up as much time as she could, Arizona stopped avoiding the inevitable and opened the bathroom door.

Barefoot, she went in search of Spencer and found him sprawled back on the couch in the living room, watching TV and drinking a longneck beer. At the sound of her approach he turned his head—and went still in that way men did while appreciating the sight of a woman.

He fought it, but his attention went over her, snagging on her legs for several heart-stopping seconds before coming back to her face.

It should have made her uncomfortable to be looked at like that. Before Spencer, it always had.

Now…now she didn't know what she felt, but it definitely wasn't discomfort. Spencer wasn't like other men she'd known. He wasn't a disgusting creep like the animals who'd taken her, or those who'd paid for her time. But he didn't deny her sexuality, either, as Jackson, Dare and Trace tried to do.

Mostly…he just seemed to accept her. And like her.

"Hey." She strode past him, going around the coffee table to put her duffel by the front door where he'd left her laptop case. With Spencer still watching her, she came back to plop down on the other end of the couch.

He stared toward where she'd dropped off the bag, then back to her with a question in his eyes.

Propping her feet on the edge of the table, Arizona controlled her smile and stared at the television. "So what are we watching?"

Silence tripped by. She could feel his rapt attention touching on her, all over her.

She made herself look at him with a raised brow. "Cat got your tongue?"

Shaking his head, he again glanced at her bag but apparently decided not to ask why she'd put it near the door. "Sorry." A slight frown in place, he half turned toward her. "Want a beer?"

She wrinkled her nose. "No. My father used to swill those things like crazy."

"It bothers you?" He sat forward as if to take the bottle away.

Arizona stopped him. "It doesn't. Actually, I kind of like the smell, just not the taste."

After gauging the truth in her words, he nodded. "Something else, then?"

"No, thanks. I already cleaned my teeth." Brushing a hand over the soft material of his couch, she said, "Am I sleeping here?"

Seconds ticked by again. He sounded hoarse when he said, "Here at my house, yes."

"I meant here, on the couch."

"I have a guest room you can use. I would have put the laptop there, but the case was wet. I can move your things in there now, if you want."

The idea of using the guest room didn't appeal to her. She wasn't really a guest so much as an intrusion. And the idea of being closed up…she fought off a shiver.

Before she could figure out how to explain her reservations, he glanced at his watch. "You ready to turn in already?"

"Not really." Dragging a throw off the back of his couch, she slouched down against the arm and stretched her legs out toward him. She stopped short of letting her feet bump his hip. "Mind if I just get comfortable here for now?"

"Not at all." He handed her a plump throw pillow. "Make yourself at home." After a long hesitation, Spencer tucked the throw up and over her feet. "I mean that, Arizona. Help yourself to anything you need or want."

"Thanks." She bunched the pillow up at her side. "So what's on the boob tube?"

Bemused, he glanced at the TV and then back to her. "Old MMA highlights. Did you want me to change it to something else?"

"This is good. I like the fights." Mixed martial arts fascinated her.

Sounding more like himself, he asked, "Why doesn't that surprise me?"

"Because you already know me, that's why." She watched for a moment and became curious about his interest in the sport. "Do you have a favorite fighter?"

"A few." His big hand came to rest casually on her foot. "If you're in a talkative mood..."

Heart racing from his touch—on her foot, for crying out loud—Arizona shrugged. "Sure."

He turned down the volume on the television. "Then let's talk about our plans for tomorrow."

What a buzzkill. She groaned. "I guess you're going to insist?"

He hesitated. "You know we need to coordinate."

Yeah, they did. To get comfortable, she turned to her back with her knees bent under the throw, her head on the pillow, and peered down the length of the couch at him. "We'll arrive separately, you in your truck, me by bus so that we can leave together in one vehicle afterward." She cautioned him, "Make sure you park away from the entrance, so no one will see us together afterward."

Deadpan, he said, "Naturally."

"I'll go in first and grab a seat at the bar. Say, five or ten minutes later, you can come in and sit at a table."

"Why don't I sit at the bar?"

"Because I've already scoped out the place, and that's where I sat before." She rolled her shoulder. "It's where I need to be to draw their attention. You can watch over things more easily, without being noticed, from the eating area."

He didn't look happy about it, but he agreed. "I'm not going to wait that long before coming in, though."

Why did he sound annoyed already? "So come in earlier, then. Just be discreet."

His thumb moved over the arch of her foot, nearly stopping her heart. "This isn't my first rodeo, honey."

She wasn't his honey, but… "What are you doing?"

"What?"

She nodded at her feet.

As if he hadn't been aware of the touch himself, he looked down at his hand and then stroked with his thumb again. "This?" He drew both her feet up to his thigh. "You're tense."

She was, but she thought she'd hidden it. "Yeah, well…"

"You don't like it?" He pressed, rubbed, worked her arches in a deep, firm massage.

And she wanted to melt. Felt like parts of her *did* melt. "Mmm. I like it."

Spencer stilled again, his gaze piercing, hot. "Never had a foot-rub before?"

"That's a joke, right?"

"So relax and enjoy."

It was a bit too personal, but she liked it too much to make him quit. "Knock yourself out." She drew a breath and tried to get them back on track. "Okay, so you know to ignore me when you come into the place, right?"

"If I did that, they'd suspect something." Setting aside the beer, he half turned toward her and, keeping his gaze on her face, worked over her feet more thoroughly.

Bone-melting pleasure stole her breath.

Watching her, Spencer said softly, "No red-blooded man is going to miss noticing you, Arizona, so forget that idea. I'll give you the same attention every other guy in the place will be doling out. Think you can handle that?"

With her heavy eyelids at half-mast, she snuggled farther into his couch. "Sure."

He half smiled. "Just so you know, I might have to pretend interest in other women, too."

That brought her out of her slumberous trance. "Why?"

"Because if the place is what we think it is, they're liable to parade out the wares. If I'm not picking up the cues, they'll pull back and we'll lose an opportunity."

He was right, damn him. She wouldn't think about it now, and tomorrow…she'd deal with it. "Fine, whatever." Her toes curled at his renewed touch. "Once you're in the bar for backup, I'll drop a few casual questions, maybe flirt a little, go for the helpless look. You know, all in all I'll make myself seem like easy pickings."

"You've done that before?"

She closed her eyes and sighed. "Yeah. Plenty of times. It works to draw out the unscrupulous scumbags."

His hands moved up to her ankles, kneading, soothing, then back down over her feet. *So* nice.

"And when the scumbags show themselves?"

"You and I can kick their…butts." She'd swallowed back the curse word just in time, which robbed the description of any real punch.

This business of curbing her language was a little harder than she'd expected.

"A near miss." Spencer's hands stilled, tightened. "But I don't like that part of the plan."

"So what'd you want to do? Sweet-talk them into falling off the face of the earth?"

"I want you to stay out of harm's way and let me handle it."

She stared at him. "Poor Spencer. Did you think the massage would make me more agreeable?" Was that why he did it? "Fat chance."

Planting one hand on the back of the couch, another near her knee, he leaned over her.

And that *did* alarm her a little. She was nearly flat on her back. She had on minimal clothing. And a man of his size and strength could be imposing without malicious intent.

She said, "Uh—" and considered bringing her knee up into his ribs.

"Here's what'll happen, honey." His tone was calm, even. "You'll ask the right questions, be suitably naive, and if anyone bites, we withdraw."

"We?" She looked at his throat, at the flexing of muscles in his chest. *Focus, Arizona.* "So you're not just cutting me out?"

He shook his head. "For now, we'll both play it cool to see how deep the operation goes."

Good idea. There were always more people involved

than those most obvious. She swallowed and pressed one hand to his left pectoral. *Solid.* "And later?"

"Once we know what we're dealing with, all of it from the bottom up, then we'll make a move. A well-thought-out move, with plenty of safeguards." He looked at her mouth, and his voice lowered. "But not until then." He straightened away again.

Arizona hadn't realized she was holding her breath until she sucked in a giant gulp. And really, that wasn't only fear she felt. She knew it, and that sort of rattled her, too.

"You either give me your word on that," Spencer said, regaining her attention, "or everything is off."

He sat there watching her, waiting, and for some absurd reason, Arizona felt like laughing. "Tell you what, Spence. After that wonderful foot massage, I'll agree that if retreat is an option, I'm all for it." Turning on her side again, she drew up her knees so that her feet no longer touched him, and she tucked her hands under her cheek. "But if anyone touches me, it's on."

"No one will."

Because he wouldn't let them? His protective nature didn't bug her as much as it should have. "No more talking. My brain is tired. Let's just watch the knockouts."

Over the throw, Spencer smoothed a hand from her foot to her knee and back again. It was a casual touch, affectionate, the way you'd stroke someone you cared for. A familiar, platonic, *exciting* touch.

Even when he left his hand there, she didn't mind. She wondered what his warm fingers would feel like on her bare skin, and shifted.

Without relinquishing the contact, Spencer turned the volume back up and they fell into a companionable silence.

Before she knew it, Arizona felt so comfortable and secure that she forgot her day-to-day grievances and her constant wariness of everyone and everything. For once, she felt…safe. She even felt *content.*

It was a pretty wonderful feeling.

IT WAS PROBABLY the earlier conversation about Spencer's wife that made her think of all she'd missed out on, all that she would never have—like family, a home of her own…children.

With the television playing in the background, Spencer a quiet, comforting presence beside her, Arizona drifted off to sleep. As she relaxed her guard, her thoughts went backward in time, and her dreams returned her to the junkyard once again.

UNABLE TO LOOK AWAY, she watched the business deal take place. The guy handing over money repeatedly rubbed his lips together. They were slick with saliva, and it made her skin crawl. The sticky evening air added to her growing nausea. Night sounds of crickets, distant traffic and an occasional barking dog closed in around her.

The degradation tried to whittle away her backbone. She would not let it.

A fast glance around showed no escape. Never an escape. High fencing topped by barbed wire enclosed the junkyard. A nearby guard, recognizing her trepidation, watched with a sick smile.

Don't look, don't look…but her gaze automatically sought the small shack where she'd be taken.

Where she'd been taken before.

Her vision narrowed, dark and fuzzy. Her throat burned, sick with revulsion. If she ran, they'd shoot her.

But…would that be better or worse?

Oh, God, by now she should've been numb.

Instead she felt it all, every leering thought, every malicious, twisted intention, each hurt and each awful humiliation.

With the transaction complete, the loose-lipped man started toward her. Her heart pounded too hard, too fast.

Her panic escalated.

And her hatred grew.

MIDNIGHT CAME AND WENT. Mired in sentiment too raw to bear, Spencer considered pouring himself something stronger to drink. Two beers hadn't done squat to numb his growing desire, both physical and emotional.

Arizona had fallen into a deep sleep; if he got drunk, it wouldn't bother her.

But it would soften his edge, and around her, he needed to stay sharp.

He finished off the beer, then leaned his head back against the couch and closed his eyes. He should have gone on to bed, but he didn't want to. Absurd as it seemed, he enjoyed soaking up this quiet, peaceful time with her.

So far, he'd seen her angry, defensive, amused and provoking. But rarely was she serene.

As she shifted, her small feet nudged his thigh. He curved his hand around her ankle, noting again her delicate bone structure, how her warmth penetrated the throw. If he touched her bare skin, she would be so soft, so silky...

A small sound escaped her.

Going on alert, Spencer turned his head and, with only the light of the television, studied her face.

Without those light blue eyes discerning his every

move, her impact should have diminished. Instead, he felt like a ticking time bomb waiting to explode.

No woman should be that sexy. In the low light, her glossy dark hair tumbled around her face and shoulders like liquid silk. And that face...thick lashes, high cheekbones, a pert nose and such a full soft mouth.

But truthfully, she could have looked like a hag, and with her body, few men would care. As Spencer drifted his gaze over her, his muscles tightened and twitched and his guts burned with need. Volatile lust pressed inside him like a tide, getting stronger and stronger every time he saw her, even when he thought of her.

Around her, he felt a craving unlike anything he'd ever known, and that made him feel guilty for too many reasons to contemplate.

Arizona's careless bravado made him hot with temper, and with lust. Her earthy way of speaking, her sexual curiosity, left him sometimes staggered, often unsettled, and anxious to school her on all she'd missed.

She shifted again, and his heart beat harder. He felt like a pervert for getting semi-hard over a sleeping woman who would be appalled if she knew the direction of his thoughts.

Then again, Arizona was insightful. She understood the way men's minds worked, so she likely already assumed he had those thoughts.

And there was the crux of his problem: she'd known nothing but immoral bastards who'd taken pleasure in forcing her, hurting her, using her, treating her without respect or concern to appease their own warped appetites.

Never, ever would he do anything to shore up her impression of men, or to add to her wounds.

As Spencer watched her, her brows pulled tight and

her jaw locked. She flinched, her shoulders stiffening, her hands drawing into fists.

"Hey." Fearing the worst, he cuddled her foot, slid his hand up to her knee. "Arizona?"

She moved again, a panicked, jerky movement that gave away great distress. A small, nearly silent cry escaped her.

Shit.

He couldn't bear knowing she suffered a nightmare. "Arizona." Clasping her knee, he gave her a gentle shake. "C'mon now, wake up."

She came around with a stifled shout, feet flying, fists aiming. His heart hammered as he dodged the blows and tried to contain her.

"Arizona!" His hands bit into her upper arms, pinning her down, keeping her still. "It's me. Spencer."

Silent, cold and so very hurt, she ceased fighting to stare up at him with big eyes and pulsing fear.

"You're okay, honey." He loosened his hold, saying again, "Everything's okay."

Her gaze went all over him—and she struggled up and away from the couch into a ready stance, shoulders forward, feet braced, her chest laboring.

Tears spiked her lashes.

Stunned by the sudden shattering of calm, Spencer watched her, unsure what to say, what to do.

She took in his sprawled posture and, in clear dread, checked her own person.

"Arizona," he chastised. Did she really think he'd molest her in her sleep? Given all she'd been through, of course she would.

Her hands went over herself, the tie to her loose shorts and the placement of her T-shirt.

Finding nothing amiss, her shoulders slumped, and

she wrapped her arms around herself. As she closed her eyes, she let out a ragged breath.

"You fell asleep on the couch," Spencer told her in the gentlest tone he could muster.

"You didn't go to bed."

Because I wanted to stay near you. He swallowed back that telling admission. "I finished my drink and watched the news. That's all."

Her laugh edged out of control. "Of course it is." Jamming rough fingers through her hair, she looked toward the front door.

"You're thinking of running." Spencer tensed, ready to go after her if she tried it. "Don't."

"Oh, God." Hands shaking, she covered her face. "Sorry, but I have to." In a rush now, she turned away.

"Arizona!"

At the harsh command in his tone, she froze, breathing hard, shivering.

What could he say? What could he do to help her? "It'll be morning in a few more hours." He sat forward, hopeful. "Let's have coffee."

She shook her head hard. "I gotta go."

"No, honey, you don't have to do anything. You can stay." *With me.* He shook his head. Searching for the right words to sway her, he said, "You probably need the bathroom, right?" She'd been asleep for hours. No way would he let her rush off into the night.

She glanced back at him. Uncertain. Worried. Incredulous. "The bathroom?"

He nodded. If she went to the john first, that'd buy him a little time to sort through his thoughts and present a more coherent and persuasive argument. "And you're barefoot. And it's still storming." Slowly, Spencer stood, determined to reach her. "Everyone has nightmares, honey. No reason to be embarrassed about it." He didn't approach her. Not yet.

Jerking around to face him fully, she shook a fist toward him. "You don't know, so stop acting like you do!"

"You could tell me."

That took her back a step. "No." She emphasized the whispered denial with a firm shake of her head. "I won't."

"Okay." Damn, but he wished he had some idea of how to react to her now. He inched forward a foot. "But if you ever want to talk about it, any of it, please know that I'd listen, and I wouldn't judge."

Her lip curled. "Great. Thanks for the offer." Again she ran a hand through her hair. Undecided, she looked around. "My stupid car is out of commission."

"Because they want you to stay here." *With me. Only with me.* "They trust me, and you should, too."

"Jackson, Trace, Dare…they're like a bunch of meddling old ladies."

Acrimony? Sarcasm? He'd take it over her terror any day. "I'll tell them you said so." Another foot toward her. "Please don't be self-conscious. Not with me."

"Why not you?" Going on the offensive, she asked, "What makes you so special?"

Good question, Spencer thought. And coming up with an answer wouldn't be easy, not when what he wanted most was to hold her close, to protect her, and…to claim her as his own.

CHAPTER SEVEN

SPENCER IGNORED his own reservations, and, because she needed it, he gave her a piece of his soul. "I have nightmares sometimes, too."

Eyes still damp, Arizona glared at him. "I doubt they're the same."

"No, not the same at all." It wasn't easy to talk about. He never had before now. Before Arizona. "In my nightmares, I see my wife crying out to me to help her, but I don't. I can't."

Arizona went still, on alert. At least he had her attention now. Her breathing eased, and she stopped shivering. "Seriously?"

Spencer nodded. "In my nightmares, I feel her fear and I see those men doing things to her that…" He worked his jaw and forced himself to say it. "Things that they may or may not have done. I hear her screaming, desperate and panicked—and I'm not there." He gave a helpless shrug that didn't even come close to expressing how he felt about it, how much he fucking hated it.

Arizona stared at him, silent, watchful.

"I didn't help her. I didn't protect her as I should have." His expression tight, his heart tighter, he admitted, "The dreams always end the same way, with her getting shot and dying in a pool of her own blood."

Arizona softened. She wrapped her arms around herself, and her voice lowered. "Not the same, but…pretty awful."

He walked the rest of the way to her. "It was one of those dreams that drove me to Marla."

"Why? I don't get that."

"Sometimes, a little human contact can help to chase away the demons." One hand on her shoulder, he stepped closer still. "I could use a little contact right now. How about you?"

"Sex?"

"No." His guts tightened. "Comfort."

"Oh." She was stiff, still. "I don't know. I've never…"

"Getting comfort isn't something familiar to you. I understand." Slowly, he drew her up against his chest, and Christ Almighty, it felt good.

It felt right.

His chin to the top of her head, he whispered, "That's not so bad, is it?"

"No."

Careful not to do anything to spook her, he kept his hands still on her back and resisted the urge to kiss her temple. "I can't know all the things you went through, or how those things affected you. But you don't have to deal with any of it alone."

She leaned into him, and, tentatively, her arms came around him. "Maybe."

He felt her small hands on his back, her soft, lush body against his. She nuzzled her face into his shoulder, maybe drying her tears. For his part, Spencer kept his touch as innocent as possible. He'd rather lose a limb than alarm her. .

After a few seconds she gave him a tighter, harder squeeze. "You're so warm."

"And you're chilled." Carefully, he rubbed his palms

up and down her bare arms. The urge to fill his hands with her long hair, to press into her, to react, burned inside him. "Should I adjust the air-conditioning?"

"No."

Nothing was ever simple with Arizona. "Why not?"

"It's your house. You should be comfortable."

Damn. "I want you to be comfortable, too. I wish you'd believe that."

She tipped back to see his face. "Guess we can either stand here being melodramatic, or sit down and get comfortable, or we could try for a few more hours of sleep." She yawned. "The last is starting to sound good to me."

Her attempt to hide her feelings didn't put him off. He understood her need to keep it together, to put up a brave front. It was so novel, so stoic, that he appreciated her efforts, knowing few would be able to manage such a show of grit.

Spencer smoothed her silky hair back, cupped her cheek. "Things can be different if you trust again, if you see a better side of things."

She knuckled her left eye. "Yeah, well, I wasn't planning to slit my wrists or anything. You don't need to break out a sermon."

When she made to move away, he gripped her shoulders. "Where are you going?"

"Bathroom?"

"Oh." She stepped out of reach, and his hands fell to his sides.

As she strode away, Spencer, feeling like a true bastard, watched the sway of her hips in the loose shorts, how her shapely legs took such long strides.

When she returned a minute later, he saw that the cool air had affected her, and he could see the jut of her nipples beneath the T-shirt. She had heavy, firm breasts made more noticeable by her slender frame.

Yawning again, she made a beeline for the couch.

Rubbing the back of his neck, Spencer asked, "Will you be able to sleep?"

"Yup." In an offhand way, she added, "As long as you mosey on to bed instead of keeping watch over me."

Somehow, he doubted she'd sleep. Was she planning something? Probably.

Spencer studied her. "Will you be here in a few more hours when I get up?"

Her brows pulled together the tiniest bit, making her look more quizzical than annoyed. "You want me to be?"

"Yes." Something darkened in her eyes. Relief? "I want that very much."

"Then I'll be here."

Still feeling uncertain, Spencer pressed her. "If you have another nightmare—"

"No, I won't wake you, so don't suggest it. It's dumb. I'm an adult. And I know how to take care of myself." She snuggled down under the throw. "But I also promise not to go running off into the night like a demented woman. Good enough?"

He supposed it'd have to be. "All right."

"Now go away or I'll be forced to group you in with the others, who really are mother hens."

Spencer moved to stand in front of her. He couldn't leave her, not like this, so he crouched down before her, smoothed her hair. "I'm just down the hall if you change your mind." *What was he saying?*

She tucked in her chin and stared at him. "Change my mind about *what?*"

Good question. Even he wasn't entirely sure what he'd meant. "If you can't get back to sleep. We can talk, or watch TV or grab an early breakfast." He tugged the throw up over her shoulder. "Just let me know."

For an answer, she rolled her eyes, dropped her head back to the arm rest, and faked a loud snore. With a small smile, Spencer squeezed her shoulder and rose to walk away.

He wanted to get her a regular bed pillow.

He wanted to sit back down and continue…just touching her. But pushing Arizona in any way would be a mistake. So instead, he adjusted the air-conditioning, then went into his bedroom, closed his door and stripped off his clothes.

It took him a little while, but he finally fell asleep.

And for once, his dreams weren't of his wife. They were all about Arizona.

And they were surprisingly pleasant.

Arizona hummed as she finished her shower. It wasn't the thought of dressing in new clothes that lightened her mood. She detested outfits meant to draw attention, but she accepted it as a necessary means to an end. She needed to be noticed at the bar, and so she'd chosen clothes that would ensure it.

So, no, it wasn't the clothes; it was Spencer who made her feel…lighthearted. Weird. Rarely did she feel so worry-free, and never because of a man.

Sure, she adored Jackson and probably always would. The poor guy had become her stand-in…everything. Big brother, best friend, comrade and semi-confidant. Jackson knew things about her that few others did, because he'd been there, witnessing it firsthand while risking his life to save hers.

It made her hot with humiliation and soft with gratitude, every time she thought of it.

Jackson had done so much for her—and she'd done nothing for him. She was a burden for him to bear. An added responsibility when he already had so many.

The imbalance of their relationship left her indebted, defensive and heavy with guilt. She needed to repay Jackson for all he'd done.

Someday, somehow, she would.

But Spencer, yeah, Spencer felt more like a true partner. There was equality. She'd had a shitty nightmare, and that sucked. But she'd also seen the expression in his dark brown eyes as he'd shared his own nightmares.

It was the sharing that made all the difference.

Almost from the get-go, they'd connected. With any luck, they could unite further over their combined efforts to bring cretins to justice.

True to her word, she'd been at Spencer's kitchen table drinking coffee when he awoke. She'd been listening for him, wondering how late he'd sleep, anxious to see him, to talk to him, so of course she'd heard him the minute he'd left his bed.

Probably thinking she had skipped out on him, he'd rushed down the hall and into the kitchen, where he'd drawn up short at the sight of her.

With whiskers on his face and his hair mussed, wearing only boxers, he'd stared at her.

And she'd seen his relief. Because he *really* wanted her there.

Her heart did that strange tumbling thing again. The whiskers were appealing enough, but what that man did for a pair of boxers should have been illegal.

He had such a great body. She'd noticed that more than once, and not in the admiring but analytical way that she'd noted the physiques of Jackson, Dare and Trace. Being strong, tall and fast, with great stamina and reflexes, they were built for enforcing their individual wills.

Spencer was all of that, but he was also remarkable eye candy. Whenever he concentrated those dark bedroom eyes on her, she felt the strangest flutter in the pit of her stomach. It wasn't unpleasant, but it was disconcerting.

And so, at the first opportunity, she'd left him.

She felt a little guilty about it, too. But reminding herself that she had to keep her independence, that she had to prove her worth to one and all—especially to herself—had helped her to walk out while he showered.

Watching for nosy creeps, she'd checked out of her old hotel, shopped for the clothes she'd wear tonight and a swimsuit for the trip to Dare's, and then checked into a new hotel. She'd kept her phone out, certain that Spencer would call—but he hadn't.

Not yet anyway.

She refused to be disappointed over that. He'd meet her tonight to help with her sting, and that's what she needed the most.

With her shower complete, her hair conditioned and her body softened by scented lotion, she wrapped one towel around her hair and another around her body. She'd just stepped out of the bathroom when her cell phone rang.

Spencer.

Refusing to dwell on the joyous racing of her heart, she took a deep, calming breath and lifted the phone. No doubt he'd be pissed that she fled while he showered. But arguing with him was almost as exhilarating as everything else they'd shared. She could hardly wait.

Smiling with anticipation, she answered with a feigned and careless, "'Lo?"

"You left me."

Her pulsed tripped at the low, oh-so-familiar timbre of his voice. She hadn't left *him*. She'd just...left. Why did he make it sound so personal?

"Just noticed that, huh? Man, Spence, you really are astute."

"You snuck out while I was in the shower."

Why wasn't he blowing a gasket? She'd managed to get past his watchful eye, and that more or less proved she was better than him—right? That should have made him furious. Instead he sounded dark and mysterious and...she didn't know.

"I had some stuff to get done." Then she reminded him, "But I was there when you woke up as promised, right? I even hung around for breakfast."

"Biding your time?"

Annoyance straightened her shoulders and sharpened her tone. "I stuck to the letter of our deal—like you did when you talked to Trace, but not Jackson."

Nothing. No argument, no reply, not even a sound of frustration.

His lack of response spoiled all her fun. On a sigh, Arizona gave up and said, "I had to go shopping so I'd have something appropriate to wear tonight."

"So it wasn't just to get even with me for talking to Trace?"

"No." Well, maybe a little. "I needed to move locations, too, and...well, a girl's got prep work to do before seducing the masses."

"I wanted you to stay."

Oh, wow. She heard his disappointment. And damn it, it ramped up her guilt a lot. "I told you I couldn't do that."

"You and I are going to have a nice long talk about what you can and cannot do."

He sounded so certain of her agreement that she wanted to turn him down. But she needed to keep the peace so that he'd continue to work with her. "Okay. When?"

"As soon as you let me in."

"Let you…" Control eroded under growing temper. "Where are you?"

One firm rap sounded on her door. "Open up, honey."

Instead, she stepped back from the door. Voice cracking with outrage, she yelled, *"What the hell, Spencer?"*

"I don't want to draw attention out here. Are you going to open up or not?"

She looked down at herself. The white towel barely protected her dubious modesty. "No, I am not." He could damn well wait for her to dress. It'd do him good to cool his heels in the shabby lobby of the motel. "You had no right to come here—"

"Have it your way." He disconnected the call.

Grrrrr. Furious—and disappointed that he'd given up so easily—she squeezed the phone, considered throwing it at the door, and decided instead to demand he come back and give her the battle she needed.

She marched toward the door, but as she reached for the doorknob, she heard a scraping sound within the lock. She knew that sound.

He was breaking in!

Sheer surprise lifted her brows and obliterated her anger. She glanced around at the room, started to retreat once more—and the door swung open.

Returning a steel pick and tension wrench to a small leather case, Spencer stepped in, used his heel to nudge the door shut again, and turned to face her.

Her startled surprise was nothing compared to his.

Finding her more naked than not, with nothing but a couple of towels covering her, he went on high alert. Except for his gaze going all over her, he didn't move. When he finally got his attention up to her face, his eyes darkened. "Hey."

Hey? That's all he had to say?

Arizona forgot her state of undress. Well, no, really she didn't. She just forgot how much she cared.

Umbrage brought her storming up to him, and she poked him hard in the chest. "Just what the *hell* do you think you're doing?"

He caught her finger and held on. "You thought you were the only one who could pick a lock?"

She jerked free of his hold—and almost lost her towel. She secured the knot above her breasts and stepped back. More subdued now, she muttered, "That's not what I mean and you know it."

One eyebrow lifted—and he pushed away from the door to step toward her. "I told you I was good at tracking."

"You *followed* me, Spencer." She didn't understand his current mood. "That's not at all the same thing."

Shrugging, he finally got his attention off her and scoped out her room instead. "Close enough."

When he eyed the laptop she'd set up on the small bedside table, she shoved it shut. She hadn't been looking at anything private, but that wasn't the point.

Ignoring that, he lifted the T-shirt she'd discarded on the bed and then her bra.

Arizona snatched both away from him. She was a tidy person and would have stored them away in her duffel once she'd gotten dressed in the new duds.

Smiling slightly, he said, "I'm relieved that you're a

fast shopper. In and out in under twenty minutes. Admirable."

He'd been hot on her heels the whole time! She grabbed his arm, but didn't have much luck turning him toward her. "You were in the shower! How did you even know I left?"

Despite her hold, he went to the window—which meant she went to the window, too.

He moved aside the curtain to look out. "You think I trusted you to stay put? No. I was listening for you. It's odd, Arizona, but I can already read you." He glanced first at her hand on his arm—until she dropped it—and then at her face. "I knew all along you were going to cut out. I saw it in your eyes."

She wanted to deny that, but too many times already he'd read her intent. The ramifications of that staggered her. "Oh, so I'm supposed to trust you, but not the other way around?"

"Give me reason to trust you, and I will." He strolled to a chair, disregarded it and moved to sit on the end of the bed.

He eyed her, smiled and patted the mattress beside him.

Arizona shook her head. She needed to get dressed before she got close to him again. Contrary to what he'd said, she did trust him, but that didn't make her more comfortable while hiding under a towel.

Spencer kept his gaze on her face. "You wanted to know what I did with Marla, what made her enjoy having sex with me?"

Her eyes flared and her jaw loosened. He couldn't be serious. But boy, he sure looked serious. "Uh…yeah." She *really* wanted to know. The sad truth was that she'd thought about it way too much, when she had other things she should have been contemplating.

"Then let's talk." He patted the space beside him again.

She looked down at her mostly bared body, touched the towel on her head. "Okay, sure. Just give me a couple of minutes." She turned toward the bathroom and her blow-dryer.

Spencer sat forward and caught her hand. "Now." He tugged her—since she didn't really resist—down to sit close beside him.

Her bare thigh pressed against the worn, soft denim covering his. She breathed in the scents clinging to his body, those of sun-warmed skin, aftershave and...earthy male.

Struggling to keep the towel closed over her thighs, Arizona waffled. "You know...I really should get dressed first."

"This won't take long." He stared down at her thighs for so long that heat crawled over her, and her toes curled. It wasn't at all an unpleasant sensation.

She cleared her throat. "Okay. Shoot."

His gaze slid up to the notch of her thighs, then to her chest, shoulders, and finally he met her eyes. "I cued into her."

It had taken him so long to say that, Arizona had to shake her head to understand him. "What does that mean?"

"A considerate man spends time on foreplay."

And he was considerate? Probably. "You mean kissing and groping and stuff." She curled her lip. In her experience, that just dragged out the inevitable.

"If that's what she likes, yes. Lots of kissing, and lots of *touching*. Doing so gives me an opportunity to pick up reactions to various things. Judging by what a woman liked most, and least, I adjust." He reached out, trailing the back of a knuckle over her cheek.

Arizona froze, then inhaled sharply.

"When I touch you like this," Spencer murmured, "you get that certain look about you."

She'd been sinking under sensation, but now she slapped his hand away. "I do *not* have a look." Except maybe a look of fear, which she fought hard to hide. Only with Spencer, she wasn't afraid. Worried a little, maybe, mostly because of how he made her feel, not because of anything he might do. But there was no real fear.

He smiled with understanding and negated her thoughts by saying, "That look tells me that you like it when I touch you, as long as I don't push things too far."

Arizona thrust up her chin. "What's the look? Describe it to me."

"Softer. Warmer." He cupped a hand around her neck so that his fingertips played over her sensitive nape. "Definitely warmer."

She swallowed hard. "I thought we were talking about you and Marla."

He grew far too serious. "I know you're unaware of it, but an honorable man doesn't discuss the intimate details of his involvement with other women."

"You big fraud!" He'd had no plan to tell her—

"But," he said, moving his hand down to clasp her shoulder and forestall her angry rise from his side, "I can give you generalities."

She crossed her arms. That'd have to do. "Better make it good."

His mouth twitched into a crooked grin, but he stopped short of laughing at her. "A smart man learns to read women. Anyone can have sex, and I'm sure you know that men get off pretty easily."

That was…straightforward. Arizona eyed him askance. "Yeah, they do." With some guys, just looking at a woman was enough. But with others…no. She didn't want to think about that.

For only a moment, Spencer looked pained. "Right. So, that being the case, the way for a man to make it more pleasurable is to make sure the woman enjoys herself, too."

"That matters to you?"

"It matters to me very much."

Huh. She couldn't imagine why, but she shrugged it off. "Most men don't care—"

He put a finger to her mouth. "Honestly, honey, you don't know what most men care about because you haven't known any real men, any good men." His voice dropped, and he looked at her mouth. "At least, I assume you haven't been intimate by choice, but I suppose you could have—"

"No." She shuddered at the thought.

"There was no one before you were taken?" He studied her. "No one since, or maybe at some point during?"

She snorted. "Before then, with my folks, it would've been one heck of a trick to pull off. During and after…" She looked away, saying again, "No."

He stroked a hand along her arm, up to her shoulder, and ended by cupping her chin. "Then trust me on this. Normal, healthy men love a woman's excitement."

"How so?" She knew as little about a woman's pleasure as she did of normal, healthy men.

"The sounds a woman makes when she comes, how she tightens." His voice deepened, turned raspy. "How she gets wet and hot and out of control…" He drew to a halt.

He sure made it sound good. "Go on," Arizona urged around the constriction in her throat, her chest and her stomach.

Spencer shook his head, his gaze intent on hers. "You understand my meaning."

Heat flushed his cheekbones, intriguing her.

She leaned away to better gauge his expression. "You turning yourself on, Spence?"

"A little." He took a deep breath, let it out and became more strident. "Getting a woman to climax is a rush, and most men will work hard to see that it happens."

Hmm. "So are you saying that every woman you screw gets off like that?"

After a long look, his abrupt laugh broke the tension. "You're priceless, you know that?"

No, she didn't know. She'd always had a price, and it wasn't all that much. "Avoiding the answer?"

"Men will lie about their success with women. Most men, anyway."

"Even good men?"

"Afraid so." He gave her such a warm look of affection, she felt it everywhere. "Because it's so important to ensure that a woman enjoys herself, too, no man wants to admit it if she left his bed unsatisfied. It'd be a major blow to the male ego. But since I promised you complete honesty, I'll admit that on occasion, it's happened to me."

Being theatrical, Arizona put a hand to her chest. "No!"

"Not often since I've matured, and not for lack of trying on my part. But women are complex. Far more so than men."

"So even a woman you didn't care about—"

"I wouldn't have sex with a woman I didn't care about."

"Oh, baloney!" No way would she let him make that claim. "Men have casual sex all the time."

"As do women," he agreed. "But there has to be an attraction, and that denotes at least some level of regard."

Given his demeanor, she felt like teasing him. "Never bought sex, huh?"

"No, I haven't. Certainly not from an underage girl."

"Don't get your boxers in a bunch. I just made an observation."

His slight frown didn't lift. "You do realize that there's a big difference between a woman who chooses to prostitute herself, and a woman forced to do so?"

"Yeah, the one choosing it must be nuts."

"More likely desperate, but not always. The point is that a real man would never try to force himself on a woman, or participate in any way when someone else is forcing her. In fact, he'd do everything in his power to stop it."

That hadn't been her experience; she'd known only men willing to turn a blind eye, willing to participate and willing to overlook the obvious. "Must be a lack of real men in the world."

"That's a jaded view, honey, and sooner or later you'll realize it." To keep her from protesting that, he continued, "I do my best physically, hope I'm reading the woman right so that I go slowly when she wants me to, harder and faster when that's what she needs, but it can still be a guessing game, and I sometimes fall short."

"You ever had a woman complain?"

He smiled. "More often than not, I'm successful."

Yeah, she could believe that. "Braggart."

"Being honest, as I promised."

He'd told her a whole lot of nuanced stuff without any of the nitty-gritty mechanics. But for now—since she was a little too overheated herself—she decided to let it go. "Thanks for the education." She slapped her hands to her bare knees. "It's been great, but now I need to—"

"Give me the kiss you owe me."

Her stomach bottomed out, her legs turned to noodles, and her backbone froze stiff. A feeling not unlike alarm, but probably more like anticipation, churned inside her.

Spencer brought her face around to his. "You cursed."

"I didn't." Did she? "When?"

"When I first got here. Twice actually, so I suppose if we're accurate, you owe me two kisses."

What had she said? What had she…oh, yeah. She remembered her outburst, and her slipups. But that was partly his fault. "You took me by surprise."

"I know. And it's bound to happen again, so you might as well get used to paying the piper."

Her pulse jumped. "I don't know if I can." God, she hated how small her voice sounded, how weak and silly. "Spencer—"

"You haven't had any pleasant kisses, either?"

"No." She amended that with, "I offered with Jackson, but you already know that."

He nodded. "And since you offered for the wrong reasons, he turned you down."

"He'd have turned me down anyway, no matter why I offered." She shrugged. "Like I said, he feels sorry for me."

Spencer let that go to say, "It's just a kiss. Why does that scare you?"

Swallowing wasn't easy. She shook her head, unwilling to spill her guts. He probably saw her as fearless; she tried hard enough to give that impression. But she knew the truth: she was a terrible coward.

"I've been honest with you, Arizona. Can't you give me the same courtesy?" He smoothed his hand up and down her arm. "Tell me. What are you so afraid of?"

She stared at the bathroom door, at the carpet, at his hand on her arm. Fine, he wanted honesty? She met his gaze. "Sooner or later, you'll snap." He was in complete control now, but what if he lost control?

Silence filled the room. She expected Spencer to deny that possibility. To maybe sweet-talk her. Maybe cajole.

"Give me your hand."

Such a calm but firm command caused her fingers to curl into her palm. "But—"

Gently, he said, "You're only making this harder on yourself."

Annoyance surfaced. He wanted to play this stupid game, fine, she'd play. She'd given her word, and by God, she'd abide by it.

Face set and cold, fingers trembling, Arizona straightened her arm toward him.

Oh-so-gently, Spencer enfolded her hand in his own. He was so much bigger, his hand twice the size of hers, rougher and thicker, too.

And so warm.

For a short time, he only held her, watching her, his thumb moving over her knuckles until her skin tingled, and the butterflies in her stomach rioted.

"Relax." He lifted her hand toward his mouth, looked at her palm, then pressed a kiss there.

Firm. Lingering.

Her pulse stuttered. Heat swelled inside her. His mouth was warm, his breath moist, his hold so incredibly tender.

Ho boy.

Suddenly he released her and stood to walk back to the window.

She kept her arm extended for half a minute before she caught herself and snatched it back. "That's it?"

Hands on his hips, his head down and his shoulders rigid, he said, "This time, yeah."

This time? She held her closed hand up against her chest, but the impression of his mouth touching her sensitive skin, how he'd looked and how he'd breathed while doing it, kept a small thrill ricocheting inside her. "There won't be a next time."

"You owe me one more."

A threat? Well, given how weak she became around him, how else could she look at it? Damn, but he left her confused!

She shoved to her feet. "Then take it now, da…darn you."

Once again amused, he turned back to her. "No, not yet. Maybe later. For now, I need to talk to you about something else. And yes, you should probably get dressed first."

"Why?" She folded her arms. "Starting to get to you?"

"I've got a boner, so lying would do me no good."

Her gaze dropped fast and hard to his lap, then stuck there. Well, well, well. Instead of distressing her, that gave her a dose of satisfaction. "Serves you right."

"Your pointed stare isn't helping."

"Poor you." But she should probably get it together. Still, it wasn't totally scary that he wanted her. Really, she'd known all along that he did. He hadn't hidden his attraction. So this was just—

"Arizona."

On a huff, she dragged her gaze upward and pointed a finger at him. "Don't move. I'll be dressed in under three minutes."

CHAPTER EIGHT

THE SECOND SHE DISAPPEARED into the bathroom, Spencer let out a breath.

The girl packed a wallop of major proportions.

After turning on her television for background noise, he sprawled out on the bed with a groan.

He'd kissed her palm, that's all. But he'd heard her accelerated breathing, felt her excited trembling, and he'd wanted so badly to devour her. Head to toes and—*oh, God*—everywhere in between.

That skimpy little towel…what the hell was he thinking, to postpone her getting dressed? When had he become such a masochist?

But he knew. Ever since first meeting Arizona, he'd put himself through hell, wanting to be with her but refusing to take advantage of her vulnerability by pushing for sexual satisfaction. If she was any other woman, he'd have already done his utmost to charm her into bed.

She had such incredibly beautiful, shapely legs.

He scrubbed his hands over his face, but still he saw those sleek muscles, her soft thighs and skin the color of rich honey.

Even her feet looked sexy to him, being small and narrow with a high arch. And those adorable knees… God, he had it bad.

Resisting her in shorts was one thing; at least last night she'd immediately covered up with the throw.

Today, in the bright light of day, in a small room mostly dominated by a bed, ignoring the insubstantial covering of a small towel was impossible.

Shit. He adjusted his jeans and concentrated on getting himself under control. Her unique brand of honesty and curiosity would be the death of him.

And thinking about her, about her body, wasn't helping with his erection. He needed to concentrate on something else—like that forbidding array of weapons in her trunk. Or her God-awful propensity for courting danger.

While slipping out the door behind her today, staying far enough back that she didn't see him, but close enough that he didn't lose her, he'd called Trace, who was very unhappy to know she'd given Spencer the slip.

With her car out of commission and Spencer keeping tabs on her, Trace had assumed she'd be safe. And he knew Arizona, so he understood the daunting responsibility put on Spencer. But Trace had wanted to ramp up the surveillance on her, and he'd wanted to have a firm discussion with her.

Knowing Arizona wouldn't appreciate either of those things, Spencer had assured Trace that one way or another, he would get her back to his house, and somehow he'd find a way to keep her there for the duration of this investigation and bust.

But if he didn't—

The bathroom door opened in a rush, shattering his thoughts. Hair wet, wearing only snug, low-riding jeans and a ribbed camisole, Arizona stepped back into the bedroom. Judging by her expression and stomping stride, *she'd* had no problem collecting herself.

Sighing, Spencer sat up. Through the thin material of her top, he could see every curve of her breasts and the plump outline of her nipples. His mouth went dry.

She stopped beside the bed, her hands on her hips. "All right, Spencer, some ground rules."

He looked up at her angry face. "Number one, you stay with me."

Her open mouth snapped shut. After blinking twice, she shook her head. "No, number one is that you back off a little."

"We made a deal," he reminded her.

Anger left her cheeks a dusky rose. "I wasn't talking about that. I was talking about you following me—"

"Overruled." Glad that she wasn't protesting his kiss, he stood, crowding into the narrow space she'd allotted between the bed and her body. "You either stay with me, or I wash my hands of the whole thing and you can deal with the dynamic trio instead."

She stared at him, and her mouth twitched. "Dynamic trio?"

Keeping his attention off her chest was a trial. "Whatever you want to call them. You know they'll be hovering over you way worse than I do."

"Yeah." She chewed the side of her mouth. "They'll smother me."

And he was counting on her to hate that. "Exactly."

She propped a hand on the nightstand, drummed her fingers. "You'd actually do that to me?"

"To ensure you stayed safe?" He'd move heaven and earth. "In a heartbeat."

She drummed some more. "They're going to be on top of things now anyway."

He wouldn't lie to her by denying that. "But if you allow me to shadow you, they'll be in the background, not breathing down your neck. Take today, for instance. If Trace hadn't known that I would follow you, one of them would have. And you'd be having a whole different conversation right about now."

The drumming stopped. "With no kissing."

Had she enjoyed it? Or was she still fighting her reactions? "Given that two of them are married and the other engaged, probably not."

She laughed. "*Probably* not?"

"They're good men, honorable men," Spencer admitted. There was no question of that. But when it came to Arizona… He shrugged. "You're hard to resist."

She eyed him up and down—and took a step back. "Jackson resisted me just fine."

God, he did not want to hear this again. Why did she keep bringing it up? Was she infatuated with Jackson beyond the platonic? Thinking that left him churning with a dangerous mix of emotions. "Let's stick to the point. To make things simpler on me and on yourself, you need to stay with me until we sort things out at the bar."

Pacing away, she appeared to think about it. "Your couch is comfortable."

"I told you that you could use the guest room."

Her shoulder lifted. "You don't want me on the couch?"

Now what was this about? Spencer crossed his arms. "I don't mind if you sleep there, but why would you want to when you can set up your own room? You can make yourself at home in there." And in case she worried about it, he added, "While you're with me, I won't push you to do anything you don't want to do—except kiss me when you curse."

She shot him a dirty look. "I won't slip up again."

"I'll give you as much freedom as I can. I'll stay out

of your hair. But if you go anywhere, I need to know. No more running off by yourself. Period."

She paced again, head down, hands on hips. When she returned to him, she nodded. "All right, fine."

He launched into the next demand. "Make no plans without me. None. We're either working together on this, or we're not working at all."

"Sure, fine. Ditto back atcha."

Being reasonable? Doubtful, so he didn't bother to commit himself to the same rule. "Tell me why you have so many weapons in your trunk."

Without missing a beat, she said, "I like to live."

That blunt answer threw him. "You need a shovel to live?"

Her chin lifted. "You know why I need that."

Yes, he probably did, but he badly wanted to be wrong. "Enlighten me."

"If I have to kill anyone, I'll need to bury them."

Oh, God. Spencer dropped back to sit on the bed. He shouldn't have asked.

Arizona, damn her, laughed. "Oh, lighten up, Spence. I was just funnin' ya."

"Funning me?" Anger stirred as he glared at her. "You think it's funny to joke about murder?"

"Sometimes, yeah. Depends on the murder victim, right?" She strolled around the room like a caged tiger. "I carry the shovel for lots of reasons. In case I get my car stuck in mud, in case I have to use my knife and need to hide it." She shrugged. "It's an all-purpose, handy tool."

Skeptical, he said, "You don't plan to kill anyone?"

"Didn't say that." Her face went carefully blank. "If someone needs killing, if I need to defend myself or someone else—"

"I'll do it." He was trained, he was a man, and...he wanted to shield her from as much ugliness as he could.

"I don't need you to. I can fend for myself."

But she didn't have to, not anymore. More firmly, to make sure she understood, he said, "If it comes to that, if the situation turns that violent, I will be the one to handle things."

Her chest rose with agitated breaths. "Just like you killed Chandra Silverman, even though it was *my* right?"

They'd already debated who had more right in that regard. But he knew his actions concerning the evil organizer of a human trafficking ring had veered from wanting revenge for the death of his wife to concern for Arizona.

She deserved to regain a normal outlook on life, not add to the nasty memories by chalking up a kill—even against someone who deserved death as much as Chandra had. She might not realize it, but it wouldn't give her closure. It'd only darken her dreams more.

Given Arizona's livid expression, she didn't agree. Spencer stood and walked to her. "Just calm down for a minute."

That damned pointy finger of hers poked hard into his chest again. "*You* calm down!"

He grabbed her hand. "That's enough."

She strained against his hold, then gave up to lean into him with her ire. "It's one thing for you to play the White Knight, but if you think you have the stones to change me, forget it."

"Change you how?" That he still held her hand—and she allowed it—surprised and pleased him. More gently now, he enfolded her fingers in his own and, drawing her closer, held them against his chest. "What do you mean?"

"I've seen violence. I've lived it. And I can take a hit as easy as the next guy."

Over his dead body. "You're *not* a guy." She was a small, susceptible female—and he couldn't bear the thought of her being physically injured.

"Doesn't matter. Now that I'm free, I plan to stay on the delivery end of things."

"Doling out retribution?"

Her jaw locked. "I will do what I think is right. What is best. You can either help, or you can stay out of my way."

No, she wouldn't get rid of him that easily. "I'm here to help, remember?" He moved his thumb over her taut knuckles, hoping to quiet her. She could make a credible fist, but she lacked the power necessary to fend for herself against brutal men, especially the immoral breed of flesh peddlers. "That's why we need some ground rules."

"I agreed to your stupid rules already."

True enough. And since he wouldn't let her out of his sight, he could keep her from using most of those weapons. Most. "What do you carry on you?"

Understanding the question, she relaxed a little. "Depends on where I go. Usually a knife, pepper spray and stun baton. The baton is telescopic, so it can fit in my purse."

She indicated the big slouch purse that looked liked it could hold the kitchen sink. "Incredible."

Shrugging, she added, "If I'm blending in but still want a gun, I carry the little Beretta Bobcat. It's easy to hide. And if I don't have to conceal things, then I carry my Glock, maybe my rifle, too. And I wear my vest. If I'm on night surveillance, I have these cool night-vision goggles that come in handy. They weren't cheap, but they're worth the cost."

Fully armed and protected, like a damned trooper. "What did you plan to carry tonight?"

"Not much, since my new clothes won't make it easy." After freeing her hand, she went to her duffel bag and withdrew a wicked switchblade. She pressed a button, and it snapped open. But closed again, the profile was slim and would be easy to hide in the bottom of her purse. "It's not my favorite, but it'll do."

He crossed his arms over his chest and surveyed her. "What is your favorite?"

Animated, she took out a leather sheath and slid free a big, dangerous knife. The fluorescent overhead light glimmered on the blade as she turned it this way and that. "My baby."

His heart grew heavy at the sight of the weapon. The fixed blade tactical knuckle knife wasn't a utility knife by any stretch of the imagination. It wouldn't be used for a quick defense. No, it was for attacking, and it would cause a lot of damage if used against someone—or if turned against the owner.

"She's a real beauty, isn't she?"

He tried to be suitably interested, rather than appalled. "Stainless steel, tanto-point. Nonreflective black powder coating."

"Yup." Arizona fit the handle over her fingers like brass knuckles. "Comfortable, too." She turned her hand, her hold secure, familiar.

Spencer grunted a reply.

Glancing at him, she said, "I have a nylon harness that gives me easy access but keeps it hidden until I want to show it." She grinned. "Sometimes that's all it takes. Most guys see this, and they back off."

Muscles coiling at her boast, he drew a steadying breath. "Sometimes?"

"Other times..." she returned the knife to the sheath and put it in back in her bag "...we battle. But for someone who knows how to use it, a knife is a terrific equalizer, so don't sweat it, okay?"

Fury stole his common sense and cool control. Her cavalier attitude defied belief. Sure, she might be able to hold her own against a man if he was drunk enough, dumb enough or completely unschooled. But for her to think, even for a single second, that she could keep a thug from turning that lethal blade back on her...

Seemingly unaware of his fury, she withdrew a catalogue. "Know what I really want?" She thumbed through the catalogue until she reached a dog-eared page. Coming to stand by him, practically leaning into his side, she pointed out a costly, custom knife. "Isn't it cool?"

Spencer only half heard her as she waxed on about bead blasted, anodized titanium handles, double thumb openers and pivot screws.

Chagrined, he dropped down to sit on the side of the bed. "You know your knives."

"I know most weapons," she agreed as she sat down beside him. "But knives are my favorite."

And the knife she favored most was one he'd already purchased for himself. The irony leveled him; love of a quality blade was one more thing they had in common.

"Soon as I can save up enough coin, I'm going to get it."

The contrasts left Spencer reeling. She sat beside him, young and, at the moment—while discussing weapons— very sweet. She was so intrinsically female, her face animated and her tone light…but she talked about buying a highly lethal weapon that, if pressed, she would use against a deadly goon.

Her thigh touched his. Her intoxicating scent filled his head.

And she wanted to debate who had the right to vengeance.

Determined to set her straight, he drew her back up to her feet, his hands on her shoulders, his expression stern—and his cell phone rang.

Damn. He waffled—but he knew he couldn't ignore it.

Shifting away from him, she lifted a brow. "Expecting a call?"

"Not really." Spencer glanced at the caller ID and saw it was Trace. Frustrated at the interruption, he answered with a succinct, "I'll call you right back."

Without a single question, Trace said, "Meet me downstairs instead." And he disconnected.

Well, hell. Definitely interrupted. "Sorry."

Arizona's eyes narrowed.

Spencer ignored her curiosity to say, "We need to get some dinner before we start tonight."

She transferred her gaze from his face to the phone in his hand and back to his face—but she didn't press him for info. "Dinner before we head to a bar and grill?"

His blood ran cold. Again. "God Almighty, Arizona. Tell me you don't eat there."

Batting her eyes at him, she said, "You think they might poison me?"

How the hell had she survived so long? "Poison you, no. At the moment they don't want you dead. But drug you? Yes."

"Yeah, well, for the purposes they'd intend, the two

would be about the same." She sniffed. "But no, I don't eat there." And then with added vitriol, "Give me some credit, will you?"

Knowing she'd just tweaked him again, Spencer growled. "Can you ever give me a straight answer?"

"Sure, and yes, we need to eat. I'm up for a burger if you are."

"How much time do you need to get ready?"

Now that she'd blown his cool, she smiled. "Twenty minutes, give or take a few." She indicated her face. "Gotta do it up a little to make sure I get attention."

She'd get attention no matter what. On top of an incredible body and breathtaking face, she had enough attitude and presence to turn heads wherever she went. She breathed, and anyone with a dick would notice. "Will you promise to meet me downstairs when you're done?"

"Cross my heart."

He looked into her eyes, believed her, then bent and put a kiss to her forehead. "Kiss number two," he told her.

"Oh." She looked dumbfounded for only a moment. "Well…good. Glad to have that out of the way."

Just to prove a point, he kissed her once more, his mouth lingering against her temple. He breathed in the soft, clean scent of her, letting his nose touch her damp hair as he absorbed her near-electric vitality.

He had Trace waiting downstairs…and maybe that was a good thing. At the very least, it served as a deterrent.

As he ended the kiss and walked away, she remained rooted to the spot. Satisfied with that reaction, Spencer opened the door and said over his shoulder, "Don't keep me waiting."

TAKING HIS TIME, Trace studied the motel that Arizona had chosen, making special note of each egress, including any windows that opened. He prowled the perimeter, scrutinizing the lighting, the nearby establishments, the ambiance, the traffic—and he had to admit, she had good instincts.

He circled back around to the lobby entrance to meet up with Jackson, who'd done his own surveillance. He found him standing just outside the front doors, smiling, lost in thought—no doubt about his impending nuptials.

He'd tried to leave Jackson behind, but given his close association with Arizona, Trace wasn't surprised that Jackson had insisted on coming along.

Though Trace hadn't wanted to admit it, he actually liked Jackson, and truthfully, it relieved him that Alani was not only in love, but with a man who could keep her safe.

Smiling, Trace clapped Jackson on the shoulder hard enough to make him stumble forward.

"What the hell?" Jackson regained his balance and scowled.

"You came along to work, so clear your head, why don't you?"

"It's clear." Jackson's scowl lifted, and he grinned. "'Cept for when I'm thinking of my beautiful bride-to-be."

"Which is apparently all the time." Trace watched a couple head into the motel, made note of another man departing.

"Lucky for you," Jackson said, "I can multitask."

Together, they stepped into the lobby. "So what do you think?"

Jackson shrugged. "It's a place I'd have chosen for myself."

"Same here."

"I told you, Arizona's not a slouch in the mental works. But physically, she's still a bitty female with more brass than strength."

"Spencer is keeping a close eye on her."

Jackson snorted with ill humor. "Yeah, I just bet he is."

Hmm. Trace studied him. "It bothers you that he's interested?" Not that Jackson should be surprised. Most single men would be sniffing around Arizona, and probably a lot of unfaithful married men.

"Not at all—unless he hurts her."

"And if he does?"

"I'll take him apart." On that foul note, Jackson stalked away to peruse the interior hallways, the restrooms, the vending machine alcoves.

Trace watched him go. Since Jackson and Arizona didn't share a blood tie, it wasn't quite the same as what he'd felt when Jackson began chasing after his sister, Alani. But close enough to fill him with satisfaction.

The satisfaction was short-lived.

Would Spencer inadvertently hurt Arizona? What she'd gone through had left her emotionally brittle, but even the most thorough digging hadn't uncovered anything in Spencer's background to show him as less than a principled man. Knowing him now, Trace recognized the protectiveness Spencer felt for Arizona, and for anyone else in need.

He was a decent man, a capable defender, and sadly, since his wife's murder over three years ago, he remained free of commitments. If he did choose to pursue Arizona, Trace had to believe he planned to go slowly and carefully.

But Arizona...well, she could tempt a saint, and no

one in Spencer's profession, with his lethal background, would ever be mistaken for such.

Luckily, Arizona's trauma hadn't stifled her independence or her ability to speak her mind. If she didn't return Spencer's interest, she'd let him know.

And Spencer would respect that.

Trace trusted that they were both adults and could decide their own relationship. But to be on the safe side, he planned to have a little talk with Spencer anyway.

WHEN HE GOT DOWN to the motel entrance, Spencer found Jackson standing there, frightening the locals. They walked a wide birth around him, and Jackson, pretending to be inebriated, gave them plenty of reason for caution.

So that was his cover? Figured he'd come up with something that allowed him to act goofy. Jackson was one hell of a fighter, with razor-sharp reflexes and an amazing intuition. But he was also low-key, laid-back, and irreverent—which made him the polar opposite of Dare and Trace.

Trace had the vibe of a keen businessman with a deadly edge. He was a driving force that couldn't be reined in—and no smart person would even try. He wasn't cocky like Jackson, but he carried himself with subdued self-assurance, and an acute awareness of his own capability.

Dare, who he'd met a few times now, was quieter, very matter-of-fact and relaxed about his ability. He didn't say a lot, and he didn't need to.

Spencer liked them all. The more he learned of their operations, the better he got to know them, the more he approved of their methods and respected their influence.

Obviously Jackson didn't want anyone to notice him

sizing up escape routes. Shaking his head, Spencer looked around for Trace. He stood with his back to the stairs, gazing out at the parking lot. Trace seemed less concerned about being observed, almost disdainful of his surroundings.

Bypassing Jackson, Spencer headed toward Trace instead.

He knew Trace was aware of him, had probably seen his reflection in the big window, so he led off with, "Sorry to keep you waiting."

Trace continued to watch the lot. "What'd you tell Arizona?"

"Nothing."

That brought him around. "She doesn't know why you walked out on her?"

"She was getting ready." He propped a shoulder on the wall. "Giving her privacy is what any gentleman would do."

"And you're always a gentleman with her?"

His brows bunched down over the way Trace asked that. "That's why you're here? Is that some sort of inquisition on my intentions?"

The slightest of smiles belied any menace. "I doubt you know your intentions at this point."

That infuriated Spencer. "I know exactly what I'm doing."

The smile turned into a grin. "Keep telling yourself that if it makes you feel better."

"What the hell does that mean?" Damn it, he'd left Arizona's room in a good mood—which Trace had quickly shot to hell.

Trace shook off his humor. "She didn't ask you where you were going or who had called?"

"She hesitates to pry too much." Then, recalling her

interrogation about sex, Spencer rethought that. "Or maybe it's just that she's selective in how and when she pries."

Trace accepted that with a nod.

With growing suspicion and tension, Spencer asked, "You want to tell me why you're here?" Trace surely had a better reason for seeking him out than idle curiosity.

"She ran out on you today."

The hell she had! He didn't appreciate the way Trace worded that. "She had some shopping to do, that's all."

"She left without telling you first."

"She's independent. You know that." Spencer worked his jaw. "I told you I had it under control."

"You should understand something, Spencer."

Oh, he understood all right. This was a warning. "I'm listening."

"Jackson has accepted Arizona as family, with Alani's blessing. Priss and Molly like her and empathize with her situation, as do Dare and I." His gaze never wavered from Spencer's. "She's one of us now."

One of us? It was the tone more than the message that had Spencer's temper on edge. "Meaning?"

"Meaning with or without you, we'll protect her."

That sounded far too close to a threat, and Spencer straightened from the wall. His shoulders bunched, and his jaw clenched. "You think I can't? Or won't?"

"I think men in lust sometimes let the wrong head make the decisions."

Jackson joined them to say, "Amen to that." He pointed to Spencer's crotch. "No thinking with the gonads."

Finding the warnings insulting—even if a little true—Spencer scowled. "Is this a case of do as I say, not as I do?"

Trace said, "No."

Jackson said, "Mmm…maybe."

On a grievous sigh, Trace shook his head. "Ignore Jackson. He's known to embrace gluttony."

Leaning in, Jackson whispered loud enough for Trace to hear, "He means in bed, but since I'm marrying his sister, he doesn't want to go into details."

And just like that, the mood lightened. Spencer rested against the wall to watch the ensuing exchange between the two men.

Trace glared. "You did get her pregnant."

"Yeah." Jackson sighed theatrically. "And knowing she's carrying my baby just makes her sexier."

Trace rudely stepped in front of Jackson, crowding him out, to address Spencer again. "For now, I'm willing to let you handle things with Arizona."

"Gee, thanks." He didn't bother telling Trace that he had no intention of butting out, regardless of what any of them said about it.

"Hey," Jackson said, his humor dwindling. "Don't I get a vote on this?"

"You've done enough," Trace told him.

Jackson opened his mouth—then grinned and closed it.

Back to Spencer, Trace added, "You can keep her safe by keeping her close. That works for me."

"It works for me, too," Jackson told him. "Close is good."

Trace spoke over Jackson. "But if Arizona decides she doesn't like that setup, then you're out."

He'd almost gotten distracted with the byplay between Trace and Jackson. Now he snapped back to attention. "I'll decide when I'm done, not you."

"Wrong." Jackson aligned himself with Trace. "Arizona makes that decision. And we'll be backing her up."

"Stay on her good side," Trace warned. "Or stay away from her."

"Won't be easy." Jackson shook his head in sympathy. "She can be pretty…trying. But you better not lose your patience with her. If you think you might, best to cut out now."

Spencer went rigid. Screw their ability and far-reaching influence. He made his own decisions, and he would be the one to decide when and if to walk away from Arizona. "You don't dictate to me."

"So you are planning to sleep with her?" Trace asked.

That pulled him up short. "None of your damn business."

Jackson folded his arms. "Course he is." He glanced toward Trace. "He's a guy. And Arizona is…well—"

"Not easy to resist," Spencer said through his teeth. "Believe me, I know. But I'm a thirty-two-year-old man, and she's not only been through hell, she's barely an adult."

Trace leveled a look on him. "So you have only altruistic motives in this? You're shadowing her out of concern for another human being, nothing more?"

He said again, "None of your goddamned business."

Neither of them was fazed by his growing temper.

Jackson tilted his head to study Spencer. "You took it upon yourself to partner up with her."

Of all the… "She came to me," he reminded them. "You already know that."

"So if she hadn't," Jackson said, "you wouldn't have seen her again?"

Damn it, he would not be cornered by either of them. "We've crossed paths a few times."

"Because of Arizona. It's not like you went after her, did you?"

He hadn't needed to, not when every time he saw one of the guys, Arizona somehow happened to be there. But he'd be damned before he continued to explain himself to them. He set his jaw and stepped forward—

"Break it up, girls. You're drawing attention." Arizona elbowed her way in past Jackson and Trace to stand directly in front of Spencer, facing him with a scowl. "You're going to give yourself wrinkles."

At his first glimpse of her, Spencer's brain went blank. "Oh, my God."

Hands on her hips, she turned a circle and eyed them all in turn. "You guys picked a heck of a public locale to compare dick sizes, don't you think?"

Ignoring the crude words, Trace tracked his gaze over her, and then slowly closed his eyes.

"Damn, girl." Jackson stripped off his jacket and tried to stuff Arizona into it. It left his gun exposed, but that wasn't as bad as Arizona drawing so much attention.

And given her outfit, her hair and makeup, she could do nothing else.

Gone were the jeans in favor of a short—*really short*—faded denim miniskirt. A low-plunging black tank made a bra impossible and emphasized the round firmness of her substantial breasts. Little strappy sandals and big hoop earrings completed the outfit. But she hadn't stopped there. Her pale blue eyes were a dominant feature on her, and now, with her lush lashes layered in black mascara and her lips a glossy pink, she looked… like a walking wet dream.

Spencer scanned the area around them and saw that they had, in fact, drawn attention. "We need to move. Now."

Trace growled a complaint as Arizona fought Jackson's efforts to conceal her. "This is going to be a clusterfuck of the first order."

Arizona stopped struggling to say, "If I can't cuss, you can't, either."

And Spencer finally pulled himself together. "Did you leave anything in the room?"

She lifted the duffel, laptop case and her purse. "I didn't see any reason to come back here after we eat, so I've got it all here and in the trunk of my car."

That meant she didn't have much. He frowned as he took the case from her, but knew he'd have to figure out the lack of personal possessions later. "We'll head to dinner now." After wresting the duffel away from her, too, he turned to Trace. "Could you—"

"Check her out, yeah. Don't worry about it. Get her well away from here before you stop to eat, though."

"Better still," Jackson said, looking everywhere as if expecting hordes of men to descend on her, "take her through a drive-thru and eat in your car."

Clustered around her, shielding her from sight as much as they could, the men led her out of the motel and toward Spencer's truck.

"Stop shoving!" Arizona complained and pushed back against Jackson.

Spencer inserted himself between them. He didn't like Jackson cozying up so close to her. Besides, Arizona was usually more reasonable with him.

Near to her ear, he said, "Hustle it up, honey. In case anyone comes looking for you later, the less notice we get, the better."

She dutifully marched ahead but continued to grouse. "You guys are the ones causing a scene."

"You aren't that naive," Trace told her.

"Never said I was," she snapped right back.

"Then you *know* how you look."

At the passenger side of the truck, she turned and gave Trace a sultry look. "So I was successful?"

Trace and Jackson both stared at her. At all of her.

"For the love of…" Spencer opened the door and lifted her inside. "Knock it off, Arizona." He knew neither man wanted to ogle her, but she made it pretty hard not to, especially when she struck a sexy pose.

After slamming the door again, Spencer told them, "I'll check in later." He circled around the hood, got behind the wheel and drove off. He didn't look back— and he did his best not to look at Arizona, either.

CHAPTER NINE

JACKSON FELT AS IF SOMEONE had just sucker punched him. He'd known Arizona had killer looks. Hell, he wasn't blind or stupid. But it went beyond that. She had an innate sensuality that, with just a single glance, roped in a guy.

If he wasn't in love with Alani, if he didn't know what Arizona had suffered, if he didn't have a deep moral code that kept him from taking advantage, well…he'd have been tempted.

With Trace silent beside him, they watched as Spencer and Arizona disappeared from sight. Still thunderstruck, he turned to look at Trace. Trace met his gaze, and he cracked.

They both laughed for a moment before Jackson shook his head. "Did you fucking see that girl?"

Reining in his humor, Trace said, "Would have been hard to miss." He grinned again. "Spencer saw her, too."

"Yeah." Jackson rubbed a hand over his head. "It's going to get interesting."

"It's going to go upside down." He turned away.

Jackson followed. "Arizona didn't even seem to realize."

"*All* women realize."

"Cynical, Trace. Real cynical." He shook his head. "Arizona is different."

"That's an understatement." He surveyed the yard, the

motel, before getting into his unassuming sedan. "Let's go before we lose them."

Jackson fastened his seat belt, then waited while Trace pulled out of the lot, keeping a discreet distance from Spencer. But it bothered him, chewing on his mind.

He didn't like for Arizona to underestimate her appeal, and he hated for her to use herself as bait. "She sees herself as a commodity, ya know?"

Trace said nothing to that.

"She thinks she's a body with a price, but not so much as a woman with boner-inspiring sex appeal."

Trace glanced at him with a lifted brow.

"Not *my* boner!" Good God, he'd turned her down, hadn't he? "Hell, you know how I feel about Alani. I don't want any other woman. I haven't wanted anyone else since meeting her."

"Let's don't belabor the point."

Jackson paid no attention to Trace's discomfort. "I mean, I can see if a woman's sexy. I'm not blind. But I'm immune to—"

That made Trace roll his eyes. "You don't have to convince me. I'm not blind, either, so I know what you mean."

"My point is that Spencer's going to have a time of it. Course, he's not in love with anyone else, so he doesn't have to feel guilty for paying attention."

"No," Trace agreed, "but his conscience isn't going to let him forget her past."

"Thank God." Jackson shifted when they spotted Spencer's truck up ahead, saying low, "If he did forget, I'd have to stomp on him. And all in all, I like him, so I'd rather it didn't come to that."

"If you tried it, Arizona might have something to say about it."

"You think?"

"We both noticed how Spencer reacted to her." He glanced at Jackson. "But did you notice how she reacted to him?"

Jackson thought about it, then groaned. "Yeah, you're right. She walked past me to him—thank God. But know what?"

Trace lifted his brows.

Jackson grinned. "Now I sort of feel sorry for Spencer."

They both laughed over that.

ARIZONA WAITED AS LONG as she could. But truthfully, the silence was getting to her. "All right, give. What's all the fuss about?"

As Spencer pulled into a fast-food lot, he glanced at her. "You."

"What'd I do?"

He got behind a line of cars waiting to put in orders. "You walked out looking like…" His gaze flickered over to her again. "That."

She adjusted the neckline of the top, tugging it a little lower, rearranging the neckline to display the most cleavage—and heard Spencer's indrawn breath.

With a roll of her eyes, she said, "Get a grip, Spence. You've seen low-cut tops before."

"Yeah, well…" He shifted uncomfortably. "There are low-cut tops, and there are low-cut tops."

"Meaning?"

"You're showing an awful lot."

"And you've seen plenty of boobs."

He groused something she didn't catch.

"If I look all prim and proper, or like my usual boring self in plain jeans and a T-shirt, how effective would that be for getting attention? I want to make sure they notice me."

He gave a grunt of disbelief. "That's not going to be a problem."

"So I look like a desperate little nympho? Like I'd be easy to pick up?"

"You look..." He trailed off, shook his head. "Never mind."

"What?" She reached over and smacked his shoulder. "Come on. What were you going to say?"

He gave her a long, slow perusal, then shrugged. "You look edible."

"Oh." She wasn't sure what to make of that. "Glad you approve."

Rubbing the back of his neck, Spencer stared out the windshield. As cars eased forward, he followed. When they were next in line, he asked, "What do you want to eat?"

"Are you buying?"

His sigh was long and dramatic. "Yes."

"Then I'll take a cheeseburger, loaded, except for onion. Fries, and a strawberry milk shake."

He gave her a long look, then rolled the truck up to the window and doubled her order but made his milk shake chocolate. "We have some time to kill, so while we talk about the plan, we'll ride to the park to eat."

"I think I have it all down, but sure, if you want to go over it again—"

"I do."

He'd been a stickler about details, something she admired. "The park sounds nice, but won't it be muddy?"

"We're staying in the truck." He gave a nod at her bare legs. "I'm keeping you under wraps."

Disappointed that they wouldn't get to enjoy the fresh

air, she wrinkled her nose. "Considering I'll soon be in a bar flaunting my wares, hiding now is sort of dumb, right?"

"This plan is dumb. If it was up to me, we'd scrap it all now before anyone sees you."

Her plan was perfect! How dare he call it dumb?

"But at least Dare agreed to come along to oversee things."

"Having Dare around is always a plus, but I figured you could handle it."

"If it was just me, if I didn't have to worry about you, then sure. No problem. But anything could go wrong, and we have no idea how many thugs might be inside the bar."

"When I was there before, I only saw a few."

"Doesn't mean there aren't more. I can handle myself, and I've gotten out of plenty of sticky situations. But not with a woman along." He flashed a hot glare her way. "And definitely not with a woman who looks like you."

She assumed he meant a woman who deliberately sought their attention. "Better safe than sorry, I guess." The last thing she wanted was for Spencer to get hurt trying to protect her.

"Exactly. So if Dare sends the code for us to get out, that's what we're doing. Got it?"

"Sure."

"I mean it, Arizona. No arguments. No hesitation. Doesn't matter what else might be happening."

"Yeah, got it. Don't beat it into the ground."

Unconvinced, he scowled. "I'm serious. No matter what—"

"I'm to turn tail and run the second you give the word. I got it already. Sheesh."

After a final long look, he rolled up to take his turn at paying for and collecting the food.

She stewed in silence while he got his change and then pulled away.

Though he kept stealing quick glances at her, he drove in silence, saying nothing for the longest time. That annoyed her, too, and finally she couldn't take it. "You realize you're playing the Neanderthal, right?"

He pulled into the park, which was all but deserted this time of the day. "And you're being naive."

"Ha!" That had to be a joke. "How naive can I be after—"

"Damn it to hell, Arizona!" After jerking the truck into an isolated area and parking, he turned to face her. "Don't say it."

Whoa. He looked really pissed, and that surprised her, but oddly, it sort of amused her. Putting on an innocent face, she asked, "Say what?"

He opened his seat belt and leaned toward her. "Don't put yourself down. Don't throw up your past as an excuse to put yourself in danger. And don't use the things that were forced on you as a way to demean yourself."

"Yeah, uh, the demeaning was forced on me—like you said."

His hand slashed the air. "And that's over. That's not who you are." His gaze raked her body. "This isn't who you are."

A slow burn started. She opened her seat belt, too, and leaned into his anger.

Anger on her behalf.

"Actually, it's exactly who I am." He started to speak, but she knotted a hand in his shirt and gave him a yank. "I am a vigilante, Spence. Get used to it."

"No."

"I'm strong and I'm smart," she added. "And my plan is *not* dumb."

Something glittered in his eyes. Taunting her, he said, "You can't even bear to have me kiss you. What the hell will you do when a stranger gets hold of you?"

Her attention went to his mouth. Was he thinking about kissing her again? "You're the one spewing taboo words."

Frustration escalating, he took her wrist, making her hold on his shirt redundant. "What the hell are you talking about?"

She locked gazes with him and took great pleasure in saying, "I haven't cussed, but you have."

"So? I already agreed to take you to Jackson's wedding." He shook his head. "And stop changing the subject."

"I will. Just as soon as I find out what your new penalty will be. After all, you've cussed twice. So I should get something, right?"

Time stretched out, and new tension filled the air. "What do you want?"

She was starting to want…a lot of things. Unusual things. Things she thought she'd never again accept, much less crave. His warm breath teased her mouth; she could hear her own heartbeat in her ears.

Dragging in a shuddering breath, she whispered, "I can bear it."

"You're confusing the hell out of me, honey."

Nothing new there. Around Spencer, she even confused herself. "When you kiss me," she spelled out. "I can bear it."

His thumb moved over the pulse in her wrist. "The way I've kissed you is not what I'm talking about."

"I know." She rolled a shoulder. "But tonight will be a starting point, a get-to-know-you period. Odds are they'll just check the boundaries, to see how much they can get away with."

"And if someone pushes past your comfort zone?"

"I'll figure it out."

He lifted her knuckles to his mouth, doing more of his specialized kissing, then put his forehead to hers. "Truthfully, Arizona, I have no doubt you can pull this off."

Matching his whisper, she said, "Then what's the problem?"

"If Terry Janes touches you, if he even looks at you funny, I might have to take him apart." He stole a soft kiss from her mouth, taking her by surprise, then settled back into his seat. "And that's a problem."

That quick, sweet smooch left her temporarily dazed. He'd done that so casually, as if they'd kissed a million times, and it took a moment for his words to sink in. She skipped past most of what he'd said—Spencer would be a professional, she had no doubt about that—to focus on the name he'd just given. "Terry Janes?"

"I told you the bar was already on Trace's radar."

No way. A little numb, she asked, "Terry is the guy running things? The tatted guy I already noticed?"

Spencer nodded. "He works the place. We don't know yet who's running the show, though."

She really, really wanted to slug him. "And you just now thought to tell me this?"

"You," he said, leaning toward her again, "snuck out on me. Otherwise we'd have hashed all this out after my shower."

Her fist trembled.

"Do it." Challenge, and something more, darkened his eyes. "I dare you."

It was *soooo* tempting to wipe that smirk off his face…but no. Why give him what he wanted?

"I should. I *could*." She checked a fingernail, the epitome of indifference. "But I'm not in my kick-ass clothes, and we have business later, so I can't get mussed. I'm remembering our purpose for being here, even if you aren't."

"It'd be tough to forget with you dressed like that."

He did seem hung up on her clothes. Arizona held her arms out to her sides and looked down at herself. "It's tame compared to what the traffickers had me wear. I wasn't sure if it was racy enough, but given how you keep going on, I guess it's appropriate."

"I want to go on the record here."

"I'm listening."

Reaching out, he fingered the hem of her short skirt. His knuckles brushed the inside of her right thigh and stilled her pounding heartbeat. "You don't need this." He nodded at her top. "Or that. You can wear your jeans and a regular top of some kind, and I swear to you, every straight guy around will go on alert."

Interesting. "You're sure of that?"

"Positive."

"What if he's a guy like Trace or Jackson—"

"They noticed." He trailed a fingertip over her knee… and then dropped his hand. "The difference is that they can appreciate how you look without thinking to take advantage of you, or put the make on you."

"I'll keep that in mind."

Blowing out an exasperated breath, he looked out the window, studying the area around them. "Arizona…" He worked his jaw before stabbing her with a look of determination. "I'm going to have to insist."

"You're doing a lot of that."

"Sorry, but I'm only a man, and I'm doing my best here."

She had no idea what he meant.

"I don't want to push you."

"And if I'm dressed sexy, you might?"

"When you dress like that, I have a harder time concentrating on what it is I want to do."

"Like tease me?" Oh, God, now she was putting ideas in his head!

"Exactly." He smiled with anticipation. "And speaking of that… You cursed."

Oh, no, she wouldn't let him get away with that. "But you did first, so we canceled each other out."

"Doesn't work that way." Somehow, without seeming to move, he crowded closer again. "Our bet was that you would curb your language, and pay a price whenever you didn't."

Refusing to act uncertain, she lifted her chin. "Fine. I owe ya one." He started to lean in, and she straightarmed him. "But you'll have to collect later."

He immediately stopped.

Nice. Not that she'd expected him to do otherwise. "I'll pay up, but fair is fair—so you owe me, too."

He sat back, his left wrist draped over the steering wheel, his right arm along the back of the seat. After a moment of consideration, he shrugged. "What do you want?"

"Details."

"Not a problem." He gave her a lazy, indulgent smile. "I was going to tell you all I could about the Green Goose anyway."

Arizona shook her head. "Not those details."

"No?" His right eyebrow lifted. "Then what?"

"We'll cover that later, too." Satisfied by his frown, she opened the bag of fast food, and fragrant steam wafted out. "Mmm. Let's eat before the burgers get cold." She handed him his share of the food, then opened up the fries and set them on the console between them.

Large trees shaded their parking spot, so Spencer rolled down the windows to let in the fresh September air. Birds flitted from tree to tree. Bees buzzed. A breeze teased past.

"It's such a pretty day after the storms."

With a sound of agreement, Spencer opened the burger and took a big bite. While she dug in, too, she watched him, amazed at how quickly he consumed his food. She imagined it took a lot of fuel to keep a guy his size going.

While studying his profile, Arizona again noted the permanent damage done to the bridge of his nose. "How did you break your nose?"

His gaze, which had been focused off in the distance, cut to her. He finished chewing another big bite of his burger, then touched the bridge of his nose with two fingertips. "It bothers you?"

Arizona snorted. "No." Not much could detract from his good looks. He was the whole package, not just a handsome face. "Actually, it makes you look rugged."

That earned her a crooked smile. "If you say so." He grabbed a few more fries.

"So what happened? Walk me through it."

"There's not much to tell." He half turned, getting comfortable with his shoulders propped against the door. "I was closing in on this guy, Willy Glassman. A world-class jerk. Domestic abuse, battery, resisting arrest...

You name it, and old Willy was probably guilty of it. After he skipped out on his bail, I tracked him for weeks. Finally found him, too, in this old farmhouse sitting out in the middle of nowhere. He and a couple of buddies were on the front porch, going through a case of beer."

"Buddies?"

"I found out later they were his brother and a cousin. They were all three loud, drunk, and I was figuring out how to grab Willy with the least amount of fuss…" He trailed off, shook his head.

"What?" Rarely had she seen Spencer look so imposing. "Something happened?"

Rubbing the back of his neck, he thought for a second, then grabbed up his milk shake. Arizona gave him time to sort through things. She knew better than most how lousy some memories could be.

"I got sidetracked."

The way he said that, it almost sounded like… "The guy got away?"

"Yeah." Putting his head back against the window, Spencer narrowed his eyes and firmed his mouth. "I never did catch him. Someone else eventually brought him in."

Incredulity took her breath. Because Spencer was a lot like her—determined to succeed—Arizona knew that wouldn't sit right with him. He was not a person who took failure lightly. Whatever had sidetracked him had to be good. "What happened?"

He chewed his upper lip, then laughed without humor. "Until I got closer, I hadn't realized what they were doing on the porch. I didn't know they had a…"

Arizona watched him swallow. She reached out and touched his knee.

He covered her hand with his own. "They were tormenting a dog."

"Tormenting?"

"Being really cruel. The poor dog was tied to a high post so that its front paws..."

Arizona covered her mouth, imagining.

"They were strangling the poor thing for sport."

"Bastards!"

He nodded agreement. "I saw that animal, saw what they were doing, and I totally lost it." He wrapped her fingers in his own, gave her a squeeze, and then released her. "Instead of biding my time and waiting for the right moment to grab Glassman, I fired a few shots so they'd take cover in the house, then I cut the dog's rope."

Thank God he carried a sharp knife. "You let them all get away?"

His laugh was harsh. "No. As soon as the dog was free, I busted into the house and beat the shit out of them."

"No kidding? I would have loved to see that."

Pausing, he gave her a funny look, laughed again and shook his head. "It was stupid. If one of them had been armed, I might not be here now."

"Not a one of them had a gun?"

"Glassman did, but he ran. I guess the other two were supposed to slow me down. And they did. I held my own, but somewhere along the way I took a kick to the face, and it broke my nose."

Enthralled, Arizona watched him with wide eyes and heightened anticipation. "Knocked you out?"

"Just made me bloody, actually, and more furious." As if he were enraged all over again, his left hand clenched. "I leveled them both, breaking a few bones and crippling a knee. But before you start looking impressed, they were punks, nothing more. You could have taken them."

Affronted by the demeaning way he said that, she scowled. "Gee, thanks."

Sidestepping her pique, he continued. "I cuffed them and called the cops. I was going to cut out after Willy, but as soon as I left the house, I saw the dog was still there. He'd left the porch and was cowering in the bushes, snarling and growling at me and..." He shook his head and his voice lowered. "I couldn't leave him."

Her heart turned over. Could Spencer be more appealing? She didn't think so.

"Turns out they had several outstanding warrants. Last I heard, they were still rotting in prison—which is where they both belong."

"Nice." Knowing better than most how badly reality could suck, she hated to ask, but she had to know. "What happened to the dog?"

"Animal control wanted to take him. He was obviously hurt, a little wild and scared." Spencer looked at her. "He didn't want to trust anyone."

Oh, no. *No, no, no.* He drew comparisons between her and the dog. Similarities existed, so she couldn't blame him, but she didn't want him to go there.

"He was a German shepherd mix, smart and, except for the signs of neglect, really beautiful." Holding her gaze, Spencer surprised her by saying softly, "I took him with me."

While Arizona appreciated his kindness and was grateful that he hadn't abandoned the dog, she didn't want him to see her the same way. Abused, yes. Angry, you betcha. Distrustful? Of course.

But she wasn't helpless as the animal had been—

because she refused to be. She'd taken charge of her life, and she wanted Spencer to see her as a capable person.

She wanted him to see her as an equal.

It took a couple of slow, deep breaths before she could find her voice. "You're a regular rescuer of strays, aren't you?" Hurt made her sound sharper than she meant to.

As if her sarcasm saddened him, Spencer focused on the woods beyond, at nothing in particular. "It took a while, but he finally healed. He started playing again, relaxing. He let down his guard."

"Where is he now?"

"A good friend of mine is a vet. He helped me work with Trooper. He kept him when I was away, and he monitored his recovery."

"Trooper?"

"That's what I named him." He shrugged. "Anyway, my friend has kids and a big fenced yard, lots of company. Trooper is happy there."

"You visit him?"

"Sometimes."

The similarities were annoying. Just like poor Trooper, Spence wanted to rehabilitate her, "repair" her and then pawn her off on someone else.

Over her dead body.

After slurping down the rest of her milk shake, she decided it was time to change the subject. "So you like animals?" That sounded innocuous enough.

"Sure." He finished off his drink, too. "But I'm not home enough to have one of my own. It wouldn't be fair."

"Same here." She'd love to actually have a home— and everything that went with it. Pets, grass to cut, windows to wash, photos to hang on the walls...

But fate had dealt her a different hand, so that'd have to be in another lifetime.

Agitated by the thought, she began stuffing the empty wrappers and paper cups back into the bag.

Spencer helped.

"I love being around Dare's dogs," she said, just to fill the sudden silence. "Tai and Sargie are total sweeties. And Priss's big cat, Liger, is such a lover-boy."

Spencer grinned. "Good thing he's friendly, since he's so big."

"Twenty-three pounds of loving," Arizona agreed.

He took the bag from her. "What do you think of Grim?"

Jackson's new cat, recently rescued in the middle of a mission, was the newest of the bunch. "The name suits him. He tries to act all dour, but he sure loves Jackson." She tilted her face up to boast, "He likes me a lot, too. Most animals like me."

Affection showed in Spencer's slight smile and dark eyes. "Animals are a good judge of character."

He sounded so sincere, so honestly admiring, that it struck Arizona—maybe fighting him wasn't the best plan anymore. Maybe, instead, she should take advantage of his unique offer. How many hunky, honorable, heroic guys would ever cross her path?

Spencer wanted her, but he put that want second to concern for her—regardless of whether or not she warranted his concern. He butted heads with her without losing his temper. He trusted in her honor enough to make deals with her.

He smiled with her, was honest, and she respected him.

Would it hurt to explore the unfamiliar feelings he inspired?

When Spencer leaned into her view, she realized she'd been staring off into space, lost in thought.

He gave her a crooked smile. "You still with me, honey?"

"Yeah, sorry." Even to her, the release of her breath sounded like a fanciful sigh. "I was just thinking."

"About?" he prompted.

"Nothing much." She nudged him with her shoulder. "We should get a move on. I don't want to risk missing the key players."

Curiosity kept him studying her until her smile faltered. "Soon as I throw this away, we can take off." He opened the truck door and stepped out to dispose of the garbage in a nearby trash bin.

As he walked away from her, Arizona indulged her own study. Everything about him drew her in one way or another: the flex of muscles in his long thighs, how his T-shirt fit across his wide shoulders, the way the wind ruffled his dark hair, his protective nature, and his badass aura of capability.

Most of all, she liked his big heart.

He'd given up a percentage of the bail on a fugitive so that he could rescue an abused dog.

How could she remain indifferent to that? She'd have done the same thing, but she knew plenty of other people who, either out of apathy, laziness, or fear, turned a blind eye to all sorts of cruelty.

But not Spencer. In the truest sense of the word, he was a champion.

She sighed as he returned from tossing away the garbage. Alert to the surroundings, his gaze constantly scanned the area, but not in a paranoid way. He looked casual, unconcerned—and so incredibly hot.

The front view was even better than the back view.

The set of those wide, powerful shoulders, the relaxed lope of his long-legged gait...the way his jeans fit his lean hips.

Spencer Lark was the real deal, an amazing mix of macho ability and tender compassion, sex appeal and physical strength, kick-ass justice and an enormous heart.

If she'd ever felt this way before, she didn't remember it. She knew no other man had ever drawn her as Spencer did. It was strange, but she couldn't deny that she looked forward to his next kiss. Would it be more intimate than the previous kisses?

Remembering them gave her a tiny shiver of eagerness.

Just a little while ago, he'd stolen a quick kiss straight from her lips.

Would he kiss her there again? Longer next time? Deeper?

Did she want him to?

Yep, she did.

Tonight, she'd be alone with him at his house again. After they finished their trip to the bar, maybe she'd tell him what she wanted. Or maybe she just wouldn't protest. This was all so new to her that she really had no idea how to proceed.

But she'd figure it out, and fast.

Spencer got back into the truck, settled into his seat and gave her a double take. "You're looking at me funny." His gaze went to her mouth. "Daydreaming again?"

"Sort of." She felt suddenly free, and that made no sense. Soon they'd be in the center of a viper's nest. Bad guys needed to be brought down, and innocents needed to be freed. And still the grin tugged at her mouth. To contain the euphoric feeling, Arizona wrapped her arms around herself. "I was just thinking that I really do trust you."

He went still, his expression inscrutable. "Glad to hear it."

Arizona had to laugh. Of course he didn't try to press the issue. Not Spencer. He still saw her as damaged goods, and he still wanted to "fix" her. But somehow, that didn't bother her so much anymore. She knew she was fine, and eventually he'd know it, too.

She gave him a nod. "Okay."

He spoke carefully. "Okay what?"

No way would she forewarn him. He wanted the upper hand, and right now, he thought he had it. That worked for her. As long as he considered himself in control, he wouldn't see her taking over.

"Never mind." Trying not to grin, she flipped down the visor and checked her teeth in the mirror. "Nothing stuck in my teeth. That's good."

"Hey." He reached for her hand, drawing her attention back to him. "Everything okay?"

"Yup." Things were awesome, better than ever, because *she* felt awesome, better than ever.

Apparently, he didn't buy that. "You aren't having reservations about going to the Green Goose?"

"Shoot, no." If anything, she was more enthusiastic than ever.

He held on to her hand. "It'd be understandable, honey. Even if Terry Janes doesn't pick up on the..." his attention moved over her "...enticement, other guys will come on to you. They'll be drinking, probably pushy."

"Yeah, I know." Duh. That was the plan. She squeezed his hand in reassurance, then let him go. "But it'll be okay. Don't worry. I've done this sort of thing before, remember? I can handle it."

Expression darkening, he pulled back and started the truck. "You handling it is what I'm worried about the most."

"Well, don't." She hooked her seat belt and gifted him with a cocky smile. "We've got the bases covered, so there's nothing to worry about. Now let's get this show on the road."

CHAPTER TEN

WORRY? HOW COULD HE NOT? Arizona showed no caution, no real understanding of the risk involved. She acted as if it was all fun and games, showing the same enthusiasm for cutthroat danger that most young ladies her age gave to a shopping spree.

She might not comprehend the temptation she presented in her sexier clothes, but he knew, and the reality of it chewed on his conscience. No matter what the final reward might be, dangling her out there for traffickers to drool over didn't sit right.

It felt more wrong by the moment.

"You look p.o.'d." With her good mood dwindling, she tipped her head at him. "What'd I do wrong now?"

"Not a thing." It wasn't what she had done as much as how she faced the world—recklessly, with no consideration for her own safety or limitations. Spencer had no idea how to rein her in. At times he wondered if such a thing was possible.

"Hmm." She shocked him with a suggestive look. "Your mouth says one thing, but your mood says another."

What the hell is she up to now? Treading carefully, he said, "Unlike you, I understand that the best laid plans have a tendency to go sideways."

"Poor Spencer." She eyed his chest, lower. "Did you want me to fall apart?"

He scowled at her husky tone. "Of course not." What was she thinking about that had her sounding so breathless? "You don't need to be overly worried, but a degree of caution would be welcome."

"So..." Deliberately teasing and intimate, she leaned toward him. "How much caution does it take to make you chill?" She stroked the side of his neck, threaded her fingers into his hair.

The touch froze him, left him so taut he felt ready to break. Spencer concentrated on driving—and on not getting a boner.

"Would it make you feel better," she continued, "if I was a little scared, maybe a little needy?"

"God, no." She'd lived enough of her life in fear. As his body stirred, he locked his teeth. "But you don't have to be so damn happy about it, either."

Her cool fingers moved over his neck. "Is that what attracted you to Marla?"

"What?" Following along wasn't easy, not while she touched him without fear. Not when her posture showed off her cleavage. Not with her voice all husky and deep.

Crossing her legs, she went more or less sideways in the seat to better face him. "Marla." In contrast to what she said, she turned her hand and drifted her knuckles over his jaw, under his chin. "Were you drawn to her because she's a typically helpless female?"

With her skirt hiking even higher, of course he looked at her legs. Again. They were so smooth, slim but shapely. And he could almost imagine them open to him or wrapped around his waist.

Or warm against his jaw...

Damn.

On the one hand, it surprised Spencer that Arizona would utilize blatant female ploys. But on the other hand…he knew better than to ever underestimate her. She used those ploys for a reason…he had to figure out why.

Unsure of her endgame, he took care with his reply. The last thing he wanted to do was make Marla more of a target; Arizona already didn't like her. "She's a successful Realtor, an independent woman who owns her own home. I wouldn't call that helpless." But Marla did like to play off the idea of a single woman alone. More often than not, the ruse compelled him to lend a hand.

"Maybe for her, *calculating* is a better word choice, then."

"Is that jealousy talking?" Given Arizona's mercurial mood swings, he had reason to worry.

Finally drawing her hand away, Arizona scowled. "Why would I be jealous?"

"I have no idea. She's just a neighbor—"

"That you *slept* with."

Right. Definitely tones of jealousy. Figuring her out could take a lifetime. "I've slept with a lot of women…"

Affront stiffened her spine. "Big whoop. I've slept with—"

"Don't." Muscles suddenly tense, Spencer worked his jaw. He did not want her drawing comparisons between consensual sex and human trafficking. "It's not the same thing."

Gently, she whispered, "Yeah, I know." She retreated to look out the window.

He missed her touch, especially since she'd replaced it with the chill of her cold shoulder. "What are you up to?"

She shook her head. "Nothing."

"Something," he corrected.

Her mouth pursed, her eyes narrowed. "Forget it."

Like hell. "Arizona…"

Shaking off her melancholy, she cut in to say, "Don't forget to drop me off near a bus stop so I can arrive separate from you."

He flexed his hands on the steering wheel. "I know what I'm doing."

"Yeah, you're kind of being an ass."

He paused before pointing out, "Now you owe me two."

"Kisses? Good. Great."

That earned her another double take. "Is that a joke?"

Her blue-eyed gaze gave away her simmering temper. "Why not?" In a tone more flippant than not, she curled her lip and said, "You kiss like a schoolboy anyway."

Well, hell. He hadn't seen that coming. "Let me make sure I understand this." He glanced at her elevated chin. "You're complaining about how I've kissed you?"

She didn't deny or confirm that. "Maybe I should really let you have it, and go for an even dozen."

"Kisses?" His heart punched into his ribs. "Yeah, maybe you should."

Mulish, she crossed her arms, swung her foot in agitation and went back to staring out the window.

"Come on, honey." He turned down the route toward where Dare waited. He'd ensure that Arizona made it onto the bus without issue, and then Dare would tail her to the bar. "Talk to me. What's going on?"

"Until you started admiring Marla, I was having a good time."

"I wasn't *admiring* her." Just like a woman to twist things around. "You asked a question and I answered it."

"Whatever."

That flippant response annoyed him even more. "Forget about Marla already, will you?" He didn't want her walking into the bar pissed off over nonsense. He wanted, needed, for her to bring her A-game by being calm and collected. "For the last time, she's only a neighbor."

"Hey, I hear you, but I don't think Marla got the memo."

"God Almighty, woman. Seriously? We don't have enough to keep us occupied tonight without you picking a fight?"

Going still, she stared at him, then groaned. She dropped her head back and closed her eyes. "Yeah, all right." A second or two passed, and she half laughed. "I didn't mean to ruin things by nitpicking."

"Things?"

She flagged a hand between them. "The little picnic was nice."

Exasperation got the better of him. "Eating fast food in the front of a truck at a deserted park prior to using yourself as bait to draw in the worst type of creep doesn't count as a picnic."

She blinked at that long string of nonsense. "Oh, well..." She opened her purse and got out a stick of gum. "It did for me."

Shit. Now he felt like a jerk. "Yeah," he reluctantly admitted. "Me, too."

"Uh-huh." She popped the gum into her mouth, folded the wrapper, and put it in the ashtray. "And here you just said you wouldn't lie."

"It's odd, no denying that, but so far I've enjoyed every minute with you. For sure, you'll never bore me." He thought it prudent to add, "Not that I share your enthusiasm for our agenda tonight."

She chewed her gum and, through the car window,

watched the scenery pass by. "You'll see. I can take care of myself."

Because she'd always had to.

But not anymore, not with him. And thinking of all the ways he wanted to care for her, he asked, "What's your favorite place to eat?" She deserved to be pampered. Dinners out, movies, maybe some dancing...

"Hmm." She gave it very little thought. "I don't know." She rolled one shoulder. "The dinner you cooked the other day was about the best I've ever had. Especially the cake."

"There's plenty left. If you want to pig out, we can finish it off tonight."

"Sounds like a plan." She gave him a quick smile. "But it was so good, I'd rather savor it."

"No need. There will be another cake at Dare's, I'm sure."

She groaned. "Don't remind me."

The small gathering was meant to make her happy, not fill her with dread. "Not looking forward to it?"

"I appreciate the sentiment, but...I hate being the center of attention, you know?"

"I'm guessing it won't be the hardship you're imagining." Once she was there, she'd enjoy herself. Somehow he'd see to it. To keep her from dwelling on it, he said, "Since you'll be staying with me, is there anything in particular you'd like me to stock up on? More sweets maybe?"

She shrugged. "If you want cookies, hey, I won't argue."

"I can make a grocery store run. And I like cooking, so if you have a preference for dinners, just let me know."

"Except for weapons, I'm not real picky."

He did not want to talk weapons with her again. "Steak? Chicken? Come on, give me a clue."

Indifferent, she offered no suggestion. "I've never really been a foodie, you know? I eat when I'm hungry, at any place that's cheap but clean. I mean, I don't want squid or snails or anything. No fish with their faces still on there. But otherwise, if you cook it, I promise I'll like it."

"Yeah, I'm not big on fish with faces, either." He turned along a road leading into a more congested commercial area. He'd have to drop her off soon—and he was dreading it already. "You specified it had to be cheap?"

"My funds are limited, remember? Especially right now. I mean, Jackson tries to overpay me for doing a little computer work, but…" She shuddered. "I detest taking charity."

"It's not—"

"Yeah, it is," she insisted, "no matter how Jackson denies it. But since I haven't held up any dealers lately—"

"Jesus, I hope not." He hadn't even considered the possibility. "If you even *think* of—"

"You're not my boss," she interjected, "*and* I haven't been focused on gambling. So…" She held up her hands, philosophical about her meager possessions. "I have the basic necessities. More than enough to get by."

Later he'd deal with the idea of her mugging criminals. For now, he wanted to talk about the few bags she kept in her trunk. "What about clothes?"

"You haven't seen me running around naked, have you?"

A clear visual struck his beleaguered brain. *No, but I want to.* Out of self-preservation, he cut to the chase.

"What you have in the trunk and in your overnight bag...is that all you own?"

"Sheesh, get rid of the long face, will you? I keep things simple for a reason."

"Being?"

"When you have things, property that's important to you, then someone can take it away."

Damn, but that was a sad attitude. "No photos? No jewelry?"

"Yeah, right. Photos of what?" She touched the hoop in her earlobe. "I have a few pairs of earrings, some bracelets and stuff that I wear when I'm working. Otherwise, that stuff just gets in my way."

Working. God, he'd never get used to her thinking in those terms. "So you don't care about fashion?"

That earned an honest laugh. "Do I look like a fashion plate to you? I have enough clothes that I don't have to do laundry every day. And once I get their attention in this getup, I can revert back to my more comfortable duds. Anything more just takes up space and ties me down."

So many times, in so many ways, she broke his heart without even trying. He pulled up to the curb. He hated to say it but knew she wouldn't turn back now. "The bus stop is around the corner, two blocks down."

She undid her seat belt. "I'll find it."

Unable to help himself, Spencer caught her arm. Her bare skin was silky soft, warm. "Promise me you'll be careful."

"You got it."

He was far from reassured. "Don't forget that I'll be watching. Don't go anywhere that I can't see you."

A huff of exasperation. "That's a given."

And still he couldn't make himself let her go. "Dare

will ghost you to the bus stop, then follow along until you get off the bus near the bar."

"If that's what he wants to do, I'm okay with it." She reached for the door handle. "I sort of figured he'd do something like that anyway. In some ways, he, Trace and Jackson are pretty predictable."

Was she disappointed that Jackson hadn't come along tonight instead? Spencer shook his head, refusing to let his mind go there right now. "The bus lets you out right by the Green Goose."

"I *know*. I scoped out the area myself."

"I have all of Dare's codes. If you see me check my phone, you know something is going on. Remember, if this plan goes off the rails—"

"Spencer, I promise. I'll be good. I'll pay attention. I'll stay out of danger."

He rubbed his thumb over her meager biceps. "I really hate this."

After an indulgent look, Arizona released the door handle and settled back in her seat. "Know what?"

Had she finally come to her senses? "What?"

She took out her gum, placed it back in the wrapper and put it in the ashtray again.

Then, before Spencer realized her intent, she turned to him, braced her hands on his shoulders and leaned in to brush a kiss over his mouth.

Everything male within him froze before going red-hot. Not grabbing her close was one of the hardest things he'd ever done. He settled his hands on her narrow waist and relished her freely given affection. "It's not too late—"

"Shh." Against his lips, she whispered, "Keep your powder dry, Spence. It's going to be fine." She kissed him again, a light butterfly kiss, and then she pulled away. "You have my word."

SITTING IN HIS TRUCK stewing, Spencer watched the entrance to the bar. Arizona should be showing up shortly.

He hated this.

Not once had he seen Dare, so he put in a quick call to the number given him.

Dare Macintosh answered on the first ring. "Problem?"

Spencer stared down the street, but the bus didn't show. "Do you see her?"

"Of course." There was a moment of silence, and then, half under his breath, Dare said, "She'd be hard to miss."

"I know." Spencer rubbed his forehead. "The outfit wasn't my idea, believe me."

"Not sure we can blame the clothes. On another woman, that skirt and top would be no big deal. On Arizona, it spells a lot of trouble."

Suffering his own twinge of jealousy, Spencer growled, "I know."

"Do you?" Dare went right to the point. "You're going to have your hands full tonight. I suggest you get yourself together."

What the hell did that mean? "You have something to say to me?"

Lacking any real inflection, almost as if he was sharing the weather report, Dare said, "You're personally invested and that's not a good thing."

The censure cut. "I know what I'm doing."

"When it comes to Arizona? I doubt it. You're letting her screw with your head."

Instead of trying to deny that, he pointed out the obvious. "You were personally invested when you went after Alani, and when you rescued your wife, Molly."

"I'm not you."

Hell, no denying that. Spencer knew he could hold his own, but Dare was in a special league, shared only by Trace and Jackson.

"Right." It occurred to Spencer that he sounded bitchy. He drew a deep breath, then another. It didn't help. "If it was any woman other than Arizona—"

"You could be detached and calculating. I know. Arizona doesn't exactly make it easy to stay uninvolved."

Finally seeing the bus, Spencer wrapped it up. "She's here."

"I know."

Of course he did. Cutting back a growl of frustration, Spencer said, "If you see anything, if you even suspect something might be going down—"

"I'll send you one of the codes we went over. Don't mix them up."

Spencer ground his molars together. He looked around again and still saw no sight of Dare anywhere. Stealthy bastard. "I've got them memorized. Later."

The second he disconnected the phone, he saw Arizona step off the bus and look around as if she'd never seen a lighted, flashy, busy bar before. Already two guys were hitting on her, one who looked around forty, one probably closer to her own age.

They both appeared charmed by her shy smiles and reserved manner.

Flexing his hands on the steering wheel, Spencer forced himself to sit still in the truck cab and observe without seeming to stare. That he'd pulled up across the street, in the shadows, helped him to go unnoticed.

Watching Arizona with the men, he had to admit that

she just might be able to pull this off. He saw her as others would; her air of confidence gone, a show of vulnerability masking her bravado. A deliberate ruse, but still, he couldn't stop staring. His chest hurt, his nostrils flared.

Despite her lack of invitation, the older man kept trying to look down her top, and the younger guy leaned back to check out her ass. Bastards.

But he'd expected no less. She looked amazingly hot while playing the innocent.

Not good.

Not good at all.

Damn, maybe he liked the helpless female act more than he'd ever realized.

For sure, he liked it on Arizona.

After giving her a minute to sidle away from the men and enter the bar, he drove up the block and around the corner to park. Later, when she called it quits for the night, they'd be able to leave together in his truck with no one the wiser.

Even knowing Dare watched over her, Spencer found it difficult to hold back, to give her time to get settled in the bar. With awful scenarios prominent in his mind, he locked up and strode along the sidewalk quietly, constantly scanning the area for any nosy onlookers.

He saw none.

Flickering white neon lights, shaped like a goose, wrapped around the words GREEN GOOSE. Beneath that, red neon spelled BAR AND GRILL, though no one would mistake the priorities of the establishment. Thick bars secured the windows, but given the area, it looked like the norm.

Above the door, a lighted banner said, EAT, DRINK, RELAX, and another sign advertised, WOMEN, WOMEN,

WOMEN! with the shapely silhouette of a busty figure beside it. Combined, the lights sent a fuzzy glow into the dark night, barely illuminating the hulking shape of an empty building on the opposite side of an alley. Beside that was a gas station. To the other side of the bar was a mom-and-pop convenience store, now closed, and beyond that, a tattoo parlor, also closed for the night.

All in all, it was an ominous, dreary, run-down area.

As Spencer approached the entrance, several women eyed him, smiling with invitation while advertising their wares.

Hookers, he decided.

Working for the bar owner? Probably. He smiled back—and walked past them into loud music and disorienting strobe lights. It took his eyes a moment to adjust.

Dim, mellow lights hung over booths in the sitting and eating area. A brighter light shone over the bar and bar stools but didn't quite reach to the seating area, leaving plenty of shadows to swallow up shady deals and lustful assignations—and with every flashing illumination, he saw a few of each.

Discreetly, he scanned the interior until he spotted Arizona at the bar. As he watched, she knocked back a shot of whiskey. Judging by the shot glasses in front of her, it wasn't her first.

Damn.

What the hell was she thinking? But when he saw the smiling bartender hand her another, he knew. Someone had already sent her the drinks. Things were moving fast. Too fast.

So SHE HAD RETURNED.

He'd hoped she would, but she was so hot, so cocky,

and so different from the others, that seeing her here now, within reach, almost surprised him.

It definitely pleased him.

Rubbing his mouth, he scrutinized her face, her body.

She'd be perfect, the best yet, the most valuable. And he would have her.

The power of it surged through his veins.

Oh, she thought herself protected. She thought herself immune.

But now that he'd set his sights on her, now that she'd come back, she would be his.

Nothing and no one would change that outcome.

SPENCER SEATED HIMSELF at a booth as far from Arizona as he dared to be while still being able to see her.

Laughingly rejecting the proffered drink, she spoke to a waiter. Spencer couldn't hear what was said, but when the waiter called over a boy with a menu, he assumed she planned to order food.

That would buy her some time—as long as she didn't actually eat much.

The shot remained on the bar in front of her.

How much whiskey would it take to get her drunk? Probably not much. The way she giggled, she was already buzzed…or pretending to be.

With Arizona, he couldn't tell.

But he could easily guess how unmanageable she'd be with liquid courage burning through her bloodstream. God help them all, she just might kill someone.

THE SECOND SPENCER WALKED IN, Arizona knew it. She didn't need to see him or hear him. He had that kind of appeal, that much presence. With him inside the spacious establishment, the stagnant air seemed to swell and churn.

Every other woman in the joint noticed him, too. Women who danced beneath lights. Women who served drinks and sandwiches. Women with other men.

Yeah, she got that. With his incredible height and those broad shoulders and that unwavering air of control, Spencer was the type of man no woman would ever ignore.

But the men became aware of him, too. Likely they saw him as a possible threat; physically he'd annihilate them, and romantically, well, he hogged the attention of all the ladies.

With just a glance, Arizona saw the big bartender zero in on Spencer with nasty intent. While polishing a glass, he spoke to the dude who'd sent her the drinks, and that idiot nodded. Then the skinny man she now guessed to be her target, Terry Janes, eyed Spencer, as well. When Janes turned to say something to the bartender, he caught Arizona watching him.

She ducked her face but smiled—and peeked at him again.

Of course the knucklehead bought it, hook, line and sinker. Men were *soooo* damn easy.

Mouth curling and dark eyes warming, Terry Janes eyed her with possessiveness.

Oh, she recognized that look well enough.

Bingo.

Up close, his thinning brown hair was more noticeable, especially with the way he slicked it back. His scruffy goatee with patches of gray gave away his midforties age. When he tugged on an earring in one ear, Arizona again saw the colorful tribal tat on his left arm.

Tonight, he looked cruel. He looked like an easy mark.

And Spencer thought this might prove tricky. Ha!

Janes leaned on the bar to talk quietly with the other men, but his intimate attention remained on her.

He was such a repulsive excuse for a human being that acidic disgust burned in her stomach. But she played it coy, letting her smile flicker as she returned his interest.

If it weren't for the loud music, she maybe could have listened in. But no way would she be able to hear unless she got right on top of them. And that'd be too obvious.

So instead, she watched him.

Not until the same boy she'd seen before approached with a menu did she look away from Terry Janes.

"You came back," he said, his voice dead, cold.

"I said I would, right?" She smiled at him and slid the whiskey aside with a laugh. "I can't do any more of that on an empty stomach."

He rubbed his neck with his uninjured hand. "Something else to drink, then?"

Arizona took in the mop of thick dark hair, the swarthy skin...the cowed shoulders. That the kid wouldn't look her in the eyes really bothered her. He had to be still in his teens. Too young to be working in a bar, but then, he probably had no one to champion him, no one to care about his mistreatment.

Being on the scrawny side, he was no match for the bullies clustered at the other end of the bar.

On his left hand, two fingers were taped together, but she could see by the swelling and discoloration of the middle finger that it had probably been broken.

When she wrapped this up, she'd repay the bastards in kind—with interest.

"How about sweet tea? Do you have that?" Leaning close to ensure he heard her, she tried to see his face.

He dodged her. "Yes." He laid a menu on the bar in front of her. For only a second, his white shirtsleeve pulled up...and exposed fresh, purpling bruises above his thin wrist. He quickly retreated. "Do you know what you want to eat or did you need more time?"

The whiskey had burned a path down her throat and into her stomach; seeing the kid's abuse burned her soul.

"If you don't mind, I'll go ahead and order now." To give the impression of desperation, Arizona rubbed her stomach as if hungry and scrunched up her nose. "What's the cheapest thing on the menu?"

She knew she had the attention of all three men; so did the poor boy, and it amplified his nervousness.

He licked pale, chapped lips. She recognized signs of malnutrition and dehydration, in his dry, flushed skin, the protrusion of his bones and lack of flesh, his obvious exhaustion. "We have chili and bean soup. House salad." One skinny shoulder lifted. "Maybe a BLT sandwich."

"Let's see..." She pretended to think about food, when really she hoped to reel in the men. She wanted Terry Janes to approach her. She wanted him to make a move. "It all sounds so good."

Janes sent a lackey instead.

Feeling his approach, Arizona handed back the menu. "I guess I'll just have the salad."

The same guy who'd sent her the drinks earlier stepped up behind her, no doubt testing the waters. "Get her whatever she wants, Quin."

"Oh." Pretending surprise at the intrusive voice, Arizona looked over her shoulder—and had to pull back so that she wouldn't bump into him. He'd crowded so close, she felt the threat of his presence even though he wore a smile. "No, really. I don't—"

"It's on the house." Music faded. The lights sent demonic shadows over his face as he visually caressed her boobs. "A pretty girl should never go hungry."

Trying to be objective, Arizona decided that he wasn't a bad-looking man. Not a troll by any stretch. But she knew who he was, what he did and what he wanted.

That made her want him dead.

"Umm…" She smiled in false appreciation. "Thank you, but…"

"I insist." With a hand on her shoulder, he leaned in closer but didn't offer his name. "Tell Quin what you want."

Quin. Was that really the young man's name? Doubtful. But it'd give her an in for setting up a contact. "If you're sure it's okay, then maybe a salad and a BLT?"

He bent a level look on Quin. "Bring her a piece of pie, too."

Before the waiter could leave, she touched his arm. "Thank you, Quin."

Haunted eyes met her gaze. He nodded and hurried off, leaving Arizona alone with the mouth-breather.

Great.

Shoring up her level of tolerance, she swiveled on the stool to fully face the douche again. Her knees bumped into him, yet neither of them moved away. He had the attitude of a man used to getting his way.

Now that he'd met her, he was bound for disappointment.

Next to Spencer, this guy looked like a complete wimp. And that brought out other quick comparisons. All around her, the usual drunks mixed, mingled or just nursed their drinks.

The creep in front of her gained power by controlling and abusing others. He gave his allegiance to a trafficker, and so did the bartender.

They were foul where Spencer was pure, and, put to the test, one on one, man to man, she knew Spencer would easily crush them all.

But cruelty gave an added edge; when a man didn't care who he hurt or how he inflicted pain, he could do a lot of damage in a short amount of time.

Though she knew the answer, she asked sweetly, with just a touch of awe, "Are you the boss?"

"No."

"Oh." Pouting in mock disappointment, she said, "You seem so much like a boss that I just assumed."

He moved to her side and leaned back, putting both elbows on the bar. The pose pulled his shirt taut over a slight gut and emphasized his scrawny chest. "Like a boss how?"

By necessity, they remained so close she could smell his breath. "You know. Very…" She smiled and allowed a slight shiver. *"In charge."*

"That's because I am in charge." Cocky, full of self-importance, he bragged, "I'm the boss's number-one man."

In a show of eagerness, she leaned closer. "You are?"

"That's right." His gaze settled on her mouth. "What's your name, pretty girl?"

She'd already thought about this, and said without hesitation, "Candy."

One brow lifted, and he gave a short laugh. "I can believe that." With one finger, he touched her chin. "You're so sweet, I think I'm getting a toothache."

Oh, puh-leeze. Could he be any cheesier? Wishing she could blush on cue, Arizona ducked her face. "Thank you."

Finally, he held out a hand. "I'm Carl."

Aha. One big fish in the barrel. "So nice to meet you,

Carl." Knowing she wouldn't get it back anytime soon, she gave him her hand.

For a heart-stopping moment, as he lifted her hand toward his face, she thought he planned to kiss the back of her fingers. Already her stomach pitched with revulsion.

She did not want his disgusting mouth on her. Her breath stalled in her lungs, and she waited.

Instead, he examined her short, unpolished nails. "No rings? No manicure?"

Asshole. If she was a young woman down on her luck, he sure wouldn't make her feel any better.

"No funds," Arizona said as if confessing a sin.

"Is that so?"

A big sigh brought his gaze back to her chest. It was easier for Arizona to conceal her hatred when she didn't have to look him in the eyes. "I've been job hunting, but so far, no luck."

"You mean a woman with your classy chassis doesn't have someone to take care of her?"

She forced a smile at the crude compliment. "I'm all alone."

Shrewd eyes narrowed in speculation. "No boyfriend?"

"Afraid not."

He studied her doubtfully. "I find that really hard to believe."

Damn. She didn't want him to get too suspicious. "It's hard, you know? I mean, I've met a few good guys who were fun to be around. I enjoyed them, but…"

"But what?"

"They started to get too…well, clingy." She toyed with the end of a lock of hair that fell over her chest. "I want to make it on my own, see some of the world, not get tied down so soon."

Guarded, he gave her long scrutiny before coming to some conclusion. "I saw you talking to Quin."

"I asked about a job."

His eyes narrowed. "What did he say?"

"That I'd have to talk to you." Quin had said no such thing, but she wasn't about to get him into trouble. "That's why I came back. I was hoping…well, do you need any more help here?"

Slowly, his mouth lifted in a smile. "As it turns out, the boss might be hiring."

"Seriously?" She perked up. "So, could I meet him?"

"Maybe." As if mesmerized, he watched the slow, playful movements of her fingers toying with her hair. "What are your job skills?"

"Well…" Speaking over the music wasn't easy but no way would she suggest they go somewhere more private. "I'm a people person. I promise I'd work real hard. I'm always respectful."

With difficulty, he got his attention back on her face. "How old are you, honey?"

She didn't lie about that. "Twenty-one."

"Hmm." His eyes glittered in speculation. "Plenty old enough, then."

"That's what I keep saying!"

His big grin showed off strong white teeth. "The only job available would be waitressing."

"Oh, I don't mind that." She squeezed his hand and rushed on with gusto. "I *promise* I'll always show up on time, and I'm *never* sick. I swear that I'm a real quick learner—"

"I'll take it up with the boss." So saying, he glanced back at Terry Janes and nodded.

So she passed muster? Fools. She couldn't wait to teach them both a lesson.

Quin hesitated with her food, hovering nearby but not intruding.

Carl motioned him in. "Your meal is here." He patted her hand one last time. "Eat up, and then you can talk to him."

"Seriously?"

He tipped up her chin. "If all goes well and he hires you, one of us will show you around the place."

Uh-oh. She was supposed to stay where Spencer could see her. In the briefest of glances, she met Spencer's gaze—and even in the darkness, with the crazy effect of the lights, she saw that he did not look happy.

Had he guessed what Carl said? Judging by his ominous expression…yes.

Well, he'd just have to trust her to keep herself safe, because she refused to blow things now.

She pasted on a beaming smile. "I would love a quick tour. Thank you!"

CHAPTER ELEVEN

SPENCER FOUGHT THE URGE to bodily remove Arizona from the bar. Had she not listened to a damn thing he'd told her?

With every hour that passed, the bar got busier, the clientele more hammered. Fewer people danced now, and even the dancers at the bar grew sluggish, sort of swaying in boredom.

It was bad enough knowing Carl's thoughts, but Spencer knew the thoughts of every other creep in the place, too. They each took turns watching her, some more subtly than others, some outright leering.

The way she sat on that stool, her heart-shaped backside outlined by the snug skirt, her long, slim, shapely legs on display...

Spencer stopped staring long enough to notice another man burning a hole in her with his hot gaze. He made no pretense of not lusting after her.

Yet another man whispered to his buddy while eyeing her, both of them chuckling with suggestive grins. Seeing their amusement stirred something dark and turbulent inside him.

He did his best to contain the primal reactions. If he went on a rampage, he'd give up the game, and Arizona might never forgive him.

Some of the men were average—clean, not too drunk.

Others had probably been at the bar all day, maybe from the night before given their red-eyed, slouched positions.

One elderly drunk in particular paced the aisle mumbling to himself and reeking of booze and sweat. Another younger guy sat quietly at a small table, doodling in a sketch pad.

Spencer wanted to annihilate them all—for doing exactly as Arizona wanted them to.

Even the barmaids cast her continual glances, some of them envious, some resentful, a few only curious. Though they weren't in Arizona's league, the women working inside the bar were mostly attractive, if somewhat worn.

When a redhead approached him, Spencer gladly latched onto the distraction. Mature enough, seasoned enough and definitely a customer, not an employee, put her in the category of safe ground. She'd help him blend in, which would give him better opportunity to watch over Arizona without anyone noticing.

"Hello," she purred.

"Hello yourself." With all his attention focused on Arizona, the woman's overblown assets and painted features didn't interest him. But he eyed her boobs, displayed in a low-cut, sheer blouse, anyway. "Can I get you a drink?"

"Honey, you can get me anything you want." She eased a full-size, shapely rump into the seat across from him. "I haven't seen you here before."

"Haven't been here before." Using the excuse of flagging a waitress, he looked around and saw Arizona attempting to engage the young waiter in conversation. She looked edgy, even a little dangerous.

Don't rush it, honey. Don't push.

Arizona had a natural-born tendency to defend the

underdog, so Spencer didn't trust in her ability to maintain control.

When no waitress approached, Spencer asked Red, "What're you drinking?"

"Rum and Coke."

"Sit tight, then." He touched the hand she'd rested on the booth top. "I'll get it."

"I'm not going anywhere."

He was so anxious to send a signal to Arizona, he almost missed the appreciative gaze of a barfly. At the last second, he winked at her.

After striding to the front of the crowded bar, he leaned past Arizona, being sure to touch all along her back, and spoke to the bartender. "A little service?"

Arizona looked up and back at him. Thank God she wasn't really eating her food, was more or less moving it around the plate. She'd nibbled on a corner of the sandwich, eaten a few bites of lettuce from her salad.

The bartender eyed his stance over her and scowled. "What do you need?"

"A drink for the lady." He nodded back at the booth where Red waited for him. "Rum and Coke."

"I'll get it right to you."

"Thanks." Easing away again, he let his body brush against Arizona. "Excuse me."

Luckily, the young waiter had used Spencer's timely interruption to escape Arizona's inquisition.

But Arizona didn't realize that yet. Her gaze went past Spencer to the redhead—and sharpened. She didn't stare, but she took in the other woman's attitude and appearance in mere seconds.

With her mouth tightening, she lifted her glass of tea, saying, "No problem" in an offhand way that didn't fool him for a second.

Perfect.

Let her stew on his possible hook-up, Spencer thought, instead of breaking heads. In the meantime, he'd keep Red company while watching everyone else in the bar, remaining alert and ready to react if it came to that.

With Arizona around, it could all go to hell in an instant.

AT THE EDGE OF AN OLD GARAGE locked up for the night, Dare stood outside his rented black van and kept watch on the Green Goose. The air felt thick with the threat of another summer storm. Dark clouds swam around the moon.

The back of his shirt stuck to his skin. Mosquitoes buzzed nearby. He could smell oil, gasoline and old refuse.

The garage sat atop a rise off to the side of a rarely used bridge. It gave him the perfect vantage point. He could see everything, and if needed, he could be down to the road in under a minute.

His phone buzzed, so he dug it from his jeans' pocket and put it to his ear. Always cautious, he said nothing.

Trace asked, "Busy?"

"Waiting. Watching."

"It should be an uneventful night."

But with Arizona involved…anything could happen.

Dare knew they all shared concern for her. In such a short time, she'd drawn them all in and won them over. It only took one look to see the vulnerability she hid behind outlandish bravado.

They also recognized Arizona's genuine courage, caring and determination to make the world a better place. Despite Arizona's rough edges, Dare liked her a lot. And he respected her.

Having her back tonight was both a pleasure and an honor. "This call is just for confirmation?"

"For Jackson. He's prowling the floor."

Dare grinned. Jackson thought of Arizona as a kid sister. Add to that his impending wedding and fatherhood, and Dare figured he had reason to pace. "So why are you the one calling?"

"Because I was wondering…after you saw her, what did you think?"

"About how she looked?" He shrugged to himself. "I definitely noticed."

"Killer, right?"

He knew Trace mentioned it as a potential problem, not out of personal interest. "She's going to make Spencer insane."

"Probably." Trace made a rude sound. "But he can handle it."

"I don't guess there's much chance that Janes will overlook her tonight."

"Doubtful anyone in that place will overlook her."

True enough. Few women looked like Arizona, but she also carried herself with a confidence that enhanced her physical appeal. "That's the point."

In the background, he heard Jackson questioning and Trace explaining.

"Spencer's got a thing for her," Dare stated.

"He's trying to deny that."

Hmm. He couldn't see denial doing Spencer much good at this point. "She's got a thing for him, too."

"More than a thing," Trace said, "if I'm reading her right."

"Does Spencer realize it?" In Dare's experience,

a lot of men never saw it coming. Spencer seemed sharper than most, but where Arizona was concerned, there existed a lot of emotional muck to wade through. It'd be easy to miss the signals in the middle of bigger issues.

"He thinks she's too young, and with her past experience, he's...wary."

"Only an idiot wouldn't be. But in Arizona's case, I can't see her age factoring in. She's lived through enough for three lifetimes." Down by the Green Goose, a white van pulled up, drove slowly down the alley between the buildings and around to the back of the bar. Dare narrowed his gaze. Not a delivery van, so what? "I think we have trouble."

Picking up on his tone, Trace asked, "Any direct threat to Spencer or Arizona?"

"Not yet." He explained about the van. "Going on gut instinct here, but I'd say the point of that nondescript van is either nabbing Arizona, or maybe to move out some of the captives."

As much to himself as to Dare, Trace said, "Spencer won't let Arizona out of his sight. Unless things explode, you can assume she's still safe."

But what about her targets? "With Arizona, chances are good that she'll be the one to light the fuse." And sorting victims from aggressors could be tricky.

"Maybe we should cut things short."

Spencer knew the codes, and he understood the situation. "We'll see. I'm moving closer, but I'll check in later."

"Thanks. I'll keep Jackson here."

Dare smiled. "Yeah, do that." He disconnected the call.

In no time, he was in front of the bar, and through the

big front window he saw the crowd but couldn't pick out Spencer or Arizona. He parked nearby, and then, moving like a wraith from the shadows, he made his way to the back lot until he could see the van.

On silent feet he edged closer, unseen but near enough to hear the quiet exchange between two men, one a driver, the other riding shotgun.

There could have been more men in the back of the van, but Dare didn't think so. Their conversation didn't include anyone else.

Near his feet, a rat scurried past. Overhead, a damp breeze cut through an old sycamore tree, stirring leaves and setting branches to swaying. Through a glass pane in the back door of the bar, light spilled through, sending shadows around overflowing refuse containers and broken brick siding.

"I heard this bitch was different. Younger." The driver laughed. *"Fresh."*

"Carl told me she's a real prime piece."

After a swig of beer, the driver tossed the empty toward a garbage can. He missed, and the can bounced off the bricks with a clatter. "You think we'll get a turn at her first?"

"Don't see why not. Once we get her under wraps, don't know why it'd matter who gets the first taste."

"I get dibs before you." And then, as a complaint, the driver added, "You're so fucking rough, you always leave them half unconscious."

"I make them *swoon*."

They shared a cackling laugh.

And though they didn't know, they sealed their fates.

Dare had no doubt it was Arizona they spoke of, but they wouldn't get a chance to hurt her.

They'd never hurt anyone ever again.

IT WASN'T EASY for Arizona to keep her attention off Spencer. Damn him, did he have to enjoy his cover so much? Several times now, even over the blaring music, she'd heard him laugh. Though she tried not to, she kept stealing discreet peeks at him. Over the top of the booth, he leaned close to the woman, close enough to kiss. Hands entwined, feet together under the table, gazes intimate...

"Did you want coffee to drink with the pie?"

Arizona let her gaze skim the rest of the room as if the bar in general interested her, not Spencer in particular.

She turned back to the young waiter. "No, thanks."

He began gathering her other dishes.

To keep him close and hopefully engage him, she asked, "Is your name really Quin?"

He faltered. "It... Yes."

She tipped her head. "Doesn't sound Hispanic."

"It's short for Quinto."

Ah, so it was his real name. "Is it always this busy, Quinto?"

He shrugged warily. "This time of night, yes. Weekends are busier."

That he'd strung so many words together surprised and encouraged her. So far, he'd been hustling from one customer to the next without a break and without much conversation. "You work the weekends?"

"Yes."

"What nights are you off?"

He seemed to miss a beat, his gaze skittish, his mood more so. "It changes."

Sitting forward, Arizona folded her forearms over the bar. "You like working here?"

His attention skipped toward Carl. Both he and Terry

Janes had moved around the bar, talking quietly with patrons, watching their workers from different angles, occasionally going into the back toward the offices. All in all, they'd made it tough for Arizona to keep track of them.

But Quin knew right where to find the most immediate threat, and that was Carl. He licked his lips. "I need to get back to the kitchen."

Thirsty customers kept the bartender busy filling glasses, and a discreet exchange of funds for drugs occupied Carl's attention. Arizona didn't see Terry Janes, but she did only a cursory scan of the area.

She didn't want to chance losing this opportunity. "So, Quin."

He gave her a cautious look of inquiry. "Yes?"

Leaning toward him, her voice low, Arizona asked, "How'd you break your finger?"

Uneasy, Quin opened his mouth, but nothing came out.

Pretending to smooth the front of his shirt, she slipped the note into his breast pocket.

The alarm in his gaze said he knew what she'd done—but had no idea why.

"If you ever want to talk, call me. I can help."

Trembling, he licked his lips again, afraid, maybe hopeful. "What are you talking about?"

She tried a sympathetic smile. "Your finger?"

He held his breath but finally said, "That was…an accident."

"I don't think so."

"I have to go." He tried to gather up the rest of her dishes in a rush and nearly knocked over the remaining shot of whiskey. "You must drink that."

Poor guy. Pity welled up; she could see his fear, even

smell it, and it made her livid, made her want to raze the place.

It also nearly crippled her with the need to help.

"You live around here?" Though already his reactions were telling enough, she pressed him. "Or do you live... *here?*"

After darting his fearful gaze around, he pushed the whiskey toward her. "Drink it. Please."

To appease him, she tipped up the glass and swallowed it back, then handed him the empty. "Okay?"

Instead of answering, Quin stared past her shoulder— and there stood Terry Janes, not more than a yard behind her. A woman hung on his left arm, and a man counted money to his right. And still he stared straight at Arizona.

Well, hell. She'd been so absorbed in the young waiter she hadn't even sensed Terry Janes getting near.

With the loud music blaring and the drone of multiple conversations, he couldn't possibly have overheard anything they'd said. But maybe Quin's guilty expression had given them away, because the bar owner's ominous intensity engulfed them both.

Oh, God, if she got Quin in trouble... "Look," Arizona said in a rush. "Let me help—"

"If you don't want anything else," Quin interrupted, "I will get back to work." He started away.

Arizona caught his sleeve. "Wait."

First miserable and then defiant, he paused. "What?"

Arizona pressed the pie toward him. "Please. I'm watching my weight, but it'd be a shame for the dessert to go to waste. Would you eat it for me?"

His jaw worked. "It is for you."

"But I don't want it. Not tonight."

Cynicism flattened his expression. "You should eat it

anyway." And with that he walked off—but he left the pie behind.

So had someone tampered with it? Did it contain something that would drug her, make her malleable, or worse?

Unwilling to take the chance, Arizona pushed the pie away. But now, without Quin to talk to and with her targets all busy, she felt at loose ends.

She'd always had a problem with impatience.

At least Quin now had the number for her day-to-day cell. Hopefully he'd call. Hopefully he'd let her help. And soon.

She wanted to act, to "fix" things however she could, preferably by stomping on some bad guys. She had new respect for how Trace, Dare and Jackson handled the involved, multileveled stings that had brought about so much justice.

She tapped her fingertips on the bar, swung one foot in time to the music, glared at one leering drunk and wished Carl would hurry up and return to her so they could get the show on the road.

"HANG ON A SECOND, HONEY." Dodging graspy hands and a wet mouth, Spencer pulled the buzzing phone from his pocket. He flipped it open to see the message: *Lights out in thirty.*

Not a code, but from Dare. What did it mean? Unsure if he should anticipate a knockout, a blackout or both, he checked the time on his watch.

Unwilling to let the redhead kiss his mouth, Spencer dodged her again—and she bit his chin.

With a hand on her shoulder, he pressed her back. "Hold on, sugar." Quickly, before things got out of hand, he beeped back a confirmation of receipt and returned the phone to his pocket.

"Business?" she asked while settling back into her seat across from him.

"Nothing important." Should he round up Arizona and say to hell with it for the night? At the very least, he had to keep her close. Right now she looked bored, and that didn't bode well for anyone.

Then suddenly Terry Janes moved on past her again, heading down a hallway toward the back of the bar, past the bathrooms and kitchen.

And Spencer knew—*he knew*—exactly what Arizona was thinking.

It was uncanny how he could read her, but when she pushed off the bar stool without looking back at him, giving him no opportunity to dissuade her with a subtle signal, he knew it was to follow Janes.

When he got her alone again...

Thoughts scrambling, Spencer prepared to go after her, and to hell with their cover.

At the last second, it proved unnecessary.

With relief, he watched as she got sidelined by a new distraction.

GODDAMNED INTERRUPTIONS... He curled his hands into fists, locked his knees and accepted the inevitable.

Stalled, yet again.

For so many nights now, he'd waited for her to return to his bar. Now she was here, but nothing was yet settled.

Frustration clawed at the surface of his calm façade, a façade of control, of normalcy. He had to have her. Sooner would be better...but if forced to it, he could be patient.

Waiting often led to the best rewards.

For now, she was too nice, giving attention to those who didn't deserve it. Stupid bitch.

When the time was right, he'd teach her better.

But it wasn't that time yet. Not yet.

Soon.

CHAPTER TWELVE

"Wait."

Thrown off by the interruption, Arizona peered down at the small, pale hand now latched onto her arm.

"Please." It was quickly retracted by a goofy little dweeb in thick glasses with an unruly head of brown hair half-hidden beneath a worn sports cap. "Wait."

Un-freaking-believable. Her brows rose with indignation. "Excuse me?"

"Look." Trembling, he thrust a large, stiff piece of paper toward her. "It's you."

She suspected the little guy had turned bright red, but low lighting made it impossible to tell. She didn't want to be rude, but she didn't have time for this. "What is it?"

Eyes darting everywhere, manner demure, he turned the pencil drawing around so that the light shone on it.

Oh, wow. It *was* her.

She eased closer to the small round two-seater table where he sat. He'd captured her likeness in profile. Amazed, Arizona studied the drawing he held.

Though she hadn't exactly posed—or sat still—he'd managed an accurate rendering that looked like her... except way better. He'd even given her a smile that seemed genuine instead of forced. And the drawing didn't emphasize her boobs or her legs.

Anyone looking at it would see no more than a young,

carefree woman. He'd drawn her as innocent, even sweet.

She'd never admit it to anyone, but occasionally she wished she was that woman.

"I don't know what to say."

A bright smile lifted his homely features. "So you like it?"

"Well…yeah. It's terrific. Really flattering."

He ducked his face. "It's not as pretty as you are."

"Pffft." She had mirrors, but she knew she had never been that…soft. Or gentle.

As if surprised by her reaction, he looked up again. "I tried, but I didn't really do you justice." And then with a puzzled frown: "You don't know how pretty you are?"

On the round table rested a stack of papers, more pencils and a drawing pad. Huh.

Curiosity got the better of her, and she lifted the top drawing, but it was a still life of the jukebox and a booth. The one below it was the moon through the big front window, obscured by the thick iron bars. In the drawing, people filled the seats around the window, but they weren't the focus.

Ignoring his question, Arizona asked, "That's what you do?" She gestured at the papers. "You sit here in the Green Goose and draw?"

"I have to order food, too." He smiled shyly. "Otherwise they make me leave."

"Why here?"

"The lighting is good."

Yeah, right. Arizona eyed the dim lamp over his table. Only the bar area boasted real light, and even there it was more for effect than illumination. "Those strobe lights can't make it easy to draw."

"They give interesting shadows. And I can draw

people without them knowing it, because they can't see what I'm doing." He frowned. "Or maybe they just don't care what I'm doing."

Sad. With his mismatched clothes and childish manner, Arizona wondered at his age—and maturity level. Definitely not a kid but…all there? She couldn't tell. "You're really good."

He adjusted his cap, shifted uncomfortably, then thrust the picture toward her. "It's for you. Keep it."

"Seriously? Gee, thanks." What the hell was she going to do with a pencil drawing of herself? Not like she could hang it in Spencer's home or on a motel wall. But no way did she want to hurt his feelings.

The noise swelled and ebbed around them. Someone jostled her, a couple edged past, two men laughed loudly.

Done wasting time, Arizona rolled it up and stuck it in her purse. The sketch was large enough that more than half stuck out of the top of her bag. She'd have to take care not to lose it. "Appreciate it."

Flickering lights gave a glimpse of his beatific smile.

Now where had Terry Janes gotten to? She'd lost sight of him, and no way could she go snooping in back rooms.

Spencer would have a fit.

But she needed to locate him. Had he known she was about to follow? Was he hiding from her? The smarmy bastard.

Before she could decide what to do, the artist caught her arm again. "I…I'm sorry. I don't mean to be pushy." Concern replaced his happiness. "But you don't want to talk to that one."

"Who?"

Swallowing hard, he hesitated, then darted a fearful gaze around the room. "The guy you were going to follow."

Damn it, was she really that easy to read? Arizona put her shoulders back in a cocky stance. "What makes you think I was going to follow anyone?"

"You've been watching him." Distressed, he removed the hat and twisted it in his hands. "I saw you."

After a more thorough scrutiny, Arizona figured him to be somewhere from his late-twenties to mid-thirties. He wasn't exactly homely, but, except for a small scar under his right eye, he was pretty nondescript.

At her lack of response, he shrugged. "Since I was drawing you, I noticed you asking about a job."

Even in the ever-shifting low lights, she could see the sincerity in his kind eyes. "What of it?"

Agonized, he looked around again, and then, rather than continue shouting to her, he pulled her in close. In a barely there breath of sound, he warned, "You don't want to work here."

An ally? Well, okay, then.

Sliding into the seat across from him, Arizona put her purse on the tabletop and leaned forward to meet him halfway. Matching his whisper, she asked, "Why not?"

"That guy you were going to talk to? That's Terry Janes. He owns the place."

This close to him, Arizona caught his scent, but it wasn't unpleasant. More like fresh honest sweat and the green outdoors. Maybe like how someone would smell after just walking in from a park or after mowing a lawn.

Her gaze went to the scar under his eye. "You know him well?"

"Sort of. I don't think he's..." He chewed on his upper lip. "Well, he's not very *nice*."

What an understatement! Arizona debated the wisdom of talking to him. It could be risky. The fewer people she interacted with, the better her chances of making a strong play and getting away unscathed.

But she sort of felt sorry for the guy; he reminded her of an overgrown puppy—too eager, too annoying, but still irresistible.

And if he knew anything helpful about Janes, that could assist her.

Giving him her most engaging smile, Arizona held out her hand. "I'm Candy. What's your name?"

"Oh, I…um…" Again flustered, he grabbed her hand and squeezed it with too much enthusiasm. "Joel Pitts. You can call me Joel."

With a name like Pitts, he'd probably been heckled a lot in school. "Okay, Joel." With an effort, she freed herself from his hold. "I'm all ears. Let's hear what you have to say."

Undecided, Joel adjusted his glasses, shifted, then leaned forward in anticipation. "I don't have proof, but I'm pretty sure—"

"At it again, Joel?"

Arizona jumped when a man clasped her shoulder. She saw Joel's eyes go round in terror, his mouth slack with dread. For a moment, it almost looked as if he'd faint.

Senses sharpening, she peered at that hand on her skin, then up the leanly muscled arm to the intricate tribal tattoo.

Finally.

Forcing herself to feign an air of uncertainty, she waited until none other than Terry Janes himself moved to her side.

Poor Joel nearly slid off his seat. Stammering, he said,

"Hey, Mr. Janes. I was just… I was only drawing her, that's all."

"Is that so?"

Keenly aware of that warm hand pressing down on her bare shoulder, Arizona said, "He's really talented." After withdrawing the sketch and rolling it out on the table, she turned her face up to Janes and met his gaze with a sweet smile.

He went still at her expression, looking her over as if enthralled.

That's it, sucker. Take the bait. She made a point of licking her lips, of lowering her lashes and playing coy.

His fingers tightened on her shoulder in reaction.

"The drawing is so complimentary. Don't you think so?"

At her prompt, a small frown pinched his brows, and he shifted his attention to the artwork.

It gave her the opportunity to study him up close.

"She said she likes it," Joel babbled. "That's why she's sitting with me."

Janes gazed from the picture to her and back again. "Not bad, Joel, but you're missing some of the raw sex appeal." His thumb caressed Arizona's shoulder joint.

Smaaarmy. His getup of snug black jeans, a snowy-white wifebeater shirt and pointy-toed boots looked absurd. She supposed the shirt was so he could show off his tat.

Bad decision.

Unlike Spencer, Janes had a scrawny chest, bony shoulders, and his biceps were far from impressive.

Arizona pasted on a smile. "So you're Mr. Janes?"

"You can call me Terry. Or Cowboy if you like."

"Cowboy?" Where the hell had that come from?

"It's what the regulars call me. I saw you in here before, and you plan to become a regular now, right?"

As if she weren't used to someone of his esteemed ilk sizing her up, she widened her eyes theatrically. "You noticed me?"

"Oh, yeah, honey, I noticed." Lifting that proprietary hand off her shoulder, he signaled the bartender.

Immediately, two shot glasses and a bottle of whiskey were put on the table between them.

She'd never been much of a drinker, but out of necessity, she'd learned to hold her own. Sometimes it got forced on her, and being drunk weakened her defenses. Right now she'd rather keep her wits, not dull them with liquor, but it didn't look as if Terry would give her a choice.

He filled both glasses.

Playing dumb, Arizona started to push back her chair. "Well, I'll just get out of the way so you two can—"

Catching her shoulder again, Janes pressed her back into her seat. "Drink up." He tossed his back and poured another.

Arizona toyed with the glass. "You don't look like a cowboy to me." More like a weasel. Or a worm. "Why do they call you that?"

Gaze dark and heavy, he stared into her eyes, and a smile curled his hard mouth. He said softly but with clear command that cut past the noise, "Drink."

Wanting to groan, Arizona lifted the shot glass, drew a breath and sipped.

"Ah-ah." He touched the bottom of the glass, keeping it at her mouth, tipping it up. "All of it."

"But…" Pushy jerk. "I'm not that much of a drinker."

"So you'll learn."

Damn it. The way he pressed the glass to her mouth,

she really had no choice. Knowing there'd be no denying him, she gulped down the whiskey and plopped the glass back onto the table.

The wheeze of her breath was only partially faked.

"Good girl." He immediately poured her another. "I got my nickname because I break in the wild ones."

"Wild ones?" Was the dumbass actually admitting to human trafficking? Would he really make it that easy for her?

Or did he somehow consider that a boast of his sexual prowess?

"That's right." His grin showed very strong, straight white teeth. "Tell me, brown sugar, you been broke in?"

Umbrage stiffened her spine and drew back her shoulders.

Oh, to slug him. Just once. *Maybe in the balls.*

No way in hell could she keep from reacting to that jibe. Forgetting her act for the moment, she stared up at him and asked with soft menace, "Was that a racist slur?"

"That was a compliment, honey. You've got striking looks—like the perfect mix of features." He ran the back of a finger up and down her arm. "Where'd you get the suntan? Momma or Daddy?"

Killing him sounded better and better. "My mother was dark."

"Was she a beauty like you?"

Good grief, how had this gotten so personal? She'd expected him to say crude stuff, to come on to her.

To be disgusting.

She hadn't expected him to talk about her parents. She hadn't expected him to expose the personal demons of her past.

"I don't really know," she lied. "We lost her a long

time ago. I barely remember her." *If only that were true.* She remembered her mother all too often.

It was her dad she'd like to forget.

"Grew up motherless, huh? So maybe you're one of the wild ones, then. Is that it? Or has some lucky bastard already gentled you?"

Arizona stared at him, refusing to flinch, refusing to look away. *He doesn't know. He doesn't know. He doesn't know.* But it sure felt as if he did, as if he looked at her and knew how her father had sold her, as if he could recognize the taint human trafficking had left on her soul.

Almost frozen in apprehension, Joel sat there watching the byplay. Janes stood right beside him, blocking any escape, using his presence to bully and intimidate.

And for poor Joel, that worked.

For her…yeah, she didn't intimidate that easily. She just anticipated the moment when she'd get to knock him off his power trip.

But for now, for Joel and Quin and any other innocent person caught in this bastard's net, she had to play it cool.

"Tame me? I don't know what you mean." Oh, Arizona, not coy enough. Play along. Tease. She forced a twittering laugh. "Whatever it is, it sounds naughty."

Janes laughed, then cast a sideways look at the artist. "This one's not for you, Joel."

"Oh, but I wasn't…" With them both looking at him, Joel cowered in on himself. "I wouldn't. I swear."

Arizona knew she had to temper her anger, but there was something about Terry Janes that rubbed her wrong, made it nearly impossible for her to play little Miss Innocent.

Understanding his level of immorality exaggerated

everything about him, every look, smile, even the way he moved his hands and the tilt of his head. He could have been someone's odd but favored uncle—instead, for many people, he'd become a living nightmare.

"Joel is fine. I appreciated his company."

Stunned by her daring, Joel gaped at her. "No, no, I...I didn't..."

"You're defending him? Really?" Janes tugged at his goatee. Tone flat, infused with threat, he murmured, "Get lost, Joel. Now."

In a near-panic, Joel started gathering up his papers. But before he'd finished, Janes hauled him out of the chair and sent him away with a shove. Papers and pencils scattered over the floor.

Mortified, Joel dropped to his knees to gather up everything.

WITH EVERY SECOND that passed, Spencer got more rigid. It was bad enough getting felt up by the woman now hoping to score with him. She thought arousal caused his growing tension. And under other circumstances, maybe, just maybe he'd have found the idea of sleeping with her a little less repugnant.

But now, this moment, he was so aware of Arizona tilting ever closer to violence that nothing and no one could divert his attention. Terry Janes's deliberate cruelty toward the smaller man would cause Arizona to see red. He knew, because he abhorred bullying, too.

A surreptitious glance at his watch showed they had another twenty-two minutes. Not much time to come up with a solid plan to extricate her from the situation without notice.

But more than enough time for Arizona to start removing heads.

LOCKING HER TEETH against the need to lash out, Arizona made a move to help Joel.

Janes said, "Don't."

He spoke with such command that she paused. But she couldn't bite back her censure. "That was cruel."

"No, that's life. Don't make the mistake of encouraging him with kindness." Leaning forward, Janes caught her hand and pulled it toward him so that she had to lean over the small round table. Now that he had her close, he didn't have to speak loudly to be heard. "Joel is like a mongrel. If you feed him, he'll never go away. Even with me kicking him every so often, he comes back."

She could practically feel Joel's trepidation as he struggled to collect his things off the floor. And she felt Janes's intention, both sexual and controlling; he made no attempt at subtlety.

The reasons to demolish him kept adding up— especially when he reached out to finger her hair.

In a low, crooning voice, he murmured, "I bet you're this silky and warm all over."

Even though her skin crawled, Arizona didn't pull away. The differences between Spencer and a scumbag like Terry Janes had never been more obvious. She should be concentrating on her next move, but instead, she thought about how Spencer made her feel. Around him, her worries lifted. He gave her respect and affection.

He gave her equality.

Such a hero.

Sure that she'd find him seething, Arizona glanced toward Spencer. He was still in the same spot, sitting in the booth.

But the a-hole now had the redhead sitting with him,

all spooned up to his side, his eyes closed as she sucked on his neck, one of his hands cupped over her rear.

That son of a...

Yeah, so maybe it was for cover, but did he have to be so convincing?

So that no one would notice her anger, Arizona let her gaze slide right on past him and turned it into a "searching for an escape" type of look.

"Now, don't go getting nervous on me." Janes wrapped her hair around his fingers, holding her like a leash. "You and I have unfinished business."

Hoping to reestablish her scam of demure naïveté, Arizona whispered, "It's getting late."

Mouth curving in a malicious smile, he tugged a little harder on her hair. "But I thought you were interested in a job?"

"Oh." Right. A job. She started this, so she needed to finish it. "I am."

"Well, honey, bars stay open late, and as a new hire, you'd have the shittiest hours. That means being on the clock until closing." Under the table, his feet encased hers. "Is that going to be a problem?"

Only then did she realize that poor Joel had slunk away. But where did he go? She peeked around and didn't see him. "No problem at all."

She made a point of not looking toward Spencer again. The way he'd been going at it, she might see something she didn't like.

Or rather, something she disliked even more than what she'd already seen.

Man, would she give him hell later.

"Glad to hear it." Janes let her hair drop and refilled their glasses. "I like you, Candy."

Yeah, well, he wouldn't—not after he really got to

know her. She batted her eyes at him. "You are so... sweet."

His expression held no amusement. "Down the hatch. Then I'll show you around the place, get you all set up. You can start tomorrow."

"That soon, huh?"

"Is that a problem?"

"Nope." Somehow she'd figure it out. She had to go to Dare's for her stupid birthday—a circumstance she'd never anticipated—but starting work at the bar would give her the perfect excuse to cut things short, to make the trip as quick as possible. "Actually, that'd be great."

"Good. Let's drink to our new association, then."

Another drink would put her over the limit. She already felt the buzz as the alcohol flooded into her system. The place felt warmer, as if the air-conditioning had died. Heat flushed her face, left her skin dewy. "I don't think I should—"

"To work here, you gotta be able to hold your liquor."

"Sure. And I can." She could hold it, she just couldn't control her temper when she imbibed too much. "It's just that I've already had a few—"

"Decide now." Intolerance put an edge in his tone. "You want the job or not?"

So he would make it a stipulation to the deal? Bastard. "I want the job. I *need* the job." More important, she needed a tour of the building. Back entrances, windows and escape routes—she had to know the ins and outs of the structure. And she needed to know if a raid would put forced workers at risk, if he stored his victims here, locked up, or if he moved them elsewhere, how many people were in the building.

There were still too many unanswered questions.

Lifting the shot in a toast, Arizona stared, unflinching, into the eyes of the devil. "To a new tomorrow."

He raised his glass. "To you, Candy—and an exciting night to come."

Yeah, a night where she'd dismantle him. "Hear, hear." Together, they knocked back the shots.

Whoa. Liquid fire cut through her, numbing her tongue and her brain, pooling like an inferno in her guts. She shook her head to clear it from the rush, wiped her mouth and set her glass next to his.

"Is that taking the edge off?"

Yeah, and she needed her edge. "Whoa." She shook her head again, but it didn't help. "I think I'm getting drunk."

"You're softening." He rubbed at his mouth, scrutinizing her. "I like it."

Before he could pour her yet another, Arizona pushed back her chair and stood. "I'm ready for my tour."

Janes came to his feet also. "You're ready, all right." He put an arm around her shoulders and pulled her into his side. They each wore sleeveless shirts, so they had a lot of skin touching.

Puke, gross, disgusting.

Her stomach actually pitched, but she drew a deep breath to settle it again, and, pretending to stumble into him, she shot an elbow into his belly.

"Shit." He jerked her around hard, and his hands bit into her upper arms. "Careful, damn it."

Giggling, Arizona flattened her hands on his narrow chest. Not much muscle there. Put to the test, she thought she could probably take him.

She relished a chance to find out.

She leaned into him and giggled again. Looking up

into his eyes, she smiled. "You know, I think maybe I've had just a little bit too much to drink."

Slowly Janes's anger faded away beneath blistering intent. "Girl, I think you've had just enough."

Romance Reading...

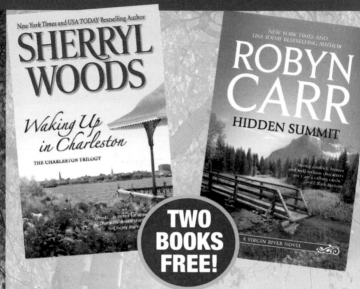

New York Times and USA TODAY Bestselling Author

SHERRYL WOODS

Waking Up in Charleston

THE CHARLESTON TRILOGY

NEW YORK TIMES AND
USA TODAY BESTSELLING AUTHOR

ROBYN CARR

HIDDEN SUMMIT

A VIRGIN RIVER NOVEL

TWO BOOKS FREE!

Each of your FREE books will fuel your imagination with intensely moving stories about life, love and relationships.

We'd like to send you **two free books** to introduce you to the Reader Service. Your two books have a combined cover price of $15.98 in the U.S. and $19.98 in Canada, but they are yours free! We'll even send you **two exciting surprise gifts**. There's no catch. You're under no obligation to buy anything. We charge nothing – **ZERO** – for your first shipment. *You can't lose!*

Visit us at
www.ReaderService.com

© 2011 HARLEQUIN ENTERPRISES LIMITED.
® and ™ are trademarks owned and used
by the trademark owner and/or its licensee.

YOURS FREE!
We'll send you 2 fabulous surprise gifts (worth about $10) just for trying "Romance"!

Yes! I have placed my Editor's **"Free Gifts"** **seal** in the space provided at right. Please send me 2 free books and 2 fabulous mystery gifts. I understand I am under no obligation to purchase any books, as explained on the back of this card.

PLACE
FREE GIFTS
SEAL HERE

194/394 MDL FNMF

FIRST NAME

LAST NAME

ADDRESS

APT.#

CITY

STATE/PROV.

ZIP/POSTAL CODE

Thank You!

EC3-ROM-12 ▼ DETACH AND MAIL CARD TODAY

The Reader Service — Here's How it Works:

Accepting your 2 free books and 2 free gifts (gifts valued at approximately $10.00) places you under no obligation to buy anythin You may keep the books and gifts and return the shipping statement marked "cancel". If you do not cancel, about a month later we send you 4 additional books and bill you just $5.99 each in the U.S. or $6.49 each in Canada. That's a savings of at least 25% the cover price. It's quite a bargain! Shipping and handling is just 50¢ per book in the U.S. and 75¢ per book in Canada.* You m cancel at any time, but if you choose to continue, every month we'll send you 4 more books, which you may either purchase at t discount price or return to us and cancel your subscription.

*Terms and prices subject to change without notice. Prices do not include applicable taxes. Sales tax applicable in N.Y. Canadian residents will be charged applicable taxes. Offer not valid in Quebec. All orders subject to credit approval. Credit or debit balances in a customer's account(s) may be offset by any other outstanding balance owed by or to the customer. Please allow 4 to 6 weeks for delivery. Offer available while quantities last.

CHAPTER THIRTEEN

SPENCER SEETHED IN SILENCE as Arizona smiled, teased and generally sucked up to Janes. She held on to him like a lifeline; he couldn't tell if she was really that wobbly, or if it was one of her insane ploys.

Either way, as he'd warned her, seeing another man's hands all over her was impossible to bear.

He got especially enraged when Janes stroked her hair with one hand, her backside with the other.

I'll kill him.

If Arizona didn't beat him to it.

She'd already landed one elbow and just now managed to get a knee into his groin. Janes looked livid, ready to punish her—until Arizona snuggled into him again.

She was so devious with her push/pull game.

Tangling a hand in her hair, Janes yanked back her head and put his face near her neck.

Spencer knew he had to do something, and fast.

How to get away from the redhead without causing a scene?

Several times now, she'd almost consumed him, and keeping her interested while stalling hadn't been easy. If anything, his delay tactics had fired her up more. At one point she'd tried to get inside his zipper, offering him a hand job right there in the booth.

Despite all her efforts, he hadn't felt a single twinge

of interest. Not when he wanted only Arizona and not while she played with danger.

Ignoring the warmth of the woman's mouth teasing his ear, Spencer quickly took in the setting of the bar.

He needed some inspiration.

Misunderstanding, Red whispered to him, "Let's get out of here."

"Yeah." Maybe he could stumble his way up front with her. Maybe he could—

Expression dark, Terry Janes turned with his hand clamped hard on to the back of Arizona's neck, keeping her pinned close to his side, half dragging her as he started toward the back of the bar.

Fuck it.

Ready to rush him, Spencer stood—and suddenly the artist was there, tripping up Janes as he tried to show Arizona another picture he'd drawn.

Thanks to the flashing of the lights, the scene played out like a delayed movie reel. Each second of darkness moved the actors, each strobe illuminated them in a new position.

The music pulsed in Spencer's temples, heightening his rage.

Janes tried to go around Joel, but he stuck close, spoiling his plans.

God bless the man—just the interruption he needed.

As the redhead stood next to him, Spencer said, "You're into threesomes, right?"

"What? No!"

"Come on." He reached for her boob. "There's a hooker down the street that comes cheap."

She stepped back, waffling...

Well, hell. He hadn't expected her to consider it. "I'll pay you, too," he offered as a desperate insult.

And that worked.

Indignation had her shoving away from him. "Forget it!" Snatching up her purse, she started to storm off but came back at the last second, grabbed his face in both hands and planted a wet one dead on his mouth.

When Spencer finally managed to lever her away, she said, "If you ever want the real thing, come and find me here." Then she turned and stormed away.

One catastrophe averted.

Trying for discretion, Spencer wiped off his mouth and began wending his way through the crowd.

He got within a few feet of Arizona in time to hear Janes tell the artist to fuck off.

The smaller man persisted. "I just want to give this to Candy." He held up another drawing.

Arizona gushed. "Oh, Joel, thank you. It's wonderful." She reached for him, intending a hug.

Cursing again, Janes yanked her back. But she'd already gotten a solid hold on the artist—Joel—and he went off balance with her.

They both stumbled.

Terry Janes held Arizona, so she didn't fall.

But Joel reeled away and hit a table. Drinks spilled. A chair overturned.

Like déjà vu from his first meeting with her, a brawl erupted around Arizona. Janes tried to get her out of the crush, but, typical of bar fights, things quickly escalated beyond the initial grievance.

Joel floundered, and he tripped up the Hispanic waiter who'd talked with Arizona earlier. The kid fell into a waitress, who landed in the lap of a disgruntled drunk, making him drop his drink.

Doing his part, Spencer tripped a man, shoved another.

As punches, glasses, even bottles got thrown, Arizona deliberately allowed herself to be jostled—and separated from the bar owner.

Forgetting about her, Janes made his getaway to protect his own ass.

Perfect.

Or at least, it was until he saw Arizona get backhanded by a drunk. She stumbled and would have fallen if Quin hadn't caught her to him.

Spencer saw blood at the corner of her mouth, and he saw the glitter of excitement in her eyes.

She enjoyed this.

Of all the—

When her artist buddy nearly went down from a random elbow, Arizona said, "Look out," and pushed the little man behind her so that he had the wall to his back, her to his front.

She kicked out at a big brute swinging a bottle, and her heel landed between the guy's legs. He dropped hard to his knees and then toppled to his back.

Half cowering behind her, Joel said, "I know a back way out."

"Not happening." Spencer wanted to get her out of the place before someone pulled a gun or knife.

In his pocket, his phone buzzed.

It needed only this.

The thirty minutes Dare had allotted were all but over. He retrieved the phone. The new message was simple: *It's over. Out now.*

He turned to Arizona just as she doubled her fists and decked another guy who'd come charging their way.

Spencer said, "Enough already."

At the same time, Joel enthused, "You're...*magnificent.*"

Accepting that as her due, Arizona swiped the blood from her mouth and grinned. "Yeah, thanks."

Before Spencer could figure out how to extricate her from the melee, he got hit in the ear.

That did it.

He had Dare calling him, Arizona intoxicated and an artist trying to play hero.

Red-eyed and feeling mean, Spencer knocked out the man with a single punch. When his buddy rushed forward, Spencer slugged him so hard he fell backward over a chair.

Arizona rolled her eyes. "That was overkill, you big show-off."

Quin stood there, agog.

Joel asked, "Who *are* you people?"

Dead serious, as if she'd totally misunderstood his question, Arizona said, "I'm Candy, remember? You drew my picture. Twice."

Damn. Spencer knew he had to get her out of there and fast, before anyone else got curious. "She's drunk. I'll see that she gets home."

Quin nodded and slipped away. When Arizona started to follow, Spencer caught the back of her shirt and drew her up short.

She windmilled her arms until Spencer steadied her.

"I can get her out," Joel said while clutching his art supplies to his chest. His face was white, his expression panicked.

"She'll be safer with me." Spencer scouted the quickest way out. He'd prefer to just haul Arizona away. He didn't see the bartender or Carl, but that didn't mean they weren't watching, so he still had to play the game.

"Candy…" Joel looked at her with worry.

"What's that?" Arizona cocked her head. "Do I hear the cops?"

Going on the alert, Joel said, "I don't hear anything."

"Sirens," Spencer said, playing along. He eyed Joel. "Anyone who doesn't want to be picked up in this scuffle ought to hightail it out of here."

"Thank you for the drawings." Arizona took Joel's hand. "I really, really love them."

With bodies flying around them, Joel asked, "Will I see you again?"

"Sure you will. I got hired, so I'll be here tomorrow."

"Oh, right." Joel started to relax. "Okay, then..."

The music suddenly died—and then Spencer really did hear sirens. Arizona's eyes widened as she turned her face up to his. "Seriously?"

"Afraid so." He watched as Joel darted toward the back and through a side door. Spencer hoped the guy would be okay, but Arizona was his first priority.

Near her ear, he said, "In case anyone is watching, we have to separate. But I'll be right behind you."

Her hand knotted in the shoulder of his shirt, keeping him close. "What about the workers? What about the waiter, Quin?"

He smelled the whiskey on her breath, felt the warmth of her, her strength and energy. "Forget it."

"I can't just leave without knowing if they're okay."

Was she kidding? "That waiter already split, remember? Joel is probably following him. But we can't help anyone if we get killed tonight," Spencer reasoned. "Now make your way to the front door. Don't engage with anyone else. Talk to no one. You got me?"

"Yup." She smiled at him, but the bruise at the corner of her mouth lessened the effect.

Damn. "You're drunk," he accused.

"Yup."

God, give me strength... "Too drunk to make your way to the front door?"

She shook her head and staggered because of it. "Nope." After smoothing out the material of his shirt, she gave him a wink and tottered off, clubbing everyone who got in her way.

Bemused, chagrined and worried, Spencer watched her go. With each flash of the lights, she progressed another foot. Almost to the door.

Almost to safety.

She left him frustrated and, damn it...admiring. Arizona let no one and nothing get in the way of her determination. She had more backbone than was healthy.

Things were coming to a head between them. In such a short time her entire perspective had changed. That had been his goal, but now, met with her innocent interest, his own reaction surprised him.

Altruism flew the coop. What he did with Arizona and why had little to do with saving her from herself and a lot to do with the incredible chemistry between them.

He wanted her, and not having her was eating him up.

Refocusing his thoughts, Spencer saw Arizona clear the front door. Far enough, he decided. He started to follow her—and suddenly the lights went out, leaving everything still, shrouded in ominous darkness.

PANIC HAMMERED against his brain, making his temples throb, his eyes burn. The little bitch wouldn't get away; he wouldn't let that happen. But with so much going on, all the noise and confusion, how could he stop her? Surreptitiously, he looked around, seeking a plan.

He could take her himself. Sure, she had some skill,

but she was still just a woman, with a woman's frailty, a woman's tender emotions.

A woman's vulnerability.

Once she'd lost her shine and, therefore, some of the profit to be made off her, he'd hoped to have her for himself. She'd be broken then, more easily manageable.

Wonderfully needy.

But thanks to the fools surrounding him, that opportunity no longer existed.

He had to act, now, or forever lose her.

And then it came to him, exactly what he would do, who he would send after her. He'd stay safe, but she would become his.

Oh, yes, a perfect plan. He laughed, knowing it would all work out.

INHALING THE MUGGY NIGHT AIR did nothing to help clear Arizona's head. In case anyone watched them, she made a point of not waiting for Spencer, of not looking back to see if he followed closely.

Plenty of people milled around out front, and the occasional car drove past. Somewhere out there, Dare kept watch. Spencer would soon follow.

She hadn't accomplished her goal, but they'd made headway. For now, that'd have to be enough.

Moving farther from the entrance, she lifted her hair off her neck and tuned out the escalating noise of rowdy brawling from inside the building and boisterous customers outside as they headed to their cars. She didn't speak to anyone, and she didn't move too quickly because Spencer wouldn't want her out of reach.

Thinking of him gave her a smile. *Spencer.*

The strange turbulence firing her blood had nothing

to do with the violence in the bar or the alcohol she'd consumed.

It had a lot to do with the impossibly hunky Spencer Lark.

Man, he was really something.

Something…exciting. And amazing.

And really appealing.

Looking up at the sky, Arizona tried to see the stars, but angry clouds hung low, rolling over one another. It would storm again, but she didn't mind. In fact, the thought of a rainy night seemed somehow…sexy.

How crazy was that? She never thought in those terms, but to think of that now, after tangling with a maniac like Terry Janes or his unscrupulous lapdog Carl, defied reason.

Sure, she always enjoyed engaging in a little violence. Blowing off steam sometimes mellowed her. But this was different.

The way Spencer made her feel was unlike anything she'd ever experienced.

As she made her way up the sidewalk a few feet more, she sighed. It was past time for her to reclaim her life—in every way.

With Spencer, all things seemed possible. With him, anticipation replaced dread.

He'd be out soon, and she had to decide what to say to him, how to convince him to get down and dirty with her.

Somehow she'd win him over. Tonight.

She didn't think she could wait any longer.

EVERYTHING HAPPENED FAST.

Something whooshed past Spencer's head, too close for comfort. Settling his chaotic thoughts, he turned to meet the danger. Trusting his gut instincts, listening, feeling the air, he prepared for what would happen. He had no idea who would attack first, but he sensed the trap and was as ready as he could be.

Suddenly thick arms circled him from behind, and he knew it was the beefy bartender. Pinning one of the bartender's arms to his side, Spencer used his other arm to bring back an elbow hard enough to crack ribs. When he heard the breath leaving his attacker, he took advantage, and in one deft move, flipped him over his shoulder.

The big man landed with a resounding crash.

Emergency lights flickered on, and added to the glow from outside illumination spilling in through the big front window, he could see well enough. The bartender lay unmoving over a broken table. Given the odd angles of one arm and a leg, he wouldn't be bothering anyone else that night.

It struck Spencer then—he was attacked, so likely Arizona would be a target, too.

To hell with subterfuge.

Breaking out in a sprint, he leapt over and around people, tables and chairs. He shoved through the doorway and into the thick, humid night air. Scanning the area, he finally spotted her down the walkway, just a little too far away.

A second later, Carl stepped out of a dark alley...and reached for Arizona.

No.

Silent, deadly and more focused than he'd ever been, Spencer charged toward her. Neither Arizona nor Carl saw his approach.

But he saw the knife in Carl's belt, and he prayed he'd reach her in time.

ARIZONA'S THOUGHTS were on seducing Spencer instead of where they should have been, so when she saw the dark, indistinct form growing into a long shadow across the walkway, it took a few seconds for the import to sink in.

Too late to take the offensive against him, Arizona realized it was Carl lurking in the night.

Well, damn. Had he taken the back exit from the bar and circled around to get her? That meant he had to have seen her leave.

And it also meant he'd been watching her…maybe Spencer, too.

If he'd hurt Spencer, so help her, she would demolish him.

As Carl made a grab for her, she played the helpless victim and let him. He snatched her into the alley with hard hands and careless strength, dragging her down to an open door.

He shoved her into a small dilapidated room.

Maybe before all the whiskey shots, she'd have been sharp enough to think of a better plan. Shoot, even two drinks ago she would have been more on game.

But even over the limit, she wasn't totally lost to skill. She wanted to get close to him.

How else could she hurt him?

Once they were out of sight from spectators, she reacted instinctively to the arm clamped tight across her throat. She went limp, dropping her weight to throw Carl off balance. When he tried to readjust, she grabbed for his fingers and, in a practiced twist, broke two with a satisfying crackle of joints.

That got her turned loose real fast.

With grim satisfaction, she ducked away while Carl let loose a string of rank curses. She knew Spencer wouldn't want her to fight, but since Carl blocked her way out of the room, she couldn't exactly tuck her tail and run, now could she?

He left her no choice but to engage in full-go contact. *Awe-some.*

Taking a stance, ready, even anxious, Arizona smiled at him.

"You stupid bitch," Carl said, and with his left hand he pulled a knife from his belt.

Great. He was an ambidextrous fiend? Figured.

Stalking her, backing her farther into the dark room, Carl said, "You thought you had us all fooled, didn't you?"

She opened her mouth to reply.

But he barked, "Shut up!"

Arizona bit back her smile.

"We saw you fighting. We saw you laughing."

We who? She lifted her chin. "So does this mean I'm not hired after all?"

His hand flexed on the knife hilt. "It means you're not worth the trouble you've caused us."

Foolish man. She knew plenty about knives, so seeing one, even in the hand of a maniac, didn't send her into a panic like it might someone else. "You're saying my value as a saleable commodity just collapsed, huh?"

Surprised by her lack of fear and knowledge of their real intent, he hesitated. But only for a second. "You're not so dumb after all, are you?"

"Well, ya know, compared to *you*…" She grinned, reminding him that she had fooled him and his cronies. "Yeah, I look like a freakin' genius, right?"

Holding his injured hand out to the side, he flexed his muscles. "You think this is a joke?"

Her back bumped up to a damp wall. "I think *you're* a joke, yeah."

A deep, angry breath swelled his chest. "You're going to regret that flippant mouth, girl."

Arizona took in Carl's aggressive stance and dark scowl, felt his mood change as he prepared to lunge at her.

Time to make a move.

Dropping her voice and her chin, looking at him through her lashes, she whispered, "And here I thought you liked my mouth." To emphasize the suggestiveness of that, she ran the tip of her tongue over her lips, leaving them moist.

That distracted him enough that he said, "I can think of better uses for it."

Men were *sooo* easy, thank God. Slowly, Arizona trailed her fingers over her chest and down into her cleavage. "I bet I could come up with all kinds of uses that you'd approve of."

Putting his attack on hold, he eyed her. "Is that right?"

She nodded, but he was busy ogling her boobs. She stepped away from the wall. "Maybe if I'm good enough—and, Carl? I can be *really* good—well, then, maybe I can convince you not to kill me?"

"Let's find out." Seeing her as no threat at all, he took a step closer. "Take off your shirt."

You'd think he would have learned from the broken fingers.

Arizona caught the hem of her top. "You want me naked? Here?"

Anticipating her nudity, he adjusted his hold on the knife, and his gaze went to her body. Murmuring low, he promised, "I will tear your shit up."

Arizona smiled, prepared to attack—and Spencer's fist came out of nowhere. It struck Carl in the jaw so hard, a tooth came spewing out.

Euewwww.

Deciding it'd be a good time to move, she slipped a few feet along the wall and away from Spencer's rage.

And he was enraged. Big-time.

Would he kill Carl? She tipped her head to survey the damage already done. Spencer held up the smaller man with one fist twisted in the front of his shirt while punching him with the other big fist. Carl's knife lay on the ground. His legs were limp, his grunts of pain dwindling.

"Hey, Spence."

He ignored her and landed yet another blow. Blood sprayed from Carl's nose. He hung boneless, unconscious, in Spencer's hold.

"Yoo-hoo, Spe-ence," she sang. "I don't mean to be a party pooper, but we did hear sirens, right? You think we should get going before the cops find us here?"

Fist suspended, he stopped hitting Carl, but his chest still heaved. Rage had bunched his muscles through his biceps, shoulders and across his back. He stood with his legs braced apart, his feet planted solidly.

Ah, he looked so sweet. All that rage on her behalf.

Arizona smiled at his back. "It's been a really great show. Seriously. I mean, nothing I couldn't have handled myself, of course, but—"

He jerked around to glare at her.

His nostrils were flared, his eyes glittering, his jaw clenched tight as granite.

Okay, so maybe she shouldn't pull the tiger's tail just now.

Gently, she suggested, "Maybe you could take me home?"

On the other side of the wall, police barked orders. They heard the thumping of running feet and the clash of a tackle. Outside, a window broke, a car horn blared.

"Any second now, someone is going to come busting in on us. And then we'll have to start explaining." Hoping to reach him, she added, "The guys really hate having to give explanations."

More breaking glass. More horns. More shouts.

Never looking away from her, Spencer exhaled, opened his fingers, and Carl collapsed in a bloody heap.

"There you go!" Arizona praised him. "And look at that. You even managed to drop him on his knife so we don't have to worry about anyone else finding it before the cops do. Good job."

Oh-so-slowly, Spencer stepped away from the carnage once known as Carl.

"Come on." She said it the same way someone would call a pet. "Come on, Spence. Let's go." Patting her thigh as she backed up to the door, she beckoned him.

Brows pulling tighter, Spencer closed his eyes for a few deep breaths, then opened them again. Through stiff lips, he ordered, "Wait." He moved around her to the door, looked out, then said, "Start walking."

"Got it." Feeling lighthearted, a little drunk and sort of…euphoric, Arizona twirled around and marched ahead.

Part of her silly mood came from recognizing, and accepting, that Spencer was the right guy for her. Not just as an ally. Not only for a friend.

He impressed her. She respected him. And she admired everything about him—but especially his ability.

She wanted him in ways she'd thought long lost to her.

She wanted him as a man.

Tonight, if she played her cards right, she just might manage to get lucky.

WELL AWAY FROM THE BAR—a few feet in front of him—Spencer watched Arizona skipping along in a drunken trot. He flexed his fists, expanding and contracting his bruised knuckles. All the volatile emotion he'd felt tonight still churned inside him. He wanted to tear apart everyone involved…while Arizona smiled like a kid at a carnival.

Keeping her within reach, while not yet touching her, and constantly scanning the area, he called Dare. The ringing stopped, but Dare said nothing. "It's Spencer."

"Done playing around?"

"Carl's in a room off the alley to the right of the front door."

"You immobilized him, right?"

That was a nice way to put it, but Spencer said only, "Yes." He rubbed the back of his neck. "I went a little overboard on him."

"No doubt he had it coming."

Spencer saw no reason to explain that Carl had dared to pull a knife on Arizona, that he'd threatened her life.

Or that she'd been in the process of bartering sex to gain the upper hand.

"I should have killed him."

Dare said, "We need him alive to answer questions. Get her out of here. I won't be far behind you."

"Thanks." He ended the call.

As soon as they rounded the corner, Spencer caught up with Arizona, anxious to ensure her safety. "Get in the truck."

She nodded but said, "That was *so* fucking awesome,

Spencer. A night I'll never forget. I'm almost giddy, you know?"

He couldn't look at her. "In the truck, Arizona."

"I'm going, I'm going." She laughed as she turned to walk backward, watching him. "Smell the rain?" She flung her arms out wide and inhaled deeply. "Seems appropriate that it'd storm again, doesn't it?"

A storm for Arizona Storm? When she tripped, he caught her arm to keep her from falling.

She snugged herself up to him. "You impressed me, Spence, and that's not easy to do."

He sighed. God, what would he do with her?

Probably not what he wanted.

Unless… He eyed her, saw the daze in her eyes and knew she was too drunk. No, definitely not what he wanted.

"Stop looking so morose, you grumpy Gus." She nudged him. "Everything is fine!"

"Yeah, just dandy." She might've been raped, then murdered in a back room off an alley. But she discounted that peril completely. "Pay attention to your feet before you fall."

"Nag, nag." When they reached the truck, she launched into chatter again. "It was so cool how you came out of nowhere like a big avenging angel. A dark angel. And bam." She threw a shadow punch. "You took it out of old Carl. One blow, and that sucker was done for."

Spencer held her door open, saying nothing. Still smiling, she slid into her seat.

"You did that in the bar, too. I should call you One-Shot Spence, or something catchy like that. Maybe when I'm more sober, I can come up with a good name for you."

Again checking the area, Spencer closed her door, then went around the truck and got behind the wheel. He immediately locked the doors and started the truck.

Oblivious to his mood, Arizona said, "I broke Carl's fingers. Did you see that?"

"No." All he'd seen was Carl dragging her away… His heart ached, just remembering. He never wanted to see anything like that again.

"Must've been after he got me into the alley." Arizona made a twisting motion in the air. "Felt damn good, getting him like that. You know he had broken poor Quin's finger, right? I wanted to pay him back in kind. But you know, I wasn't even thinking about that when it happened. He tried to choke me—the dick—and I went on auto-drive." She gave him a fat smile. "See, training pays off. Told you everything would be fine."

Adrenaline still pumped through Spencer's veins, making everything she said feel like nails on a chalkboard. "Put on your seat belt."

After a long look, she huffed at him. "You are being such a pill." She latched the belt.

A pill? He wanted to raze that goddamned bar and half the men in it, yet he held on to his temper—just barely. Spencer put the truck in gear and, deciding he needed to get moving before he blew, pulled out to the road.

"Wish I could have stomped on old Terry a little more, too. *Cowboy*." She snorted in utter disdain. "What an ass."

Grinding his teeth, Spencer tuned her out and concentrated on his driving. They got a few blocks more before she started in again.

"He thought he'd break me in. That's what he said. His exact words. Can you believe that? *I'd* break *him*."

She laughed. "Just like I broke Carl's fingers." She reached over and patted Spencer's thigh. "And just like you broke the rest of him."

At her touch, his whole body tensed more.

The pat turned into a tentative stroke, moved to his inner thigh, and Arizona gave a bold and curious squeeze. While playing with him, she said, "I hope when we go back, I get a shot at Terry—"

Primed to the breaking point, Spencer snapped, "Enough!" He knew he wouldn't make it until they reached his home, so he jerked the truck off to the side of a busy street. He put it in Park with jarring impact.

Clenching the steering wheel, he struggled, striving for a calm that remained well out of reach.

CHAPTER FOURTEEN

ARIZONA TIPPED HER HEAD to study him. "Damn, Spence, what's the matter? You get a bee in your boxers?"

He ignored her question. Something felt wrong—something beyond Arizona's cavalier disposition and inebriated boasting. He searched the streets, watching for a tail, but saw nothing.

When his cell phone rang, he grabbed it up, expecting the worst. "Yeah?"

"You're clear," Dare said. "A cop started to follow you, but I took care of it."

He looked around and still saw no one—not even Dare. "Just like that?"

"Yes."

Itching for violence, needing release, he breathed hard.

"You okay?" Dare asked.

"Yeah." He ran a hand over his face. More curious than alarmed, he said, "About that cop..."

"We work with them when possible. Sometimes we have to exclude them so they don't get in the way, but we do not commandeer their authority when it's avoidable, and we never consider them expendable."

He knew they didn't harm innocent bystanders, but the rest was news to him. From what he'd observed so far, the trio recognized only their own command. "Good to know."

Arizona turned in the seat and treated him to a dreamy-eyed smile.

Places on his body that were already jumpy twitched in redirected interest. She reached for him, but Spencer caught her hand and held it still. Thinking of how the lights had gone out, he said to Dare, "So it all went down already?"

"It did. I can explain later, but a situation arose that forced my hand and gave us enough reason to move in ahead of schedule."

Arizona stiffened. "What do you mean it went down? What? The bar?"

He shushed her while rubbing his thumb over her knuckles and, then to Dare added, "You got Carl?"

"I sent two officers around to that room off the alley to collect him. I got Terry Janes myself." Amusement entered Dare's tone when he said, "You can tell Arizona that Janes resisted."

No, he wouldn't tell her a damn thing. Not yet anyway. Resistance would mean Dare had had to restrain Terry, and that meant he'd probably pulverized the guy. The last thing Arizona needed was more encouragement toward fighting.

Instead, Spencer concentrated on getting the facts. "He was the one running things?"

"He hasn't admitted as much yet, and we don't make assumptions."

"What do you think?"

"My gut tells me something more is going on."

"Damn."

"We'll have confirmation soon."

"The workers?" Arizona asked.

Spencer repeated her question.

"Everyone we could find is now safe."

He nodded to Arizona and saw her slump back in relief. It touched him that she'd been so genuinely concerned for people she didn't know.

Dare added, "We got info on another group of young Hispanics in transit. They would have mostly been used for labor at a nearby motel, but a few of the females were intended for trafficking. They should be freed within the hour."

Incredible. "So Janes spilled his guts about that?"

"No, but he will." Before Spencer could ask, Dare said, "Actually, it was two bozos I found around back in a van. But I can catch you up on that later."

Like hell. "Tell me now." His gaze landed on Arizona. And because he already knew it, he said, "They were there for her, weren't they?"

"Afraid so." Dare didn't mince words. "The driver did most of the spilling, but both men were anxious to share." He paused, then added, "I can be convincing."

Again, he had to reach for lost control. But he had to think of Arizona. He had to get her to his house, and he had to find a way to convince her to stay away from dangerous situations. "So now what?"

"Whenever we can keep a low profile, we do. We'll continue to oversee things, to ensure we get the results we want."

"Meaning no one walks away?"

Dare didn't reply to that. "We have a good relationship with the special agent in charge. He's organized an effective task force, and he has all the contacts he needs to take this through the proper legal channels."

Catching Arizona's wandering hands again, Spencer shook his head at her and whispered, "Stop that."

Dare laughed. "She enjoyed herself?"

"Seems like."

Still amused, Dare said, "Get her home safe, Spencer."

"Working on it." Since he held the phone, he ended up playing one-handed patty-cake with Arizona to keep her from molesting him.

His resistance was on shaky ground already—he didn't need her enticement, too.

She pretended to pout, then put her head back and closed her eyes on a lusty yawn.

"We're heading to my place now." The sooner he got her tucked in for the night, the sooner he could loosen his knotted muscles.

"Great. For the time being, keep her there. At least until we meet at my place. We'll catch up then." And with that Dare was gone.

Frowning with new concern, Spencer folded the phone and put it back in his pocket.

"What now?" Arizona asked.

He shook his head. Did Dare want Arizona to continue staying with him because someone had gotten loose? Or was it just a precaution?

"You're keeping something from me." Resentment chased away her lethargy and had her gathering steam.

"No." To forestall the fireworks, Spencer said, "I'm just a little amazed that it's all over."

"Did they have to kill anyone?"

He frowned over her bloodthirsty tendencies. "Dare said he'll fill us in on the details when we get to his place tomorrow." He hesitated, but he needed her cooperation right now. "For the time being, he wants you to stay with me."

"Mmm." Rather than argue, she asked, "And how do you feel about that?"

"It's not a problem for me." Hell, the only problem would be if she tried to leave him now.

At his answer, Arizona gave him such a wanton look that his guts cramped. He felt tortured, bordering on a loss of control, and she wanted to...flirt?

Trying not to stare at her mouth, he said, "What's up with you?"

With a secret smile, she lifted one bare shoulder. "I did a side-by-side analysis, that's all."

He had no idea what to make of that. "I don't follow."

She released her seat belt to turn toward him. After taking her gaze over him, his chest, his shoulders—his lap—she looked into his eyes and said huskily, "You, Spencer Lark, stand out."

"Among those scumbags?" He turned toward her, too. He had one arm along the back of the seat, the other draped over the steering wheel. "Jesus, I hope so."

"Definitely when compared to them, but from all other men, as well."

Her admiration put another crack in his already weakening resolve. Spencer tried scoffing at her. "You're drunk."

"Yeah, a little." Easing closer still, she said, "But it's not like I'm totally shit-faced or anything."

Did she curse on purpose? "You're not thinking straight."

"Actually, I was thinking about it a lot even before the whiskey. Even before I walked into the bar."

Good God. Feeling cornered by her intent and his own heated interest, he asked, "About *what?*"

"You. How you look. The things you do, and why you do them." She drew a breath and her eyes grew heavy. "How you make me feel."

"I panic you," Spencer reminded her. Okay, so during

that last kiss he'd given her, she hadn't exactly been fighting him. And before going in the bar, *she'd* kissed *him*. A barely there kiss, but still… "I have to coerce you into every single—"

"No, you don't." She shook her head. "Not anymore."

Spencer considered her assurances. She might think that now, but she wouldn't if he put it to the test. If he kissed her as he wanted to.

The way he craved.

"Okay, then." He'd give her a more thorough taste that would help to remind them both of how she really felt and of everything she still had to overcome. "Maybe you ought to pay up?"

She gave a quizzical look.

"You cursed, Arizona." Trusting that she'd shy away, he pushed her. "A whole lot of curses, actually."

"Hmm. Well, damn." She breathed a little harder, a little faster. "Guess I forgot myself."

Could she find a more inventive way to make him suffer? "Arizona…"

"But what the hell, right?" Her twitching smile proved a taunt; she deliberately threw out the curses. "These are extenuating circumstances."

Anticipation rode him, amped up his determination and his lust. "You're playing with fire."

"I know. But not cursing has been a real…" long, dark lashes lifted, and her gaze locked on his "…bitch."

That did it. She asked for it.

Hell, she *begged* for it.

And why not? It'd probably take no more than one real kiss before she'd be backing up and rethinking her brazenness.

She didn't really want him.

She didn't really want any of this.

Set on his course, Spencer said, "Time for me to collect, then, so sit still."

But she didn't. As he leaned toward her, she licked her lips and suddenly launched herself at him.

Taken off guard, he didn't resist as her mouth landed on his, not brief, but open, hot. He tasted the sharp bite of the whiskey first and then the sweetness of her tongue as she took his mouth without reserve.

Oh, God.

He tried to pull back.

Sort of.

He got his hands on her upper arms…but didn't quite push her away as he meant to.

She made a sound of hunger and deepened the kiss.

Heat flared, and his dick twitched to attention.

So did his conscience.

The easiest explanation for her quick turnaround was that on top of the adrenaline high, she'd had way too many drinks.

But damn, her mouth felt good and tasted good, too. Before he even realized it, he had his hand tangled in her long hair, his mouth slanting over hers, their tongues dueling.

He pulled her closer as he leaned back so that she sprawled over his chest. Instead of recoiling, Arizona moaned.

Shit.

He freed his mouth, then had to hold her away as she tried to crawl up onto his lap. "Honey…wait."

"No."

"We have to stop."

"Can't."

Honest need sounded in her tone, and Spencer's control fragmented. A kiss hadn't dampened her enthusiasm at all. Hell, it had spurred her on.

Because of the alcohol.

Never in his life had he taken advantage of an inebriated woman, and he sure as hell wouldn't start with Arizona. He had to pull it together and fast, or he'd do something they both might regret. "Arizona, *stop.*"

He held her back the length of his arms.

The look she gave him would have reduced most guys to a puddle. Hurt, embarrassment, even desperation—he saw it all in her beautiful blue eyes.

He shored up his resistance and touched her cheek—and prayed that he was the only one to notice how his hand shook. "You promised me you'd be okay."

Confusion overtook embarrassment. "What are you talking about?"

"Before you went in the bar. You gave me your word that you'd be fine."

Overflowing with frustration, she held out her arms. "And I *am.*"

"Bruised and bleeding is not fine. It's a long way from fine." He gave the corner of her mouth one last stroke, smoothing a darkening bruise with his thumb. "You got struck."

"A little backhand, that's all." She reached for him again. "It's nothing."

"Maybe not to you." He held her at bay, and this time she let him. "But to me it's a lot. It damn near killed me when that bastard hit you."

"Yeah?"

Telling her too much would only encourage her. "I want to get you home, cleaned up, and then you need to sleep off the whiskey."

She leaned in to put her head on his shoulder, cuddling close—and he let her.

"I don't want to."

The rejection stiffened his spine; her nearness, the scent of her, stiffened everything else. "You don't want to come home with me?"

She shook her head. "I don't want to sleep."

Spencer could see the wheels turning. So she no longer minded kissing—that didn't change anything else, not her past, and not the fact she was drunk.

Besides, he couldn't delay things any longer, not here, out on the street, exposed to danger.

He looked out the back window but saw no one and nothing. Was Dare still following them? If so, Spencer couldn't even imagine what he'd think.

He lifted Arizona back to her own seat. "Sorry, honey, but I need you to put your seat belt back on."

"But—"

"I'm done arguing, Arizona. Just do it."

She resettled herself with angry movements. "You're a real killjoy, you know that?"

Spencer fought a reluctant grin as he put the truck in gear and pulled back out to the road. God help him, it was getting more and more difficult to play this game.

And with every minute, it felt less like a game anyway.

Everything about her appealed to him, especially her independence. She went after what she wanted, whether it was a new knife, a fight with a scumbag like Janes, or…a devastating kiss with him.

If it weren't for the danger, he would have loved watching her work. She pulled off the "look at me, I'm so helpless" act to perfection. But when necessary, she was ballsy to the extreme, with the skill to back it up.

He didn't hear from Dare again, but he assumed he still followed.

Taking a disjointed route back home took longer but felt safer. No way in hell would he lead anyone to his place.

By the time they reached his driveway, Arizona was almost asleep. She'd curled up toward the passenger door, her long hair hanging down to hide her face, her arms folded around her middle, her sandals discarded on the floor.

Sexy. Like a slumbering kitten—but with sharp claws.

"We're here," Spencer softly told her.

"Whoop-de-doo."

Okay. Not so asleep after all.

"Let's go." He got out and walked around to her side of the truck, but she'd already opened her door and started a zigzagging stride up the walkway. Barefoot. The turbulent night air swirled around her, lifting her long hair and sending leaves to scuttle past her ankles.

Rushing to grab her purse and sandals, Spencer caught up to her and took her arm. "You're hammered."

"Yeah, the booze is sort of sinking in, ya know? I feel it more now than I did when I first left the bar." Then she paused, looked toward Marla's and gave an exaggerated wave. "Hey, neighbor!"

Spencer turned his head around in time to see a curtain drop. He did not need this conversation tonight. "Keep going."

"What? You don't want to chat with your lover?"

God, no, he didn't want that. Unless Arizona became his... He put the brakes on that provocative thought. "Inside."

"Yes, sir. Right away, sir. Thank you, sir."

His mouth twitched again. "I am not that bossy."

"Ha!" She nearly knocked herself over with that exaggerated exclamation. "Bossy, and arrogant, and a...a *tease*."

Hauling her into his side, Spencer supported her while they went up the porch to the front door. "You need sleep a whole lot more than you need anything else."

"But we were going to eat cake."

He got the door unlocked, opened it—and she almost fell inside. "That'll have to wait." Giving up, he scooped her into his arms.

"Wait." She straightened her neck to look around. "You're going to carry me? Seriously?"

Shrugging, Spencer looked down at her, their faces close. "Seems easier than rolling you to bed."

"But since we are going to a bed..." She touched her forehead to his. "I can think of better things to do than..." She burped, then snickered. "Sorry."

"Right. Hold that thought." After pressing her head to his shoulder to remove a modicum of the temptation, he kicked the door shut and started forward.

Through the silent, dark house, Spencer carried her—and he enjoyed it. A lot. Probably too much.

"Not the couch?" she asked when he passed it.

"Not tonight, no."

"I don't want to sleep in your guest bedroom," she rushed to say.

"I know." He hugged her just a little. Sooner or later he'd find out why she hesitated to use the room. "I'm taking you to my bed."

"Really?" Her arms tightened around his neck, and she whispered, "Change your mind?"

"No." But God, he wanted to. Holding her like this felt…right.

And dangerous. To him and her, both.

The steady drumming of her heartbeat, the lush press of her breasts to his chest, her warm thighs over his forearm…all combined to ramp up his awareness.

With regret, he let her legs slide down until her feet touched the tiled bathroom floor. He dropped her sandals and set her purse on the vanity. "Why don't you do…whatever you do before bed, and I'll be right back."

She lounged against the sink. "Where are you going?"

"To lock up. I'll just be a minute."

"Okeydokey." She closed the door on him.

Taking his time, Spencer turned the dead bolt on the front door, checked the windows and then went to his bedroom to turn down the bed. He'd just finished when Arizona emerged.

Her hair was damp around her face, so she'd splashed it—but hadn't removed all her makeup. She stopped in front of him, swaying just a little.

He tipped up her chin and examined the place where she'd been hit. Even in the dim light, he saw the darkening bruise that colored the side of her mouth and along her jaw.

He touched it with his thumb. "I hate it that you got hurt." Again. Under his watch.

Damn it, he wanted to protect her, not let her suffer more abuse.

Her mouth tilted. "I've had a lot worse, so quit worrying about it."

Her breath smelled of toothpaste, and her eyes looked dazed. "You're not making this any easier on me." Bending down, he brushed his mouth over the bruise. She started to lean into him.

Before he got carried away, Spencer said, "Don't go anywhere. I'll be right back," and he left for the bathroom to wash up and brush his teeth, too.

Because he didn't completely trust her not to bolt on him, he left the door ajar and listened for her while he did a rush job of preparing for bed.

Less than two minutes later he came out to find her curled on her side in his bed.

The jean skirt lay crumpled on the floor.

She hadn't even bothered to get under the covers.

His heart punched hard at seeing her like that—deeply asleep, in his bed, wearing only black panties and an insubstantial tank top that hugged her lush curves.

Drawn to her, Spencer approached the bed, stood at the side of the mattress and took his time looking over every inch of her. A fully naked, well-posed centerfold model couldn't have been more tempting.

Silky panties barely covered her, leaving much of her smooth hips and bottom on display. His hands curled with the need to touch her, to stroke over that honey-colored skin.

She had her long, sleek legs bent at the knee, one drawn up to expose her almost like an invitation. Visually he traced the rise of her proud shoulder, down the dip to her tiny waist and then back up again to the curves of that sexy backside.

Physically, he wanted her so much he hurt.

And emotionally… God, he choked on the thick emotions, they so overwhelmed him.

Because he had to touch her, he aimed for safe ground and drifted his fingertips through her hair, tucking it back so he could better see her beautiful face. Leaning down, he pressed a gentle kiss to her brow. She felt baby soft and smelled woman warm—an intoxicating mix.

Now, right at this moment, she was dead to the world, at peace, her expression utterly relaxed.

Young.

Carefree.

All the things she should be—even when awake and aware.

If she saw him standing there with a jones, admiring her in her sleep, she'd probably deck him. Grinning over that probability, Spencer dropped his hand and took a step back, then slowly opened the snap to his jeans and slid down the zipper past his erection.

He would sleep with her, he'd hold her, but he would not take advantage.

There wasn't anything he could do about the boner except suffer it.

Would she still want him in the morning?

Without drink clouding her judgment, would she still be able to push past her demons and overcome her reservations to take what she wanted?

And if she did, then what?

All his reasons for not indulging that final intimacy still remained. Taking her, being inside her, would only make it more difficult to do what was right—what was best for her, what would be honorable for him.

Because her past skewed her perception of any intimate relationship, Arizona didn't—*couldn't*—know her own mind. Her history hampered clear thought and insight the same way too much alcohol did. He shouldn't take advantage of either.

Spencer shook his head. All the arguments made sense; they were valid, of course. But he fought a losing battle, and he knew it.

In her unique, kick-ass way, Arizona personified temptation.

Pulling the covers out from under her, he tucked her in and turned out the low light. What would she think when she awoke with him in the morning?

Anticipating her reaction, he skinned off his jeans, put those and her skirt on a chair, and in boxers only, he stretched out beside her.

She didn't stir.

Though Arizona wasn't a fragile woman, she was so much smaller than him, her bone structure slight in comparison. He slid an arm under her head, another around her waist, and pulled her up close against his body so that he spooned her.

Amazingly enough, wrapped around her protectively, affectionately, *lovingly*...it was the most comfortable he'd been in a very long time.

ICY RIVER WATER CLOSED over her head, but she kicked hard and broke the surface long enough to gulp in much-needed air. Fierce rainfall stung her face; laughter sounded over the thunder. A bright flashlight beam hit her in the eyes, momentarily blinding her.

Panic sank its claws deep, but she fought it off. Think, Arizona, think.

Her next breath was the most immediate need, but, God, the river pulled at her, and without her arms to help, staying afloat was not only awkward, but nearly impossible. She choked on dirty water, shivered from the bone-deep chill.

Where was the shore? Which way and how far?

And if she made it there, then what?

They'd only throw her back in.

Probably with the added disadvantage of a bullet or knife wound.

Suddenly the chatter, the heckling, even the laugh-

ter stopped. Despite the rushing sounds of the river and the night and the raging storm, the loss of human words clamored against her brain.

Thighs screaming with exhaustion, despondency strangling her, she broke the water again—and saw a skirmish on the bridge.

It so surprised her that she went under again and swallowed a mouthful of the foul water. She kicked, but her legs felt leaden. Her lungs screamed, her shoulders ached so horribly from the unnatural pull of the tight bonds...

So tired that every muscle in her body cramped, she almost gave up—and then a splash sounded near her. Forgetting to kick her legs, she went under once more—and strong arms closed around her.

Fear surged, giving her renewed strength.

"Shh," he said as he pulled her toward shore. "I've got you now. I swear it's okay."

A man, big and so incredibly strong that he controlled himself and her against the deep tug of the river.

But who, and why?

Unwilling to trust anyone, she head-butted him, making him curse. But he didn't loosen his secure hold.

Oh, God, oh, God...

She kicked, and her heel connected a few times but gained her nothing. Thrashing, fighting, she did everything she could to get free, and still he dragged them nearer and nearer to the shore.

The moment his feet touched ground, she felt it. Seconds later hers did, too.

She didn't scream, didn't call out or cry. Instead, she did everything in her physical power to get free.

While continuing to shush her in that oddly soothing

voice, he pinned her down in the muddy ground, immobilizing her legs, making her arms hurt more.

So tired. Muscles aching. Lungs burning.

Giving up seemed more and more likely.

"I'm going to cut you free now. Be still."

A knife! But true to his word, he crouched over her, lifted her wrists and sliced through the nylon restraints.

Then he moved quickly out of her reach.

With her backside sliding on the muddy bank, she scrambled away. Her arms were useless, numb and tingling. Her legs were heavy with fatigue.

"It's okay," he said. He didn't follow. He held his arms out and waited. "You can trust me."

He couldn't be serious. She trusted no one. No one. No one...

CHAPTER FIFTEEN

ARIZONA AWOKE AS SHE OFTEN DID, with a near jolt, her heart thumping, adrenaline surging. She sat upright, and her gaze darted around, searching for any and all threats.

She found none.

Taking in the room with a sense of confusion, she tried to orient herself. Soft sheets covered her, so unlike the usual overstarched bedding in hotel rooms. Gray dawn flooded the room; gentle morning rain trickled over the window panes.

Cozy warmth surrounded her.

And now that she was awake, she felt unaccountably...*safe*.

Nice feelings. Unfamiliar, but...she moved her hand over the sheet. Something in the room smelled wonderful, and she filled her lungs on a deep breath—

"Morning."

Shock took her pounding heart to a standstill. Sucking in air, she placed that deep, recognizable voice—and then oh-so-slowly turned her head to see Spencer stretched out beside her. Oooookay. The sheet just barely rested over his hip. One big hairy leg stuck out.

Her jaw loosened. "You're naked." The second she spoke, she felt the stiffness of her jaw. She touched it and knew she was bruised.

"In my boxers actually." He lifted the sheet to show her. Yeah...not much better. Spencer in boxers was enough to stop her heart. Especially when aroused. And he was.

Again.

Lord have mercy.

Marla hadn't joked about his size. The man was big all over, a fact she'd noticed more than once.

Well. He sure got her heart going again, even faster than the damn nightmare had. By the moment, she became more alert.

"You're okay?" he asked with concern.

"What?"

He nodded, his gaze on her face where she touched her jaw.

"Oh. Yeah." She dropped her hand. "I'm fine."

As he shifted, his brows pulled down in worry.

Seeing all that exposed flesh, so sleek over taut muscle, Arizona automatically breathed in deep again—and her stomach did a crazy little flip.

Mmm. Yup, that's what she inhaled all right—the stimulating scent of warm skin and relaxed muscles on a supersized sexy male bod.

Deeee-licious.

He said nothing else. She didn't, either. Who could talk? She'd rather soak up the sight of him.

Like the morning she'd first awakened him, he looked good with rumpled hair and beard shadow. Unlike that morning, a sort of banked heat smoldered in his dark eyes.

Hello! What had Spence been doing to look all turned-on and primed that way?

Propped on one elbow, he appeared clear-eyed and alert, as if maybe…he'd been watching her.

For a while now.

As she slept.

Wow.

Her thoughts went chaotic, but then, with Spencer, there was nothing new in that. He often left her brain jumbled and her heart confused. She rather liked it, especially since, before Spence, she'd sometimes doubted she had a heart.

Last night was only a vague memory, her last clear thought of being in the bar and seeing him with another woman.

So how'd they end up in bed together? If they'd done the deed and she couldn't remember it, she would be seriously annoyed.

Suspicious, she looked down at her partially stripped body, then again, more leisurely, at his. Cocking a brow, she tried to brazen through the awkwardness. "Do I need to kick your butt?"

Unconcerned with the implied threat, his tone merely curious, Spencer asked, "For what?"

"Taking advantage of me while I was drunk?"

Smiling, he reached out and tugged on a hank of her long, disheveled hair. "No, baby, you don't."

Baby?

"But I might need to turn you over my knee for trying that very thing."

"Yeah, that'll never happen." Not only wouldn't she allow it, she knew Spencer would never do it. But he had said it, so… "What do you mean?"

"Last night, you tried to insist that I take advantage of you."

"No kidding?" Now that he said it, she sort of remembered making some hot and heavy offers. Before going into the bar she'd decided she wanted him. Shoot, looking at him now, listening to that deep, even voice, being so close to him, she *still* wanted him.

Big-time.

And why not? She couldn't stay celibate forever, and she did want to be as whole, as normal and functional, as any other adult.

Spencer claimed to want to help her with that—up to a point anyway.

She wasn't going to give up her work, so who knew if she'd end up caught again? Before that happened, it'd be great to know how it should be.

How it could be with Spencer.

His dark eyes warmed even more, and his voice dropped. "You were awfully hard to resist."

"But you resisted anyway, huh?" Jerk. Way to make her feel like chopped liver. He sure hadn't resisted the bimbo at the bar, never mind that he'd been undercover.

"You'd had way too much to drink," he pointed out.

And that was that; he wasn't an opportunist, especially not with women.

Had she thrown herself at him? Looked like a fool? Suffered humiliating rejection? Gawd. Maybe it was better that she not know.

His big hand stopped toying with her hair and instead dropped down to rest warmly on her knee. "I tried to reason with you, but then you passed out on me."

"Here?"

"You don't remember any of it?"

She screwed up her face, thinking hard… "I kicked Carl's butt. I remember that."

"You broke his fingers." His expression darkened with the reminder. "I did the rest."

An indistinct memory intruded. "Dare had something to do with us cutting the night short…" No wait… Her eyes widened. "It's over, isn't it? Dare shut them down?"

Spencer nodded. "He moved in early and took over."

He filled her in on the details he had. "You drank so much with Janes, it's a wonder you recall anything."

"Bits and pieces are coming back to me." Curiosity crowded in around the relief of knowing innocents had been saved. "So if nothing happened between us, why am I in bed with you?"

"I thought it'd be prudent to keep you close."

"And…how close were we?" Because really, she'd always figured sleeping with a guy—in the literal sense—would make her too edgy. Sleep meant exposure. Lack of defense. Sleep meant she had her guard down, and she plain didn't do that. Not with anyone.

But then, Spencer wasn't just anyone. Not anymore.

Almost from the moment she'd met him, he'd affected her differently. Sometimes she hated it, but most times, she kind of liked the way he made her feel.

"I enjoyed holding you, Arizona." His thumb moved over her knee. "You're very soft and warm."

No way.

Mistaking her wide-eyed incredulity, he frowned again. "You had a nightmare?"

"One I lived through, yeah."

"About?"

"The river. Almost drowning." She waved it off as insignificant. She'd had that damned dream so often, she'd gotten used to it. "Jackson saving me and all that."

"Damn. I'm sorry."

"Same old, same old." She looked around, saw his jeans on a chair, then lifted the sheet and found she wore only her underwear with her top. Her mouth went a little dry. "So…did you undress me?"

"You did that." He gave the sheet a slight tug. "I was noble and covered you up."

"And then crawled into bed with me?"

"It's my bed."

Right. So he did or didn't want her? She couldn't tell. He seemed different today, maybe more susceptible to intimacy, but she didn't relish the idea of asking, only to be turned down again.

What if he'd only slept with her out of convenience? She tried to broach things subtly. "So…what now?"

"That depends on you."

Interesting. Well, she knew what she wanted to do, but she said nothing and instead just waited.

"You have a hangover?"

"Nope." Running her fingers through her tangled hair, she yawned, then flopped down to her back beside him. "My jaw is a little sore, that's all."

His expression flattened. "A bastard at the bar caught you."

Never would have happened if she'd been sober. But she didn't dwell on that, not now, not with Spencer close enough that the heat of his body touched all along her side.

Her heart started doing that crazy thumping thing again.

She looked over at him. "I'm maybe a little muzzy-brained, but no real aftereffects."

"Good." His dark gaze went to her chest, and his nostrils flared.

She still didn't know where this little morning chat was headed. "You're asking because…?"

"We have unfinished business from last night."

Awwwwe-some. But to be certain, she asked, "Sex?"

Pausing, he clarified, "You want me?"

"Oh, yeah."

"Good." He leaned toward her.

Yay! But now that Arizona had it confirmed, nervousness set in, and she held him off with one hand. "Hold up, Spence."

That got his attention back on her face. He studied her, and whatever he saw—or thought he saw—banked the fires. "Things look different in the light of day, now that you're clearheaded, don't they?"

"Not really." As yet unmentioned stipulations aside, she still wanted to devour him from head to toe. But he sounded so self-righteous, so…condescendingly male, as if he expected her to act the part of a swooning virgin or something, that she couldn't keep from messing with him a little. "It's just that I can't… I don't…"

"Shh, I know, baby." He drew a deep breath and nodded. "I understand."

"Do you?"

"Of course I do." All too serious, he curled his fingers over hers. "It's okay."

Arizona snickered at his restraint, and when he eyed her with confusion, the laughter bubbled out. "C'mon, Spence. I'm just funning you."

"Funning me?"

Turning on her side to face him, she mimicked his pose with her head braced on a hand. "Of course I'm still game. Shoot, I'm dying to do the nasty with you."

He scrutinized her. "But?"

Boy, he was good at reading her. "But…" Trying to find the right words, she cleared her throat. "The thing is…I need…"

He didn't rush her. He didn't move. It almost looked as if he didn't breathe.

Deciding to just spit it out, she said, "It's gotta be lights on. Me on top. You got a problem with that?"

No reaction.

"Spence?"

He visibly shored up his self-control. "I don't want to pressure you. I don't want you to do anything before you're ready."

"I'm ready. And trust me, I want to do this. I just have a few glitches, that's all."

"Glitches?"

"Like I said, lights on."

"Tell me why."

Seemed obvious to her. "So I can see you—that way, there's no...confusion in my memories."

She saw it in his eyes, the realization that without lights, she would remember other men, doing other things.

Far too grave, Spencer closed his eyes, but only for a moment. "No problem."

He took that so well, she expounded on the rest. "And me on top because, really Spencer, hunky as you are, I still have some trust issues, you know? I gotta know I have control."

His brows lifted in disbelief. "Being on top lets you think you're controlling me?"

She let his arrogance slide to say, "Yeah. I mean, why should I make it too easy on you?"

He snorted. "Let me assure you, Arizona, you have *never* been easy, not in any way."

"And," she said, talking over him, "before you answer, know this—if you turn me down again, I'm going to feel really rejected."

His big hand cupped the side of her face. "No man in his right mind could ever reject you."

Relief turned her bones to noodles. "So is doing it my way a problem?"

"Lights on, with you on top?"

"That's how it has to be."

Understanding softened his stern expression. "Doesn't sound like too much of a hardship."

Was he mocking her? Arizona rolled over atop him. "Is this going to be fun, Spencer? Because seriously, you don't look real excited." She pressed a firm but fast kiss to his mouth. "I want it to be fun."

"Got it. Well-lit, you in the dominant position—and plenty of laughs. Any other demands?"

Her temper sparked. "You don't like the stipulations? Fine. Forget it." She started to roll away.

"So bossy." He caught her, holding her still against him while fighting a smile. "I like your stipulations just fine."

"Baloney."

"I want to see you, Arizona. Hell, I'm dying to see you. So lights on would be my preference anyway. And you over me just gives me a better view."

She hadn't thought of that.

He focused on her mouth. "Far as the laughs go, well, I'm hoping I don't inspire hilarity, but I very much want you to enjoy yourself. What do you think?"

She scowled at him. "You're sure?"

"I know trust doesn't come easy for you." Slowly, tenderly, he smoothed back her long hair. "You might want to remember that I only want the best for you. In all things."

Oh, she could hardly wait. "All-righty, then." Hesitant on how to proceed, she asked, "Should I get naked now?"

His hands moved down her spine to the small of her back—then just rested there. "Is that what you want to do?"

His patience wasn't helping to put her at ease. Why

couldn't he be a little more…frenzied? Like she was? "I don't know. It's what I normally did when—"

His hand covered her mouth. Face tight, his expression a little pained, he drew another breath. "I want you to forget all that."

Fat chance. Did it bother him more than it bothered her? Seemed possible. For a big macho protector like him, it'd be a tough reality to get past.

She took his wrist and pulled his hand away. "Are you trying to forget?"

He opened his mouth—then frowned. With regret, he said, "We're rushing things."

"So?" If he'd rush a little more, they could be halfway through it already.

"You need to get a shower."

Was he already pulling back? Well, he could forget it. "Shower with me."

He shook his head. "Why did I think you'd be more reasonable sober?"

"No idea." She ran her hands over his chest. She *loved* the feel of his crisp chest hair. "You must not have been paying attention." She also loved the feel of his strong bones and firm muscles, and just looking at him made her insides quiver.

She wanted to do this, she really did.

"Oh, I've paid attention all right. Count on it."

Having no idea what he meant by that, she leaned down and teased her nose over him. His scent left her more intoxicated than the whiskey had. "I gotta tell you, Spence, you are one sexy dude."

His smile came reluctantly. "Thank you." Then he caught her and eased her back. "But I think maybe I should shower and shave, and—"

"You're looking for excuses, aren't you?" Disgruntled, she scowled at him. "You sure you want me?"

"Very sure." He again looked at her mouth. "More than I've ever wanted anything."

That surprised her. So did he mean, like, more than he had wanted Marla? And what about his wife? And that bimbo he'd been cuddled up to in the bar last night? Or did he just mean recently? "So you're saying—"

"I want you, Arizona Storm. Never doubt it. I'm dying to kiss you, to get you naked—even though you smell of stale whiskey."

"I do?" But of course she did. Unwilling to breathe on him more, she pursed her mouth. Good grief. She hadn't even thought about that.

He smiled. "I want you even though you have makeup all around your eyes." Regret replaced the smile. "And a few colorful bruises."

She scowled, then pushed up to sit on the bedding. "The bruises bother you?"

"Of course they do, because it means you got hurt again." He came up beside her and stroked her hair over her shoulder. "I'm going to kiss each and every one of them. It won't really help, but it'll make me feel better."

He sounded all husky and affected, and that affected her. "It'll make me feel better, too."

He pressed small kisses along her jaw, to her ear and then over her shoulder. "You sure about that, honey?"

She shivered. "What do you mean?"

He continued kissing her, soft, damp kisses in surprising places that left behind a tiny tingle. "Forget about your past for a minute, okay?"

Not really possible, but she shrugged. "Yeah, okay."

"Do you understand what I want to do to you? How different it's going to be?"

She thought she'd known, but now… "Um…maybe?"

"You're trying to rush through things, but I want to take it slow." He lifted her hair away, and she felt his tongue on her nape, then the edge of his teeth. "I'm glad you want the room well-lit, because I want to look my fill."

"Me, too." She couldn't wait to explore his big, strong body.

His hand touched the inside of her knee, drifted up her inner thigh.

Sensation chased ahead of his fingertips; anticipation left her breathless.

But he stopped short.

With his mouth touching her temple, he whispered, "I want to touch you, and kiss you. All over."

Her stomach seemed to tumble. "All over?"

"Yeah." His smile came slow and easy. "Everywhere."

The way he said that curled her toes.

"I want to know your taste, and I want to breathe in your scent. Here." He nuzzled the side of her neck. "And here." He trailed a finger down between her breasts. "And especially here." His hand opened low over her belly.

She bit back a groan.

Then he put some space between them. "And as hard as it'll be to hold back, I don't want to be rushed. *You* won't want me to be rushed."

None of that sounded like what she'd expected based on her experiences. "I don't see…"

"It's early yet. We have hours before we need to leave for Dare's."

Oh, crap. Her birthday gathering. She'd forgotten all about that.

He brought her chin around to look into her eyes. "It's

not as long as I'd like. I'd rather have the whole day to focus on you, to show you how things should really be. But we'll spend what time we have in bed. So if there's anything you want to do beforehand, I suggest you do it now."

She gave it quick thought—and decided she needed a few minutes to get a grip. "Okay, so how about I go shower and you put on coffee, and then we'll take it from there?" She rolled out of the bed and headed for the bathroom. "Make the coffee strong. I think I need it."

"Arizona?"

She paused at the bathroom door, looked back and saw him staring at her backside. "Yeah?"

"I can maybe wait while you drink one cup, tops." His gaze lifted to hers. "After that, I make no promises."

A SHOWER REVIVED HER physically, but she'd used every single second to go over what Spencer had said and how he'd said it.

Now…now her hands shook, and a slow burn smoldered inside her. She couldn't stop thinking about what they'd do, couldn't keep the visuals from her mind.

She had a feeling Spencer had done that on purpose just to work her up. Diabolical. And oh-so-hot.

Rather than wash her hair and take the time to dry it, she put it in a high ponytail. Wearing a T-shirt and shorts, she sat at the kitchen table and tried to enjoy her coffee.

But Spencer was in the shower now. *Naked*. And every second that passed torqued her tension a little tighter.

A sweet ache curled inside her.

Her lungs constricted so that she had to breathe harder, faster.

So this was lust? Who knew?

It was better than she'd ever figured. Sure, she knew stuff happened differently between two willing people. She wasn't a dummy. What she'd done as a captive, forced by traffickers, was not at all the norm.

There'd be pleasure. She'd seen plenty of movies, talked to lots of people.

And she knew how Jackson and Alani behaved with each other. Dare and Molly. Trace and Priss. They sure liked getting up close and personal.

Very soon that'd be her. With Spencer.

She closed her eyes as sensation swelled inside her, sweeter, hotter.

But he wanted her to wait?

Screw that.

She plopped the now-empty coffee mug down on the table and started down the hall. Along the way, huffing fast with need, she peeled off her shirt and then paused long enough to push off her shorts. Reaching up, she pulled the cloth-covered rubber band from her hair and it tumbled down her back.

Still in panties, she knocked at the bathroom door.

Spencer said, "Yeah?" as he opened the door for her.

Shock kept him still for a heartbeat, then his gaze dropped fast, moving all over her. He inhaled, and his face tightened.

A white towel circled his hips, another hung around his neck. Steam wafted upward, caressing his damp skin. He'd just finished shaving.

They stared at each other.

Or more precisely, he stared at her boobs, and she stared at that happy trail of dark, fine hair that disappeared into the towel.

Without looking away from her, he put aside his razor

and, taking the towel from around his neck, wiped the remaining shaving cream off his face. He discarded the towel on the floor.

Licking her lips, Arizona reached out, hooked her fingertips into the other towel, and pulled it away from his body. It hung loose in her hand.

Holy smokes, he hadn't been kidding. He really did want her.

The man was impressive—in all ways. "You're big."

"Yes."

He sounded awfully cavalier about it. "So…" She couldn't get her gaze off his jutting erection. "Looks like you're ready, too."

"I've been ready since the day I met you."

What a relief, since she'd felt the same. Oh, she'd done her best to ignore it. But not anymore.

She let the towel slip from her fingers. "That's…nice."

His hands fisted. "You're not afraid?"

"Nope." Anxious, needy, desperate even, but not afraid. She met his gaze. "Not with you."

Some sharp emotion brightened his eyes. "At all uncertain?" He brought her face up. "Because, baby, I know you were uncertain earlier."

Ah, so that's why he'd suggested the shower and the coffee and the excruciating delay? *For her.*

What a guy. "Yeah, I guess I was. A little."

"I don't want you to be." Still he didn't touch her. "Not at all."

"I'm not anymore." A little shakily, she added, "Honest to God, Spencer, I appreciate the concern. I really do. But I don't think I can wait a single second more."

He nodded—and continued to resist. "Has any man ever spent his time just kissing you?"

"No." Her heart beat so hard it hurt. "Thank God."

He took a step closer. "Has any man ever touched you, just for you? Just to make you feel good?"

"Of course not. Men don't—"

"Shh." Calm personified, he pressed a warm kiss to her mouth. Slow, lingering.

As he drew away, Arizona lifted her heavy lashes, took a breath and whispered, "Damn."

Wearing a half smile, Spencer closed in for another kiss, a little hungrier, a little less cautious.

Now, that was more like it. Her breath shuddered in, came out in a sigh. "Oh, hell."

He caught on to her game. "Are you asking for another kiss, honey?"

"That's the deal, right?" She leaned into him, her mouth almost touching his. "For every curse—"

"Yes, that's the deal."

"Well, I know a lot of curses." She played her hand down his chest, over to his side. God, she loved the feel of him. "So what's it to be, Spence? Should I singe your ears, or do you just want to—"

His mouth settled over hers without reserve. And she accepted with a hardy groan, clinging hands and the press of her body to his.

"Spencer…"

He drew her in closer. "Tell me what you want."

"This is all so curious."

"This?"

"Sex." She turned her head to meet his gaze. "I gotta admit, until you, I hadn't been a fan of the idea."

"I know." Pain filled his gaze. "I'm sorry."

"Wasn't your doing, now, was it?" She leaned into him, enjoying his strength, his heat. His appeal. "But with you? I dunno. You make me feel funny."

His big, hot hand opened over her belly. "Here?"

"Yeah." She pressed her hand over his, absorbing the warmth of his palm while breathing in his delicious male scent.

"Funny, how? Tell me."

"All warm and...slippery."

He bit off a groan. "Perfect. That's exactly how I want you to feel."

"And how should you feel?" Teasing, anxious to touch him, she reached for his erection.

He caught her wrists and held her hands away.

"Spencer?" He looked pained. He looked...stoic.

A heartbeat of silence passed. "Let me show you, okay?"

Something in the way he said that made uncertainty take hold. "Whoa." She stepped back from him. "Show me what?"

With shaking hands he smoothed back her hair. "How good it can be for you."

"But not for you?"

"No matter what, I'm going to enjoy this, too. Never doubt it."

Shaking on the inside, she tucked in her chin. "This?"

Firm, he said, "Giving you pleasure. Taking you to orgasm."

No freaking way. "What, with you all uninvolved and stuff, and me being some sort of a sacrifice?" He had to be joking. She shoved against his chest. "Thanks, but no thanks."

He caught her to him. "It wouldn't be like that."

"I want you inside me, damn you. I want you with me all the way."

Breathing harder, he locked his jaw. "I can hold off,

Arizona. I can do what's right—for both of us. But not if you…"

"Well, I *am!*" Humiliation washed over her. She gave him another hard shove and finally freed herself. "I'm not a damn project for you to work on!"

"I didn't—"

"I'm not playing this stupid game of yours. Either you want me, or you don't." Thumb to her naked chest, she shouted, "I'm an all-or-nothing woman."

More than a little aware of her nudity, she turned to depart on a dramatic exit.

Before she'd even taken a full step, he pulled her back around and scooped her up against him. His own measure of frustration deepened his voice, sharpened his tone. "Your stipulations mean you *aren't* all-or-nothing."

"So instead of calling them stipulations, just call them a fetish." She went on tiptoe, leaning into his anger. "Lots of people like to take control in bed."

"It's not the same thing and you know it."

Deflated, hurt, she muttered, "I wanted to feel you inside me. I wanted to be a part of you." Tears burned her eyes, scalding her with humiliation. "Thanks for nothing."

He breathed hard, his nostrils flared, his eyes bright. "I tried, Arizona. God knows I did."

She started to tell him to go to hell, but his mouth landed on hers, not tentative, not gentle, but hungry and demanding.

Suddenly on fire, she groaned her approval and clenched her hands on his shoulders.

He stroked down her back to her rear, lifted her up and pulled her in snug against his erection. Against her lips, he said, "I need you, Arizona. Right now."

Ah, now *this* was what she'd wanted. She could

handle the overwhelming physical stuff better than all that knee-weakening emotion or, God forbid, his nobility. "You have a funny way of showing it."

"I'm sorry." He lifted her completely off her feet, and she just naturally wrapped her legs around his waist. "Arizona…"

"I've got you now." She knotted her fingers in his damp hair and said with carnal demand, "Kiss me again."

"I will." He licked her neck, drew her skin in against his teeth. "But, remember, you have to trust me."

"I do." She moaned, squeezed him tighter. *When had her neck gotten so damned sensitive?* "If you even think about—"

"I won't." And then, resigned to his fate: "I can't." He kissed her mouth again, devouring her, his tongue bold.

He tasted so incredibly good that Arizona didn't realize he'd headed for the bedroom until he stretched out on the mattress, her atop him. Since her legs had been around him, she ended up straddling him, her knees pulled up along his sides.

Keeping one hand on her head, he moved the other down her spine—and into her underwear.

Startled, she made to straighten her legs, but he said, "No, leave them open. Let me touch you." And then with a growl, "I *need* to touch you."

Everything inside her clenched. "Yeah, okay." But because the idea of him touching her *there* excited her so much, she took his mouth again.

Nothing could be as nice as kissing Spencer.

And true, she did have a few twinges of trepidation. But they were nothing compared to the searing urge to get closer to him, to taste more of him, to learn his body and *feel* him, all over.

He kept stroking her bottom, leisurely touching her as if he enjoyed her skin—right up until he delved down, his fingertips playing between her legs, over her sex.

Gasping, she freed her mouth and arched her back.

He murmured, "You're wet."

"Yeah," she said with wonder. When she looked down, she found him staring at her intently. Gazes locked, he pressed in one finger.

Oh...wow.

Who knew? She all but panted, amazed at how that felt. "That's..." But she didn't have words.

Spencer slid his free hand over her thigh, pulling her leg up higher along his hip. "Scoot up so I can get to your nipples."

Um...she didn't think she could do that. If it weren't for her stiffened arms keeping her over him, she'd collapse in a boneless heap of sensation.

"Arizona. Come on, baby. Scoot up here."

"I can't."

"I'll help." He took his fingers from her, making her moan, and clasped her waist. "I sort of cut corners on this anyway."

"This?"

"Enjoying you. Doing things right." He gave her a crooked and very sexual smile. "A man should always start at the top and work his way down. But you threw me off, standing there in the doorway all but naked."

"You *are* naked."

"Because you stole my towel." He cupped one breast, ran his thumb over her stiffened nipple. She felt the jolt of it all through her body. "Since you want to be on top, this is how we'll do it," he told her while watching the play of his hand at her breast. "Come here."

On a groan, she slowly leaned forward, closer, her

body tensed and her heart thundering. Knowing what he would do and so eager to feel it, she leaned in—ahhhh.

Without teasing, with no prelude, his hot mouth closed over her, drawing her in, sucking on her gently. Her lashes sank down and her lips parted. "Oh, God, Spencer. That is so…"

"What?" He licked, circling his tongue around her, kissed her nipple one last time and switched to the other breast to start sucking again.

"Awesome." No wonder people chose to do this. Okay, so she'd expected it to be nice, but she hadn't expected this.

When his hand went back into her panties, his fingers back between her legs, it was almost too much.

The intensifying ache built, growing and ebbing like a tide, making her gasp and rock against him. Tighter and tighter, until she thought she might break—and wanted to.

Eyes squeezed shut, teeth clenched, she groaned in mounting frustration and acute need.

Suddenly Spencer moved her back.

It startled her, his abrupt withdrawal, and she inhaled a broken breath. Confused, she stared at him. "What's the matter?"

"I need a condom, honey. Now." He lifted her off him and sat up to rummage in the bedside drawer.

A little lost, turbulent sensation still churning through her, Arizona rested there on her knees. Spencer had his broad, muscled back to her as he took care of business, and then he turned toward her again. "Let's get rid of these panties."

She swallowed hard. "Okay. Sounds like a plan." She started to push them down, but he moved her hands away.

"Let me." He eased her to her back on the mattress,

saying, "I know you don't want me over you, so don't worry. But I'm going to enjoy removing them a lot more than you will."

She didn't understand him. How could he be so calm when she was so urgent? "Will you get on with it?"

"No." Lazily studying her everywhere from below her chin to above her knees, he opened his hand over her belly. "You are incredibly stacked, Arizona, without a single flaw anywhere. I've never seen a woman so damned...perfect."

She snorted at that. She knew she was about as far from perfect as a human being could get.

He ignored her sound of disagreement, saying, "But even if you weren't so gorgeous, I'd still want you."

"Really?" Then why wouldn't he end the frustration?

Palming each breast, he toyed with her nipples, making her crazed. "Absolutely." He went back to her belly, then lower, cupping his hand between her legs. He closed his eyes a moment. "You're appealing in ways you don't even realize."

She'd have asked for details, but with his fingers touching her, she couldn't think straight, much less talk.

He opened his eyes again. "But seeing you like this now, how drop-dead sexy you are, is a nice bonus."

"I think you're pretty damned sexy, too." She twisted under his teasing hand and gasped out, "I guess big alpha studs really do it for me."

His gaze flickered up to hers for just a moment. "All alphas, huh?"

No way. Was he actually comparing himself to Jackson? "I can't see me being drawn to a wimp. But the fact that I bullied you into this says that you're different, right?"

"I guess it does." Staring down at her, his gaze intent,

he moved her thighs farther apart. "Will it bother you if I bend down to here—" he traced a fingertip around and over the crotch of her panties "—to kiss you?"

Her toes curled again, her throat tightened in expectation. Shaking her head, she gasped, "Knock yourself out."

Another crooked smile, and then, "Thank you. I think I will." Bending, he nuzzled his nose against her, breathing in deeply of her scent before opening his mouth over her.

Through the thin barrier of her panties, she felt his hot breath and then the press of his hotter tongue. It made her a little crazed. Her thighs fell open more. "That's... Yeah." Biting off a ripe moan, she tipped back her head and stared at the ceiling, happy to absorb this new experience.

"I've been dying to taste you," he said in a guttural voice thick with need.

"I didn't expect..." What? Any of this? Or more to the point, the impact of it on her senses.

He drew his teeth carefully over her, and her back arched on a sharp ache. He soothed with his tongue, and the moan broke free.

Turning his face, Spencer took a soft love bite of her inner thigh. "I think we better put this on hold."

"Damn you, Spencer." Only half jesting, she said, "I own both a knife and a gun, you know!"

He disregarded her implied threat. "Sorry, but with you, now, I'm high on need and short on control. I can't do this." With a growl, he kissed her thigh, her hip bone. "Not without ending up over you, and possibly dredging up a bad memory." A second later, he whisked her panties down and off her legs. "And not while I need you so much."

Bummer. She should have kept her big mouth shut about that little issue of hers. Maybe it wouldn't even have mattered. Maybe with Spencer—

In a rush, he sat up against the headboard and caught her wrist. "Ready?"

She turned her head toward him. "For what, exactly?"

"You laid out the rules, honey, so I need you to ride me."

Oh. Right. *Boy, that sounded super-sexy.*

She licked her lips in anticipation and moved up over him again. She'd been so close, all that pulsing pleasure escalating toward something monumental. But she didn't begrudge him this.

Of course he wanted to get off. When it came right down to it, he was still just a man.

He helped her to settle over him.

Heart rapping madly, she braced herself with her knees outside his hips, her hands on his hard shoulders.

Opening her with his fingers, he guided himself to her.

Thinking of his size, she swallowed, preparing, knowing he'd thrust up into her, bracing for it…

But Spencer stopped. When she opened her eyes to look at him again, he gave her a tender smile. "Arizona?"

Her throat tightened more, but she managed to say, "Hmm?"

"Will you kiss me?"

Yeah, kissing would help. Sometimes, when she kissed Spencer, she forgot everything else.

"Okay, sure." She leaned down to him. Any second now he'd be deep inside her. Would it hurt?

She didn't think it'd be too bad, because seconds after that he'd be done.

A little pain? No big deal. She couldn't wait to have

him fill her up. But she didn't want it to end, not yet, not so soon.

Taking her mouth in a deep but gentle kiss, he began slowly rocking into her. She would have gasped, but he had his tongue in her mouth, one hand on the back of her head keeping her close, the other on her hip, guiding her.

He took his own sweet time about it, too, easing into her, teasing her with the slowness of it, making her want him deep, forcing her to groan again in frustration.

Yup, as a really big guy, he was…proportionate in all ways.

But it was actually pretty wonderful, more so than she'd ever imagined. No pain, just sweet, sharp pleasure.

As he filled her up and then some, she squeezed without meaning to and drank his groan of pleasure. Deeper, deeper, until he'd buried himself inside her.

Indescribable.

Unfamiliar. Exciting.

New and hot.

She freed her mouth and whispered, "Ohmigod, that's…" She breathed hard.

Spencer kept his dark, glittering gaze locked on hers. "I want your mouth, Arizona. Don't stop kissing me."

"Okay. But don't you want to—"

"Not yet."

His mouth was wonderful; he kissed her in ways she'd never known, in ways that…involved her. Pleased her.

It felt more *about* her than she'd known was possible. He kept kissing her more and more, as if he couldn't get enough, couldn't give enough.

He was inside her, yet he didn't thrust. No loss of control. No rush to the finish line.

Except to cuddle her breasts and stroke her skin and

make her insane with those drugging kisses, he didn't move at all.

When she moaned, he finally freed her mouth, but only to kiss her throat, her shoulder.

How the heck could that be so wonderful?

He lifted her breast and closed his mouth over her nipple again, tugging hotly, teasing with his tongue and then with his teeth.

All those remarkable, wonderful aches deepened, building up, expanding, until *she* had to move.

And when she did, Spencer helped her, clasping her hips and guiding her so that she rode him just right, pulling away and then sinking down again, getting all of him on each long stroke.

Heat rose from their bodies. They both breathed harder and faster, moved harder and faster.

And through it all, Spencer touched her, watched her, encouraged her.

Focused on her.

That was so new—and so exciting.

Her eyes closed and her fingertips sank into his shoulders. "Don't you dare stop again."

"I won't." With both hands on her breasts, he teased her nipples, his gentle touch making her wilder, hotter. "I could look at you like this all day."

All day? No way. "I can't…" Her thighs strained and her body clenched around him. The pleasure peaked— and ebbed. Oh, God, oh, God. "I need…" *Something.* Her thundering heartbeat rocked her body. "Spencer…"

"Shh. It's okay. I'm going to help you." He slipped a hand between their bodies, his fingers sliding over her wet sex until he touched her clitoris.

"Right here, Arizona?" He watched her face and smiled. "Yes. Right here."

Crying out, she rode him hard as she sought release. He found a rhythm that sent her heartbeat skyrocketing. She tried to be quiet and couldn't. She tried to center on him and couldn't. Everything narrowed, spiked.

His voice rough, Spencer whispered, "I want you to come for me, Arizona."

And amazingly enough, she did.

CHAPTER SIXTEEN

SPENCER WATCHED HER FACE, saw the moment the pleasure overtook her, and much as he wanted to let go, he couldn't give it up, couldn't miss seeing her like this.

Never one to be inhibited, Arizona came with deep guttural groans, her face tight with release, her long dark hair tumbling everywhere. He felt her squeezing him tight, and he felt her wetness.

More than that, he felt her surprise.

As she eased, her cries quieted, and her body quivered in small aftershocks. Limp, a little sweaty, she came down over his chest with a moan. "Oh, my God."

Moved by her honest response, he smiled and kissed her temple, then rearranged her a little, keeping her legs bent but stroking her spine and smoothing back her hair. It was the oddest thing, being so primed and so incredibly turned on, but content just to be with her, to hold her.

"I have no bones."

"Mmm. Well, I still have one particular bone that I'll continue sharing with you."

She snickered. "I meant that I'm limp."

"In a good way, I hope." He kissed her temple again with affection and caring, though he doubted she knew it.

Could she recognize genuine caring? He just didn't know.

"A very good way." She stirred enough to run her fingers through his chest hair. "I like this."

Damn, given the slick, snug way she still held him, when she moved her hand, even a finger, he felt it on his cock. "The release?"

"Actually, I meant your sexy, hairy chest. God, Spencer, I do love touching you." She lifted her head and smiled at him. She had a glow about her, her blue eyes lazy, her honey-colored skin flushed a dusky rose. Almost timidly, she said, "But, yeah, the other was pretty amazing, too."

Damn, but she pleased him. "I'm glad."

"It was a surprise, you know? Sort of blew my socks off. At least it would have if I was wearing socks."

Nervous chatter from Arizona?

Talking while still buried inside her sweet body wasn't easy, but he managed. "Sometimes surprises are nice."

She now had both hands running over his chest. "I mean, of course I knew about it. But getting that, going all goosey and tingly and that breathtaking wave of sensation, with you inside me, well, that was a big old first for me."

Damn it, he couldn't bear it. Hearing her talk about it was making him hotter. He caught her face and pulled her in close for another devouring kiss. He wanted to brand her in some way, to make her his and only his— and he wanted to treat her as gently as possible, to cherish her and show her that love didn't hurt.

Love?

Oh, God. Determined to block that from his mind, Spencer tangled his hands in her hair and ate at her soft mouth. Not turning her to her back took great concentration on his part. He desperately wanted to be over her, in her, driving hard and deep...

His control shattered.

"My turn," he whispered, and it took little enough for him to clasp that lush ass and press up into her. She still had her knees drawn up along his sides, her full, firm breasts pressing against his chest.

As he thrust, she moaned, clenched around him, and opened her mouth on his shoulder.

Surprised, he asked softly, "Again?"

As an answer, her short nails dug into his muscles, and she began rocking her hips in a cadence with his.

Amazing.

Holding back wasn't easy, but no way would he cut her short. He hugged her closer so that she ground against him with each movement of their bodies, her clit on his shaft, her stiffened nipples against his chest. With her scent surrounding him, she got wetter, her body hotter, and he had to grit his teeth to keep from exploding.

Just when he thought he wouldn't last a second more, she gave a vibrating moan and treated him to the slight sting of her sharp little teeth. *Perfect.* He let himself go with a harsh, guttural groan.

Coming was great.

Coming with Arizona was...hell, maybe life-altering. He felt a part of her, connected in an alarming way.

After what seemed an eternity, they both went lax, melting into the mattress with pounding heartbeats and labored breaths. Arizona was a warm, gentle weight on his chest, her scent spicier now, filling his head.

Seconds ticked by.

He didn't want to move. Ever.

He didn't want to talk, either. Not yet. Not until he'd reconciled all the ways she leveled him.

Nothing had really changed, and yet it felt as if everything had.

Sluggishly, Arizona pushed up on straightened arms and looked at him. With an amused shake of her head and a groan of near-discomfort, she unbent her legs—and collapsed again.

And even that, feeling her slim but strong limbs around him, her full breasts and now soft nipples on his sweat-damp chest…it moved him. A lot.

In myriad ways.

While trying to calm his chaotic thoughts, Spencer idly caressed her dewy skin. He could span the width of her back with one hand, and yet she had more courage than most grown men.

At six feet, five inches tall, he towered over a lot of people. His job as a bounty hunter, his demeanor of grim resolve, gave most reason for pause. But not Arizona. From their very first meeting, she'd gone head to head with him, her pride, her determination and confidence matching his in spades.

She'd been smart enough for wariness; she had a very real understanding of her own limitations. But she'd had no real fear of him.

Mostly because she thought she had little enough to lose. But also because she had real skill. Granted, the skills were limited by her size and strength, but put to the test, she'd do well under pressure or in a situation rife with danger.

He admired her.

And now, knowing she also matched him sexually… it was more than any man should have to deal with.

"Holy smokes, Spence." She gave him a playful

love bite, then rubbed her nose over his chest hair. "I'm almost speechless."

Relishing all the tantalizing dips and curves of her body, he ran his hands from her shoulders to her ass and back again. She was the sexiest thing he'd ever seen.

The most fearless. Most reckless.

And the most endearing.

What the hell was he going to do with her?

Unlike with other women, he couldn't just decide to enjoy his time with her while it lasted. He squeezed his eyes shut, but he couldn't shut out the reality of their relationship.

Complicated, difficult and important—to her, to her future and how she accepted life. How she valued herself.

He was the biggest fraud imaginable, because he'd known from the onset that he couldn't play this game without eventually bedding her. He wasn't superhuman, and that's what it'd take to resist a woman like Arizona, especially while getting closer.

So he'd known, and still he'd used the excuse of trying to help her over the hurdles of emotional and physical abuse as a way to get her under him. Because he'd *had* to have her.

God, that sounded awful, even as it rang true.

And that made him a grade-A bastard.

Arizona would be the first to deny it, but she was by far the most vulnerable woman he'd ever met. She had no understanding of common courtesy, much less genuine kindness. She expected little and told herself she wanted, and deserved, nothing more.

For her, affection was an unfamiliar, even alien concept. As a grown and experienced man, he could decipher what he felt. He could deal with it.

He understood it.

But Arizona didn't have the advantage of healthy relationships to contrast against this. Her emotional growth had been so badly stunted by traffickers that she might misconstrue sexual satisfaction for something…more.

She deserved all those exciting first discoveries that most girls started building in their late teens. Arizona deserved to have comparisons, to really know what she felt and what she wanted.

She should expect the best, because she deserved it.

"You've gotten awfully quiet."

He cupped a big hand over her backside, palming one cheek. "You wore me out and my brain is sluggish."

Sounding far too young, she asked with forced insouciance, "Not disappointed?"

Her uncertainty stabbed like a knife. "No, baby." He kissed her crown, then the bridge of her nose. "I'm as far from disappointed as a man could get."

"Good." Relief lightened her tone. "Because I liked it, too."

That made him smile. "I know."

"You do?"

"I figured coming twice was a positive sign."

"Oh. Yeah, I guess." She propped herself up with her pointy little elbows on his chest. "I've never done that before."

"Come with a man?"

Nodding, she toyed again with his chest hair. "By myself, well, that's different. But the idea of getting with a man willingly…"

"I understand." And he was very glad to be the man who shared that with her.

"You surprised me."

The room was quiet, the gray day intimate, the tumbled sheets comfortable. He ran his fingers through her tangled hair. Everything about her, physical and emotional, fascinated him more than he'd ever thought possible. "Give me an hour or so, and I can surprise you again."

She didn't smile with him. "So…"

That particular serious look on Arizona had him really curious. "Something on your mind, honey?"

She chewed her lower lip, then blurted, "Jackson is pretty notorious sex candy."

Sex candy? *Jackson?* That wasn't at all what he'd expected, and for a moment, he stalled. While exploring the curve of her behind, he explained quietly, "You probably don't know this, but when you're sprawled out over a naked man after having sex with him, it's really bad form to talk about another guy."

Her brows scrunched down. "But I'm curious."

Worse and worse.

He didn't want to discourage her—not in any way—so he tried to hide all disgruntlement. "About Jackson?"

She studied him, and her face brightened with a mocking grin. "Not *that* way." Laughing, she slugged his shoulder. "It's just that I was thinking of him being such a panty-dropper."

The things she said could make his brain swim. "*Former* panty-dropper."

She looked at him in confusion. "What?"

Because it was important for her to understand the distinction, which reflected not only on relationships in general but also highlighted the difference between honorable men and cheaters, Spencer tried to explain. "Jackson is in love with Alani. You know that, right?"

"He doesn't exactly hide his feelings about her. So what?"

"Being in love means that Alani's panties are the only ones Jackson wants to drop from now on."

Perplexed, she thought about that. "So a guy has to be in love to give up variety?"

He had no idea about the direction of her thoughts. But he wanted to be patient with her, and he wanted her to feel comfortable asking him anything. "What's this about, baby?"

She veered offtrack to ask, "Why are you calling me baby?"

Leaning in to put his nose in her neck, Spencer smelled her. Touched her. Tasted her skin. "You are so soft, and so sweet. It's just an endearment. You don't like it?"

"I don't know. I guess it's okay."

He kissed her to keep from smiling. "So what are you thinking about?"

After a long hesitation that built the tension, she blurted, "Are you going to be doing this with any other women? I mean, while you're doing it with me?"

Jealousy? Possessiveness? He suffered both, but he hadn't expected it of her. Pretending to misunderstand, he mused aloud, "I did offer that redhead in the bar a three-way—"

She slugged him again, not so playfully this time. "Not funny, Spence."

The grin got away from him. "It's a little funny."

She started to leave him, but he held on to her, and after the briefest wrestling match where he chuckled and she groused, she gave up. "Fine." Plopping down on him again, she snapped, "Do whatever you want. Screw whoever you want."

"I need a few minutes first, but thanks."

Her mouth opened, then closed. After a second, she asked, "Me?"

"I'm a one-woman-at-a-time man." He lifted her face and kissed her lightly on her mulish mouth. "Right now, you're the only one I want."

"Really?"

She looked so hopeful, wearing her heart on her sleeve, not bothering to protect herself. She would protect the world, anyone she thought needed her help.

But she wouldn't protect her own heart.

"Silly Arizona." He cupped her face, stroked her jaw with a thumb. "How on earth could I want any other woman when you're around?"

Her mood lightened, and she surprised him by sitting up with a smile. "Let's go eat some cake. I'm hungry." She eyed him from head to toe and back again. "And maybe the sugar will speed along your recovery."

So she wanted him again? Nice. "That particular hungry look from you might have done the trick." He reached for her—and his doorbell rang.

Her expression went from impish to suspicious. "Who is that?"

"No idea." Bodily, he lifted her out of his way and stood. "Why don't you stay put and I'll go find out?"

"Like that?" She nodded at his crotch. "Probably not a good idea."

"Smart-ass." He removed the spent condom and dropped it into the waste can, then reached for a pair of boxers.

Fascinated, Arizona watched him intently. "Well, you *know* who it is."

He had an idea, but it wasn't easy to banter with her while she sat there naked, in his bed, still warm from sex and staring so fixedly at his junk. "Who?"

"It's Marla."

"You don't know that." He pulled on jeans as the bell rang again. "Could be the postman." And just to tease her, he said, "Or maybe Jackson decided to visit you."

"Nah." She sprawled to her back, one leg bent, arms over her head, and stretched. She was utterly comfortable in her nudity. "He'll visit with us later today at Dare's."

Spencer had to take a turn staring. "I don't suppose you'd want to stay exactly like that until I get back."

She went still, then smiled. "You plan to take long?"

"No." He wanted Arizona again, and he didn't trust her to her own temper, so he'd send Marla on her way as quickly as he could.

"Will you bring me some cake?"

In two long strides, Spencer reached her. Without thinking about it, he leaned over her for a quick smooch and ended up kissing air when Arizona bolted to the other side of the bed.

She stood there, shoulders back with pride, face pinched with embarrassment.

Spencer straightened. They stared at each other. "I'm sorry. I forgot."

Her mouth tightened, but she nodded. "It's okay."

No, it wasn't, but the bell sounded again. "I was only going to kiss you."

Suddenly bounding up and over the bed to land in front of him, she grabbed his face for a hard kiss. "I'm sorry I…reacted. Now go. But hurry back. If you're gone long at all, my imagination is going to really tick me off."

That made him grin. He left the room before he changed his mind and didn't go at all. That would be unkind to Marla.

THE SECOND HE CLEARED the room, Arizona dropped back on the bed with a groan. Why did she have to act like a putz just because Spencer tried to kiss her? God, she despised her own weaknesses. She knew without a shadow of a doubt that he would never physically hurt her.

But deep down, in places where reason didn't exist, it didn't matter. Some fears remained, and they gnawed at her peace of mind, keeping her from true freedom.

Disgusted with herself, she lay there in the bed for a minute before jumping up to creep down the hallway, going far enough to listen in.

Sadly, she couldn't hear a thing other than the soft drone of voices. Definitely Marla—not that she'd had a doubt.

Did Spencer still want that woman? Did he have fond memories of his time with her? Lustful memories? For certain, Marla didn't go fleeing the bed in a panic over a kiss.

Marla, damn her, would not have hang-ups that limited what Spencer could do.

Turning to face the wall, Arizona clunked her head once, then stalked into the bathroom. She stared at herself in the mirror, but her frown looked the same, as did her eyes, mouth, nose. And other than a few whisker burns here and there, and a possible hickey on her neck, her body didn't look any different, either.

She touched the interesting passion bruise on her neck and went all soft and mushy again.

Man, oh, man, Spencer knew how to play it in the sack. The guy had some serious skills. With his mouth, his hands.

Skills he'd used with other women.

How had Marla put it? *If you'd ever had him, you'd feel differently about having him again.*

Yeah, she got that.

Now.

Because she definitely wanted him again.

But what did she know about hanging on to a guy? Before Spencer, she'd just wanted men to keep their distance. Shoot, she would have kicked their butts to ensure they didn't get too close. Well, except for Jackson, but that was different. She and Jackson were...friends. Almost like family.

But not exactly.

Now, with Spencer, she wanted to get as close as two people could get.

Sure, he'd seemed content enough with their little go-around in the sack. But Spencer had told her all along that he wanted to normalize her—her words, not his—and that once she got over her hang-ups, he intended to send her packing off to some other nameless, faceless dude.

Arizona curled her lip. Not happening. No other guy appealed to her like he did. If forced to it, she could screw another guy, and she'd survive it just as she always had.

But she would never crave another man the way she craved Spencer.

She wouldn't enjoy anyone else like she did Spencer. She snorted. *Enjoy*. What a wimpy word for how she'd felt.

Wrapping her arms around herself, Arizona thought of all the ways he excited her senses. She *loved* looking at him. The man had a seriously hard, sexy body. He was so damned big. All over. And his body hair...fascinating. It added to his manliness, not that he needed any help with that. He was so macho, he could define the word.

Breathing in his hot scent made her tingly all over.

Other than noticing unpleasant odors, like sweat and alcohol, she'd never paid attention to a man's aroma. But Spencer smelled so delicious that she practically hyperventilated when near him, because she kept breathing deep, filling her lungs with him.

Oh, and his taste… A flock of butterflies rioted in her stomach with just the memory of his kiss, the stroke of his damp tongue, the heat of his mouth. Knowing how good his sleek flesh tasted under her tongue, she wondered about tasting him everywhere. Maybe, once she got more used to him, she'd give it a go. Would Spencer like that? She snorted again.

All guys liked the pleasure of a woman's mouth.

But most of all, she really, *really* loved touching him. All over. With her hands, her mouth. Sliding her body over his—

The unexpected peal of her cell phone nearly stopped her heart.

Good grief, she'd been totally immersed in a stand-up, vivid, hot-and-bothered fantasy. All about Spencer.

A guy she'd just had sex with and who was, at this very moment, standing in his doorway wearing nothing but jeans, showing off his awesome bod while chatting with Marla, a woman who'd shared his bed.

Bleh. She'd have to visualize stomping them both later. Right now, she had to answer her phone. Because her separate phones had distinctive rings, she knew it was a social call. But because she had few enough people who ever called her, she assumed Jackson wanted to make sure she wouldn't back out of the visit today.

She managed to find her purse and dig out the correct cell on the fourth ring.

Without checking the caller ID, she said, "What's up?"

"Candy?"

Oh, no. No way.

Luckily the bed was right there, because her backside landed on it before she'd even realized her knees were bending. "Yes?"

"It's Quin."

No reply came to mind.

"From the Green Goose."

Her tongue felt thick when she said, "Quinto?"

"You gave me this number. On a note, in my pocket. Last night. Do you remember?"

Yeah, *now* she remembered. But until she'd heard his voice, she'd forgotten all about that. *What did the call mean?*

And what the hell had she been thinking?

"I am sorry to bother you," Quin said with strained apology. "You were drinking, so you probably do not—"

Thoughts scrambling, Arizona interrupted him, anxious to keep him on the phone. "No, it's fine. I'm glad to hear from you." Trying for cheerfulness to cover her shock, wishing she could order her memories so that they made sense, she asked stupidly, "What's up, Quin?"

Audible breathing, along with a lot of hesitation, filled her ear. "Since I will not be able to see you at the bar again, I wanted to thank you."

Her mouth went dry as dust. *Think, Arizona, think.*

She cleared her throat. "Why wouldn't you see me?" Oh, God, that sounded lame, not at all convincing. But was she supposed to know of the raid? Should she remain undercover? Hadn't Dare busted that whole gig wide open?

Think, think, think.

Hoping for inspiration, she said, "Maybe you don't know, but I got hired to work there. I report in tonight."

She heard some shuffling, as if he'd muffled the

phone, or his groan, then Quin whispered, "No, you do not."

"Why not?" Somehow she knew, absolutely *knew,* that Quin was in big trouble.

"The police came, with others. You were a part of that, right?"

"The police?" She'd drunk so much that she couldn't recall if she was supposed to be aware of the raid or not. Rubbing her forehead, she asked, "What are you talking about?"

Hadn't she and Spencer covered their connection even then? Or, no, wait—they'd sort of fought together against a few of the rowdier drunks. Joel had been there, but far as she could remember, he hadn't gotten hurt. Spencer's bimbo had already split, so she hadn't been around.

But Terry Janes...no, she hadn't come across him again. She hadn't seen Carl, either—not until he tried jumping her in the alley outside the bar.

She had no memory of Quin being about at all.

"The raid that shut down the bar?" Quin prompted. "You were with the artist, and with Mr. Janes. There was a fight, and then the police came."

Oh, God. She didn't know whether to trust him or not. He sounded like Quin, but the boy she'd met had been almost silent. She couldn't imagine him calling her for a chat.

After chewing her lip, Arizona asked, "Is this really you, Quin?"

Flat, with no inflection at all, he replied, "Who else would it be?"

If only she had a few minutes to think, or if she'd anticipated this—but she'd gone straight from waking, to wanting Spencer, to indulging her first full-participant carnal encounter—with no time for configuring various scenarios about her performance of the night before. "I don't know. What happened to Joel? Did he get hurt in the fight?"

"I can not say."

"What about Terry Janes?"

"Again, I do not know."

She chewed her lips, weighing his answers, trying to find the truth in them.

At her continued silence, he asked, "You did not want me to call you?"

"Sure I did." But the circumstances had all changed. She didn't need to get closer to him now, because thanks to Dare, it was shut down. Permanently.

Quin was safe. Or...at least he should have been.

Why hadn't they gathered Quin into the net, though? Why wasn't he in some kind of safe house, getting questions answered? Being reunited with loved ones? She'd thought—

"Candy? Are you still there?"

"Yeah." She had to get it together. Now. "Sorry. I drank way too much last night and I'm still a little hungover."

"I know. I saw." With sympathy, he added, "You had no choice but to drink, and I had no choice—"

"It's okay." Quin had to play along, or he'd be hurt. She got that. "So I don't have a job?"

"You truly do not remember?"

"I remember I got hired." Without any real despondence, she added, "Bummer that the job is gone."

He drew a breath, then shattered what remained of her cool composure. "Do you think I could see you, Candy?"

Oh, no, no, *no*.

"See me?"

"We could meet somewhere. And...talk. I can tell

you about the raid, explain all that has happened. I could even help you find another job. A better job."

She needed a viable excuse, and she needed it fast. She needed a plan even more. "Umm…"

"It is important that I speak to you," he stressed, and a certain strain sounded in his tone. A strain of desperation. "I…I need your help."

"Okay, yeah, I'll try." To stall for time, she asked, "Will you give me a number where I can reach you?"

Another long pause and more shuffling. "The best that I can do is a pay phone. Will that work?"

"Sure." She snatched a pen and paper from her purse. "Where is the phone?"

"It is in the south side, by the gravel pit. Away from the bar." He read the phone number to her.

Not a great neighborhood, but she was familiar with it, so that was a plus. Was he hiding out there? Or setting up an ambush?

She could scope out the area, find the best way in and out of the locale, all the side streets and dead ends. And using the program Jackson had given her, it'd be easy enough to check up on Quin's info.

She pressed him, asking more questions. "Is it by a business? Someplace that'll make it easier for me to find it?"

"There is a pawn shop. Harry's Hocks." He drew an audible breath. "You cannot miss it."

"When?"

"Today," he suggested in a rush. "Right now, even."

"Sorry, no can do." She wanted to help him, but she wasn't a fool. "I already have other plans."

He fell silent for such a long time that she thought he might have hung up. Then he asked, "Tomorrow, then?"

"Sure, I can probably do that." Somehow she'd figure it out. "What time?"

"Noon."

Because he hadn't taken a single moment to think about it, Arizona knew he'd already had that time specified to him.

But by who?

Knowing he was pressured made up her mind more than anything else could have. Guessing how Spencer and Jackson, even Dare and Trace, were likely to react, Arizona closed her eyes. "I'll be there. And, Quin?" Even though he wouldn't understand, she said, "Don't worry too much, okay?"

She waited, but he didn't answer. The phone died with a soft but deafening click.

CHAPTER SEVENTEEN

"YOU DID WELL."

Relief made him shaky. Slowly, Quin sank down onto the park bench. If only she could have made it tonight... waiting was hell. Worse than hell.

Tomorrow seemed a very, very long time away.

"Quin, Quin. Don't look so worried. This is all working out beautifully. Better than I had hoped, even."

Quin nodded. Actually, it had been easier than he had expected, too. Candy was either very foolish or foolishly brave. He didn't know which.

"She's perfect and you know it. Perfect! You saw her."

Yes, he had seen her. Very different from the others. Somehow...stronger. Almost defiant.

But she would not be strong enough or defiant enough for what would happen.

Impatience cramped his muscles. He put his head back and closed his eyes. Tomorrow.

He would wait, and tomorrow would come.

And then it would all be over.

SPENCER PEELED Marla's hand away from his chest. Again. "Did you try calling someone?" Someone else. Someone other than him.

"Who?" She appealed to him with big eyes and a lost expression. "The storms caused so much of a mess all over, everyone is busy."

Cocking a brow, Spencer stepped around her and out to the porch. Humid air washed over his bare chest. Dark clouds continued to roll across the sky.

Well, hell. Trees were down, branches and debris everywhere. And sure enough, a massive limb lay across Marla's driveway and the path to her porch.

He ran a hand over his head. He'd heard the rainfall in the middle of the night, but he'd been so enthralled watching Arizona sleep, so caught up in the pleasure of having her close, in his bed, that he hadn't realized...

As if she'd read his mind, Marla said, "I guess you were too *busy* to notice?"

Ignoring the innuendo, he turned back to her. "Actually, yeah. Late night and all." He stepped out of reach when she leaned toward him. "It was barely raining when I got to bed."

Jealousy sharpened her tone. "Not alone?"

"Not your business," he corrected as gently as he could. But hell, he'd slept with her, more than once, so he felt like a complete bastard for being so brusque with her now. "Marla, listen—"

She went all tearful in a heartbeat. "I'm sorry, Spencer." Bordering on desperate, she leaned closer to him. "I don't know what I did to turn you away."

God, he hated these types of confrontations. "You didn't do anything wrong."

"I thought we were getting along great. I thought things were good between us."

"It was never like that." His own frustration ripened. "I made that clear up front."

From the doorway, Arizona said, "Yeah, well, apparently not clear enough."

Both he and Marla swiveled around to see Arizona lounging in the door frame, dressed in her shirt and shorts, tangled hair around her face, her gaze direct, challenging and a little…sympathetic.

For Marla.

It surprised Spencer, seeing that level of compassion; such a contrast to her balls-to-the-wall, take-no-prisoners attitude about most issues.

It also pleased him.

Arizona had such capacity for caring, and that had probably made her past abuse that much worse.

Right now, though, her presence would only complicate the awkward situation even more. "Back inside, Arizona."

"Screw you, too," she replied with no animus at all and stepped farther out to the porch. She sent him a sardonic smile. "You don't give me orders."

Wide-eyed and uncertain, Marla edged closer to Spencer's side. "I, ah…"

"Men can be such dicks, huh?"

Since Marla appeared ready to faint over the easy way Arizona insulted him, Spencer said, "You're not helping, Arizona."

"Was I supposed to help?" She made a rude sound—and stopped directly in front of Marla. "Why are you here?"

Arm limp, Marla pointed at her house. "Tree limb."

"Yeah? What tree limb?"

Spencer scrubbed both hands over his face. "There were storms last night. You," he said, stressing the word, "were too hammered to hear them." He didn't bother telling her that he'd been oblivious, as well. "They blew half the damn tree into her yard and one really big limb is blocking her driveway and front walkway."

"I was pretty drunk," she confirmed to Marla, then she went to the edge of the porch to survey the damage.

In her short shorts and the soft T-shirt, she made a

real sight leaning there on his railing. A breeze lifted her silky ebony hair. It tumbled down her back toward that perfect rear.

He was staring at her ass, a little lost, when she whistled.

"Holy cow. You can't even get your car out with that blocking the way, can you?"

"Ah…no."

Arizona turned back to Marla. "So what'd you want Spencer to do about it?"

Poor Marla looked from Arizona to Spencer and back again. "Help move it?"

"You aren't sure?"

Still uneasy, Marla swallowed. "I really don't know. I've never had it happen before. But I know it's too big for me to take care of on my own."

Evaluating things, Arizona eyed Marla up and down, then looked at the limb again. "Probably." She cocked a brow. "You got a chain saw, Spence?"

So now he was Spence again? "Sure." He strolled over to join her at the railing. "Doesn't every guy?"

That made her laugh. "Every guy with a house and big trees in his yard." Close to his side, aligning herself with him, Arizona leaned back on the railing and addressed Marla. "We were just about to grab some cake and coffee. And in a few hours we have to head out to see friends."

"Friends?"

"I know, right? Seems odd to me, too, but somehow, I have them."

Marla blanched. "Oh, I didn't mean anything insulting—"

Arizona waved that off. "Give us a few minutes, and we'll come over and help clean it up."

"We?" Surprised and somewhat desperate, Marla looked to Spencer for help.

Knowing Arizona well enough to know he'd have a fight on his hands if he tried to exclude her, he shrugged. Once she'd made her mind up about something, she could be pretty stubborn.

"You might want to change clothes," Arizona told her. "Looks like messy work." She turned to Spencer with a gaze full of challenge. "You ready for that coffee?"

Amazing. Was there any situation—other than having a guy over her—that unnerved Arizona? She grabbed control of a socially awkward, uncomfortable scene and just played it out like it was nothing.

"Yeah," he said slowly, doing his best to figure her out, "I'm ready." He gave Marla a salute. "An hour or so ought to do it."

"Oh. Okay." She stood there, befuddled. "Thank you."

Once inside, Spencer shut the door and snagged the back of Arizona's shirt, halting her stiff stride toward the kitchen. "Hold up."

Silent, strangely distant, she kept her back to him.

Undeterred, Spencer again eyed her backside. "Care to tell me what that was all about?"

She shrugged. "Neighbors are supposed to lend a hand to their neighbors, right?"

Using his hold on her shirt, he reeled her in, then wrapped his arms around her from behind. She stayed stiff—until he nuzzled the side of her neck. "You know I'm not interested in Marla, right?"

"I heard you tell her so."

"I wouldn't lie about it."

While she thought about that, she rested her hands over his. Finally she nodded. "Okay."

And yet she still sounded somehow distraught. "So what's wrong?"

"Nothing," she said too fast.

Something—but pressing her now would get him nowhere. She'd share her thoughts in her own sweet time. "Want to know what I think?"

"If it has anything to do with admiring Marla, no."

God, keeping up with her would be a challenge. "Why would I— No, forget that." He propped his chin on top of her head. "I was admiring you, actually."

"Me?" She twisted to see him. "Why?"

Too many reasons to count, but he said, "You sympathized with her."

"Pffft." As an invitation to nuzzle her neck more, she tilted her head.

"You did." He obliged with a soft, openmouthed kiss. "And it was very kind of you."

"She's probably an okay person."

Spencer hid his grin against her. "She's nice enough." But too manipulative, and too damn clingy. "It was wrong of me to let her think—"

She bolted away. "Cake, Spencer. And coffee."

In one deft move, he caught her again and tossed her over his shoulder. "Sex, Arizona." Already anxious to have her again, he smoothed a hand over her ass, then up and inside the leg of her shorts so he could fondle one firm cheek. "And maybe, after that, cake and coffee."

Hanging over his shoulder, Arizona stiffened, and then she relaxed. "Yeah, okay." Her hands smoothed down his spine. "That works just fine for me."

UNABLE TO WAIT, Spencer got her into his bedroom and pressed her up to the wall, his body against hers, his mouth almost touching hers. "Does this bother you?"

"No." She tried to kiss him.

"Arizona. Wait." He held her face. "I need to know if this is okay."

"It's great." She wiggled free so she could kiss him. "Awesome." Her tongue moved over his lips. "Just don't crawl on top of me and we're good to go, so...*go*."

Always in such a rush. He brushed back her hair. "If you feel even a twinge of—"

"I'm not shy, Spencer. I don't like something, you're going to hear about it, scout's honor." Pressing him back, she grabbed the hem of her T-shirt and jerked it off over her head. "So let's move on."

Lord have mercy. Her breasts were so large and firm for her slender frame. He reached for her.

She deflected him. "How about you play catch-up first?" She hooked her thumbs in the waistband of those skimpy shorts. "I'm pretty sure this'll work better if we're both naked."

"Agreed." In record time, he shucked off his clothes— just as Arizona straightened from doing the same.

"There." Beautifully bare, she kicked her shorts to the side. "What do you want to bet this'll be better than the cake?"

His gaze went all over her. "It already is." He put a hand to her narrow waist and soaked up the incredible sight of her. How long would it take for him to get used to the impact of her body? "Stand still, okay?"

"No way." She spread her hands out over his chest, and started to trail them down his body.

Drawing a quick breath, he caught her wrists. "Let me taste you." His voice roughened. "This time without your panties in the way."

Their gazes held; her pulse visibly quickened as the

seconds ticked by—and she braced back against the wall. "Yeah, okay."

"I love it when you're agreeable, honey." But because the L-word made him feel too much, even when used in banter, he quickly took her mouth.

Kissing her offered a unique pleasure, especially when she arched up against him, naked flesh to naked flesh, her soft curves touching him everywhere.

He had to cup her behind, had to cuddle her heavy breasts. Every single part of her tempted him.

While exploring her body with his hands, he kissed her for a long time, deeper and hotter. He stroked over her skin, the supple curves of her waist, her hips.

Her thighs.

He teased his fingertips down her spine, down, down, and then inward to her moist sex.

She went to her tiptoes against him.

Trailing damp kisses down her throat to her collarbone and then to her breasts, he took his time enjoying her until she became fevered, until he knew she neared her limit.

That meant he'd almost reached his limit, too.

Going to his knees, Spencer hugged her hips and rubbed his face over her belly.

She drifted her fingers through his hair and whispered his name.

When he teased her hip bone with his tongue, she twitched. Was she ticklish? He smiled as he said, "Hmm?"

"I think we need to get on with it."

"Not yet." And then with a growl, "You smell so good."

Her hand fisted in his hair. "You keep teasing me and I don't like it. Or maybe I like it too much."

"You'll enjoy this, I promise. Not as much as I will, but still…" He nudged her legs open wider, then looked up at her. "Lean back on the wall for support, then bend your knees a little."

She hesitated—and finally did as he asked, stepping her feet apart, flexing her knees.

Heat washed over him. "That's it." He opened her with his fingertips, teasing more, stroking over—into—slick, hot places, before leaning forward for the most intimate of kisses.

Her long, vibrating moan turned him on as much as her taste.

Licking his tongue over her, in her, he gave them both what they wanted. She grew wetter, her breathing more ragged. He teased her clitoris and heard her loud gasp.

Cupping her hips to help support her, he kept her upright and slowly drew her in, rasped his tongue over her, sucked.

In less than two minutes, she couldn't hold back her escalating cries.

As she came, she called out his name. Spencer clenched his fingers on her luscious behind, holding her still, relishing her honest reactions and how quickly she came for him.

Not until she knotted her fingers in his hair again did he let up. He stood and lifted her in one smooth move, taking her to the bed and putting her on her back.

She quickened, but he said, "Shh. It's okay," and moved back for a condom before she could get too wired about their positioning.

Soon as he had that covered, he turned back to her and pulled her to the edge of the bed, her legs open around him.

She eyed him with uncertainty. "I'm not riding this time?"

He shook his head, words beyond him. Putting her ankles up to his shoulders, he bent his knees, guided himself into her, and pressed deep in one long, smooth, slick thrust.

She arched up. "Ah, God."

"I know. It's deep this way." He locked his arms around her raised thighs, keeping her from retreating. She was already so wet, but still he worried. "I'm not hurting you?"

"No. No, it's…" Her teeth sank into her bottom lip, and she groaned harshly. "Don't you dare stop."

"I won't." He pulled back, then hammered in again and again.

He watched the bounce of her lush breasts, the hollowing of her flat belly as she tightened her muscles, the way her face drew taut in harsh pleasure.

She grabbed fistfuls of the sheet to anchor herself and shouted, her back bowing as she already came again.

That was enough for Spencer. Hell, it was almost too much. He joined her with a guttural groan, and it was so mind-numbing, he barely had enough wits left to sprawl beside her, instead of over her.

But that was too much space between them, so he rid himself of the condom and pulled her over to his chest.

His whole body still buzzed, his brain at rest, when Arizona muttered, "I have to tell you, Spencer, that was way better than cake."

MARLA PACED THE YARD, wondering if Arizona had spoken code with her "cake and coffee" nonsense. Were they having sex right now, while she waited on them?

Was Spencer, even at this moment, doing all those

awesomely wonderful, carnal things to Arizona that he once did with her?

She hated herself for being so jealous.

Arizona, damn her, had surprised her with her willingness to help with the fallen tree. Who did that? What woman willingly put her man in contact with another woman who openly lusted for him?

But of course she knew: a confident woman.

A woman with no fear of losing the man.

Damn them both.

Things had been going along so nicely before Arizona had shown up. Okay, so Spencer had been clear that he didn't want involvement.

He looked plenty involved with the little half-breed.

Marla bit her lip, guilty over the unkind thought. But how could she compete with Arizona's exotic looks? The younger woman had that smooth as coffee with cream skin, silky dark hair, and sharply contrasting pale blue eyes.

And her body? God, she detested comparisons. She wasn't a troll, and she knew it. She had generous curves that men enjoyed, she had no doubts about that.

But Arizona was sleek and strong and still very shapely as only the young could be. Not that Marla considered herself old at thirty. But standing next to Arizona aged her dramatically.

Why didn't the little twit just go away? Spencer would come back to her then, she was sure of it.

And if he did…then what? She just didn't know. But she disliked having her ego trampled, and that's how she felt—trampled into the ground.

Wondering what took them so long, Marla walked across the yard—and the driver of a passing car, forced to slow around the debris, whistled at her with bold admiration.

Well. Very nice. That little tease went a long way toward soothing her self-esteem.

So she still had it? Of course she did.

She didn't acknowledge the admirer, but she added a little swing to her step as she went to investigate the tree limb.

Then Spencer's front door opened, and Arizona strolled out and the stupid driver almost hit a tree.

Furious, Marla heard the squealing breaks and glanced up long enough to witness the driver's admiration. Arizona showed no interest. Spencer came out right behind her.

They were both smiling.

The car sat there a moment longer, the driver no doubt staring at Arizona, and then finally drove away. Face tight, eyes burning with animosity, Marla considered what to do.

Arizona approached. "I'm going to cut off the smaller branches. We'll let Spencer do the heavy work. Sound like a plan?"

Knowing she couldn't keep giving her the cold shoulder, Marla shook her head. "This was a bad idea. I've rethought it. Maybe I can hire someone—"

Arizona laughed.

Spencer said nothing. He just walked past them to his garage while pulling on thick gloves.

For only a brief moment the sun came out, sending a blinding reflection off every wet surface. Steam rose around them.

Marla lifted a hand to shield her eyes. With Spencer otherwise occupied, she shored up her courage and said to Arizona, "When are you leaving?"

As if the question didn't throw her at all, Arizona said, "Not sure yet. Guess it depends on Spencer, you know?"

Such honesty floored Marla. She licked her lips. "So, when he asks you to go, you will?"

"He won't have to ask," Arizona assured her. "I don't hang around where I'm not welcome." Curious, she met Marla's gaze. "My visit bothers you?"

Considering what Arizona said, Marla shook her head.

A visit.

Not a permanent, move-in situation.

Hmm. Since Arizona sounded sincere, Marla thought she just might be able to advise her, to perhaps hurry her along on her way. She ventured forth carefully. "Spencer doesn't want to settle down, you know."

"Yeah, no kidding." Laughing, Arizona took a cloth-covered rubber band off her wrist and used it to tie back her hair. "He's been as up front with me as he was with you."

That left Marla floundering.

"You realize that he's still in love with his deceased wife, right?" With her hair contained, Arizona put her hands on her hips. "He's got some real issues with that. Even if I split, I'm not sure it'll matter for you."

Good God, did Arizona feel…sorry for her? Was she trying to prepare her for disappointment?

How dare she?

"I can help him get over the loss!"

"You think so? Well, I'll concede the possibility," Arizona told her with a flat smile. She studied Marla a moment longer. "Can you be trusted?"

"With what?"

"The context matters, huh?" Sardonic, Arizona waved

a hand. "Never mind. Trust comes in layers. I get it. I just meant with Spencer, with having his best interests in mind."

"Of course." Especially since she believed Spencer's best interests were also her own. "Why?"

"I need to know if you'll be working tomorrow morning."

Marla shook her head. "I'm off until midafternoon."

"Okay." Arizona thought about it a little more. "That might work, then. Thanks."

"That's it?" She wasn't going to explain?

"For now, yeah. See, Spencer's coming back, so we should wrap up this little chat. He wouldn't like us gabbing about him. But honestly, Marla, when I do bounce—because I'm pretty sure that I'll have to eventually, maybe even sooner than I'd hoped—I wish you luck with him. But only if you can make him happy." She leaned in closer, her gaze direct, even threatening. "If you can't, then stay the hell away from him. Got it?"

Marla leaned back from the intensity of Arizona's stare—and she nodded.

And then Spencer was there, shoving oversize lawn bags toward Marla and giving Arizona a level look while handing her a bow saw. "Everything okay?"

"Just dandy."

He watched her a few seconds more. "If you want to cut off the smaller branches at the top there, I'll start on the other end."

"Got it."

"You know how to use that?"

She eyed the tool with a smirk. "Put it to the branch and…start sawing? Easy peasy."

Spencer shook his head. "Don't give yourself blisters, okay?"

Irate over their intimate chitchat, Marla loudly shook out a bag. "Shouldn't we get started?"

"We should," Arizona agreed, and she walked away from Spencer—leaving Marla there with him.

The humidity was such that already his shirt stuck to his wide chest and broad shoulders. "Thank you for doing this." The big branch trembled as Arizona began sawing away.

"No problem." He surveyed the branch, which was more like a small tree. "I just hope we can get it all done before we need to take off."

As he went to the largest section of the branch and knelt down to prime the chain saw, Marla followed him.

"She's a peculiar girl."

"I'd say unique." He dismissed her to pull on safety goggles.

Marla touched his shoulder to regain his attention, then couldn't stop herself from rubbing her fingertips over the sensual feel of soft cotton covering solid muscles.

No one wore a T-shirt like Spencer. He was so deliciously big and solid and…hard.

Going still, Spencer glanced toward Arizona—who literally paid them no mind at all—then looked up. "What are you doing, Marla?"

He truly had no interest in her. None. Not a spec. He didn't enjoy her attention now, not even to spur Arizona's jealousy.

When she forced herself to be honest, she had to admit that he'd never been all that interested. Willing on occasion, sure, because she'd thrown herself at him every chance she got. But he'd never been in hot pursuit.

Mostly her success at getting into bed with him had been based on catching him at moments of weakness.

Not that a man like him had any real weakness. But Arizona was right: he still loved his deceased wife—and she'd played on that.

God, that made her sound awful. Like an opportunist. Like a user.

Her pride saved her. She dropped her hand and lifted her chin. "I just wanted to ask if you put on sunscreen? The clouds are parting finally. It's going to be a scorcher."

He squinted up at the sun, then turned toward Arizona. "Do you need sunscreen?" he called over to her.

Arizona smirked and, without looking at them, said, "Not if you two stop playing around over there, so we can get done with this sooner rather than later."

Ah. So she hadn't been so oblivious after all. Marla forced a smile. "I'll start picking up the debris." She hated yard work, but she couldn't very well ask for Spencer's help, then go off to her air-conditioned living room.

Once the chain saw started, there was no more talking, and they made quick work of it. Arizona finished with the smaller branches and, beaded with sweat, went straight into helping Marla fill the bags.

Wilted, Marla used her wrist to brush her hair away from her face.

"I'm dying of thirst," Arizona said. "You got anything cold to drink?"

"Colas or iced tea."

"Iced tea sounds great. Why don't I finish up here while you go get some glasses for everyone?"

Marla eyed the remaining work. "If that's what you want." She'd be thrilled for any reason to get out of the heat, even one fabricated by Arizona.

"Thanks. Take your time. We're just about done here." While Spencer stacked the wood in her side yard, Arizona went one further and found a rake to get up the rest of the mess. She even whistled while sweating, as if physical work in the hot sun was a pleasure.

So very peculiar.

And damn it, almost likable. *Almost.* More disturbed than ever, Marla went inside to fetch the tea. God willing, they would be done with all the dirty, heavy lifting before she returned.

CHAPTER EIGHTEEN

HE WOULD NEVER UNDERSTAND HER. She'd been too am-
icable at Marla's, too accommodating, and it worried
him. How could she go from jealous and uncertain one
moment to supremely uncaring the next?

She couldn't.

And that meant she was up to something, but what?

While driving, Spencer repeatedly glanced her way.
Now that he'd had her, his fascination had grown instead of lessening. All the ways he'd touched her, he
wanted to touch her again. And he had many questions,
but they'd been in the truck for nearly an hour now, and
she'd barely said two words.

Noting that she'd gotten too much sun on her nose,
he felt a reluctant smile pull at his mouth. She looked
cute—if a little female warrior with her devastatingly
sensual looks could ever be called that.

Killer gorgeous, cocky, capable—and cute. Yes, the
words all described Arizona.

When she looked at her palm, he asked, "Did you get
blisters after all?"

"Maybe a few. I was enjoying it so much, I barely noticed."

"Enjoying it?"

"Yeah. The fresh air, using my muscles, working up
a sweat." She peered up at him. "You have a house and
yard and all that, so you're probably used to it."

But she had…none of that. Yes, he often took it for granted. "I see." One day, he hoped she would take such things for granted, too.

He wondered what she would think of Jackson's intended birthday gift. Would she love it, accepting it as something she desperately wanted, that Jackson could easily give?

Or would she balk at the extravagance?

"I take it you didn't enjoy it, huh?"

Actually…he had. But mostly because she'd been with him. There'd been a certain peace in doing something so mundane, so *normal* with her.

Instead of answering, he reached for her hand, lifted it so he could see her palm. He shook his head at the sight of several blisters, then brought it to his mouth and kissed each one. "I shouldn't have let you saw."

"Let me? Get real, Spence. You couldn't have stopped me."

Grinning, he laced their fingers together and compared their hands. His engulfed hers, leaving her looking so fragile, when she was anything but. "I'm probably twice your size."

"Yeah, so?" She winked at him. "The bigger they are, the harder they fall."

He divided his attention between watching the road and the surrounding area, and playing with Arizona. God, it had been so long since he'd played. "Make a fist for me. Let's see how credible it is."

She balled up her hand, then offered sweetly, "Want me to plant you a facer so you can judge my strength?"

That made him laugh. "No."

"I wouldn't anyway." She opened her hand on his jaw, then stroked down to his neck, his shoulder, down his arm to drop her hand on his thigh. "If it came to it, I'd aim for your boys." And she slid her hand up his inner thigh. "More likely to slow you down that way."

"I'll take your word for it." He remembered how, in the past when they'd first met, he'd avoided one such attack by her, only to get caught with the next. She'd laid him low with her deadly aim.

To keep from wrecking, he caught her hand and held it on his knee.

"And if you dodged that," she continued, "well, then, I'd punch you in the throat. It's way softer than a chin or jaw, and gagging, gasping men are a lot less trouble."

Hating the thought of her ever again being in such a conflict, Spencer smoothed a thumb over her knuckles. "Any guy who knows how to fight would block that punch."

"He could try." Suddenly she said, "So if you're done stewing, can I ask you something?"

Is that what she thought? That he'd been disgruntled in some way? "I wasn't stewing."

She snorted, making her disbelief plain.

"You do that a lot, you know? Make that obnoxious, rude noise. You may as well call me a liar."

Smiling wickedly, she put her head back against the seat and, staring over at him, taunted quietly, *"Liar."* Before he could get too riled over that, she half turned toward him. "You were stewing, Spence. Admit it."

"You're wrong. I was actually wondering about something."

"What?"

"You first. You said you had a question for me. Shoot."

"Okay." She took her hand from his knee to his midsection. "How do you keep in such great shape?"

Her praise warmed him. He adored her body, so it was

nice that she felt the same about his. Shrugging, he said, "I work out occasionally. I jog every couple of days. And without much leisure time, I stay more busy than not."

"So…" She stretched the length of her seat belt to reach for him. "No time to get soft, huh?"

Spencer caught her hand so she couldn't get too intimate. Even after all their sexual excess, it wouldn't take much to get him primed again. He already felt twitchy, just thinking of how she had looked in his bed, how she reacted, the sounds she made…

And now, minuscule shorts, a scoop-necked tee and her high ponytail all worked to emphasize her body.

A body he'd touched, tasted.

Taken intimately.

He appreciated her interest now, but he wouldn't take chances with her, not in any way. "Back in your own seat, honey. I want you buckled in right and tight."

Her expression turned mulish. "You still treat me like a kid."

That had to be a joke. "How can you say that with a straight face after the morning we had?"

She softened. "Yeah. I guess you're right." She tipped her head. "We'll do it again?"

Hell, yes. But because he never made assumptions about Arizona's thoughts, he asked, "Did you want to?"

She studied the blisters on her palm again. "Well, the thing is, if everything is settled at the Green Goose, then…I probably don't need to stay with you anymore, right?"

"Yes, you do." Damn, he'd said that too fast. She watched him with curiosity—and so much more. He needed a plausible argument, a way to convince her without giving her ideas. "At least until Dare and Trace figure out if anyone else was behind the setup there. Until that happens, who knows if it's safe?" That sounded more rational, and he let out a breath. "All right?"

"They have Terry Janes and his pathetic henchman, Carl, so it probably won't take them long to file it away as a job well done."

Not long enough. But how much time with Arizona would be enough? "Probably not."

"Then I guess it'd be okay, and yeah, if we're shacking up, even on a temporary basis, no reason not to reap the rewards, right?"

He grinned—with relief and with need. "Then definitely, we will." But for how long? He couldn't let her get so enmeshed in his life that she mistook things—more than she probably already did.

More than he was starting to, because damn it, he was beginning to hate the idea of letting her go.

"Back to staying in shape." She stroked his biceps. "I think we should grapple sometime."

Slanting a look her way, he took in her small bones, her slim frame and soft curves, and shook his head. "No."

"C'mon, Spence. Think about it. While I'm staying with you, I have no way to practice, unless you practice with me." And to further convince him, she said, "You don't want my skills to get rusty, do you?"

He'd prefer that she have no need for deadly skills but didn't think she'd be receptive to that preference. "You'd be comfortable grappling with me?"

"Sure. I was comfortable having sex with you, right?"

"You wore me out. I'd say more than comfortable."

Happiness filled her smile. "I know. Crazy, huh?"

It shouldn't have been crazy. He remembered again

how amazed she'd seemed as she came, the sheer… wonder of it. And he'd given that to her.

It should have been enough for him, but with Arizona, nothing felt like enough.

"So what do you say?"

He shook his head. "No grappling." It was too much to ask him to promote her violent tendencies. "But this leads into what I was thinking about—if you don't want a guy on top of you, how do you fight?"

A little peeved that he'd turned her down, she said flatly, "I don't let anyone get on top of me."

As if she'd always have a choice in the matter. He shook his head again. "Is there anything else that still bothers you?"

Shrugging, she acted as if it didn't matter, then said, "A few things."

"Will you tell me?"

"I guess I should. I mean, staying with you and all, you're bound to notice, right?" She sighed long and dramatically. "I'm not a fan of closed space. Like, maybe… your guest room? The one you keep trying to stuff me into?"

"I haven't—" He shook his head. No, forget that. He'd offered her the use of the room, and she'd declined, that's all. He hadn't pushed her, because he'd had suspicions. But it didn't matter now. "I don't ever want you to do anything you don't want to do."

"Great. Then can I just keep sharing your room? While I'm staying with you, I mean? Would you mind that?" And in a rush: "Not that I'll be there all that long anyway."

So where would she go? Another motel? He hated that thought. "Trust me, Arizona—having you in my bed won't be a hardship." Whenever he thought of how she'd been hurt, anger burned bright inside him. "Will you tell me why you dislike the room?"

"Seriously? You can't figure it out?"

Yes, he had a good idea why enclosed rooms bothered her. But he wanted her to confide in him, to tell him everything rather than keeping it bottled up. "You were locked in rooms. Small rooms?"

"Yeah." Despite the restriction of her seat belt, she drew her knees up and wrapped her arms around them.

Spencer said nothing.

"I'd sit there alone, listening, never knowing what would happen or when. I'd hear people walk by outside in the hall. Or talk. I'd hear other girls taken, or people put into the rooms with them."

Jesus, he wanted to... He drew a breath. "I'm sorry."

"Yeah, me, too." She patted his shoulder. "Whenever I rent a motel room, it has to have windows that open— not only for an escape if I have to make a hasty exit, but so that I don't feel trapped. I'll leave the bathroom door open, too. Rooms that are just a...a box, give me the creeps." She held silent a moment. "Nights are always the hardest for me. A lot of times, I'll take a long drive, just to kill time. Sometimes I end up at a bar, sometimes I just troll the neighborhoods."

Thank God she would be sleeping with him. He'd hear her if she tried to slip away. "Being in my bedroom doesn't bother you like that?"

"No." She studied him. "It's strange, but I don't think about most of that stuff when I'm with you."

Her admission humbled him. "I'm glad."

After that somber, sad exchange, Arizona turned to look out the window.

It was odd, but he already knew her well enough that

he could read her and her moods, picking up on her thoughts and her worries.

They'd reach Dare's soon, so better to get all said before that. "What else, honey?"

The seconds ticked by without her making a sound, and then finally, so quietly that he could barely hear her, she said, "I don't want to swim."

"What's that?"

Anxiety brought her around to face him, and raised her voice. "I haven't been in a freaking body of water since major a-holes did their best to drown me." And with more venom: "I don't want to swim."

Of course she didn't. He should have thought of that himself, but her easy acceptance of storms had thrown him off. "Then don't. Everyone will understand—"

"No way." She held up a hand to cut him off. "I don't want anyone knowing that I'm too chicken to swim."

Of *course* she didn't. Arizona was the proudest, most independent woman he knew. Admitting to a fear or weakness would never sit right with her.

He held on to his frustration, and rather than explain to her that the others would understand, that they wouldn't judge, he asked, "What can I do?"

She glared at him. "Did you bring trunks?"

"I'm afraid so." It was supposed to be that type of gathering. Hot summer day, friends together on a lake... swimming was expected, even anticipated.

"Yeah, that's what I figured, too. I wore a suit under my clothes, but even if I didn't, I'm betting one of the other women would have a spare."

And that would rob her of any good justification to forgo a dip in the murky water. "Want me to make up an excuse of some kind?" For Arizona, he'd think of something.

"No, but you can swim with me. And I mean *with* me. As in really close. As in don't leave my side even for a second."

He could do that. Hell, he'd enjoy it, as long as he knew she wasn't suffering at all. "If that's what you want, sure."

She gave a roll of her eyes. "Do you think you can act like you *want* to be there, not like I'm forcing you?"

Would she ever understand her own appeal? Or for that matter, his strength? "You can't force me, Arizona, so yeah, no problem. I was looking forward to swimming with you, anyway."

"Great." Her shoulders loosened a little. "But I guess we'll never know if I could force you, since you won't spar with me."

"Arizona," he warned.

She grinned. "So now you know the sum of my personal kryptonite. Small rooms and swimming. Pretty pathetic, huh?"

"I'd say admirable. Most people have things that scare them. Bugs, heights, fire, the dark. Hell, even the boogey man. And that's just from life, from living, not from…" He cut himself short.

"What? You were going to say trauma or some melodramatic puke like that, weren't you?"

Lying would be pointless. He wanted to give her honesty—as much as possible, whenever possible. "Probably, yes."

"Well, you can put a lid on that right now. And while you're at it, stow the sympathy, too. Don't need it, don't want it."

"I'm afraid you have it anyway, along with anything else you want or need."

She dropped her feet back to the floor and turned her

shoulders toward him. "Sex," she enunciated plainly. "I'll take that."

"Already done. Will be done again. No problem."

A slow grin replaced her frown. "Thanks for being so agreeable, and for working around my…glitches."

Is that how she categorized her fear of losing control? He thought of giving her new memories, maybe making love in the lake. It'd be tough, what with the dynamic trio lurking about, but maybe he could finesse it somehow.

Would she be agreeable? He broached the possibility by saying, "There are a lot of ways to have sex."

"Don't I know it. But somehow, no matter the way, the guy's usually still controlling things."

"Not always."

Intrigued, she said, "Yeah? Interesting." She looked him over. "So far, you've controlled things, but I barely noticed because I didn't feel controlled."

"How did you feel?"

She gave it a lot of thought. "A little wild, I guess. Like maybe I wasn't me anymore. Like maybe all that really mattered was touching you and tasting you and having you do the same to me. I forgot about so many things because it was all so…"

"Consuming?" Damn, talking about it with her made him hot.

"Good word choice. Yep, that's about it. Very consuming, but in a great way. Not like consuming fear or pain—just consuming pleasure."

Every muscle in his body twitched. Every time she opened up to him, his heart felt trampled, and he wanted to get hold of the ones who'd hurt her.

Impossible, since they were long gone.

At the same time, he wanted to promise her that she'd have that pleasure, with him, for a very long time.

Also impossible.

He made a point of not looking at her. "It should always be that way, honey." He gripped the wheel tighter and forced out the words, as much to remind himself as her. "Any guy you sleep with should be equally concerned with how you feel."

ARIZONA FLINCHED at what he said.

Any guy she slept with.

Meaning he still wanted to fob her off on that nameless, faceless other dude.

The idea repulsed her. And it infuriated her.

But facts were facts: Spencer wanted to rehab her, and that's all he really wanted. Oh, yeah, she knew it wasn't a chore for him to sleep with her. She wasn't a hag, and her hang-ups aside, she wasn't too weird or obnoxious in bed.

But what she'd told Marla was true; he was still in love with his wife, and a woman like her would be only a temporary substitute—in bed. Nowhere else.

Nowhere that really mattered to his life or to his own personal issues.

She wished she could help him as he wanted to help her. Not that there was any real comparison. Spencer was one of the greatest, most awesome, incredible guys she knew.

And, Jesus, didn't she sound like an infatuated sap?

Well, unlike Marla, she had pride galore. Pride had kept her going when others might have given up. She stared at Spencer for a long time, willing him to meet the accusation in her gaze, but he kept his attention on the road.

Screw it. She wouldn't debate sleeping with other men, so instead she just said, "Good to know. I'll try to remember that when I sleep with someone else."

An interesting muscle clenched in his jaw, and his big hands—hands that could be so gentle and so hot when he touched her—squeezed the steering wheel.

Possessive. That's what he was. She knew all about that because Jackson was the same. For as long as she slept with Spencer, he didn't want her sleeping with anyone else. Not like he'd let her out of his sight long enough for her to go carousing anyway.

And that could be a problem, given she had to meet Quin tomorrow.

"So other guys are on the list," she said, "but for tonight, soon as we can wrap up this nonsense at Dare's—"

"Your birthday is not nonsense."

"—I want to try out this control reversal you mentioned."

He opened his mouth to further explain the importance of her birth celebration—and then her words registered.

Going silent, he clamped his mouth shut. New tension coursed through him—but this was tension of a very different kind.

All sexual—the fun kind of tension.

Grinning, Arizona watched him.

He pawed the steering wheel, his jaw flexing, and he flashed her a glance of heated comprehension. "You want to see how far you can push things?"

"With *you,*" she stressed, because whether he wanted to hear it or not, she didn't want to roll with anyone else. "So…yeah, that's what I want."

Two slow, deep breaths expanded his chest. He tried for a cavalier shrug. "Okay, sure."

She smirked. Of course he was agreeable about it; she hadn't expected anything else. Men were *so* predictable.

To up the ante, she whispered, "How you kissed me, Spence? *Where* you kissed me? I want to kiss you like that, too."

He cleared his throat. "You mean…?"

She nodded. "You on your back, hands to yourself, letting me make you nuts." She tipped her head. "You think you'll like my mouth on you?"

"Yes," he said without hesitation.

"You think you'll be able to keep your hands to yourself?"

"I'll try. But for now, let's stow that, okay?" Shifting in his seat, he adjusted his jeans. "We're at Dare's, and I don't want to face them all with a boner."

Her gaze dropped to his lap, and sure enough, she'd gotten him all stirred up. "Nice. I have skills with this, too, huh?"

Her boasting made him laugh. "I suppose you do. But around you, I'm pretty easy, so don't let it go to your head."

A nice confession. She'd enjoy taking control of him—later, after she survived this little celebration.

Ugh. She made a face and peered out the windshield at the heavily wooded area.

Regardless of her personal preferences, she had to admit that Dare had a terrific place. Uneasy, she said, "I can see the lake already."

"And smell the air?" He took the window lower. "Fresh."

"Everything smells green." She filled her lungs and tried not to think about swimming.

As he pulled into the long drive leading to Dare's impressive home, Spencer reached for her hand. "Try to relax, okay? Just forget about the lake for now—we'll deal with that later. You're here with friends, with people who care about you. Enjoy their attention, and yes, their gifts."

She groaned. Gifts? "My birthday is over already. This is dumb."

Understanding and, as usual, soothing her, Spencer lifted her hand and kissed her knuckles. "Whatever happens today, honey, know that I'm right here with you, okay? You aren't alone."

Yeah, that helped. For now.

Today.

But she'd soon be all alone again—sooner than even Spencer suspected.

CHAPTER NINETEEN

THE SUN BLAZED AGAINST the pale blue sky without a single cloud in sight. A light breeze stirred the air, sending the surface of the lake into mesmerizing ripples that glinted like diamonds.

From swaying treetops, blackbirds swooped down to peck at insects. Chattering squirrels scurried around, gathering berries and nuts. A cicada chirped relentlessly.

Laughter, casual conversation and lots of love surrounded her. For most, it'd be the perfect day.

But, God, she felt like a fraud.

Like an interloper.

She didn't belong in this cozy family atmosphere. She didn't really belong anywhere.

As beautifully wrapped gifts were pressed toward her, she tried not to be too conspicuous. But her smile felt wooden, her face stiff.

She detested being the center of attention—at least for something like this. If she drew attention kicking ass, well, so be it. *That* she didn't mind so much. She was good at that. In the middle of a low-class bar, she fit right in.

Here…not so much.

On this hot afternoon, near a lake, after dinner off a grill, eaten from a patio table, her inexpensive shorts and top should have been appropriate. But next to the other women, even though they wore similar outfits, she looked...cheap. Their casual clothes were somehow classier. Richer. Better-fitting.

They had polished fingernails and pedicures. They had salon-styled hair and lotion-rich skin.

She'd never cared about that stuff. She wanted her clothes to be comfortable, period. She made sure that the legs of her jeans hid her ankle holster, and her tops had to be long and loose enough to conceal the sheath for her knife, usually fastened at the small of her back. That mattered.

Style did not. Keeping up with fashion had never been her forte.

Now she sort of wished she'd put some thought into it instead of stewing over the whole swimming thing.

With her long red hair in a thick braid, Priss looked elegant, especially in the breezy and colorful cover-up she wore over her swimsuit. And Molly in her white cotton capris and tailored halter defined chic.

In her feminine sundress and designer sandals, Alani was the classiest. Even the way the breeze teased her pale blond hair seemed affected for style. Right now, Alani had a hand protectively over her middle—and Jackson had his hand over hers. Though she wasn't showing yet, they were both so excited about the pregnancy.

A baby.

The idea boggled Arizona's mind. The only thing she knew about kids was that they scared her. But Jackson assured her over and over that she'd be a great aunt. He didn't seem to find that whole idea absurd—and oddly, neither did Alani.

But who knew? She might not even be around by the time the baby was born, so why should she worry about being a bad influence?

In her ear, Chris, Dare's right-hand man, said, "Chin up, kiddo, or everyone will think you're glum."

Crap. Arizona glanced up and found them all waiting on her. Their expressions varied from indulgent to amused to concerned.

Chris, always easy to be around, sat to her right. He gave her a nudge. "Start with the small packages," he suggested, "and you can work up to the bigger stuff."

Bigger stuff? No, she didn't even want to know. Accepting the box he handed to her, she gave a gruff, "Thanks," and untied the ribbon.

It surprised her to find three gifts inside: a camera, an empty photo album and a framed photo of her with Jackson and Alani. She stared at it blankly.

"I snuck and took it," Chris told her, "because Alani wanted you to have a family photo, but she also wanted it to be a surprise."

Her heart lodged in her throat. Jackson and Alani stood together, facing the camera, full of smiles, while she wore a silly smirk, her gaze on Jackson. It looked as if she'd been laughing at something he said.

"I love that crooked grin," Alani told her.

Jackson reached across the table to tweak a long hank of her hair. "It's cute."

Cute. Not a word usually applied to her, and maybe that was what she loved most about Jackson—he saw her differently than others did.

It was also a problem, because in the most important ways—like attitude and determination—she wasn't different at all. And for a woman to be like Jackson...well, it was hard for others to accept. It was especially difficult for macho, protective guys.

Like Jackson, Dare, Trace...and Spencer.

But, yeah, in the photo, she didn't look bad. She actually looked...happy.

Swallowing hard, she forced herself to face Alani. "It's great." More wonderful than she'd ever imagined anything could be. "Thank you."

"So you like it?"

Luckily it was a five-by-seven, not larger, because she didn't have a wall to hang it on. She lived out of her trunk, utilizing motel rooms and other various dives. But, yes, she liked it very, very much. Maybe she could attach it to the dash of her car somehow.

Words seemed impossible, so she nodded.

"It's a digital camera, so you can hook it up to any computer and print off more pictures. Eventually you'll fill the album." Alani smiled at her. "It'd be nice for you to have photos of all your family."

Leaning in, Chris bumped shoulders with her. "She means us, you know. We're adopting you whether you like it or not."

"Hey, what's not to like?" Jackson grinned at her. "If she can tolerate Trace, the rest of us are cake."

"Ha!" Priss stretched across the table to smack Jackson. "Trace is the best part and you know it, Jackson Savor!"

"Depends on who you talk to," he told her while ducking another swat from her. "You can't take Trace's word for it."

Trace pulled Priss back to his side.

Playful insults ensued, along with lots of camaraderie and laughter. They all interacted so comfortably. They were a family, in the truest sense of the word.

But she had no idea how to fit in.

Her heart aching, Arizona glanced over at Jackson. In so many ways, he'd tried to include her. But he would soon marry Alani, and not long after that, he'd have a baby.

His own family. A *real* family.

Not for a second was Jackson oblivious to Alani—what she did, how she moved, probably her every thought. All through dinner he had watched her eat, his intense scrutiny of her mouth almost embarrassing. His awareness of her was palpable and very sweet.

How could she ever intrude on that?

Chris bumped his knee into hers, jarring her from her melancholy yet again.

She eyed him and caught his look of understanding.

"Don't let the inmates get to you." He handed her another gift.

"I like hearing everyone joke around," she admitted.

"There you go," Chris said. "Can't beat 'em, so you may as well join 'em. Now stop hedging and open another gift."

She received some funny T-shirts from Priss and Trace. One said, "Power in a Ponytail." That made her laugh, especially since that was how she often wore her hair. Another said, "A Real Princess Can Save Herself," and that was so absurd, she snickered. "Nice. I love them."

From Molly and Dare she received a small bottle of perfume that smelled like heaven, along with some very feminine hair clips that, oddly enough, she liked, even though they were far more girly than anything she'd ever purchased.

Chris took one from her and stuck it awkwardly in her hair, making Molly laugh.

Dare leaned in and repositioned it. "Very pretty," he pronounced.

"Really?"

Jackson laughed. "You could shave your head and still be stunning, Arizona, but, yeah, it looks great."

"You have such amazing hair," Molly said.

And everyone agreed.

Blushing, Arizona glanced at Spencer.

He winked, then handed her another gift. "This one is from me."

She accepted the gift. "When did you have time to do this?"

"I found a website that'd expedite things, and then had it sent here overnight."

"No way."

"Way." He smiled. "The hardest part was using the internet without you catching me at it."

"Sneaky." Amazed that he'd managed it without her knowing, Arizona took care not to rip the pretty paper as she peeled it away. Moving aside layers of tissue, she unveiled a stunning silver jewelry box with her initials ornately engraved in the lid.

It looked expensive, and incredibly personal.

Since she had only a few pieces of jewelry, none of it costly, she didn't understand. But because it was from Spencer, she loved it. Coasting her fingertips over the engraving, she said, "It's amazing."

"Look inside," Spencer told her.

"Oh, okay." Without even realizing it, she held her breath as she lifted the lid—and found a matching jewelry set of bracelet, necklace, earrings and ring, all with her birthstone.

The pieces were delicate and so very, very pretty.

Sunlight glinted on the stones and in the silver. She lifted out the bracelet. "It's all… It's…" Moisture gathered in her eyes. Damn it, she would *not* cry. "I've never seen stuff so pretty."

"Maybe someone should have gotten her a mirror," Chris quipped, and the women quickly shushed him.

Spencer reached for her hand, took the bracelet from her and latched it around her wrist. Still holding her fingers in his, he said, "Everyone should celebrate their actual birth date."

"Not a made-up date," Jackson told her. "With us, it's the real thing."

"Although much as I like a party," Chris added, "we could always celebrate birthdays real and staged."

Arizona looked around at everyone, marveling at them.

Molly sat on Dare's lap. He accepted that as ordinary, as expected, looping his arms around her and kissing her ear with honest affection. "Same here. Any excuse to get together with friends and family is okay by me."

"Next will be the wedding," Alani said, and she looked at Spencer. "I expect both of you there."

"Arizona has already agreed to bring me along."

Right. Spencer was the one who'd agreed so that she wouldn't have to attend alone. But she appreciated his discretion.

When Alani spoke of her pregnancy next, Trace just smiled, hugging Priss closer into his side. She whispered something in his ear that made him go still, and, his eyes glittering, he whispered back, "Behave." But he kissed her, and Priss, wearing an evil grin, rested her head on his shoulder.

Despite their career paths, the men were generous and attentive.

Despite the husbands they'd chosen, the women were confident and happy.

For Arizona, it was all such an alien concept—to be… content.

She'd never known contentment. She'd never known that level of peace. She tried to fake it around them, but even now, even with them going out of their way to include her, she knew she didn't belong.

Given the way Spencer watched her, he probably knew it, too.

Now that she'd opened her gifts, Arizona thought about slipping away before they decided to swim. But... they'd only follow. Earlier, before they'd eaten, she'd tried that. But everywhere she went, they followed like she was the Pied Piper or something. They were determined to include her.

She didn't want to be the spoilsport, not when they were all relaxed and comfortable.

"Thank you all so much. I don't even know what to say about all the fuss and—"

Chris stood. "You're not done yet." He unearthed one more gift from beneath the piles of wrapping paper. "You still need to open my present to you."

"Another gift?" Never in her life had she been given so much. "I'm speechless." Unnerved by all the attention, Arizona opened the gift—and stared in disbelief. She almost forgot to breathe.

Grinning like a sinner, Chris said, "Well?"

"Oh, my God." She wheezed in air, and each word she spoke rose higher and higher. "Are you freaking *kidding me?*" She lifted out the heavy knife, the same one she'd been saving for, and hefted it in her palm. "Oh, my God, Chris, it's *awesome!*"

Silence fell around the table.

Neither she nor Chris cared.

"You like it?" Chris asked.

"Are you serious? Look at that blade! Look at the an-

odized titanium handles, the double thumb openers."
She turned it this way and that. "What's not to like?"

"Glad to hear it."

Dumbfounded, moved by emotion, she shook her
head. "How did you know?"

"I listen. I heard you talk about it." He gave a telling
look to the others. "And I knew it'd make you happy."
He bent to see her face. "At least, I hope it did."

Over the moon with incredulous joy, she carefully set
the knife back in the box.

"Arizona?"

She threw herself against Chris's chest and felt his
arms come around her. Fighting off tears wasn't easy.

She loved the gifts, all of them, but that knife…it was
as if Chris actually knew her, really knew her—and
liked her anyway.

He chuckled at her tight hold. "I take it it's the right
one?"

"I was saving for it!"

"Now you can spend your money on something else."

She hugged him so fiercely that he groaned and pretended to collapse, so she levered back and grabbed
his face. Despite his look of surprise at her intent, she
planted a big, five-second smooching kiss right on his
handsome mouth, ending with a loud, "Mmmwwah!"

"Whoa," Chris said once she freed him. "Try that
with any other guy and you'd probably find yourself
hauled off to bed."

"No other guy could be you." Joy clogged her throat.
"You're amazing, Chris. Just…amazing."

"Like the knife?"

"Yes, amazing like the knife." Arizona released him
to beam at the others.

Jackson stared. Trace cleared his throat. Dare rubbed his mouth. The women watched wide-eyed.

But so what? For once, she didn't give a damn what any of them thought.

And then she saw Spencer's dark expression. So he didn't like her kissing Chris?

Or was it the knife he didn't like?

Well, tough titty. She didn't care what he thought, either. "It's *the* knife," she told him. "The one I told you I was saving for. I showed it to you in a magazine, remember?"

"Yes, I remember."

Chris paid no more attention to his disapproval than she did. "There's a sheath to go with it, but I didn't get that. Sorry."

"I have one that'll do." She reached back, realized she'd left the knife at home, and shrugged. "I left it at Spencer's, but really, this is already too much. Too extravagant, too—"

"I can afford it," Chris told her, sounding serious for the first time. "And you deserve it."

Why she would deserve such a gift, she couldn't imagine. But then, she knew she didn't deserve any of it.

Yet here she was, in the middle of her very first birthday party, surrounded by gifts.

Any second now, the dampness filling her eyes would fall. She held the knife to her chest, a cherished gift. "Thank you. Everyone. Seriously. It's all great. I'm just…" Overwhelmed, she let out a shaky breath. "I'm floored. I never expected…"

They smiled at her.

Crap. One more second of their kindness, and she'd be a goner. "Yeah, so, thanks. Again. A lot." Her throat felt tighter. "So…I'm going to take this stuff to Spencer's truck. You know, to make sure nothing happens to any of it."

Feeling like the biggest coward alive, she turned and literally ran so fast that Tai and Sargie perked up. Excited by a possible game, the dogs chased after her.

Arizona knew she'd have to return, and very soon, otherwise they'd all come looking for her. But God willing, she'd get her emotions under control before then.

She'd rather be thrown into another river than let everyone see her weeping like a girl.

HARRY'S HOCKS HAD SHUT down weeks ago, but that only made it cheap to rent.

For a few hours.

He needed no more time than that.

After she'd been made…*suitably pliable,* he'd move her. He'd get her settled in, and he'd enjoy her at his leisure.

Thinking about it, imagining how she'd be, how he'd make her be, he rubbed his hands together. She might not be grateful at first, but eventually she'd be thanking him, maybe even begging him.

He laughed with pleasure at that image. Once he explained to her how he'd saved her, taking her from a worse situation, accepting her when no one else would want her, then she'd show proper gratitude. Now, with him, she wouldn't be sold.

He would offer her comfort, and in return, she would give him…everything.

He would demand nothing less.

SPENCER WANTED TO GO after Arizona, but he knew she wouldn't appreciate that. It was bad enough, watching her draw comparisons, knowing she thought she didn't fit in. But seeing that wealth of emotion in her expression had nearly leveled him.

All because of a knife.

And not just any knife, but a knife meant to do damage. A knife meant for a skilled combatant.

A knife she knew how to use and had wanted for just that purpose.

A gift that damn near brought her to tears.

He didn't know what to do.

Chris began gathering up the torn and discarded wrapping paper.

Jackson stood to scowl at him. "What the hell, Chris?"

Spencer sat back, content to think about things, about Arizona's reaction—and Chris's obvious insight.

"Did you see her face? I'd say, so far, today has been a success."

Dare shook his head. "You realize you just set us all back, right? We're trying to get her away from danger."

"Not encourage her into it," Trace added.

"You're trying to change her," Chris pointed out but not with much accusation. He looked at Spencer. "She doesn't want to change."

"Just where the hell do you think she'll use that knife?" Jackson asked.

Chris paused in his clean-up efforts to give Jackson a direct look. "She does not want to change."

"What does that mean?" Trace asked. "You actually think it's okay for her to get involved in this stuff?"

"I think she's a very special girl with a unique background who can make her own decisions."

"Chris has a point." Spencer lifted a long, curling ribbon from the table. "Can you imagine how it makes her feel?"

Nodding, Molly whispered, "She is who she is, and yet we've all made it clear that she should be someone else."

"But given what she's been through, how life molded her…" Priss closed her eyes a moment. "Changing is probably impossible."

His guts cramped at what he'd inadvertently put her through. "Disapproval isn't easy for anyone." Spencer crushed the ribbon in his fist. "She needs acceptance first."

"Well, hallelujah. You get the prize." Chris threw a balled up wad of paper at Spencer. "How can she trust that any of you care, when you don't accept her for who she is?"

"There's an order here," Spencer agreed. He slouched in his chair with a groan. "And I for one have gone at it ass-backwards."

"Well, damn." Jackson stood, then rubbed the back of his neck. "I just wanted to protect her."

"It's what you do." Alani took his hand. "But Arizona isn't like most women."

"Or most victims," he agreed.

Amen to that. She was unlike…anyone. Stronger, thank God. More resilient. And so incredibly proud.

"Damn it, I still have to give her my gift." Jackson started to go after her.

But Spencer said, "No, leave her be."

Looking very put out by the idea that Spencer would dare try to give him an order, Jackson slowly pivoted to stare at him. "Come again?"

Not the least intimidated, Spencer rolled his eyes. "Give her the time she needs."

Forestalling any hostilities, Chris said, "She'll be back."

"Her pride won't let her dodge us for long." Spencer stared toward where she'd gone. "But she won't appreciate you seeing her upset."

JACKSON HAD TO ADMIT that Spencer was probably right. Arizona could get real prickly over any perceived weakness. But damn, it went against the grain. Every instinct in his male-inspired repertoire told him to console her.

She'd probably have a fit if he tried that, though.

And she'd be more embarrassed. He couldn't do that to her.

Patience was one of his strong suits. When necessary, he could wait for hours, even days, on a stakeout. But now, he had a hell of a time waiting for Arizona to return.

In his pocket, the keys jangled. He paced, constantly watching for her.

By silent agreement they had all decided to give her the space she needed. She'd return when she was ready. It had only been ten minutes. But still…

Finally she came back around the house, both dogs trailing her. She stroked Tai while talking to Sargie.

She liked dogs. Maybe that could be his next gift.

He wanted to take care of her for a very long time. He wanted to shower her with presents.

He wanted her to be in his life, for the rest of his life. As Alani had pointed out, she was like a sister to him. He felt responsible for her, loyal to her. He trusted her.

He loved her, damn it.

Hopefully his gift would help to convince her.

She stalled when she saw them all still lounging around the patio. "I figured you guys would go swimming or something."

"That's next," Chris told her. "But Jackson has one more surprise for you."

Jackson saw her bite off a groan, and it amused him. "None of that, now." Throwing an arm around her shoulders, he brought her into the group. "Indulge me a little, will you?"

"Well, sure, but..." She let out a long breath. "Seriously, Jackson, it's already so much. My trunk will be full!"

Alani, bless her beautiful heart, grinned hugely. "That's the best part, Arizona."

"The best part of what?"

"You'll have more room. All the room you need."

Seeing that she didn't understand, Jackson added, "I don't want you to live out of your trunk. Not anymore."

Her gaze sought Spencer's—why, Jackson didn't know. Was she seeking additional support? Or was that look more about what she kept in her trunk?

He glanced at Spencer, but that sly dog kept all expression hidden.

Deciding that he'd check out her trunk at the first opportunity, Jackson withdrew the keys. "You know how Chris has a house here with Dare?"

Shock filled her features as Arizona took a step back. "No."

It was an act of denial. She knew all about Chris's house; in some ways, she was no different from him. Within minutes of her first trip to Dare's, she'd taken in everything, including the property. She'd explored the boathouse, the dock, the shed, the garage...and Chris's place.

Eyeing the keys in his hand, she shook her head. "No, you didn't... You wouldn't..."

Disbelief had her stammering.

Too bad. Eventually she'd get used to being loved.

At least, Jackson hoped that was true.

He pulled Alani into his side. "We did."

Chris shrugged as if it were no big deal. "I have my own place for privacy, but I'm here, nearby, so I can keep up with everything Dare needs done."

"He's only a shout away," Molly said. "It works out great."

Arizona shook her head again, harder this time.

"I want you to continue working for me." Ignoring her disbelief, her stricken expression, Jackson forged on. "You're thorough. You catch on quick to the computer programs we use. And you get it."

"It?" she asked.

"The whole biz. What to look for, what to consider. You put the pieces together."

"You know what trafficking looks like," Trace pointed out. "You recognize the signs."

"Right." Jackson jumped on that as a way to convince her. "I need you working with me."

"You mean *for* you." She couldn't hide her sneer. "Like a secretary."

Yeah...regardless of what Chris said, he wasn't ready to toss her into the middle of it all; she'd spent too much time there already.

He looked to Spencer for help but got none. In fact, the poor dude looked pained. Jackson got it; Spencer might not want to admit it, but he'd been caught in Arizona's web. Her special brand of vulnerability and bravado, the way she fought the world, just reeled a guy in.

Of course, Spencer looked at her in a way Jackson never had. At times, it made him uncomfortable and gave him just a hint of what Trace must've felt when he was hot and heavy on Alani's tail.

Spencer wanted to do what was best for Arizona, which meant he had to fight his instincts—the gut-driven urge to protect her, even from herself.

Jackson could tell him that it'd be easier to give in, to redirect all that energy into loving Arizona instead. But he had a feeling Spencer needed to figure that one out on his own.

And if he didn't…well, then, he didn't deserve Arizona.

"I'd say as an assistant, actually, not a secretary—which you make sound like a dirty word."

"I do assist," Arizona said warily. "I'm not behind on anything, right? I went through all the files you sent my way."

Alani hugged up to his arm. "You've been wonderful. Jackson told me so."

Jackson nodded.

"But we'd also love to have you close."

Arizona shifted her feet, took one stance, then another. "Yeah, well…" Again she glanced at Spencer. "I appreciate that. The thing is—"

Unable to take all her waffling, Jackson dropped the keys onto the table. "Those go to a lock. For a front door. That'll go into the house we're having built for you on our property—and don't you give me that look." He pointed at her. "You can't keep running around the streets."

Arizona's eyes narrowed. "No." She looked from him to Alani. "But thank you."

Jackson ignored that. "I have more than enough land, damn it. Like Chris said, you'd have your own privacy—"

"No." She swallowed hard, breathed fast. "You're too generous and too…" At a loss, she shook her head.

"Appreciate the gesture. Really. But I can't. Thanks anyway."

It wasn't a damn gesture, but when he started to speak, Alani squeezed his arm. "Please think about it, Arizona, okay? The keys are symbolic. We haven't broken ground yet on the new structure."

"We wanted you in on that," Jackson explained. "Alani wanted you to help design the house."

"Oh, God." She rubbed her forehead.

Alani left him to approach her. "Don't make a decision right now. Take a little time to think about it, that's all I'm asking. Could you do that, please?"

Jackson knew Arizona wanted to refuse, but Alani had a hand on her shoulder, her tone was soft and sincere, and Arizona wasn't immune to her.

Who could be? His fiancée was one special lady.

Damn, he was lucky.

Smiling, he came up to put an arm around each of them. "Great idea. Take a little time to get used to the idea before you decide."

"And until then," Chris said, "let's eat some cake!"

CHAPTER TWENTY

THANK GOD THEY DIDN'T make her suffer through any singing, or blowing out of candles. After helping to clear away the last of the birthday mess, Arizona finally started to relax.

At least, on that score. She still had to find out what she could about Quin and the sting and that suspicious phone call she'd received.

"So, Dare." With all birthday celebrating now out of the way, Arizona sought a way to ask the necessary questions. She moved her glass of lemonade a little, seeing the ring of condensation left behind on the patio table. "Did you wrap up everything at the bar?"

"The Green Goose?"

How many trafficking rings was he currently busting up at bars? Dryly, she said, "Yeah, that one."

"Not completely." Dare shrugged. "But everyone is safe, and there are good people working on the details."

Everyone wasn't safe, or Quin would've had no need to call her.

"We're staying in contact with the head of the new task force," Trace told her. "He's still interrogating Terry Janes, but I doubt they'll find out anything else."

Huh. Trace had probably already questioned the guy, and he wasn't held back by legal restrictions. "You figure if you couldn't make him talk, no one can, right?"

Scowling a little, Trace avoided the question. "It's being handled."

"Right. I'm sure it is. But if there's nothing else to find out, why interrogate him?"

Jackson frowned at her. "There's always more to find out. Like who owns the place."

"Janes doesn't?"

"Nope."

She ran her finger through the condensation on the table. "So…who does?"

"We're still working on it," Dare told her. "So far, no one we nabbed seems to know, so we'll have to search the records."

Arizona considered that. "You got Janes and his henchman, Carl, and the bartender…"

"And a couple of other thugs who drove a white van. Dare grabbed them out of the back alley."

Arizona looked up. That was the first she'd heard about a white van.

"But," Jackson said before she could start asking questions, "you don't need to worry about any of that. Those bozos are shut down for good."

Unfortunately, she had reason for doubt. She turned to Dare again. "Okay, so you got the creeps. But do you remember the workers you rounded up?"

"There were over a dozen people, hon."

She deflated. "So you can't account for them all?"

Intuition sharpened his gaze. "I can place most of them. Why?"

Oops, time to retrench. "I was just wondering." She brushed away a bumblebee that tried to land on her arm and summoned her most casual expression. "Was Quin in there?"

"The Hispanic kid?" Dare thought about it and then shook his head. "I don't recall seeing him, no."

"Isn't that odd?" Forget subtlety; she *needed* to know. "I mean, he was there that night. He served me."

"He probably split the second he heard the sirens," Jackson said. "Maybe he's an illegal. Bastard traffickers convince them they'll be arrested if they're caught."

"Is there a reason you're worried about him, specifically?" Trace asked.

"No, not really." Her thoughts churned a little more. To make her lie more convincing and throw them off the scent, she asked, "What about that goofy little artist, Joel Pitts?"

Dare shrugged. "I don't know the names of the people, but I can find out if it's that important to you."

No, it wouldn't matter. She knew Quin was free because he'd called her, so why put Dare to the trouble of gathering info? "That's okay. I was just curious."

"Why?" Spencer asked quietly.

She slanted him a look. "Quin and Joel were the two I talked with most. I spotted Quin right off as a victim and then, since Joel drew pictures of me..." She shrugged. "I feel like I sort of know them both."

"What do you mean, he drew pictures of you?" Priscilla asked. "What kind of pictures?"

"I was going to ask the same thing," Alani said.

"I'll show you. They should still be in my purse." To give herself a moment, Arizona went inside and hunted for them. They were now badly creased and smudged a little, but she brought them back outside anyway.

As she rolled them out on the table, she explained. "I was pretty hammered when we left there, or I'd have thought to take them out before they got messed up."

Everyone gathered around. "Wow." Priss admired the drawing. "He's really talented."

A different topic was to her advantage, so Arizona kept it going. "Even without me posing or anything, the drawings look like me, except better."

"Not true," Dare said.

"Hard to imagine that's even possible," Jackson told her. "You looking like you do and all."

"You really are beautiful," Alani agreed. "There's nothing to improve on."

"Yeah, well…thanks." Uncomfortable with the compliments, Arizona gave her attention back to Trace and Dare. "I was hoping to see them both again. Just to see how they're doing."

She glanced at Spencer. He was far too quiet as he scrutinized her with piercing interest.

While trailing his fingertips up and down his wife's arm, Trace asked, "You're worried for them?"

Ignoring Spencer's watchful gaze wasn't easy. When Trace picked up one of the drawings to study it, she tried for a shrug. "They both seemed pretty lost, that's all. It'd make me feel better to know they're okay."

"Arizona?"

She tried not to wince at Spencer's tone. "Hmm?"

"Why are you asking about Quin and Joel?"

"I told you." She didn't want to lie to him—but neither could she tell him the truth. As she again rolled up the drawings, she settled on a partial truth. "Curiosity, that's all."

"Uh-huh." Spencer caught her gaze and held it. "What else?"

As if they only then felt the tension, everyone went still, watching them, waiting.

Arizona pressed the drawings back into her purse.

She'd just gotten done being the center of attention; damned if she'd let Spencer put her back there again. "Why does there need to be any other reason?"

"With you, there are always ulterior motives."

She thrust up her chin. "Bull. I didn't have an ulterior motive when I asked you to spar with me. I just wanted to hone my skills. And still you refused."

His eyes darkened, maybe with irritation. "Because I don't want you using yourself as bait."

"Why not? That's the easiest way to catch a man." Her voice dripped with sugary sweetness. "It apparently works for Marla." And then to the group at large, she explained, "That's his neighbor."

Spencer sawed his teeth together.

Jackson pulled back. "What does his neighbor have to do with anything?"

Arizona said, "She wants him."

At the same time, Spencer said, "It's Arizona's way of deflecting."

Wow. He saw right through that, huh? So he wasn't a mental slug. She'd already known and admired that about him.

She said to the group, "I wanted to work out with Spencer." She gave her attention back to him. "But I guess that's one more thing I'm supposed to do with the next guy, right?"

Spencer went rigid, his jaw flexing, his gaze cold.

And he withdrew. Arizona felt it, saw it, and it wasn't pleasant.

Uh…yeah. So maybe she'd pushed him just a little too far with that jibe. But seeing his set features, she didn't know how to regroup.

"Speaking of computer work…" Chris cleared his

throat. "I wanted to show you a new program, Spencer. I'm thinking it'd be pretty valuable to a bounty hunter."

Spencer slowly pushed away from the table and stood. Without a word, he walked away with Chris.

Holy cow. Ice could have formed in his wake. He left behind so much tension, the air crackled. *Talk about awkward...*

She might have felt more uncomfortable, but damn it, instead she felt guilty.

The urge to go after him left her fidgeting in her seat. Even if she did, what would she say? *I'm sorry you don't want to keep me around for the long haul?* She snorted and didn't even care that the others gave her funny looks. She knew zilch about this relationship crap, what was the right thing and the wrong thing to do.

And damn it, she had few choices now. Given that she'd meet with Quin tomorrow, what could she say that'd make a difference anyway?

Dare stepped away from the patio table. "I'll go with you."

Not understanding, Arizona glanced back at him, then did a double take at his expression. Molly beamed with pleasure, confusing her more. "Go where?"

"Head to head." All business now, he beckoned her from her seat. "Come on. Let's see what you've got."

Trace sat back with a smile. "I have to admit, I'm curious."

Jackson groaned.

Arizona couldn't believe her luck. Dare Macintosh wanted to spar with her? No way. "Do you mean...?" She waved a hand between them. "Me and you? Seriously?"

He gave a sharp nod. "Let's grapple."

Despite the circumstances, anticipation bubbled up. But she didn't trust the offer. Narrowing her eyes, she asked, "Why?"

"Why not?"

Trace sided with Dare. "All things considered, Arizona, you need to know how to fight."

She didn't point out that she already knew how to fight. "What things?"

"Being around us," he said. "Working with Jackson."

And Dare added, "Poking your little nose where it doesn't belong."

Now *that* she couldn't let pass. "Who says it doesn't belong?" She had as much right as they did, maybe more, to work at bringing down traffickers.

Jackson opened his mouth, but Dare interrupted whatever he planned to say. "Are we sparring or not?"

Her heart beat rapidly. "Oh, definitely, we are." She left her seat and strode toward him.

"You mind the others watching?"

"In most bar fights, there's a crowd." She shrugged. "I've never let an audience get in my way."

"Oh, my God," Priss said. "You actually fight in bars?"

"I keep my knife on me," Arizona explained. "It's a great equalizer."

The men said nothing, but the women couldn't hide their disbelief—probably disapproval, too. Not that she gave a flip.

Only…she kind of did.

No, screw that. She shook out her arms and took a stance across from him.

"Now that I know you like knives…" Dare picked up a sturdy twig about as thick around as his index finger. He broke it until it was close to ten inches long. "We'll pretend this is your favorite blade." He flipped it over once and then held it out to her.

A stick? Okay, she'd play along. After tossing it from hand to hand, Arizona worked her fingers around it until it felt right. She nodded.

"Try not to poke out my eye, okay?"

Satisfaction filled her smile. "Don't worry," she taunted him. "I won't hurt you."

Dare didn't take the bait, but then she already knew he had a cool, controlled temperament.

They stood in the yard. It wasn't flat but instead sloped down gently toward the lake. No problem; real fights seldom occurred under ideal situations. Dare adjusted for the terrain, so she would, too.

She felt the sun on the top of her head and bare shoulders, but it didn't blind her.

She felt the rapt stares of the others and dismissed them from her mind.

Drawing a calming breath, she braced her feet. "Ready when you are."

Probably hoping to startle her, Dare lunged forward in a head-on attack. Reacting automatically, Arizona released the twig with the same deadly accuracy she utilized with her knife. Like an arrow, it struck Dare solidly in the chest—right where his heart would be.

Stunned, he stopped in his tracks.

Smug, vindicated, Arizona whispered, "Gotcha." Maybe now he'd take her seriously.

Trace barked a laugh. "Not bad, Arizona." He sat forward. "But if that wasn't a killing blow—and it rarely is, at least not right away and not against a guy like Dare—then you're in trouble, because now you've lost your weapon."

Oh, well…yeah, maybe.

Trace nodded at her. "Try again."

Expression enigmatic, Dare handed her the makeshift knife and resumed his stance. "Ready?"

She set her feet apart and rolled her shoulders to loosen them. "Yup."

This time, the second he moved, she dashed in, ducked under his arm and used the side of the twig to simulate a slash across his crotch. She rolled out of the way.

She felt pretty good about her speed, until she came up and found Dare right behind her, saying, "I might be bleeding out, but now I'm really pissed, too." Effortlessly, he contained her in a choke hold. "And then we'd die together."

He didn't hurt her, but no way could she get out of his hold, either.

Near her ear, he asked, "What would you do now?"

Still held tight, she said, "Normally I'd stomp an instep, or deliver a head butt. Or even just drop my weight so you had to readjust your grip. But you've already taken away those options."

"True enough."

"I guess I'd just bide my time and wait for an opening." She tipped her head around to smile at him. "Everyone slips up eventually."

"Maybe." Dare released her. "Unless I snapped your neck without missing a beat." He smoothed down her mussed hair, then lifted her chin. "And that's the thing, Arizona. You never know how trained someone might be. Most idiots in bars are without skill. But not always. It's not something you can take for granted."

Feeling her blood sing through her veins, Arizona grinned. "Okay, so school me." She shook out her limbs. "I'm all ears."

Trace laughed again. "You're all something—not sure ears are the right description."

Over the next few minutes, as she and Dare tried several different moves together, she was *almost* able to put aside her conflict with Spencer.

But not quite.

Where was he now? What was he doing?

Was he so angry that he'd avoid her the rest of their trip?

Like hell. She wouldn't let him brood. If he wanted to argue, fine, she'd argue. But she wouldn't—

She grunted when Dare caught her unawares and tripped her to her back. She bounded right back, jerked to the side and kicked him in his sexy butt.

The women started cheering; it was Arizona they wanted to see come out ahead.

They booed Dare when he again took her legs out from under her, even though he brought her down easy to the grass. "You're distracted," he scolded. "And that could cost you your life."

They hooted and hollered when she rapidly squirreled around and locked her arms tight over Dare's throat. "Not that distracted," she said as she used her knees in his back for leverage.

Dare laughed. "You are fast."

"Cry uncle?" she asked outrageously, just to egg on the women.

"I don't think so." Dare flipped her over his shoulder and tossed her high into the air, making her squawk loudly in surprise.

Trace roared with hilarity even as Dare caught her again, and the women joined in.

Jackson came to stand over her. "You said something about crying uncle, Arizona?"

Exhilarated and gasping for breath, she shouted, "Never!"

Sargie and Tai wanted in on the game. The big dogs started bounding around them to the point that Grim the cat hissed and ran off, and even Liger turned up his nose and moved a safer distance away.

On her back, grass in her hair and the sun in her eyes, Arizona fended off the dogs and laughed till her sides hurt. It was so much fun. She couldn't recall the last time she'd...played.

Maybe she never had.

Shaking his head, Dare threw more grass at her while Tai and Sargie both tried to get in his lap. "I'll concede that you have some skill, brat."

"And just think." Wearing a proud grin, Jackson stood over her, his hands on his hips. "If you lived close, I could work with you until you're good."

Ha! She looked up at him. "I'm already good."

"Yeah, maybe." His grin widened. "For a girl."

Grabbing his ankle, Arizona jerked him off balance, and he ended up on his butt beside her. For a second, he sat in stunned silence while Trace and Dare chuckled and the women heckled him.

Then Jackson's eyes narrowed with wicked intent. "Paybacks are hell, honey."

Uh-oh! Snickering, Arizona shot to her feet, but she didn't get far. She squealed again as Jackson easily brought her to the ground, but instead of grappling, he... *tickled her*.

Until that moment, she hadn't realized she was so incredibly ticklish. She laughed and struggled, kicked and punched, and did her best to get away.

She was no match for Jackson.

He caught her wrists and pinned them down. "Cry uncle," he insisted with unrelenting good humor.

"No, never!" Around her laughter, she said, "I'll get you somehow. I'll—"

Jackson contained both her wrists in one big hand. He half loomed over her, using one leg to trap hers in place.

Too late, Arizona realized her precarious position.

The laughter died; her heart started a mad drumming and her lungs compressed.

But no matter what she tried, she couldn't get free of him.

LAUGHING SHRIEKS INTERRUPTED Chris's efforts to distract Spencer by waxing on about the in-depth program. Not that he'd been able to concentrate much anyway. It had been clear to Spencer that the entire birthday celebration was difficult for Arizona, so he'd tried not to take her cutting remarks to heart.

But damn it, was she serious?

Send her to another man? Hell, no, he didn't want to do that. Ever. The idea of her with someone else ate him up inside.

Long before he'd made love with her, he'd fought that internal battle over doing the right thing or being selfish.

"Is someone skinning the cats?" Grinning, Chris headed for the back door.

"That was Arizona." Frowning, Spencer followed. He'd recognize Arizona's voice anywhere, but shrieking? That was so unlike her. "Something's wrong."

"They're probably just playing."

Spencer hastened his step. He had hoped that eventually Arizona would realize how these people cared about her.

But he hadn't expected it to happen today.

He drew up short at what he found.

He'd been inside less than twenty minutes—and somehow, in his absence, she'd ended up on the ground with Dare and Jackson both.

He'd heard her laughter...so why did he feel so uneasy now?

Chris, still holding a stack of printouts from the computer program, grinned when he saw the antics in the yard. "We're missing all the fun."

Spencer didn't return the grin. The closer he got, the tighter his tension grew.

Finally, as Dare stood, Spencer got a good look at Jackson straddling Arizona's hips. Her hair was now more out of the rubber band than in it. With one hand Jackson kept her arms over her head, and with the other he attempted to tickle her bare midriff while she twisted and turned.

Even more than that, Spencer saw her face. Pale, drawn. She fought silently, trying to free herself without giving away her terror at being under a man.

An anomalous emotion, blistering hot and explosive, coursed through Spencer. *Get the hell off her!*

"Whoa, subtle, dude," Chris told him. "Real subtle."

Not giving a damn what anyone thought, Spencer reached her in three long strides. Catching Jackson by the upper arm, he literally hauled him up and away from Arizona, freeing her from his hold.

In an instant, she was on her feet, sucking in much-needed air, still shaky but, again, trying her utmost to conceal it.

She kept one fist pressed to her stomach, the other stiff at her side.

Heaving beside her, Spencer marveled at her strength, her pride. He fought the urge to grab her close—and the urge to flatten Jackson. He wanted to hug her, to shield her against his body.

Everyone now stood around them, watchful, their gazes ripe with sudden understanding, concern and... sympathy.

Fuck.

Arizona would *hate* that. She'd rather suffer through the terror than have anyone look at her in pity. Any second now someone would reach out to her.

She looked as if she'd fracture if that happened.

As a distraction, Spencer turned to Jackson and crowded close to ask hotly, "Are you out of your mind?"

Slowly, his every movement precise, Jackson straightened to his full height, which remained a few inches short of Spencer's near six and a half feet. His expression darkened, but he looked beyond Spencer to Arizona and then back again.

Spencer held his gaze, willing him to understand. Praying that he would.

And he did.

Though still edgy, Jackson pulled it together. "She's good," he quipped in a tone that was *almost* congenial. "Against an average guy, she just might hold her own."

Relief rolled through Spencer. He dragged in a breath, and nodded. To maintain his own role, he said, "If she stays out of trouble, she doesn't need to hold her own."

"No guarantee that she'll do that."

"Not with her skill set," Dare added, doing his part to ease the situation. "She lacks strength, but she makes up for it with speed."

"And daring," Trace added. "If what she showed us just now was accurate to how she'd be in a real battle, then she's not a cautious fighter. That's both good and bad."

Arizona pushed back her hair—and took a firm step forward. "I'm standing right here, you guys." Only a faint trembling gave away her lack of composure.

"What Chris said makes sense. She's going to be around danger. It's in her nature. You know that."

"What did Chris say?" she asked, but no one gave her an answer.

In that moment, Spencer's respect for each of the men doubled. They were ruthless when need be, but they were also kind and caring. "There's danger, and then there's danger." Without looking at her, Spencer reached for her hand and tugged her into his side.

And she let him.

"You said it yourself, she lacks the strength to go toe to toe with a psychopath."

"It's my decision, Spence." She looked up at him. "Not yours."

"Actually it's theirs." He nodded at the men—and prayed they'd find a way to let her down gently. What she'd just gone through proved she wasn't ready, emotionally or physically, to run the risk of getting caught again. "And they don't look like dummies to me."

Jackson said, "Don't push your luck." His smile was mean.

Trace shouldered Jackson aside and spoke to Dare. "Now might be a good time to ask him."

Spencer smoothed his thumb over Arizona's chilled knuckles. "Ask me what?"

"If you'll join us."

Proving he wasn't really pissed at all, Jackson nearly

felled him with a whack on the back. "The pay is a shit-load better than what you're used to, man. And you get to exercise your alpha dog." He winked. "A real win-win."

Well, hell, Spencer thought. He hadn't seen that one coming.

He looked down at Arizona and found her beaming—with pride. Huh.

No jealously. No resentment.

Never the expected from her—because she rose above the expected, over and over again.

Incredible.

He'd think about her astounding acceptance later, but for now, she'd been distracted from her fear, and that was what mattered most.

CHAPTER TWENTY-ONE

NEEDING A FEW MINUTES, Arizona excused herself and went inside. In the bathroom, she splashed her face, straightened her ponytail, put a little more makeup over the bruise on her jaw.

And she took time to breathe.

But honestly, excitement for Spencer overshadowed everything else.

They wanted him to sign on.

Damn, she was *soooo* proud of him. She couldn't imagine a bigger compliment or a better testament to Spencer's ability and his honor. They trusted him, and that meant so much.

And if he worked with the guys, then maybe she could convince him to partner up with her. Yeah, he wanted to cut their time short, she knew that. She hadn't forgotten his motives or what he'd told her from the get-go.

But now she had a good excuse to try to talk him around.

She now had hope—and wow, hope was a scary thing.

On her way back out, she heard the women talking in the kitchen, laughing and chatting so amicably. At least they weren't gossiping about her—yet. If she got the opportunity to stick around long enough, though, she knew they would.

She pasted on a smile and stepped into the room.

Priss immediately asked, "Did you bring a suit? We're getting ready to go down to the lake."

"Yeah, it's under my clothes." And with any luck, it'd stay there.

But luck wasn't with her today.

"Soon as the guys are done talking, we're all heading down," Alani told her. "I think Chris wants to ski, and I wouldn't mind cooling down with a swim."

Molly rinsed a glass and put it in the dishwasher. "I'll be ready in just a minute." She left the room.

Priss stood. "I need to find the sunscreen. Trace gets apoplectic if I burn."

"I have some," Alani told her.

"You two go on." Arizona had other interests than swimsuits and sunscreen. "I'll wait for you outside."

"You just want in on the conversation out there," Alani teased, but without any insult. "Go on then, and we'll join you soon."

But when Arizona stepped out, the yard was empty. Frowning, she followed the sound of low voices over to the side yard—and overheard Dare and Spencer talking. Curiosity got the better of her, and she hoped to glean a few details about the offer.

Wearing a half smile, she inched closer.

"You shouldn't fight it," Dare said. "I can tell you from personal experience, it's impossible once you've met the right one."

That didn't sound at all work-related. Arizona started to interrupt, and then Spencer replied.

"Unfortunately, I had to bury the one that was right for me, and I'm not looking for a replacement."

Arizona staggered back. Her heart dropped and her stomach cramped.

Whatever Dare said in return was lost on her. A ringing sounded in her ears. She'd known. She wasn't stupid.

But hearing Spencer spell it out like that…well, that hurt.

So maybe she was pretty damn dumb after all. Why else would she have let herself get emotionally involved? Spencer hadn't misled her. He'd been brutally honest every step of the way.

Praying the men wouldn't hear her, she turned away. Disgust carried her halfway down the hill before she even realized where she was going.

Her jumbled thoughts kept her stomach pitching.

Tomorrow, she'd defy Spencer's trust. She would sneak away and meet secretly with Quin.

For a guy like Spencer, that in itself would be a deal breaker, not that they'd had any sort of emotional deal. But…God, she wished they did.

Maybe, since he enjoyed having sex with her, she could convince him to…what? Keep sleeping with her?

Hadn't Marla tried that trick? Why should she think she'd be any more successful?

Because she wouldn't make demands. Yeah, so desperation drove her. She'd never really wanted anything, or anyone, the way she wanted Spencer Lark. He was worth fighting for.

Problem was, she didn't know how to engage in that type of fight. She sure couldn't pound him into agreement. And she already knew he disliked games and despised dishonesty.

What tools did that leave her?

She could let Spencer know that she wanted, needed, nothing in return. Just great sex. Just…his company on occasion. Maybe the casual arrangement would work for him.

No matter what, she had to try, because the alternative, never seeing him again, was far too crushing to consider.

ARIZONA FOUND CHRIS sprawled on the dock looking as lazy as the dogs when they sunned themselves. He'd obviously taken a dip in the lake; water beaded on his wide shoulders, dripped from his wet hair and left a small rivulet down the deep groove of his tanned back, all the way to his still-soaked shorts, which now drooped low on his hips. So low, in fact, that she saw a strip of paler skin that they usually covered.

"Stop staring." Eyes still closed, voice languid, Chris added, "I'm starting to feel naked."

"All but," Arizona told him, and she sat down at his side. She thought about putting her feet into the lake, looked over the edge of the dock at that dark water, and shuddered.

"The vitals are properly covered." He shifted a little, squinted one eye against the glare of the sun and resettled himself.

She'd never paid much attention before, but Chris looked good. Six-two, black hair, blue eyes, lean but muscular build. From what she knew of him, he spent as much time in the water as out of it.

At the sound of a fish jumping, she pulled her attention away from his body and instead looked at the lake. "You ever skinny-dip in there?"

Indolent amusement curled his mouth. "What do you think?"

"I bet you do."

"Not so much now that Molly's around." Rolling to his back, he scratched his chest, put his arms over his head and let his legs sprawl.

She couldn't help noticing that his shorts were a little low in the front, too. Odd that her intimate involvement with Spencer increased her awareness of other male... attributes.

Chris caught her peeking but didn't comment on it. "What about you? Got the urge to commune with nature?"

"No." Before she even considered getting in the water, she wanted Spencer with her. No matter what else happened, he'd promised her that much.

"Where's everyone else? The guys still talking shop?"

"I guess." Would Spencer join up with the others? Arizona just didn't know. "Molly and Alani are changing into their suits, and Priss was going to put on sunscreen."

"What about you?"

"I don't burn easy." And she had no intention of staying in the water any longer than it'd take to prove... what? That she wasn't a chicken?

"Me, either." A dragonfly buzzed close, and Chris watched it until it zipped away. He closed his eyes again, and it almost looked as if he dozed.

"Can you sleep in this heat?"

"When people aren't talking to me, yeah."

So she was bothering him? Well, tough. She needed some advice, and who better to ask than Chris?

If she tried talking to any of the guys, they'd either rat her out to Spencer, or they'd start issuing him warnings. She didn't have a single doubt. It was like some macho, protective code they had. Buttheads.

And the wives...well, nice as they were to her, she felt almost dysfunctional around them. Other than being female, she had zip in common with them.

So that left Chris.

He groaned out a laugh. "Come on, Arizona. Spit it out." Shielding his eyes with a forearm, he squinted toward her again. "You're down here with me for a reason, right?"

After rolling a shoulder, she asked, "Where's Matt?"

He gave her a long stare, then dropped the arm over his eyes and rested back again. "No idea."

"He wasn't invited?"

Exasperated, he half sat up to glare at her. "Why is it if you put two gay guys in a room together, everyone assumes they're a couple? I can have friends, you know."

She blinked at him. Wow. What a reaction. "So... touchy much?"

In a priceless expression of bemusement, he huffed. "Not usually, no." And then, turning the tables on her, he said, "But look who's talking about being touchy."

Her shoulders stiffened. "What's that supposed to mean?"

"Oh, no you don't. Don't go looking all pugnacious and put out. You covered it well, but not well enough." Sitting up cross-legged, he draped his forearms over his knees. "So you don't like being pinned down? Big deal. Get over yourself already."

She had no idea what to say to that. Denials would be absurd and cowardly. She thrust up her chin. "I'm working on it."

"Yeah, so work on it with Spencer. You trust him, right?"

Trust had nothing to do with it. Why had she ever wanted to talk to Chris anyway? "You are such a smart-ass."

"Only when I'm right." He grinned, leaned forward and gave her shoulder a shove. "Admit it."

After she righted herself, Arizona glared at him. She

wouldn't admit a damn thing. Not yet, anyway. If he wanted admissions, he could go first. "I only wondered about Matt because I know Priss is fond of him."

"Oh." He shrugged. "Yeah, well, he's only a friend and this was a family thing, and if I'm touchy about it, that's because everyone seems to think otherwise."

"That you two are…?"

"Yeah."

"But you're not…?"

He rolled his eyes. "No, we're not. I like being a bachelor."

"Yeah. I get that."

"Somehow I don't think you do." Going all serious and solemn, he tipped his head. "So…about Spencer?"

Screw it. She needed his input. Trying to figure out the right words, she said, "What if a guy enjoyed kissing you and…stuff? Could you assume he wanted more?"

Much arrested, Chris gave her a blank stare. "Of course he wants you." Stretching out on his back once more, he folded his arms over his head. "You know that already."

Since he wasn't looking at her, she stood and skinned off her shirt and shorts, then sat beside him again. "I'm talking about…more than sex." When he groaned, Arizona slugged his arm. "Come on, Chris, stop making those ridiculous noises. I can't talk about this with anyone else."

Dropping his arms, he half sat up—but fell back at the sight of her. "Jesus, girl. Give a man a shock, why don't you?" His gaze moved all over her. He shook his head, and his voice dropped. "No wonder the guys are having fits."

Damn it, now *she* felt naked. "You're gay!" And

really, the suit was as plain as she could find, dark so nothing would show through, not overly skimpy...

"Doesn't make me blind." He frowned at her. "You do realize you're incredibly sexy, right?"

"I don't care about that!"

"You're awfully screechy today." He eyed her critically. "So what's the problem, anyway?"

A deep breath didn't alleviate the sense of desperation. She did not want this to be her last night with Spencer. "I need to know what I can do to make Spencer like me."

Tiredly, Chris said, "He already likes you."

Not enough to tolerate deception, to put up with her peculiarities, to keep her around beyond the time it took to "help" her. But she couldn't say all that, not to Chris.

He caught her chin and lifted her face. "Hey, what's not to like, right?"

Too many things to count—and that was the problem for her. She didn't think she could change, not enough anyway. "You don't have to sugarcoat things for me."

"Me?" he asked dramatically. "I'm honest, always." Smiling, he smoothed back her hair. "And I'm telling you that you're a nice person, not too pushy, totally loyal, and *hot*. Trust me. Spencer likes you plenty."

Avoiding his gaze, Arizona picked at a splinter of wood on the dock. "Is there anything I can do to make him...more than like me?"

"I don't know," he said carefully, watching her. "How much more are we talking?"

"Enough that he'd forgive...other things." Before he could ask what other things, she drew a deep breath and forged on. "Enough that, even if he gets really peeved at me, he'll still want to have sex."

"Yeah, well, that'd cover most guys. No worries there. Men let very little get in the way of physical pleasure."

"Damn it, Chris, I want him to *care*."

The teasing ended. "So it's like that, huh?"

God, she was afraid so. Truly afraid. She didn't want to care about Spencer, but she couldn't seem to help herself.

She looked at Chris and nodded.

His expression of sympathy had her fidgeting, and then he glanced up the hill. With a satisfied smile, he said, "I think what you're doing is working just fine."

SPENCER TOOK IN Chris's amusement and Arizona's guilt and he felt his blood boiling. What was she up to now?

And where the hell had she gotten that swimsuit?

More than anything, he wanted to stuff her back into her discarded shorts and T-shirt and haul her off somewhere, out of view of the others. He did not want everyone else seeing her. Sure, he trusted the other men, otherwise he wouldn't even consider working with them.

And he wouldn't have allowed them to butt in on his relationship with her.

They wanted him to commit to her.

He knew Arizona deserved more.

But his arguments about her age, her past, had sounded as hollow to him as they had to Dare and Trace and Jackson. In fact, Jackson had stalked off in annoyance, and Trace had given him a pitying look before walking away.

Only Dare had remained, telling him what he already knew: that fighting his feelings was useless.

Spencer had dissuaded him the only way he knew how, by bringing up his deceased wife.

He'd no sooner said the words, than he wanted to see

Arizona. He needed to hold her, to talk to her, to…what? Value what time he had left?

Shit.

Even knowing it was his bad mood driving him, he rocked the dock with his heavy footfalls. With silky menace, he asked, "Am I interrupting?"

Laughing, Chris stood and stretched with a complete lack of concern. "You guys have selective memory about my sexuality whenever you choose to play caveman." He shook his head. "It's pretty hilarious." He turned, went to the end of the dock and jumped in.

Arizona chose to watch Chris instead of looking at Spencer. He stepped closer and only when his shadow fell over her, did she finally turn her face up to meet his gaze.

God Almighty, she looked like temptation. The bright sunlight glinted in eyes so blue, they matched the clear sky, emphasizing the contrast to her naturally darker skin. As he stared down at her, she pulled away the band that held back the mass of her long hair. It fell free around her shoulders.

It seemed impossible, but every minute around her made him want her more and in more ways. Physically, yes. He couldn't look at her without getting a jones. But it was so much more than that.

So much more than he could handle in a crowd.

"The others will join us soon." Spencer crouched down in front of her. Her gaze went to his bare chest, his abs, over his thighs. "I need to get in the water, honey."

She licked her lips. "You don't want to wait a bit?"

"I would have." He eyed the swell of her breasts above the bra top. Could a woman be more stacked, more lush? He shook his head. "Seeing you in that suit changed things."

She touched a hand to his chest hair. "Okay." Concern about the swim kept her from commenting on his obvious interest. "I guess I'm ready."

He knew he was. More than ready, in fact. Damn, but this wouldn't be easy.

She was nervous enough without his lust, which, considering the setting and circumstances, was inappropriate in the extreme. Doing his best to keep his attention on her face and off her body, Spencer said, "How about I get in first, and you can climb down the ladder next to me?"

She lifted a hand to shield her eyes. "You're going to dive in?"

Pausing, he tried to figure the direction of her thoughts, but he just didn't know. He went with the truth. "Probably."

Her small but proud shoulders squared. "Then I will, too."

Before today, he might have tried to talk her around. Not anymore. With every minute, he better understood her. The will that drove her was the same will that had allowed her to survive. Her pride was important to her, so that made it important to him, as well.

Best to just get it over with.

Dread of something was often worse than the actuality. Once she was in the water, held close to him, she'd be fine. She would realize there was nothing to fear, not with him nearby.

She would trust him.

Without another word, Spencer nodded, then stood, went to the end of the dock and dove in. Chris floated on his back, probably to give them privacy; he paid no attention to Spencer.

Looking up at Arizona there on the edge of the dock, he waited.

At this time of the day, the sun backlit her body, showing off every shapely curve as she folded her shirt and shorts and put them on a bench. As if preparing for battle, she came to the edge of the dock and stood with her feet apart, her arms loose at her sides, her hair cascading down around her shoulders and over her breasts.

The black two-piece fit her to perfection, and kept his gaze riveted. He didn't rush her, but neither could he take his eyes off her.

When she heard the others chatting as they walked down toward the dock, she firmed her mouth, took three quick, deep breaths—and made a clean dive into the lake.

"MESS THIS UP, and I'll kill you."

Quin tamped down his defiance in favor of survival. Not for a second did he doubt the truth of those words. He'd seen evil, plenty of times.

This was something more. "She said she would be there tomorrow."

"She better be."

Knowing he'd done all he could, he licked his lips and tried to still the quaver in his voice. "Where is Joel?"

"Forget Joel. We don't need him."

Please, please don't let Joel be gone for good. "He won't be back?"

"Maybe later, I don't know." He paced, saying almost as an afterthought, "You should be worried about your sister."

That jolted him. "I am. Very worried."

He smiled, and the smile turned into a laugh that quickly faded. He waved a hand. "She's safe."

That sounded like the truth; Quin prayed it was so. But he just didn't know. From one second to the next, lies mixed with reality, and madness overshadowed sanity.

His stomach growled and cramped, and he pressed a fist to his guts.

"You're hungry! Of course you are. It's been forever since I've fed you." Like he would a pet, he rubbed Quin's head. "I've been so excited with the thought of getting Candy back. She ruined everything, you know? It was all part of her plan. She's not like the others. She duped everyone. Probably even you, right?"

Knowing better than to disagree, Quin nodded—and he prayed for the food. He needed his strength to get through this.

His survival depended on it. His sister's well-being depended on it.

Candy…well, she would hopefully fend for herself, because he had nothing more to give.

THE SECOND ARIZONA'S HEAD cleared the water, Spencer drew her in close, their bodies touching at the waist, his legs moving to keep them afloat. "Okay?"

Water spiked her dark lashes and left her hair slicked back to show off high cheekbones. He could see the fear in her eyes and the resolve to ignore it.

She gave a jerky nod. "I'm fine."

"You're beautiful. And amazing." He kissed her, soft and quick, feeling the chill in her full lips. "Sexy." He kissed her again, lingering a little this time. "Incredible." One more kiss, longer, deeper. "Hot…"

"You're nuts." She snickered while treading water, and her feet bumped against his.

Her laugh felt like the greatest gift ever given to him. "You really are okay?"

"I promise I won't freak out and drown us both."

"I'm glad."

Voices carried as Jackson and Alani walked onto the dock. Trace dove in, followed by Priss. Molly sat on the end and let her feet dangle. Dare tossed in a float and then jumped in next to it.

"They actually think this is fun," she whispered, and her fingers dug into his shoulders.

"Let's go over this way." Holding her waist with one hand, Spencer used his free arm and his legs to move them to the other side of the dock. It wasn't really private, but it kept her from getting splashed.

Someone turned on a radio; conversation and laughter filled the air around them.

Once his feet touched bottom, Spencer stopped. He smoothed back her hair, brushed her cheekbone with his thumb. "Feel good?"

Surprised, Arizona nodded again. "It isn't too bad."

"No?"

"Not with you." She draped her forearms over his shoulders, leaning into him. "Did the others...you know. Ask questions?"

He knew exactly what she meant. "They're concerned for you, that's all."

Her nose touched his chest, and she nuzzled against him. "What did you tell them?"

"That you were the strongest woman I know."

She gave a strangled laugh before she tipped back her head to smile at him. "You know what I mean."

"I do. And that's what I said." Without really meaning to, he let his hand drop to her behind. "They're not stupid, honey. More than most, they understand what you went through, and why some things will be difficult for you."

"I guess." She glanced over at Jackson when he did a cannonball into the water, making the women screech and Chris laugh. "That's what they think? That it's just…difficult?"

Actually, they'd recognized more than Arizona did herself. "Like me, they think you're pretty amazing." He kissed her temple. "I gather you impressed them with your ability."

She shrugged. "Compared to them—"

"That's not a fair way to judge, and you know it." He waded farther to the side of the dock, opposite of the boathouse. The others couldn't see them now, but they had no real privacy, not for what he wanted, what he needed. "They're in a skill set unlike any I've ever seen."

Arizona looked around at the quiet cove. "Know what I'm thinking?"

"I know what I'm thinking." He softly kissed her neck, her shoulder. If he could distract her from her nervousness about the water, that'd have to be good enough.

"I'm thinking that you've helped me conquer a lot of stuff."

If only that were true, maybe he wouldn't feel so damn tortured now. He caught her face, and, after a hungry kiss, he leaned her back in his arms. God, he wished he'd been there with her when she'd needed him the most. But he couldn't give himself too much credit. "You faced all the hardest battles alone—and that says a lot about you, Arizona."

"Maybe." Tightening her hold, she again tucked her face in close to his neck. "Some stuff, though…it's harder."

"I know, and I'm sorry I wasn't out there with you."

He hugged her tighter. "I'm sorry that I walked off and left you alone."

"Because Jackson played around and I panicked?" He felt her smile against his skin. "Not your doing, Spence. But, hey, thanks for covering for me with the caveman routine."

No reason to explain that it wasn't all feigned. Though he knew it was irrational, he didn't like seeing other men touch her. "You liked that, did you?"

"Yeah, I kind of did." She looked up at him, her gaze too serious, too solemn.

"We could work on that, you know." Spencer breathed in the scent of her sun-warmed skin, felt the way her firm body aligned with his own, and he concentrated on not reacting physically. "With me getting on top of you, I mean."

For a second or two, she looked incredibly sad— before she forced a smile. "Are you trying to dodge my turn at controlling you?"

Oh, hell. The water wasn't cold enough to keep his erection at bay. With sizzling visuals in his mind, he looked at her mouth, leaned down—and icy water doused his head.

He glanced back.

Only a few feet away, Chris grinned at him. "Break it up, you two. This is a public area."

Spencer bit off a groan. Beyond Chris was Jackson. Alani, floating on a raft, had joined them, as well.

Dare was climbing the ladder up the dock, where Molly waited for him.

"We're going for a ride," Priss announced from the boat. "Will you guys join us?"

He wanted to refuse, but Arizona whispered, "Finally we can get out of this stupid water."

He had no real choice but to nod. "Sure, why not?" As he slogged through the water to the rock retaining wall, he whispered to Arizona, "But only if you wrap up in a towel or something."

"All the women are in swimsuits," she pointed out.

Spencer glanced around. True enough, and while the women were all physically different, they were each attractive—but they weren't Arizona. They could have been buck naked, and still they wouldn't affect him the way she did.

"Somehow, that doesn't seem to matter." Spencer snatched up a towel and bundled it around her. Chris mocked him with a grin, but Jackson gave him a salute as he did the same with Alani.

Dare and Trace ignored them as they helped their wives into the boat.

Soon, Spencer thought. Soon he'd get her back to his place, and then he'd show her just how different she was. And after that…he didn't know.

Luckily he still had time to figure it out.

CHAPTER TWENTY-TWO

PARTICULAR IN HOW he did things, he worked late to ensure he had everything prepared.

Curtains at the front windows hid the empty interior; Clever Candy wouldn't know that "Harry's Hocks" was abandoned until it was too late. She wouldn't realize that it would be her temporary holding place, a place for her to adjust to her new circumstances.

He checked the restraints he'd fastened to a grommet screwed into the floor in the back room. With both feet planted, he tugged, pulled.

It held secure.

"Good. Very good." He repositioned the mattress. She'd be able to recline comfortably even with her hands restrained. "Put clean bedding on that mattress."

Quin did as told, tucking the soft white sheet around the flat, twin-size cot mattress.

"Pillow and blanket, too. All the comforts of home." He laughed. "I know she likes whiskey. But what else?"

Quin shrugged tiredly. "Water? Cola?"

"We'll get both. Keep them in a cooler with ice."

"All right."

"Go back outside now. Wait at the bench." He paced the floor, peered out the window cautiously. "She is a very clever girl. Very clever."

"You think she will come early?"

"To check us out? Definitely. The question is when."

He turned to Quin. "But you will play your part, and you will do nothing to alarm her."

"Yes."

"Talk to no one else. No one."

"No."

"Christ, your parroting is getting on my nerves. Go, then. Sleep out there if you want. I don't care. But wait there until she comes."

Quin looked toward the door. "It is dangerous?"

His eyes narrowed. "More dangerous if you mess this up. Do you understand me?"

"I understand." And with that, Quin shuffled out, his feet dragging, his shoulders slumped.

Yes, it had been a long day filled with preparations. But he was far too excited to sleep. The men he'd hired would show up first thing in the morning, just in case she caused any problems.

In case she didn't at first understand her good fortune.

After that…she'd be his. And nothing, no one, else would matter.

IT WAS NEARING MIDNIGHT by the time they got home. Arizona had been too subdued, almost as if something had happened.

But what?

After the dip in the lake, she'd seemed to genuinely enjoy herself, especially during the boat ride. Like the ultimate free spirit, she'd turned her face into the wind, closed her eyes and relaxed.

Later she'd laughed as Jackson rode on a tube behind the boat, getting bounced over the wake and waves. And Chris had impressed them both with his slalom skills, cutting sharply over the wake as if born in the water.

Afterward, there'd been quiet conversation around

a bonfire, with the night insects buzzing and the occasional splash of a fish in the water. A million stars had filled the sky, making the night magical.

During the visit, Arizona had insisted on taking several photos with her new camera. Before they left, she'd hugged each of the dogs, the cats, and then suffered through the human affection, too.

Jackson, especially, had held her overlong, talking quietly to her until Spencer wanted to flatten him.

Only when Chris had given him a laughing shove had he realized how he'd glared at them. Arizona, with her sullen silence, had given nothing away, so he could only guess what Jackson had discussed with her in such depth.

Something about her goodbyes bothered him. They had seemed too permanent, as if she didn't plan to see any of them for a long time. In the normal course of things, she was not a huggy type of woman. Most times, she shrugged off emotion as if it made her uncomfortable.

On the ride home, they listened to the radio, both of them mellow from all the sun and fresh air. At times, he'd thought Arizona dozed. But then she'd sigh, or yawn, or stretch, and he knew she was lost in thought.

"Tired?" Spencer asked after parking his truck.

"Relaxed." She smiled at him. "I feel almost as boneless as I do when you have sex with me."

That left him mute with arousal.

Not Arizona. "Do you mind if I leave my gifts in your truck for now?"

So she was tired. "I could carry them in."

She shook her head. "That's okay." Holding her sandals in her hand, she opened her door and got out. "It's late. We can get them tomorrow."

"All right." And though his suspicions grew, he couldn't put his finger on the reason why.

As they went up the walkway, she glanced at Marla's place several times, and when Marla peeked out the window, Arizona lifted her hand in a wave.

Not a "gotcha" wave but more like a genuine greeting.

Marla dropped the curtain without reciprocating, and that made Arizona sigh. "She's so hung up on you."

"I don't think so, but if she is, she'll get over it." Marla was not a woman to pine long for a man, and she wouldn't waste her time on a lost cause.

Spencer was lost. So damn lost that he didn't know if he was coming or going anymore—all because of Arizona.

He didn't understand her. Nothing new in that, though. He could spend every day with her for the rest of his life, and he wasn't sure he'd ever completely know her.

Finding that a disturbing thought, he unlocked the front door and stepped inside. He flipped on a light.

Dropping her shoes by the door, Arizona took one of his hands in both of hers and started backing toward the bedroom. "So, Spence Are you going to keep me in suspense?"

He knew exactly what she meant, but she'd gone so long without asking, he decided to tease her. "About what?"

"Don't make me force it out of you." Once in his bedroom, she stepped up close and went on tiptoe to twine her arms around his neck. "Not when there are other things I'd rather be doing to your big gorgeous bod."

So up front and honest in her desire; he'd accomplished that much, anyway. He liked it. He liked her.

Probably too much.

Was Dare right? Should he look at things from a different perspective?

Arizona bit his bottom lip. "Spill the beans, already. Are you joining up with the guys or not?"

He clasped her waist. "I told Trace I'd think about it, and I will."

"Oh, come on." She leaned in and took another soft bite, this time on his chest. "You know if you're in or not."

"And you care…why?" He liked her in this playful mood. But hell, he liked her when she was prickly and when she was obstinate, and when she blustered with bravado, too. "Because of the money?"

"Pffft. Get real."

But he was half serious. On a bounty hunter's pay, he lived a frugal lifestyle, not at all as posh as the others. Their homes were like vacation destinations. Dare had more than one boat, each probably costing twice what Spencer had paid for his truck when it was new. Jackson made enough that he wanted to give Arizona a house for her birthday.

They could all retire now and be set for life.

But Spencer knew they wouldn't. In fact, they wanted to expand their enterprise—with him.

"You don't like the idea of financial security?"

"Sure, I guess." Grumbling, she left him to sit on the side of the bed. "But apparently, if Jackson gets his way, I'll already be a homeowner and stuff. What else would I need?"

She wanted so little from life. Did it truly not matter to her at all? Hands on his hips, Spencer dropped his head. "I don't know."

"About their offer?" She studied him. "About what you're going to do?"

"There's a lot to consider."

"I know." She smoothed a hand over the blankets to keep from looking at him. "Like whether or not you want to be stuck that close to me, right?"

Ah, hell. What could he say to that? It definitely factored in—but as an incentive. A dangerous incentive.

At his hesitation, she went on, saying, "I mean, Jackson is all into claiming me as a little sis, and the other guys...they've sort of accepted me."

"They've *totally* accepted you." Spencer needed her to understand that and to believe it.

"Yeah." She looked up at him. More sun colored her nose now, as well as her shoulders. "And the women...I think I scare them a little, and they pity me, but they're nice enough."

Spencer sat beside her. The bed dipped, and her hip pressed into his. "You're wrong. They're in awe of you, they told me so. They admire you, same as I do. And yes, they're sorry for what happened to you, but they know it hasn't slowed you down. If anything, it's made you stronger."

"Yeah, right." She folded her hands between her knees and swung her bare feet. "So strong, I'm afraid of a lake."

God, she'd become so precious to him, in such a short time. Spencer brought her chin around. "So strong that, afraid or not, you got in the water."

"Only because you were there with me."

That soft admission leveled him. He whispered back, "You're so strong that it scares the hell out of me."

"Why?"

Because he *had* to, he kissed her. Short and sweet and

nowhere near satisfying. "I know there's no reining you in, much as I'd like to."

Looking far too serious, she said, "You realize that, do you?"

"I also realize that you're not a woman to sit on the sidelines, and I'm doing my best to accept that."

Breathing a little faster, she touched his chest. "I don't mean to make things difficult."

"I know." Slowly, he went to his back on the bed. "Why don't we put this conversation on hold for a while?"

Her beautiful blue eyes shone with a smile. "Got something else in mind, do you?"

"Definitely." He stacked his arms behind his head and got comfortable. "You want your turn at controlling things? Well, I'm more than ready. I'm already hard thinking about it."

"Yeah?" Luckily for him, she put aside the seriousness of their talk in favor of lust. "Well, all right, then."

As she crawled up over him, resting full on him until she covered him as much as she could, Spencer breathed in the scent of her skin, her hair. With his nose near her neck, he said, "You smell so good."

"I should probably shower."

"No." Hell, they'd been in the sun all day, in and out of the lake, wind-burned by the boat ride. "You smell earthy, and sexy, and it turns me on."

She rubbed against him. "I love how you smell, too. So good, I could just eat you up." She followed up those provocative words with a lot of openmouth kisses on his throat, down his chest.

Sitting up on his thighs, she said, "Off with the shirt."

"All right." Leaning up as much as he could, he

reached back to snag a handful of the shirt, then jerked it over his head.

"There you go," she whispered and spread her hands out over him, exploring his clenched abs, down over his hip bones...down to his erection.

Spencer bit off a groan.

As she moved off him, she ordered, "Lift your hips. I want to lose these shorts, too." She looked at him, her gaze bright. "I want to be able to get to you."

His chest expanded, his hands curled into tighter fists, and he raised his hips.

Having Arizona undress him was a unique pleasure. She rushed, rough in her urgency, and the second she had his shorts off, she stopped to stare.

It wasn't easy, not when he wanted her so much, but this was her time, and he wouldn't rob her of it. "You want to take off your clothes, too?"

"Sure, why not? Just remember to keep your hands to yourself, okay?"

Gently, watching her as she stripped, he whispered, "Whatever you say, baby."

She went still, then grinned. "I like the sound of that." After literally tossing her clothes away, Arizona asked, "Where do you keep the condoms?"

"Nightstand." He was strung so tight, talking wasn't easy. "We don't need it yet, though."

"I don't want to have to fumble for it." She set the box out, then turned back to him. "Open your legs a little."

Damn. She'd taken right to this. Spencer opened his legs and immediately felt her hands coasting up his calves, then the insides of his thighs.

"You are so powerful." She sat between his legs and

leaned forward to explore his chest, down his ribs, his abs. "But you would never hurt me."

"Never," he reiterated.

"I know it. I mean, I *really* know it." Her long hair teased over his skin when she kissed his throat, across his shoulders. "I think that's why I can be with you. I mean, I trust Jackson, and still I freaked out today."

God, he wanted to hold her. "I'm sorry—"

"Shh." She licked his nipple, then took a soft love bite of his pec muscle. "I think, if it was you, I'd be okay. For whatever reason, you're special."

He had no idea what to say to that. Was he special enough to help her move beyond her awful past? Special enough that she could enjoy a normal life with him?

Or just special in this, in sexual involvement? Did she want to experiment? "Remember, I told you, whatever you want."

"Right now, I just want to get my fill of you."

And she could do that in one night? Because he couldn't. He knew it, accepted it, but had no idea what to do about it.

For a good ten minutes, she kissed him everywhere, and the touch of her mouth, her small, sharp teeth, her hot little tongue, competed with the lure of seeing her like this. The silky fall of her dark hair continuously drifted over his body.

Her nipples, puckered tight, teased his skin whenever she leaned against him. Each time she repositioned herself, she gave him a tantalizing peek.

By the time she focused all her attention on his cock, he was damn near a goner.

She curled both hands snug around him, and he groaned.

Watching him, she stroked, and his hips lifted off the bed.

She gave a wicked smile of satisfaction. "You're close, aren't you?"

"Yes." He labored for breath—and prayed she'd put her mouth on him. Through a red haze of lust, he watched her and waited.

She cupped his balls in one hand, held his cock with the other and lowered herself down across his legs.

Rubbing her downy cheek against him, she asked, "Am I being suggestive?"

"You're being diabolical." He shuddered as she licked him, from the base all the way up and over the head. "Arizona…"

She opened her mouth over him and drew him into the heat of her mouth.

"Ah, God, baby…" He felt the stroke of her tongue, the firm way she held him in her hand, and he knew he wouldn't last. "Sorry, Arizona." He twisted away.

Eyes dazed and hot, she looked up at him. "You didn't like it?"

"I liked it too fucking much."

"Oh." Breathing hard, she looked down at him, still held tight in her fist. "Hmm." She kissed him again, and he went taut from his head to his toes.

"I won't last. If you don't stop that, it'll be over, and that's not what we want."

"You don't know what I want."

Slowly, he lifted one hand, and when she didn't protest that, he cupped her cheek. "You're breathing hard. Your face is flushed and your nipples are tight. If I put my fingers in you right now, I'd find you wet and ripe and ready. Admit it."

She swallowed and nodded. "Yeah."

"You want me. And I love it that you do."

Her eyes flared a little at that word, but she remained mute.

"That means we need to finish this together."

Again she looked at his cock. "With you inside me?"

"God, yes."

"All right." But she tortured him more by saying, "I'm still in control though."

Obligingly, Spencer put his hand back behind his head.

Arizona took her time putting the condom on him. "You are so impressive, in so many ways."

He didn't want her under some misplaced delusion that he was more than himself, more than a hardworking guy, trying to do the right thing whenever he could. Especially with her. "I'm just a man."

"Not even close."

He forged on. "And right now I'm a desperately horny man."

She laughed.

He didn't. "I need you, Arizona. Right now. No more playing."

Her gaze met his, and it was…profound. He felt it, whether she did or not.

"I want to be inside you."

"Yeah, okay." In a rush, she moved up over him.

"You need me to touch you."

"No." She shook her head even as she guided him in. "I just want to watch you."

But he was big, and this way was so deep…

"All of me, honey."

Her bottom lip caught in her teeth, she eased down onto him. Lifted again, eased down more.

"Sit down, Arizona." Hands knotted behind his head,

his shoulders, chest and abs tense with the strain, Spencer watched her, saw the heightening of her color, and though he didn't mean to, he took over. "Brace your hands on my chest."

She did, arms straight and stiff.

"That's it." His voice sounded gravelly, but he couldn't help that. "Now put your legs out. Relax. More, honey. Yeah, let me all the way in."

Fully seated on him, she pressed down more, grinding until Spencer couldn't help but give a harsh groan.

"Okay, sure," she panted. "That did it for me."

Fighting the urge to drive up into her, he asked roughly, "What?"

"Hearing you sound all turned on."

"God, Arizona, how could I not be?" He stared at her body, at her face. "Do you know how you feel to me? How damned good it is to see you like this, to be with you like this?"

"Yeah, okay." She held out her arms. "You can take over. Feel free to get as touchy as you want—"

Before she'd finished, he dragged her down to him and wrapped his arms around her, touching her with his hands, his mouth, holding her steady as he thrust up feverishly…

Her nails bit into his shoulders, and she cried out.

The second he felt her coming, Spencer wanted to join her, but instead he held back.

It wasn't easy.

Clamping his hands onto her bottom, he helped her maintain the rhythm so that she felt every single ripple of pleasure.

Very soon, he decided, it would be his turn. But this time would be different.

And it would be important.

WHILE IN A DREAMY FOG, their heartbeats still pounding together, feeling soft and limp, Arizona smiled. "Better and better."

Spencer stroked her hair lazily, and then, slowly, he turned them until he'd moved over her. Still deep inside her, he positioned himself on his elbows, keeping the weight of his chest lifted off her. He watched her, his hand gentle at the side of her face.

Funny, but just like that, just because it was Spencer, she realized that it wasn't so terrifying after all.

He kissed her forehead, the bridge of her nose, her lips. "Okay?"

She felt the trembling in his big body and nodded. "I want to watch you come."

He put his forehead to hers and slowly withdrew, slowly sank back in. She felt his strenuous breaths against her lips, felt the heat pouring off him.

In a way, it felt more secure, having him over her like this, covering her with his size and strength; it felt... protective, instead of controlling.

Without really thinking about it, Arizona lifted one leg around him.

He thrust a little harder, a little faster.

Incredible. She twined the other leg around him, too, and tightened.

"Arizona," he whispered, and he kissed her, hot and languid, deep and hungry. Two strokes later, he put his head back and growled out his release.

It was pretty amazing. She smiled as her legs slipped away from him, smiled that even now, after coming, he thought to stay on his elbows.

Protecting her. Always thinking of her.

Caring for her.

Damn it, emotion got a stranglehold on her.

He took several deep breaths, kissed her neck, her mouth again, and looked at her. "You're okay?"

Eyes closed, she nodded.

Spencer brushed her hair away, smoothed her eyebrows with his thumb. "I want you to look at me, honey. I need to see that you're okay."

But she couldn't do that.

Tears burned her eyes, and she didn't want him to misunderstand.

"Arizona?" Soft, insistent, he said again, "Look at me, honey."

Instead, she wrapped her arms tight around him and squeezed to keep him close. "I never cried before meeting you."

He didn't ask her not to cry. He said nothing at all.

He just held her as he rolled to his side, tucking her in close, surrounding her with his heat, his size, his affection.

And to her mortification, it all boiled over. She heard the first sob and wanted to die. But the second sob came, too, and then more, until she was soaking his chest and shaking with racking sobs.

Somehow Spencer sat up and, holding her close in his arms, put his back against the headboard. He did her a solid by turning off the bright bedside lamp, leaving them with only the intrusion of the hall light. He pulled the sheet up and over them, one hand fisted in her hair, rocking her gently.

And he kissed her forehead, her ear, the top of her head while stroking her back, her hip, and hugging her.

Over and over again.

"God, this sucks," she complained around a hiccuping wail.

"Not with me," he said softly. "I'm special, remember?"

She laughed and buried her face against his throat to cry some more. Yeah, he was special, all right. So special that it was killing her, when nothing else had.

Finally, after what felt like forever, her breathing evened, and the wave of turbulence passed. Spencer shifted, reaching out, and came back with a tissue box. He offered it to her in silence.

After she'd cleaned up her face, she felt too foolish for words. "I'd apologize—"

"But you don't need to." He squeezed her...protectively. "Not with me. Ever."

"I figured." She snuggled in again and sighed. Her thoughts ran this way and that, but she couldn't seem to nail them down. "I guess you're getting tired?"

"No."

"Me, either." Against her nipples, she felt his sexy chest hair and the reassuring thump of his strong heartbeat. "Or are you just saying that, because you don't want to interrupt my crying jag?"

"No." He looked down at her. "And you're not crying anymore anyway."

"Pretty repulsive, huh?"

"No. Not ever." He squeezed her. "And don't say things like that. It pisses me off."

"You cursed."

Shrugging, he said, "And you cried. So we're both human."

Was that how he saw her excess of emotion? As just being human? "Well, I feel dumb."

"Please, don't."

She frowned at him. His short replies were starting to bug her. "Not feeling real chatty?"

"I'm just enjoying holding you."

Had to be a joke, right? Was that really how he felt? He wasn't disgusted, wasn't uncomfortable—

"Whatever you're thinking, Arizona, you're wrong." He brought her face up and pressed his mouth to hers. "I'm glad that I was the one here with you, not anyone else. And I'm humbled, because you trust me that much."

Trust, huh? Okay, so maybe it did have to do with trust. But it also had to do with knowing that tonight might be her last night with him. "So…" She traced a fingertip over his throat. "Do you feel up to a shower?"

"Sure."

"And then maybe…" She cleared her throat. "This is awkward. I mean, after me bawling and all."

His smile touched her forehead. "You want me again, baby?"

Perceptive men were so sexy. "Yup, that's about it."

With no effort at all, he left the bed while still holding her in his arms. "I'll need an hour or so. But I figure it'll take me that long just to kiss you all over, so we should be good to go."

And he called her diabolical?

CHAPTER TWENTY-THREE

THE SECOND HE AWOKE, even before he got his heavy eyes open, Spencer knew she was gone. It hit him like a tsunami of ice water.

The bed, the house, the very air felt empty.

Arizona's vitality, the energy that surrounded her even while she slept—all gone. The void left him feeling empty, too.

He sat up and checked the time. Only nine o'clock. They'd stayed up well into the night making love, and he'd gone to sleep with her wrapped around him.

Her eyes had still been swollen from crying. Her nose still pink.

Damn it, she should have been exhausted, and instead, she'd used his exhaustion to sneak out on him. In fact…had that been her plan all along? Had she insisted on the excesses just to wear him out?

Or maybe to get her fill before leaving him?

"Jesus." Her departure could only mean one thing: trouble. He snatched up his cell phone from the end table and punched in her number—but he didn't get an answer, and he wasn't surprised by that. He tried her other number. Still nothing.

Throwing off the sheet, he left the bed with his mind whirling as he tried to decide what to do first. Look the house over for clues? Call Jackson? Wait for her? What?

He yanked on his jeans and cursed again, all too

aware of the yawning dread that threatened to take over. Maybe Jackson could trace her cell if she had it on. Or maybe Jackson even knew of her whereabouts.

But what if he didn't?

The knock on his front door got his feet moving, and he bolted into the living room.

He threw open the door—and came face-to-face with Marla. Impatience boiled over. "Marla." Regulating his voice wasn't easy. He ran a hand through his hair and started to turn away. "I don't have time right now—"

"It's Arizona."

He snapped his gaze back to her. "Tell me."

"I'm sorry, Spencer. I didn't know. But yesterday she asked me if I'd be here this morning. She told me she might have to leave…bounce, I believe she said…earlier than she'd anticipated. She asked if I truly cared for you, if I could be trusted—"

"Where is she?"

Marla flinched.

Damn it. He held out his hands, soothing her. "I'm sorry." It took a great effort, but he calmed his tone as he drew Marla inside. "She's gone, and that isn't a good thing. She has a knack for getting into dangerous situations. The sooner I can go after her, the better, so if you know anything—"

"That's why I'm here. Arizona said she should be back by lunch, but…" Marla thrust a note toward him. "She gave me this. She said if she didn't make it back, I was to give it to you then, but I…I admit I opened it."

Spencer took it from her hand and unfolded it. Arizona's handwriting was big and bold, but perfectly spaced, neat and legible.

Marla grabbed his wrist. "She didn't want me to show

it to you yet, but after reading it, even though I don't understand it all, well, I didn't think I should wait."

He nearly crumpled the note. Rage chased away the despondency. When he got hold of her, and he would, he'd… "Thank you. You did the right thing."

Marla stopped him as he again started to turn away. "Spencer?"

"What?"

"You and I…we were never going to happen, were we?"

He shook his head. "I'm sorry, but no."

She accepted that. "Arizona said as much." She drew a breath. "You're in love with her?"

Oh, God. He drew a breath. "Yes."

"She doesn't know that."

"No." He'd been such a stupid fool. But given her note, he had a little time to fix things.

"You should probably tell her." And then in a censuring tone, "Women need to know these things."

And Arizona needed to know it more than most. "I've been an ass." He needed to call Jackson, and he needed to get on the road.

Marla nodded in agreement. "Is there anything I can do?"

He started to shake his head, then thought to say, "Call me if she shows up here."

"Okay." She forced a smile. "I hope it works out, Spencer. I mean that."

"Thanks." Damn, she really was an okay person. Arizona knew it, but then, she was a good judge of people.

Was her judgment enough to see her through the trap this morning? He prayed so.

But he'd do what he could on his end, and he'd see that the others were there, as well.

Arizona wasn't alone anymore.

One way or another, he'd get her to understand that.

AN EARLY-MORNING SUN, blazing red, pierced the sky, turning hazy clouds pink and mauve and reflecting off the pavement. It'd be a scorcher, hot and humid and typical for this time of year. She wouldn't complain. She liked hot weather better than cold.

Too many layers hindered her ability.

Arriving at the site early, Arizona drove slowly down the street, looking around for a possible ambush. She spotted Quin right away, sitting on a bench in front of "Harry's Hocks" pawn shop. Though someone wanted her to think otherwise, she knew that Harry's was shut down, had been shut down for a while.

So why the sign in the window stating he'd open at noon?

One possible setup.

To the right of that building, a drive-thru convenience store with a multi-locked front door and an iron grate on the one remaining window boasted bright, graffiti-covered bricks. The drive-thru window, layered in bulletproof glass, had a sliding metal tray for taking money and handing out products. But that was on the opposite side of the building, near a corner street.

To the left was an abandoned florist shop, the lot overgrown with weeds, the front sign hanging crookedly, the once-ornate script faded to near invisibility.

Beside that was a pay-at-the-pump gas station that had seen better days. Then an auto parts store, a cigarette shop, and a place that cashed checks. All were run-down, all looked disreputable.

So early in the morning, few people were out and about. Only sluggish traffic moved past, and they weren't travelers who'd give a damn about crimes committed, petty or otherwise.

They were the "see nothing" crowd, the "mind my own business" denizens who either didn't care, or knew better than to get involved for fear of retaliation.

On other buildings, some of them used as homes, cardboard and plywood covered the windows. Porches barely remained intact to structures. Refuse had gathered in every nook and corner.

Quin sat slumped on a bus bench in dirty clothes, his hair matted, his legs pulled up so that his face rested on his knees. Massive oak trees, their roots breaking through the buckled sidewalks, separated him from an empty parking lot, no longer used thanks to broken glass. It looked as though he'd slept there, seeking the shelter of the trees.

Had he been homeless in the recent storms?

Trying to find relief from the unrelenting sun and heat of the day?

He'd somehow escaped Dare's net when the police closed in at the Green Goose. Maybe Quin had something to hide, something in his past that made him wary of the law, even when it tried to rescue him.

Or maybe someone else had gotten to him first.

She circled the block, then parked her car well away from the area, about half a mile down, closer to a grocery store. After locking it tight, she strolled back to where she'd seen Quin. That morning, in the dark at Spencer's house, without making a single sound, she'd dressed in worn jeans, unlaced sneakers and a big loose T-shirt. To keep it out of her way, she'd contained her hair in a high ponytail.

The sun baked down on her head, bringing perspiration to the back of her neck, down her spine.

All along the way, she marveled at the trees. Despite the devastation of the area, there were so many of them, big and healthy and beautiful. At some point in time, the area had probably been really pretty.

Like her, time and abuse had forever changed it; it would never be the same.

Quin didn't hear or see her approach—which made Arizona doubt any willing complicity on his part. Anyone versed in criminal activity would have picked her out several blocks away, since she didn't bother with stealth. Shoot, trying to slide in and out of the neighborhood would mean utilizing alleyways and darkened doorways, and that'd be more dangerous than coming down the middle of the street.

After scrubbing his hands over his face, Quin pushed up from the bench to pace. Arms folded around his middle, shoulders hunched, limping slightly, he made his way nervously out to the curb, back again.

What are you up to, Quinto?

Her jeans hid the gun at her ankle. Snug against the small of her back, she felt the sheath for her knife digging in with each step she took. Not the knife Chris had just given her. No, she wouldn't risk losing it. It was too precious to her.

She'd left it, and all the other gifts, in Spencer's truck.

When, *if* Spencer started looking for her, would he understand the significance of that? Would he see it as a sign that she wanted to come back?

To him. With him?

No, she hadn't taken her new knife. But various other weapons filled her pockets, some obvious, some less so.

At the moment, her best weapon was rage.

When she got close enough, she hid it all with a smile. "Hey, Quin."

Startled, he jerked around so hard he almost fell. He froze at the sight of her standing there. Staring at her wide-eyed, something awful shone on his face, something akin to paralyzing fear.

She went still, too. He looked…ravaged. Her eyes narrowed. Her voice soft with menace, she asked, "What happened to you, Quin?"

A hot breeze sent the enormous tree limbs swaying, leaving dappled sunlight to dance over his dark skin. He shook his head without answering. "You came early."

An accusation? His eyes looked wild, filled with fear. Knowing the gig was up, that Quin was part of a trap, Arizona shrugged. "I'm not a real trusting sort."

Almost sick, he lifted a shaking hand to his face, and his eyes closed. "I'm sorry."

"Because?" She walked past him to the lone bench, all the while keeping watch. All of the surrounding buildings offered concealment for creeps; the danger could come from anywhere.

But if she didn't face the danger, she couldn't very well combat it.

"I had no choice."

"Yeah, I figured that, ya know? I can tell the good guys from the bad. So how about we get away from here now? I could help you, if you'd let me."

He shook his head. "I can't."

"Because?" she asked again.

"I…" He swallowed hard, went through an internal battle, and then blurted with remorse, "I have a sister. A young sister. She is all I have."

Ah, that figured. "So someone's using her to make you toe the line, huh?" Sympathy welled up, but she hid that with the rage. She didn't have a sister. She had…no one. Well, maybe Jackson—but God help anyone who tried to use him. "How old are you, Quin?"

"Sixteen."

She sat down on the bench. "You're working with someone."

His face went pale.

"I already know it. The thing is, I don't know who. The raid you talked about at the bar? How'd you get out? How'd this other person get out? Or was he ever there?"

He shook his head. "I had no choice."

"Yeah, I know. We already covered that, right?" She kept her senses open, alert to any intrusion of danger. "I'm not blaming you, you know."

"But you will!"

So much fear. She understood it, because she'd felt it before. Who was she kidding? She sometimes felt it still.

Otherwise, she wouldn't have gone to Marla, trusting her to cover her ass. If this all went wrong, and it very well might, well then, Marla would tell Spencer, and he'd let Jackson and the others know, and one way or another, they'd find her.

She'd left enough info for them to easily track her.

And if she got hurt in the bargain…well, at least Quinto would be free. At least a scumbag would pay.

If she'd gone to the others first, no way would they have let her be involved. Going to the bar was enough to get their panties in a bunch. Meeting in this neighborhood?

No, they'd have nixed the deal to try something else, and while she trusted they'd have eventually been successful, what would have happened to Quin in the meantime?

"Come, sit down, Quin. Let's talk, okay?"

Shaking his head, he took a step back.

Her senses prickled. "I'm at least an hour early, so I'm guessing we have a little time, right?"

He breathed faster. "Actually..." His dark eyes lowered. He shook his head again. "No."

Arizona felt the shift in the air.

Oh, shit.

She sprang from the seat just as three men approached, all from different angles.

Three! Well, they weren't taking any chances with her, the buttheads.

She grinned as the first guy got close, and when he reached for her, she kicked out, catching him in the balls. He doubled over. At the same time she ducked a meaty fist from another man and spun around. She kicked him in the knee. It hurt him but not enough.

She could draw her knife, but she had no illusions about getting away.

Not from three men.

Showing her knife now would only put her at a disadvantage—she'd lose the knife for sure, and she had a feeling she'd need it later.

A hard arm wrapped around her neck, wrenching back her head, while others grabbed for her wrists. A cloth-covered hand clamped over her mouth.

She didn't understand...until she breathed in the sickly sweet scent, and dizziness assailed her.

Chloroform.

No, hell, no! Anger gave her strength. She tried to hold her breath as she doubled her efforts, stomping toes, gouging shins, but the dizziness got worse.

She managed a solid head butt, got her heel into a soft groin...

Someone cursed while someone else laughed.

Off to the side, a man said, "Get her feet, you moron!"

A *fourth* man? What the hell? Had they sent a battalion after her?

Unfortunately, Quin was cowed enough that he jumped to obey, struggling to grab hold of her feet. She kicked him in the face, bashing his nose and sending him backward. Poor Quin crumpled to the ground, blood flowing.

Someone laughed even harder at that.

"You're useless," the man said. "Utterly useless." And then, out of nowhere, she got clubbed in the temple.

And even as she faded, Arizona feared for Quin.

She also recognized the voice.

Joel Pitts. The homely little creep from the bar. The kindly, goofy artist.

Well, hell.

Now it made sense.

From the top of an abandoned building, his eyes burning, Spencer watched Arizona being dragged into the pawn shop. Each of the men who'd dared to touch her would pay dearly. He'd see to it.

He had himself under icy control, because that's what was needed.

But as soon as he had her safe again—

Jackson crept up beside him. "How many?"

"Counting the kid and the fucked-up artist, five. The artist and the kid went in with her."

"So the others are just guards, huh? That's convenient."

"She maimed them," Spencer said, and he tried not to sound admiring. But damn, she was a handful and then some. If there hadn't been so many of them, she just might have pulled it off.

Jackson leaned up to look over the roof and grinned

at the sight of one guy rubbing his crotch, another still bent double, holding himself, and the third limping on a damaged knee as he went around to the back of the building. "Girl's got deadly aim, ya know?"

Yes, he did know. He'd once been the recipient of that aim.

Before she'd come to trust him. Before she'd come to stay at his home.

Before she'd given herself to him.

Knowing he had to block those thoughts or emotion would overshadow deliberation, he shook his head. "Dare is watching the back exit?"

"Yeah. He'll have that third guy covered, too. Unless they have an underground tunnel, they aren't going anywhere with her."

The building they'd dragged her into was square, squat and visible on all sides.

With the note she'd left, Arizona also had left detailed info about the area. She must have gotten up early enough to run the neighborhood through a program check. In one sentence she'd apologized to Spencer for not telling him her plans, and in the next she'd told him that if he insisted on getting involved, he should follow her instructions.

And he did.

"Could be a basement." It amazed Spencer that he managed to string together coherent words with such blazing rage squeezing his throat and surging through his bloodstream. Trust went both ways, but Arizona would learn more about that once he had her safe.

"Probably is. At least a cellar or something like it. Most of these old shitholes have them." Jackson chewed his bottom lip and shocked Spencer by deferring to him. "So what do you want to do?"

"Kill them all."

"Seriously?"

Damn it. Jackson hadn't sounded particularly shocked or disagreeable about that idea. Spencer shook his head. "No, not the kid." He rubbed his tired eyes and accepted the truth. "I believe that's Quin, the waiter from the bar. Arizona...cared for him, that's why she's here. He could be in a forced situation. And she'll kick my ass if I let him get hurt."

"And if it turns out he's not forced?"

"Then she can do whatever she wants with him."

"Gotcha." He sent a code to Dare and Trace, then looked through binoculars. "Huh. I can see them."

Spencer took the binoculars from Jackson and was relieved to see Arizona's eyes open, a mean smile on her mouth.

Thank God. The relief was enough to rob him of composure. He hadn't wanted to consider any alternative other than her being dazed. Now that he could see her—looking brazen as always—he could breathe a little easier.

"We could force our way in—" Jackson said.

"But she could get hurt in the process." They didn't know if Quin or the artist might be armed. "No, we have to do this right. And her note did ask us to give her some respect."

Jackson snarled something indistinct but nodded.

"Doesn't sit right with me, either." Spencer kept his gaze on her, willing her to caution. "But she didn't think we'd let her do this on her own—"

"And we fucking wouldn't have!"

"—so this is her way of proving herself." Of getting the respect she needed.

The respect she deserved.

No more trying to change her.

They both fell silent as they considered the setting.

Her idiot captors had her on a thin, narrow mattress, in a middle room, but in view of a window. Quin hovered near her side, traces of blood now smeared over his face, and his nose, upper lip and chin purpling with bruises. The kid probably had a broken nose—not that Spencer would spare him any real sympathy. Not yet anyway.

Joel Pitts stood at the foot of the mattress, staring at Arizona and literally rubbing his hands together.

Clichéd prick.

Lowering the binoculars, Spencer asked, "You got a clear shot from here?"

A crack sniper, Jackson lined it up, and said, "Yep." He continued to look through the scope, then lowered the rifle. "The thing is…you won't like this, Spencer."

His heart slammed to a standstill. He put the binoculars up again. "What is it? What's wrong?"

"Arizona is giving me the signal to wait."

Tension vibrated through him. *There's a fucking signal for that?*

Jackson scratched his ear. "There's pretty much a signal for everything."

He couldn't believe it. "So she knows we're here?"

"She's sharp as a tack, so, yeah." He rolled to his back and pulled out his cell. "And it looks like she's awake, pissed off and determined to call the shots."

CHAPTER TWENTY-FOUR

ARIZONA DID HER BEST to ignore the pain in her head. It throbbed, pulsed, and every so often, her stomach cramped as if she might puke.

But since her hands were tied behind her, and she didn't have a bucket handy, that'd be really gross.

"I think you scrambled my brains."

At hearing her speak, Joel jumped in delight, expectation bright on his face. He drew a shuddering breath of excitement when she sat up straighter. "You're awake!"

"Barely, asshole. What's your deal, anyway?"

He shriveled back. "Listen to that language. What is wrong with you?"

"Me?" He had to be kidding. "You're the lunatic, bud."

She struggled upright a little more, relieved to realize that while her hands were tied behind her, the idiots hadn't taken her knife. She felt the familiar pressure of the sheath against her spine and the shape of the handle against her wrists.

Real observant, bozos. "Oh, God." Her head felt like it might topple right off her shoulders. Through narrow, pain-filled eyes, she looked around at her surroundings. They'd planned for her. They'd planned the whole thing. "What did you do?"

"I brought you home. Well, not really home. Just

where I can see you more—and see more of you." He reached out to touch the top of her shirt.

Arizona used her feet to kick him backward. "Paws off!"

Her venom surprised him. He stumbled, barely catching himself, then rubbed his midsection where her heels had struck him. "You're angry?"

"Angry?" Yanking at her bindings only made her head hurt more, but it'd be expected—and then, when she wiggled her knife free, they wouldn't suspect anything. "Cut me loose and we'll see how angry I am."

"But…" Bewildered, he shook his head. "You're not afraid?"

"Of a dead man?" She snorted. "Get real."

That surprised a short laugh out of him. He held out his hands. "But I'm not dead."

"Yeah, you are. You're just too stupid to know it yet." To be on the safe side, she again looked toward the window and gave another abrupt shake of her head. She'd seen the glint of sunlight—probably off binoculars, or a rifle barrel, or a scope—the second she'd come to.

Spencer had found her. Earlier than expected. So did that mean Marla had tattled early?

And if she had…well then, Marla must not want her gone for good. *Friend* was a word she didn't quite trust, but she could maybe count Marla as an ally.

"You should stop struggling, because you can't get your hands free. And now that you're awake, I'm going to fasten them to the grommet in the floor."

"Yeah—not happening." She'd kick in his face before she let him do that—or die trying. "Come near me, and you'll be sorry."

One brow lifted with interest. "How?"

"Try touching me and you'll damn well find out." Best bet was that Spencer had Jackson with him. And maybe even the other two...

Her stomach roiled again, and she had to breathe fast to settle it. Barfing was *not* an option. Off to her side, Quin cowered, silent and sad, his face a mess.

Arizona spared him one look of apology, then dismissed him. He wasn't a threat. "Look, Joel—" She paused. "Not your real name, I don't suppose?"

"Actually, it is."

"Great." How had she so badly misjudged him? "You're not only a psychopath, you're an idiot, too."

His eyes narrowed. "You will stop insulting me."

"Or what? You'll kidnap me? Hit me in the head?" She looked around. "Tie me up in a dirty room on a lumpy mattress—"

"Shut up!"

She huffed out a long breath while wiggling again as if trying to get her hands free.

She *almost* had her knife. "So where'd the other goons go?"

"They're keeping watch."

"Outside?" Wow, that'd be...too perfect.

"Yes."

Satisfaction tipped up her mouth, but she quickly wiped it away. "Listen up, Joel. If you let me loose now, I can maybe keep you alive, otherwise—"

In a startling, unexpected move, he jerked to his feet and viciously backhanded her.

Given the earlier bonk to her brain, well, yeah, she reacted sluggishly—so he got her good. Her head snapped to the side.

Blood dripped from her lip, and she licked it away, then worked her jaw. Hopefully that was the best he had.

"Know what, Joel?" Through narrowed eyes and a distinct lack of generosity, she met his gaze again. "Now I hope they do kill you."

Quinto took a shivering breath. "He is not Joel anymore."

Whoa… "Come again?"

"Joel is an idiot," said…Joel.

Arizona lowered her chin, stared at him anew and wanted to howl in frustration. In an aside to Quinto, she asked, "What's this? *Who's* this?"

"I'm one and the same," Joel drawled, "but I'm stronger. I'm not a fool. I'm not a weak, mewling artist."

Oh, for the love of… It needed only this. Arizona couldn't help but laugh. When his face tightened, she laughed some more. "Here I was, doubting my instincts, thinking I'd really blown it. But of course I didn't know you were a bad guy. I mean, the dude I met wasn't, right? So how could I have known?"

"You couldn't."

Amazingly, she felt better about things. At least now she knew her judgment wasn't completely screwed. "So you're…what?" She snickered. "Like Jekyll and Hyde?"

"You dare to laugh at me?" He bunched up in outrage, his hands fisting, his face flushing. "You're insane."

"Yeah—says the kettle to the pot." She spat blood and got her fingers around the hilt of her blade. "Jesus. My head is throbbing like a marching band."

"You're not natural."

"Yeah, I know." She looked at the window again and gave another shake of her head. Neither Quinto nor Joel paid any attention. They assumed she was clearing her thoughts. "So, Joel-number-two, did you know they ran a trafficking ring?"

He went still.

"Yeah, stow the surprise. I know all about their dirty little business." In tiny increments, she slid her knife free of the sheath. "Those morons? Terry and Carl and everyone else associated with selling humans, well, they'll be rotting in hell right about now. But you, you walked free."

"Yes."

"So tell me, did you know what they did? Did you know they bought and sold people?"

"Since I own the place, of course I knew."

Her thoughts reeled. "*You* own it?"

Joel shrugged. "That's why Joel hung around. To comfort the ones that got away."

Oh. My. God. He really was totally cuckoo. "That'd be Joel-one, right?"

"We are one and the same!"

"But Joel-two," she said, ignoring the bite of his insanity, "you didn't comfort them?"

His lip curled in disdain, making him look very, very different from the needy artist. "They were used up, destroyed. Dirty. I took care of them when no one else wanted them any longer."

"You mean you preyed on them, right?"

"After being in service, they're weak. They need me." He stepped closer and looked her over with sick intent. "Easy pickings."

Oh, to nut him real good. But he was so unstable, she didn't know what he might do. He could kill Quinto before the others could get to him.

No way did she want that death on her conscience; Quinto had been through enough. So instead of striking out, she engaged him in conversation. "What do you want with them? You rape them? Prostitute them out?

What?" If she could keep him talking, the chances of survival were a whole lot improved.

"Of course not. That'd be unseemly." He looked beyond her. "I make them...pets—just as I've done with Quin."

Imagining Quinto's shame at hearing that taunt, she rushed her movements. In the process of slicing through the bindings, her sharp blade did a little damage to her hands, too, but nothing all that serious.

Nothing that would slow her down once she was free.

"You've got something else on Quin, though, don't you?"

Joel shrugged as if it didn't matter, as if telling her would have no consequences at all. "He has a sister. Or rather, I have his sister." He laughed.

"Huh? No kidding?" No way would she tell him that Quin had already shared that info.

She felt the binding loosen. *Almost free.* "Where is it you have her?"

"I keep most of the girls at my home, in the cool, comfy cellar."

"Where is that exactly?"

He tipped his head. "Still plotting? Still thinking that you might get away?" His laugh had a demonic ring to it. "Foolish girl."

"I know where he lives," Quinto whispered, his gaze going a little wild. "I know."

"Yes, but your sister isn't there, is she Quin?" Smiling, he checked a nail.

"Why not?" Arizona asked as if it didn't really matter. "You have her somewhere else?" *Where?*

"Actually, she was on a delivery truck due to come in, but with Terry Janes shut down..." He shrugged. "I'll be able to find out, though, and then I'll get her."

Quinto deflated.

Arizona did not. She took great pleasure in saying, "Yeah…guess again." She stared him in the eyes—just a minute more, and she'd have her hands loose. "That truck has already been recovered."

"No."

"Yup." She turned to Quin. "Everyone on it is safe."

"Safe?" For several seconds Quin stood there, then he collapsed to his knees beside her. "You are sure?"

"She's lying!" Joel yelled. "She can't know that."

"Actually, I can and do know all sorts of things." Through the window, in the distance, Arizona saw Spencer come over a crumbling concrete wall, Trace right behind him. That meant Dare was watching the back, and Jackson, no doubt, remained hidden with a sniper rifle.

Her priority now was getting Quin out of this cluster-fuck without him getting hurt. "Everyone who was on that truck is safe—and you're as good as dead."

Joel's hands bunched into fists. "No one is going to kill me." He took a purposeful, threatening stride toward her.

She was ready—but then Quin lurched forward, putting himself in the way. "No, don't."

God save her from heroes. "Uh, Quin…how about you move?"

Joel heaved with anger. He withdrew a small gun from his pocket. "Get out of my way."

Quin braced himself, saying, "I cannot. You've done enough."

Joel aimed the gun, and Arizona rushed to say, "Quin, seriously, dude, stand back, okay?"

He kept his back to her so he could continue to watch Joel. "I am so sorry."

"I know. Don't sweat it."

He looked over his shoulder at her. "I don't understand you."

"Yeah, I get that a lot. Just do me a favor and don't stand too close to me."

Before he could oblige, Joel slugged him in the temple with the gun, and Quin staggered, falling to one knee. Joel used his foot to shove him aside.

She felt for Quin, but she wouldn't let him distract her. Her gaze bored into Joel. "You never stood much of a chance. But now you've sealed your fate."

"Big talk—for a woman bound."

Her head didn't hurt anymore. Nothing hurt. Fury obliterated every other feeling. She held his gaze, refusing to let him look away. "Even with my hands tied, I will annihilate you."

Quin groaned.

Joel said to him, "Shut up." But then, showing his concern, he started to the front to look out the window, asking, "You were followed? You brought friends to help you?" He saw his two guards still standing there.

Reassured, even cocky, he returned to Arizona. The gun held loosely in his hand, he crossed his arms and grinned at her. "You almost had me. I was almost convinced that you'd brought along an army."

"Not an army, no." But given their skill, they might as well have been. "So, come on, then. I can see you're feeling feisty. Let's see what you've got." Though she kept her posture relaxed, her hands behind her, she was ready, more than ready.

Haltingly, a little unsure despite his boastful words, Joel took a step toward her, raising his fist to strike her—and she kicked him hard in the balls. As he grabbed for himself, she kicked up again, and this time got him in the solar plexus. He wheezed and fell backward.

She was off the mattress in a heartbeat, her knife held in her now bloody hands.

Hysterical at seeing her free, Joel scuttled backward, screaming, "Guards! Get in here!"

One big bruiser burst in from the back, a gun in his hand—but before Joel could get too excited about that, the glass in the back window shattered. As if in slow motion, the man lurched forward from the force of a bullet. Blood bloomed on his chest—and he collapsed face-first to the floor.

Smug, Arizona said, "Told you so."

Shaking, Joel took aim, but she moved fast, slicing his wrist with her knife. The blade cut through tendons and muscles with ease.

He screamed as the gun dropped from his hand, blood streaming along his arm, his face going white in shock and pain.

"Oh, my God," he wailed. "What have you done?" Holding his wrist, big tears in his eyes, he whimpered as he fell back against the wall and then slowly slipped down to the floor. He looked at her, his expression wounded. "Oh, my God."

Annnnndddd...Joel the artist was back.

"Geeze Louise." Arizona collected the gun from the downed guard—who was moaning, so apparently alive—and then kicked Joel's gun well out of his reach.

A glance back at Quinto showed him staring at her in awe. "You okay?"

"Yes." He nodded. "Yes, I am okay."

She hunkered down in front of Joel. "What about you, buddy? You okay?"

Suddenly Spencer was there, bolting through the

door. He made quite the entrance, all decked out in weaponry, a bulletproof vest, his gun aimed, his face set, ready for…anything.

Joel screamed again, but she understood that.

Spencer was a large, dark force, heaving in rage. He looked really, really awesome.

"Wow," Arizona said to Joel. "Will you look at that?"

Spencer stopped short at seeing her position in front of Joel. He began to breathe hard.

Slowly, Arizona stood. She felt…well, awkward. She nodded at his loaded ammo belt. "Got your party dress on, I see. Expecting trouble?"

He pulled his attention from her to survey the room, taking in Quinto, then the fallen body on the floor, with a glance. His gaze came back to her face, searching her expression before going all over her body. His eyes narrowed, and he started toward her with a heavy stride.

Arizona blurted, "There are other women. At his house. Quinto knows where it is."

Spencer halted again.

Quin nodded fast.

She gestured at Joel with the bloody knife. "He's… well, he's nuts. Totally whacko." She winced. "You can't kill him, okay?"

"I wasn't going to."

"Oh." And here she'd been all set to be noble and defend the jerk. Sort of took the wind out of her sails. "Well…good."

"I figured if you needed him dead, you'd have taken care of that."

"Um, yeah, I would have." Was he serious? Did he truly trust her to make that call? Thinking about that, she said, "Can you maybe tell the others not to kill

anyone, either? I mean, it'd be so messy and everything—"

In one long stride, Spencer reached her and gathered
her into his arms.

"I'm a mess!" she protested, already knowing she'd
get blood on his shirt and on him.

"You're mine," he said in return.

Okay, hold the phone. She drew in air to ask him what
the hell *that* meant, but he hugged her tight, so tight she
could barely breathe, much less talk.

Her head protested, but really, her heart liked it just
fine.

"You disarmed the wounded goon?" Spencer quietly
asked.

She squeaked, "Yup."

"The crazy guy is unarmed?" He kissed her temple,
her ear.

"I took his gun, so, yeah."

His big hands opened on her back, stroking, cuddling, then squeezing again. "And the other one, he's
not a threat?"

She shook her head.

Jackson came in then. He was dressed much the same
as Spencer—kick-ass and prepared.

His presence in the small building meant that they'd
already "secured" the guards.

He saw them and rolled his eyes. "So what are we
doing here?"

Spencer eased her back, cupped her face in his hands
and smoothed her hair. "Do you have a concussion?"

"Eh…probably," she admitted. "I'm a hair away from
chucking, seeing two of you, and I've got a wingding of
a headache."

He groaned and kissed her forehead. "What do you

want them to do? Tell me quick, so I can get you to the hospital."

"Hospital?" But she didn't want to go to the hospital. She needed to get to Joel's house, she needed to see about the women he held captive. She needed—

"Shh. Give your orders, honey. It's your call. I understand that."

"You do?"

"I'm not a slow learner." He gave her a look of reprimand. "The purpose of your note was crystal clear."

Ho boy. Yeahhhh...she'd meant it to be a statement: she was available if he wanted her, but she couldn't, wouldn't, completely alter her psyche. She was who she was, formed by life experiences and a strong personality, and an even stronger will to make a difference. She'd try to buffer her take-charge attitude, but she could never become a mere observer.

"I, uh..." She cleared her throat, certain that she wanted to go on seeing him and not too proud to say so. "If you were interested, I could maybe meet you halfway."

"One thing at a time, honey." Spencer gave her a gentle smile. "The task force agent is on his way with a team, and so is the ambulance. I'm holding on by a thread, so you *will* go to the hospital. Okay?"

Seeking a little guidance, she looked toward Jackson, but he'd already pulled off his shirt to swaddle Joel's arm. "Where are the guys?"

"Awaiting instructions." Jackson glanced at her. "But since you were preoccupied...I'm assuming you don't want him to bleed to death?"

With Jackson looming over him, Joel looked ready to swoon. Arizona waved a hand for Jackson to continue and turned back to Spencer.

Damn it, why did she feel shy? She didn't know what any of this meant, and she hated being unsure. She made to push her hair from her face—and Spencer sucked in air.

"Jesus." He caught her hands, lifting them for a closer scrutiny.

More blood had trickled from her wrists, snaking down between her fingers, going under her nails. It looked really gross and made her want to groan.

"All superficial, I promise. I just nicked myself a few times while getting free." She didn't know what to do with her bloody hands, but then Spencer followed Jackson's lead and pulled off his shirt. He ripped it cleanly in half with little effort.

Arizona stared at how the bulletproof vest fit him. It fastened with wide strips of Velcro just under his pecs and over his abs. His muscled shoulders flexed as he took her hand.

"Trace insisted," Spencer said, explaining the vest. "I had other things on my mind."

"Yeah, like…?" Hopeful, she waited, her breath held.

He smoothed the strips of cotton around her left wrist, down and around her palm. "Getting to you." He lifted her other hand and, in hoarse tones, said, "That's all I could think of."

She'd scared him? Well, yeah, of course she had. Spencer cared for everyone, and from the day she'd met him, he'd been trying to keep her safe. "Sorry."

"You're forgiven." He'd just finished wrapping her hands when they heard the police sirens. "What now?"

She turned to see Quinto leaning on the wall, his eyes closed, his entire demeanor waning. "He's got to eat," she told Spencer, trying to think of his most immediate needs. "And he needs to see his sister. And rest. And—"

Trace put a hand to her shoulder. "I'll see to it."

Since she hadn't heard him come in, she jumped.

After studying her eyes, he gave her shoulder a squeeze. "You did good, Arizona, but even the best soldier knows when to retreat."

Her face went hot, and she mumbled, *actually mumbled,* "I'm not a soldier."

"No, but you are doggedly persistent, intuitive and capable." He drew her forward to kiss her brow. "Now, how about you put Spencer out of his misery by sitting down until the ambulance gets here?"

Put him out of his misery? She eyed Spencer's expression and frowned. Yeah, he did look pretty miserable.

And it was her fault. She didn't need guilt on top of a splitting head.

Jackson said without looking back, "He's giving you the deference you want, doll. Accept it with good grace."

"You can both leave her the hell alone." His mood growing blacker by the moment, Spencer put his arm around her. "Come on. Let me take you outside for some fresh air. We'll wait for the ambulance."

"Yeah, okay." She went along willingly, doing her utmost not to wince over the excruciating pain in her noggin. "I really do feel like crap."

He started to say something, but then they stepped outside and into the growing crowd. Police, task force, locals…they combined to make quite an audience.

Chaos consumed them. Paramedics rushed inside to see to Joel and to the man Dare had shot. Other EMTs came to look her over and, after a cursory exam, insisted that Spencer was right, and she needed to go to the hospital.

"Great," she grumbled. "Just freakin' great."

Spencer bent to kiss her brow. "I'll be right behind you. You aren't going to get away from me again."

And that confused her enough that she didn't complain as she got loaded into an ambulance, and it drove off for the hospital.

CHAPTER TWENTY-FIVE

SPENCER SAT IN A PLASTIC CHAIR, coffee cooling in front of him, Jackson pacing back and forth around him.

Dare and Trace were busy wrapping up everything with Quin and Joel—because they insisted on it, and even the official in charge of the elite task force didn't try to dissuade them.

They would, supposedly, keep a low profile—if you could call maiming guards and shooting a thug in the chest a low profile. But they would also ensure that it was handled to their satisfaction.

Always.

They had such power—and Arizona was now a part of that.

They wanted him to be a part of it, too. It'd mean relocating for the sake of anonymity. It'd mean starting over, burying the past for good.

Moving on with his life.

Moving on with Arizona…if she'd have him.

Spencer rubbed his face. Arizona had only been away from them for an hour or so—long enough for the docs to examine her and run some tests—but it still worried him.

Knowing her, she could sneak out. Again.

She could refuse medical attention. She wasn't dumb, but she did seem to think herself invincible.

Or disposable.

She could—

"Stop it, damn it." Harried, his blond hair standing on end, Jackson snarled, "You're stressing me out."

Slowly lifting his brows, Spencer looked up at Jackson. "I haven't done a thing."

"You're brooding." Jackson dropped down beside him, his mood black, his expression fierce. "Jesus, what is taking so long?"

Spencer eyed him with disgust. "You're going to be miserable when Alani gives birth. You know that, right?"

"Just…shut up." He got up to pace again.

Spencer joined him.

"If she was a guy…" Jackson said.

That deserved a short laugh. "Then I probably wouldn't be here."

"Well…yeah." He suddenly grinned. "She really proved herself, didn't she?"

"I'm thinking that was the point."

"I hate it when Chris is right." Jackson jammed his hands, palms out, into his back pockets. "He's never going to let us live it down."

Spencer rolled his shoulders. He still wanted to take Joel apart, but more than that, he wanted to show Arizona how important she was to him.

"What are we going to do?" Jackson asked.

We? "I want her back," Spencer said, distracted with his thoughts.

"Oh, really?"

That got him focused real quick. "I'm *getting* her back," he amended, challenging Jackson with a look. "And I'm keeping her." God, he made her sound like a pet. He manned up, stared at Jackson, and said, "I love her."

"Is that supposed to be news to me?"

Nonplussed, Spencer shrugged. Hell, it was sort of news to him. "I'm just saying."

"Yeah, so why tell me?"

"Hell if I know," he muttered and rubbed his face again. "The best we can hope for is to know where she's at and what she's doing. If we try to shut her down—"

"She'll just move on to another cluster-fuck." Jackson went to look out the window at the boring parking lot. "Alone."

Spencer couldn't bear that thought. "At least if she's working with you—and I don't mean computer work—I can partner with her. That's what she wants anyway." Partners, in more ways than one—though Arizona might not know that yet.

Jackson lifted a brow. "She said that?"

"Yes." Back when he'd been too arrogant to listen. Back when he thought he'd somehow help her along... and out of his life. "We can keep tabs on her. We'll know who's involved."

Nodding, Jackson said low, "She won't fall off the radar again."

Knowing he had no choice, Spencer drew in a deep breath. "It's the only solution, because I don't think Arizona is capable of taking a passive role."

"She can't, any more than I can," Jackson said, and then he added, "Any more than any of us can."

"That's about it."

"Hell...I guess she's in."

His quick agreement surprised Spencer. "You don't need to discuss it with Dare and Trace?"

Jackson turned to laugh at him. "No. They've just been waiting for us to get resigned to it. They figured it the same way you did—keep her close, work with her..."

"Accept her and love her." Spencer smiled. "I intend to do just that."

The doctor came out to greet them, and he was smiling but frazzled. Yup, Arizona could do that to you.

She was an exciting, unpredictable, sexy and precious woman.

And whether she knew it yet or not, she was his.

SHE HAD HER JEANS back on but unfastened, when Spencer came around the curtain. She wrinkled her nose at him. "Stupid bandages on my hands. I told the doc I didn't need to be all trussed up, but he wouldn't listen."

Without a word Spencer brushed her hands away and fastened her jeans for her. After brushing the backs of his fingers over her belly, he smoothed down her T-shirt. "You'll be healed up in time for Jackson's wedding."

"Yeah, sure. Told you it's just superficial." She rolled a shoulder in dismissal of the little cuts. "No biggie."

Framing her face in his hands, Spencer bent to kiss her.

Gently.

Sparingly.

Mega nice. But the second he lifted his mouth, she asked, "So what's going on? What have I missed?" She expected him to protest, and she had her arguments all lined up.

This was her rodeo, so she had a right to know the deets. She'd missed enough already, playing the patient.

Instead, he said, "Jackson is waiting to talk with you, but I wanted to go first. He's been downright neurotic, waiting to know that you're okay."

"Pffft." Somehow she couldn't imagine badass Jackson worrying. "Of course I'm fine."

"Dare and Trace are doing what they do best."

"Excelling?" she asked with a grin.

He nodded. "Taking charge. Making certain that Joel doesn't slip through the legal cracks to wreak anymore havoc. They already freed the women from his house, and they're reuniting Quinto with his sister."

"Ahhh…man, I wish I could see that."

"I hear tell Quinto is doing much better, now that he knows his sister is okay. He's in better shape than you, for sure." He bent his knees to look her in the eye. "How do you feel?"

He was being reserved and so incredibly cautious. "No worries. I'll survive."

Far too somber, his hand smoothed over her head, cupped her cheek again. "You are a survivor, aren't you?" He brushed her skin with his thumb. "But how do you feel? Head hurting still?"

"It's bearable." Man, she felt so tongue-tied. She had no clue where this was going, if anywhere. Sounding like an uncertain sap, she asked, "You hung around to drive me home?"

"If by home, you mean my house, yes. You will come with me, won't you?"

He still held her face, still stared into her eyes, so serious and so attentive. "I, uh—"

"The doctor said someone will need to watch over you for a while, in case you get dizzy or start throwing up." He kissed her again. "You need someone to care for you, Arizona, so you don't overdo it. Let me be the man who does that."

With him being so tender, her knees felt like noodles. "Yeah, okay, knock yourself out. If you want to play nursemaid, it's no skin off my—"

A longer, softer kiss quieted her defensive chatter. When he lifted his head, she felt herself swaying. *Get a grip, Arizona.* She cleared her throat, more baffled and flustered by the moment. "I—"

"I'm selling my house."

"You're *what?*"

Instead of explaining, he pulled her in closer again, tucking her against his chest. "I accepted the job offer. Are you okay with that?"

Joy exploded, making her flinch. "Ow, damn." A hand to her head, she pushed away from him. "Yeah, I'm okay with it. Shoot, I'm thrilled." She rubbed her temples.

Spencer caught her wrist and led her to sit on the edge of the hospital bed. "Will you partner with me?"

Agog, she stared at him. *Good thing he'd gotten her to sit down before dropping that bomb.* "Come again?"

"I'm taking the job with a caveat that you work with me. And I'm selling my house because, as of right now, I'm too well-known in it. Too many trails that lead to too many details."

"Oh…well, yeah. Maybe." But his house? He loved that house. Shoot, *she* loved that house. "All of your wife's things, I mean, it was your house with her—"

"Shh." He kissed her forehead, the bridge of her nose. "I figured we could buy new things and put them in a new house. Our house."

Her stomach bottomed out. "Our…?" She wagged a finger from him to her and back again. "Meaning us?"

He gave a firm nod. "Us. You and me. Partners." He stepped between her legs and pulled her in against his chest.

He did seem to have a thing about keeping her close.

"I love all the stuff your wife put in the house to make it a home."

"I love *you,* Arizona."

Whoa. She struggled out of his tight embrace to look up at him. "Did you get hit in the head, too?"

"No. I woke up and you were gone and I knew I'd been an idiot. But actually, even before that, I knew it. I realized that I'd been trying to…" Self-disgust tightened his mouth. "I wanted to help you get beyond the past."

"Yeah, and you did. I've been making all kinds of progress—shoot, except for getting slugged in the head, I'd be about ready to leap tall buildings in a single bound."

He didn't laugh. "If you decided to, I've no doubt you could figure out how."

"Eh…it was a joke, Spence."

He smiled. "You must be feeling friskier if you're back to butchering my name."

"Friskier?" She narrowed her eyes, but not much because that hurt.

The smile widened into a grin. "You are so beautiful."

"And you're acting really weird." *Had he really said he loved her?* Like, maybe he loved her the same way Jackson did? Only, Jackson hadn't slept with her. Jackson hadn't made her melt with wild pleasure. Jackson hadn't—

"I love you, Arizona. I want to be with you."

"You mean as…partners, right?" Because really, none of this was making much sense. But she really wanted to work with the guys. It'd be like a dream come true.

"And lovers."

If he hadn't been holding her, she might have slid right off the side of the bed. "Seriously?" She had *no* problem with that. "That'd be *awesome!* I was sort of hoping, but I didn't want to push…and then I had to do this thing with Quinto, and I sort of figured that'd queer the deal, ya know? But if you—"

His hand covered her mouth.

"Whether we work with the dynamic trio or not, I want to partner with you."

"And have sex with me," she reminded him.

He nodded but added, "In sickness and in health."

Her eyes flared. *No way.* That sounded like some sort of…proposal. Not that she knew jackola about proposals. She gave a nervous snicker. "Does that mean…?"

Spencer lifted her chin, bent and kissed her once more. "I thought you were too young for me."

She snorted. "That is *so* dumb."

Another kiss, this one ticklish because he laughed. "God, I need you, Arizona. No, you're not too young. You're perfect. For me. And I love you."

There it was again! Flat-out. And Spencer said it as if he meant it and *not* in the same way that Jackson said it. "I wasn't sure—"

"I am. Very sure." He wrapped her close so that her nose was against his chest, and she breathed in his wonderful scent. "I thought I wanted to help you get beyond a past so tragic, it shredded my heart."

"You did! I am past it. Mostly anyway." Spencer deserved full disclosure. "I still have nightmares, probably always will."

"But from now on, you won't be alone when you do, because you'll be with me."

"Oh. Okay." Yes, she was forever changed by the past, but she no longer felt wounded, not if… She peeked up at him. "You accept me as I am?"

"I *love* you as you are. I hope you'll show more caution, but—"

"I'm always cautious!"

He gave her a stern frown. "No more leaving me notes. No more sneaking off without me."

"Well, as to that, I had to. I needed you to see that I could handle myself."

"I figured that out. You're a woman meant to champion others. And you were pretty amazing."

No way could she bite back her grin, and she didn't give a damn if it made her head hurt more. The compliment left her beaming. "Yeah?"

Spencer sighed with fond exasperation. "What I'm trying to say here is that I thought I'd help you, and instead you helped me. You brought me out of the past. Now all I can see is the future."

Her toes curled, and she squeaked, "With me?"

"Today, tomorrow and for the rest of our lives."

"That would be...*awesome*."

His grin came slowly. "You think so?"

Before Spencer, she couldn't imagine saying the words, but *with* him, it was pretty damn easy. "Yeah, since, you know, I really love you, too."

Spencer's grin widened. She smiled, too, because now that the words were said, she felt totally...free.

Gently, he cupped the back of her neck and kissed her. "Come on, honey. Let's go home."

PROPPED AGAINST A WALL with Dare at his side, Spencer watched as Arizona held the tiny newborn. She looked in awe, and she looked incredibly soft. Like a woman.

His woman.

She would be the most amazing aunt ever.

"Man, Jackson, she's beautiful."

Jackson sat beside Arizona, his free arm around her shoulders while his baby girl held on to his pinkie with her tiny hand. "She smells awful good, too, don't you think?"

Arizona put her nose to the mop of downy soft blond hair and inhaled. "Mmm. Yeah, she does." She cuddled the baby closer. "We could bottle you up, little girl, and make a fortune."

Jackson grinned. "She looks like Alani."

Trace stood behind the couch, leaning down to do his own marveling at the new addition to the family. Alani, who'd only recently finished feeding the baby, was in the other room with Molly and Priss, going through yet more gifts.

Chris came in, fresh from a shower. He pulled on a clean T-shirt and crowded in close to Arizona's other side. "You have all the right instincts, Arizona."

Arizona smiled, but when she turned her attention to Chris, it was to say, "You did the background check on the owner of the massage parlor?"

"Yeah. Dare says it's worth investigating." He touched the baby's toes. "Forced labor at the very least, but probably trafficking, too, given the owner's connections."

"I'll go by and check it out," Trace added. "Do a visual. Get some firsthand evidence if I can."

"How do you plan to get evidence at a massage parlor?" Jackson asked. "You going to pay for a 'happy ending'?"

"I already have my happy ending, you ass."

"Oh, real nice. You don't want me to curse in front of Alani, but you can do it in front of my daughter?"

"She's too young to understand."

The baby stretched, and Arizona said, *"Ahhhhh…"* in a meltingly sweet voice before looking back at Trace. "You'll let me know what you find?"

Trace flicked the end of her nose. "You'll be the first I tell."

"Thanks."

Dare nudged Spencer, disturbing his silent reverie. "Giving you any baby ideas?"

He was so content, so happy, it almost scared him. He and Arizona would move into their newly built home later in the week. She had stacks of family photos ready to decorate the walls.

So far their working arrangement was perfect. It worried him every time she went after a scumbag—but it made her happy, and she was good at it. Really good.

Now that she'd been accepted, she coordinated with the others, which cut down greatly on the risks. And she'd had only a few nightmares; each had quickly faded once they made love.

So with great sincerity, he said, "Whatever Arizona wants."

Dare smiled. "An attitude like that is liable to get you into trouble."

That attitude had gotten him everything he never knew he wanted, because as it turned out, all he ever really wanted was Arizona.

* * * * *

Don't miss RUN THE RISK,
the first in Lori Foster's sizzling new series,
coming soon from HQN Books!

PEPPER YATES FELT THE INTENSE scrutiny stroking over her as she made her way to her apartment building. She'd been feeling it ever since her new neighbor had moved in, but she'd never get used to it.

Dangerous anticipation crawled up her spine.

She didn't acknowledge the man leaning over his balcony, muscular arms folded along the railing, shirtless, smiling—tracking her every move.

But of course he called out to her. It made no sense, but her rebuffs hadn't dissuaded him at all.

"Evening, Ms. Meeks."

When she'd taken the alias, it hadn't been a big deal, because she wasn't a big deal. Few ever spoke to her.

But he did.

She peeked up at him. "Evening."

He disappeared off the balcony and she just knew he was coming inside to corral her in the narrow hallway.

She went slowly up to her second-floor apartment, and… there he was.

He lounged back against his door, which was right next to hers, arms crossed over his bare chest, his brown hair disheveled. He wore only wrinkled khaki shorts that hung low on his lean hips—and he took her breath away.

She had to avoid his gaze or—humiliating thought—he just might see everything she felt, everything she thought.

About him. About the incredible body that he insisted on displaying.

And how she'd like to rub *her* body all over his....

Don't miss RUN THE RISK,
the first in Lori Foster's sizzling new series,
coming soon from HQN Books!

PEPPER YATES FELT THE INTENSE scrutiny stroking over her as she made her way to her apartment building. She'd been feeling it ever since her new neighbor had moved in, but she'd never get used to it.

Dangerous anticipation crawled up her spine.

She didn't acknowledge the man leaning over his balcony, muscular arms folded along the railing, shirtless, smiling—tracking her every move.

But of course he called out to her. It made no sense, but her rebuffs hadn't dissuaded him at all.

"Evening, Ms. Meeks."

When she'd taken the alias, it hadn't been a big deal, because she wasn't a big deal. Few ever spoke to her.

But he did.

She peeked up at him. "Evening."

He disappeared off the balcony and she just knew he was coming inside to corral her in the narrow hallway.

She went slowly up to her second-floor apartment, and... there he was.

He lounged back against his door, which was right next to hers, arms crossed over his bare chest, his brown hair disheveled. He wore only wrinkled khaki shorts that hung low on his lean hips—and he took her breath away.

She had to avoid his gaze or—humiliating thought—he just might see everything she felt, everything she thought.

About him. About the incredible body that he insisted on displaying.

And how she'd like to rub *her* body all over his....

These cowboys are tough...but not too tough to fall in love!

In these timeless romances from bestselling authors

JAYNE ANN KRENTZ,

LINDSAY MCKENNA

and

B.J. DANIELS,

three women will discover that the West has never been so wild....

Available now!

REQUEST YOUR FREE BOOKS!

2 FREE NOVELS
FROM THE ROMANCE COLLECTION
PLUS 2 FREE GIFTS!

YES! Please send me 2 FREE novels from the Romance Collection and my 2 FREE gifts (gifts are worth about $10). After receiving them, if I don't wish to receive any more books, I can return the shipping statement marked "cancel." If I don't cancel, I will receive 4 brand-new novels every month and be billed just $5.99 per book in the U.S. or $6.49 per book in Canada. That's a saving of at least 25% off the cover price. It's quite a bargain! Shipping and handling is just 50¢ per book in the U.S. and 75¢ per book in Canada.* I understand that accepting the 2 free books and gifts places me under no obligation to buy anything. I can always return a shipment and cancel at any time. Even if I never buy another book, the two free books and gifts are mine to keep forever.

194/394 MDN FELQ

Name	(PLEASE PRINT)

Address	Apt. #

City	State/Prov.	Zip/Postal Code

Signature (if under 18, a parent or guardian must sign)

Mail to the **Reader Service:**
IN U.S.A.: P.O. Box 1867, Buffalo, NY 14240-1867
IN CANADA: P.O. Box 609, Fort Erie, Ontario L2A 5X3

Not valid for current subscribers to the Romance Collection
or the Romance/Suspense Collection.

Want to try two free books from another line?
Call 1-800-873-8635 or visit www.ReaderService.com.

* Terms and prices subject to change without notice. Prices do not include applicable taxes. Sales tax applicable in N.Y. Canadian residents will be charged applicable taxes. Offer not valid in Quebec. This offer is limited to one order per household. All orders subject to credit approval. Credit or debit balances in a customer's account(s) may be offset by any other outstanding balance owed by or to the customer. Please allow 4 to 6 weeks for delivery. Offer available while quantities last.

Your Privacy—The Reader Service is committed to protecting your privacy. Our Privacy Policy is available online at www.ReaderService.com or upon request from the Reader Service.

We make a portion of our mailing list available to reputable third parties that offer products we believe may interest you. If you prefer that we not exchange your name with third parties, or if you wish to clarify or modify your communication preferences, please visit us at www.ReaderService.com/consumerchoice or write to us at Reader Service Preference Service, P.O. Box 9062, Buffalo, NY 14269. Include your complete name and address.

LORI FOSTER

77647	FOREVER BUCKHORN	___	$7.99 U.S.	___	$9.99 CAN.
77612	BUCKHORN BEGINNINGS	___	$7.99 U.S.	___	$9.99 CAN.
77582	SAVOR THE DANGER	___	$7.99 U.S.	___	$9.99 CAN.
77575	TRACE OF FEVER	___	$7.99 U.S.	___	$9.99 CAN.
77571	WHEN YOU DARE	___	$7.99 U.S.	___	$9.99 CAN.
77495	BEWITCHED	___	$7.99 U.S.	___	$9.99 CAN.
77491	UNBELIEVABLE	___	$7.99 U.S.	___	$9.99 CAN.
77444	TEMPTED		$7.99 U.S.	___	$9.99 CAN.

(limited quantities available)

TOTAL AMOUNT	$ _____
POSTAGE & HANDLING	$ _____
($1.00 FOR 1 BOOK, 50¢ for each additional)	
APPLICABLE TAXES*	$ _____
TOTAL PAYABLE	$ _____

(check or money order—please do not send cash)

To order, complete this form and send it, along with a check or money order for the total above, payable to HQN Books, to: **In the U.S.:** 3010 Walden Avenue, P.O. Box 9077, Buffalo, NY 14269-9077; **In Canada:** P.O. Box 636, Fort Erie, Ontario, L2A 5X3.

Name: _____

Address: _____ City: _____

State/Prov.: _____ Zip/Postal Code: _____

Account Number (if applicable): _____

075 CSAS

*New York residents remit applicable sales taxes.
*Canadian residents remit applicable GST and provincial taxes.

HQN™   ◆ HARLEQUIN®
™ www.Harlequin.com

PHLF0412BL